"Jessica Joyce has gifted all of us with an electrifying debut, and the perfect summer read! If you love your flirting paired with a healthy dose of roasting, rivals-turned-lovers, road trips that become journeys of self-discovery, hilarious but sexy banter, and steamy love stories, this is the beach read you want to pick up! A million out of five stars, Jessica Joyce is a new and forever fave!"

—Ali Hazelwood,
New York Times bestselling author of *Love, Theoretically*

"Sometimes all it takes to get back on track is a road trip with your oldest rival . . . Jessica Joyce's debut, *You, with a View*, stole my heart and had me absolutely sweating at the chemistry between Theo and Noelle. I will never see a vintage red Bronco, a TikTok travel video, or a man's thighs the same way again."

—Alicia Thompson,
national bestselling author of *Love in the Time of Serial Killers*

"Stunningly heartfelt and sexy beyond words. Jessica Joyce writes with a deeply empathetic pen, drawing each character with profound tenderness and crafting the perfect amount of rivals-to-reluctant-road-trip-companions-to-lovers tension—incidentally, my new favorite trope. I want to live inside this book."

—Rachel Lynn Solomon,
New York Times bestselling author of *Weather Girl*

The Ex Vows

JESSICA JOYCE

BERKLEY ROMANCE
NEW YORK

BERKLEY ROMANCE
Published by Berkley
An imprint of Penguin Random House LLC
penguinrandomhouse.com

Library of Congress Cataloging-in-Publication Data

Names: Joyce, Jessica, author.
Title: The ex vows / Jessica Joyce.
Description: First Edition. | New York: Berkley Romance, 2024.
Identifiers: LCCN 2023048269 (print) | LCCN 2023048270 (ebook) |
ISBN 9780593548424 (trade paperback) | ISBN 9780593548431 (ebook)
Subjects: LCGFT: Romance fiction. | Novels.
Classification: LCC PS3610.O974 E9 2024 (print) |
LCC PS3610.O974 (ebook) | DDC 813/.6—dc23/eng/20231016
LC record available at https://lccn.loc.gov/2023048269
LC ebook record available at https://lccn.loc.gov/2023048270

First Edition: July 2024

Printed in the United States of America
1st Printing

Interior art: Vines © Ohn Mar / Shutterstock.com
Book design by Kristin del Rosario

For past me,
who didn't give up,
and for future me,
who will look back on all of this and be so proud.

The
Ex Vows

Prologue

I hate thinking about the way it ended, but sometimes I think about the way it began: with me walking through the door of someone else's house without knocking.

This has always been a typical move of mine, wandering latch-key kid that I was in my early years. But in every other way, the beginning was an atypical day.

When I let myself go there, I watch it in my head like a movie. I let it feel like it's happening now instead of thirteen years ago, where the real moment belongs, where fifteen-year-old me is turning the doorknob on a house I've burst into hundreds of times before. I find no resistance, because by my sophomore year of high school—when this memory takes place—my open invitation into the Cooper-Kims' home is implied.

My best friend, Adam Kim, is somewhere in here, probably still sweaty and gross from cross-country practice. At least I went home and showered.

I greet Adam's three rescue dogs, Gravy, Pop-Tart, and Dave, my ears perking at the dulcet tones of a video game played at full volume, two voices rumbling below it. The dogs trail me as I make my way to the den, the tags on their collars jingling. It's a sound as familiar as my own heartbeat.

Adam's house is warm and sun-filled, often noisy, with a lingering, faint citrus scent. The first time I walked in, something unraveled in my chest; it felt like *home*, not a place where two people lived with sometimes intertwining lives. My house is quiet and often empty, just as it was all the years between when my mom left when I was three years old and now.

The times my dad and I do sync up are great; he asks tons of questions and tells me what a great kid I am, how easy I've been, how proud he is of my grades and the extracurriculars that keep me busy. He listens to every story I can get out of my mouth, his phone facedown on the dining room table while it buzzes and buzzes and buzzes. Eventually the phone wins, and I'm left craving more time.

It's why I've made a habit of making other people's houses my home, and why I love the Cooper-Kims' house best.

In this memory, I'm nearly to the den, wondering who Adam has over. I sincerely hope it isn't Jared; I keep telling Adam what a dick he is.

With the power of hindsight, I know what's going to happen seconds before it does, so I always hold my breath here—

Right when I turn the corner and run face-first into a broad chest. It has so little padding it makes my teeth rattle.

"Whoa," a voice breathes above me, stirring the hairs at my temple. Warm, strong hands grip my arms to keep me upright.

I look up . . . and up, into a face fifteen-year-old me has never seen before.

Whoever this is, he's beautiful. He's tall (obviously) and broad-shouldered, with limbs he hasn't grown into. In this moment, I don't know that he'll fill out in a painfully attractive way—his chest will broaden to become the perfect pillow for my head. His thighs will grow just shy of thick, mouth-wateringly curved with muscle, the perfect perch for me when I sit in his lap.

But the eyes I'm looking into won't change. They'll stay that hypnotic mix of caramel and gold, rimmed in deep coffee brown and framed by sooty lashes and inky eyebrows that match the hair on his head. They'll continue to catch mine the way they are in this movie moment—like a latch hooking me, then locking us into place.

"Oh. Hello," I say brilliantly.

His mouth pulls up, which is wide and meant for the toothy smiles I'll discover he doesn't give away easily. He's prone to quiet ones, or shy, curling ones, like he's giving me now. "Hey."

I step back, my heart flipping from our crash and the warmth his hands have left behind on my skin. "Sorry, I didn't know Adam had someone over."

"Never stopped you before, Woodward," Adam calls distractedly, his eyes glued to the TV screen.

I roll mine, turning back to this stranger. "I'm that doofus's best friend, Georgia."

"Like the peach," he says, his voice lifting at the end. It's not a question, but a tentative tease. In my life, I've heard that joke a million times and hate it, but here, I like the way he says it, as if he knows how ridiculous it is and is in on the joke.

I grin. When I'm watching this, I think about how open my expression is, how hopeful and full of sunshine. "Good one. No one's ever said that to me before."

His eyes narrow, like he's trying to figure me out. I make note of how quickly he does, a tendril of belonging curling around me when he laughs. "You're joking."

"Yes," I laugh back.

He pretends to look disappointed. "So I'm *not* the first?"

"More like lucky number ninety-nine," I shoot back, and he grins. A toothy one. "Should I call you by the number or do you have a name, too?"

"That's Eli— mother*fucker*," Adam shouts.

My gaze slips from the stranger—Eli Joseph Mora, I'll find out—to Adam, whose tongue is sticking out while he furiously pounds on a game controller. A second one lies next to him, a decimated bag of Doritos next to that.

When I direct my attention back to Eli, our eyes click. I hear it in my head, feel it in my chest, both in the memory and for real. Whenever I let myself think about the beginning, I want to get out of this moment as much as I want to wallow in it.

Fifteen-year-old me smiles up at fifteen-year-old him. "Hey, Eli. I hope *you're* not the motherfucker."

"Not that I'm aware of," he says. His eyes spark with amusement and other things, and the spark transfers to me, burrowing somewhere deep. It'll wait there for years while we go from strangers to friends to best friends. It won't catch fire until our junior year of college, when he joins me at Cal Poly after two years at community college.

"Who are you, then? Other than a stranger until"—I look down at my watch, a Fossil one I bought with the Christmas cash my dad gave me because he didn't want to get the wrong one—"three minutes ago."

"The new guy, I guess?" I notice his nose is sunburned along the bridge when he scrunches it. "I just moved from Denver, started at Glenlake two days ago."

He doesn't tell me now, but later he'll divulge that his parents moved him and his two younger sisters to Glenlake, a city in

Marin County just north of San Francisco, to live with his aunt. His dad lost his job as a mortgage broker when the economy crashed, starting a relentless financial slide until they lost their house. At fifteen, Eli's sleeping on a pull-out in his aunt's rec room; later, when we buy our first bed together, I talk him into splurging for a king.

I always notice the way his shoulders pull up toward his ears, maybe wondering if I'm going to ask questions. He doesn't trust me with his heavy stuff yet, but eventually he'll trust me with a lot of it, before we both start hiding ourselves away.

"Adam's already got you in his clutches?" I raise my voice. "You work fast, Kim."

Adam grins, but doesn't spare us a glance.

Eli looks over his shoulder at his new friend, then back at me, rubbing the back of his neck. "Yeah, I think he kind of adopted me."

"He does that," I say, remembering that fateful day in sixth grade when Adam and I met, a month after my best friends of three years, Heather Russo and Mya Brogan, unceremoniously dropped me. Halfway into our inaugural year of middle school, the friends I thought were forever suddenly decided I was too needy, that my desire to hang out at their houses all the time was burdensome, and my occasional emotional moments were supremely irritating.

In the end, Adam saved me from my loneliness. It makes sense that he'd save Eli, too, though I don't know yet that he's also lonely, or that Adam's house will become his home as much as it is mine.

"All right, Eli," I say, looking him up and down. He's wearing scuffed Nikes, gym shorts, and a T-shirt with a tear near the neck. I can see a sliver of collarbone pressing sharply against his golden skin, the glint of a fragile gold chain. "I guess I'm kind of adopting you, too."

His eyes move over my face. "Probably a good idea, since I've already got a nickname picked out for you and everything."

"Does Adam have one?"

"Slim Kim," Eli says automatically, and I laugh as Adam scoffs. He's all elbows and knees at fifteen. "Still workshopping it, though."

It'll morph over the years—Slim Kimmy, SK, Kiz, or Kizzy. I'll watch him test versions of nicknames with other friends, but mine will only ever be Peach. When I eventually ask him why, he'll tell me it's because he knew exactly who I was to him from the start.

I glance at Adam. "I can't believe I'm saying this, but I think I won the nickname portion of this adoption process."

My chest warms at the way Eli's grin widens. It's an addicting feeling, knowing I'm in the middle of meeting a person I'll get to hang on to.

Adam looks at me over Eli's shoulder, his mouth pulling up, and I know he feels it, too: the three of us are going to be friends. Something special.

Years later Eli will tell me that he fell in love with me right then, and in this movie-like memory I always see it—how we can't quite break eye contact, the flush along the shell of his ear when I sit next to him on the couch minutes later, the way his eyes linger on me when Adam and I bicker over control of the TV, the steady bounce of his knee. The beautiful, shy smile he gives me over the pizza we have for dinner later.

He'll hold on to it for years, but eventually that spark will become a wildfire.

And then we'll burn it all down.

Chapter One

Thirteen years later

This wedding is cursed

"Not again," I mutter.

To the untrained eye, this text probably looks like a joke, or the beginning of one of those chain emails our elders get duped into forwarding to twenty of their nearest and dearest, lest they inherit multigenerational bad luck.

In actuality, it's been Adam's mantra for the past eight months.

Adam is the brother I never had and I'm truly honored to be along for the ride on his wedding journey. But had sixth-grade Georgia anticipated I'd be fielding forty-seven daily texts from my more-unhinged-by-the-minute best friend, I would've thought twice about complimenting his Hannah Montana shirt the day we met.

My Spidey senses tingle with this text, though. It hasn't been delivered in aggressive caps lock, nor is it accompanied by a chaotic menagerie of GIFs (my kingdom for a Michael Scott alternative). Whatever has happened now might actually be an emergency.

Then again, the wedding is ten days away. At this point, anything that isn't objectively awesome is a disaster.

I pluck my phone off my desk, typing, *What's the damage?*

A bubble immediately pops up, disappears, reappears, then stops again.

"*Great* sign."

It's nearly four p.m. on Wednesday, the day before my week-long PTO for the wedding starts, and I still have half a page of unchecked boxes on my to-do list, plus a detailed While I'm Away email to draft for my boss. I can't leave Adam hanging in his moment of need, though. What kind of best woman would I be?

No better than the largely absent best man? comes the uncharitable punchline. I slam the door on that thought. It's not like I've minded executing most of the best-people activities; it's been a godsend for multiple reasons. It's just so typical of him to—

I catch my own eye in the computer's reflection, delivering a silent message with the downward slash of my dark eyebrows: *Shut. Up.* I'd rather think about curses than anything tangentially related to the subject of Eli Mora.

Not that I believe in curses at all.

Except . . . deep down, I do worry that Adam's been hounded by bad vibes since he proposed to his fiancée, Grace Song, on New Year's Eve. Their plans have involved a comedy of errors that have escalated from *bummer* to *oh shit*: the wrong wedding dress ordered by the bridal salon, names misspelled on their printed wedding invitations twice, and—the one that nearly got me to believe—their wedding planner quit three months ago because his Bernedoodle had amassed such a following on social media that he was making triple his salary as her manager.

For Adam, whose natural temperament hovers somewhere near live wire, it's been a constant test of his sanity. Even Grace, who's brutally chill, the perfect emotional foil for Adam, has been fraying.

But then, she would've been fine eloping. Every new disaster probably only further solidifies the urge to book it to Vegas.

Adam's texts tumble over one another:

Georgia

Our fucking DJ

BROKE THEIR HIP

LINE DANCING AT A BACHELORETTE
PARTY

IN NASHVILLE

I need to know what I've done in my
28 years on this dying earth that is
causing this to happen

I start to type, but he beats me to it.

That was rhetorical, Woodward,
DON'T

Clearly Adam's shifting out of his panic fugue, so I shift into fix-it mode. It's the reason he came to me out of everyone—he knows I'll step up without hesitation.

Deep breath. Nothing's burned to the ground, right? I text back. This is problematic but not fatal. We'll come up with a new list.

The bubbles of doom pop up again and I wait. Again.

I wish I could say my eagerness to jump into this shitstorm is fully altruistic, but since I got back from a six-month work stint in Seattle three months ago, I can count on one hand the number of times I've seen Adam, all wedding-related. This has been the only way to reliably stay in his orbit.

For now, anyway.

Here's the thing: I'm a list girl. I learned the magic of them long ago—the way they can streamline tasks and expectations. Needs and emotions. How they can take a messy, chaotic thing and make it manageable. They've been my coping strategy since I was a kid. They quiet my mind and untangle my emotions so that I stay cool, calm, and compartmentalized. So *I'm* not a messy, chaotic thing.

Needless to say, it aggrieves me that I can't list my way out of my recent realization: my closest friends have fully shifted into phases I'm not in—falling in love, cohabitating, building social circles with other happy couples that make me the extra wheel, a feeling I avoid as resolutely as Trader Joe's on a Sunday. My time in Seattle only made it more obvious, and I hate that there's no checklist that'll pivot me off this path.

It's not that I expected an epic welcome home party, but I *did* expect to come back to my favorite people still living in the same city as me. Instead, I returned to an entirely different landscape: Adam and Grace moved to Glenlake from their apartment in the Inner Richmond six blocks away. Jamie Rothenberg, my other best friend and roommate for the last five years, went and fell in love while I was gone, too, and moved into her girlfriend's Oakland bungalow right before I got back.

Really, though, it's fine.

Okay, sure, loneliness is gnawing at me, a feeling that's been familiar since I was old enough to know what it was (kindergarten, when my dad couldn't make it to my holiday concert and I sang my solo to our neighbor, who showed up in his place). Yes, I can feel it curling up next to me at night in an apartment that used to echo with Jamie's honking laughter instead of the reruns of *New Girl* I put on a timer so I can sleep. Absolutely, watching two of my best friends find the kind of love I once thought I had is fairly soul-destroying. As is being knee-deep in my best friend's wedding festivities, knowing that in ten days I have to stand beside—

My phone buzzes. I jump, shaking off that unwanted, side-swiping thought, and turn my attention to Adam's text: Can you help with a DJ list that isn't shitty?

That deserves a voice message. "Can I help with a list? Seriously?"

Like all the other times Adam's called me in for support, it's a serotonin hit that chases the lonely feeling away.

And once the wedding is over, what happens then? a quiet voice asks. Like all my messiest thoughts, I wrestle it into submission.

Adam's follow-up text comes as a Teams notification dings politely on my computer. My head swivels on instinct, ponytail sweeping across my cheek.

NIA OSMAN: can I borrow you for 5?

Adam and my boss needing me play tug-of-war on my people-pleasing tendencies, but only one of them is paying me.

Nia needs to chat, I text. Take a deep breath, listen to your Calm app. I'll come back to you on the broken DJ ASAP.

My phone chimes twice, but I ignore it, mentally apologizing to Adam as I start the short trek down the bright white hall to Nia's office.

"Georgia!" a voice calls when I'm nearly at her door.

I turn to see Shay, a recent engineer steal from our biggest rival, walking up.

"Hey!" I say, clocking her wide smile. A gold star materializes on my mental chart; somewhere, an HR angel gets its wings. "How's it going?"

"*Amazing.* I love my team and my boss and—" She laughs self-consciously, tucking a blond curl behind her ear. "Actually, it'd probably be easier if I listed the things I don't like." Her green eyes widen. "Which is nothing!"

I smile, feeling the familiar endorphin rush of a role well filled. I adore my job. I've been here nearly five years and knew as soon as I interviewed with Nia that it was the perfect fit; now I get to do the same for the people I bring in.

"These are the updates I live for." Gesturing to Nia's office, I say, "I have to go, but let's grab lunch when you've settled in, okay?"

"Sounds perfect," Shay calls as she strides away.

Nia is seated at her sleek white desk when I enter, chin propped in her hand. Behind her, the floor-to-ceiling windows frame a view of Chinatown and North Beach, and beyond it, the Golden Gate Bridge stretching across the sun-blanketed bay.

"Another satisfied customer?" she asks as I sink into the acrylic chair facing her, a black eyebrow rising over her thick red frames.

I buff my nails on my shoulder. "The Georgia Woodward streak continues."

She smiles, but it fades as she removes her glasses. "Listen . . ."

My stomach drops. Am I in trouble? While I can't say the same for my personal life, I've transitioned seamlessly back into my role here. I'm good at my job. I rarely make mistakes, and when I do, I own them. They're never repeated; I make sure of it, because I have a Mistakes Never to Make Again list I reference often.

My mind flashes to the item at the top: those fifteen months I spent in New York right out of college, the apartment lease with two scrawled signatures, shaky from excitement. A pair of warm brown eyes meeting mine, locking into place, full of happiness and love—

Nope. No, no, no.

I focus on Nia, who isn't wearing her mistake face. It's not a good face, but I don't think this is about me.

"Oh god, are you leaving?" I blurt out. She's not only my boss but my mentor, the kind of kickass human resources leader I hope to be someday.

"No, I'm not leaving. And you've done nothing wrong, before you ask. I want you to . . ." Nia pauses, spreading her arms wide. The thick gold bracelets on each of her wrists jingle musically as she continues. "Take in what I'm about to tell you."

I wipe my sweating palms on my pants. "Okay."

"You know that our Seattle office has been massively growing, considering you're responsible for filling at least half those seats."

I nod, anxiety creeping up my throat.

"Arjun"—our CEO—"wants to shift the workforce focus to the Seattle office and eventually make San Francisco a satellite location. There are state-to-state financial implications I won't bore you with, but the company is in the process of making strategic role transfers." Nia leans back, her mouth twisting. "You led the build of the Seattle team perfectly, and you were a rockstar while I was out on maternity leave before that."

"Okay," I repeat, drawing out the word.

"The recruiting director in the Seattle office quit a couple weeks ago," she says, looking straight at me, her dark eyes penetrating. "They want to fill the role internally and dissolve the senior manager position here."

It's as if she's dropped one thousand puzzle pieces into my hands with five seconds to solve it. "Senior mana— that's my position."

"Turns out you're so good at your job they're taking you away from me, Georgia. You're getting a promotion, your own team to lead." Nia pauses. "But that promotion is in Seattle."

All the blood drains from my body.

Seattle is not San Francisco. Seattle is in *Washington*, eight hundred miles away. I'm fated mates with the Bay Area—I was born here, grew up here. My apartment is here, my friends and my dad, too, though I rarely see him thanks to his thirty-years-and-running devotion to his job as a public defender. I like being here when he needs me, though; it's been just the two of us since the day my mom decided parenting was too much for her. He relies on me in his way.

The point is, all my connection points are here. My *life* is here, one that took a significant hit during my six months in Seattle. What if I made the move permanently? Would I ever see Adam and Jamie, or would I lose them to time and distance and domestic bliss, the way so many adult friendships fade away?

"What if I don't take it?"

Nia's eyes soften with apology. "There won't be a position here. I wouldn't be able to keep you."

I'm close enough to Nia that I can be real, at least with my swirling work-related worries. "You seriously think I can lead a team on my own?"

She gives me a look. "Georgia, you already have."

She knows I mean forever, not temporarily, but I let that sink in anyway, remembering the anxiety I felt when I took over while Nia was on maternity leave, the way it melted when Arjun said he'd heard I was doing a great job a few weeks later. Being handed the opportunity to lead recruitment in Seattle and the sense of accomplishment I felt when I left a thriving team there. The restlessness I've felt since I came back. I spent the majority of the last eighteen months stretching myself to the limit and loving it. These past few months have been like hitting cruise control at fifty-five after an extended jag at one hundred.

Nia must see it on my face. She leans forward for the hard sell, elbows resting on her desk. "I've worked with you for almost five years. You're the best employee I've ever had, and that's not an exaggeration."

"You're allergic to exaggeration."

"Exactly," she says, her burgundy-painted mouth pulling up. "This move is the culmination of your hard work. You deserve this, Georgia. It's just a matter of whether you want it."

The panic and misery ebb, replaced by an addicting feeling: pleasure. My response to praise is Pavlovian; when I get it, I want more. Nia is feeding it to me on a silver platter.

They want me to move back for good. But they're doing it because I'm fucking awesome at my job. Because I *killed* it. Because they need me.

I swallow against the anxiety and pride knotted in my throat. "That means a lot coming from you."

Her smile is warm, but then she straightens, turning no-nonsense. "I know you're going out for your best friend's wedding and I'm sorry for dropping this on you the day you leave, but they need to know by the beginning of September if you plan to take it, so I had to tell you now."

"That's in three weeks," I wheeze.

She nods. "Think about it while you're out. Weigh the pros and cons with one of your lists, then enjoy the wedding. When you get back, you can tell me what you want to do."

That's great. But who the hell is going to tell *me*?

Chapter Two

My getting-home routine in Seattle was a dance I never thought I'd have to replicate once I returned to San Francisco. But with Jamie gone, I do it every night: flip the hallway light on right away, then the kitchen light, the living room lamps. Turn the TV on before removing my music-blasting earbuds.

I'm eternally grateful to Grace for introducing me to Jamie when I moved back from New York five years ago, and forever thankful to Jamie for giving me a room to rent without hesitation, then becoming my best friend, something I needed more than ever. I miss the way she'd careen from her bedroom after her full day working as a freelance graphic designer, all golden retriever energy as she greeted me at the front door.

This place feels so empty without her. I wish she was here tonight, but she's across the bay instead, out at a dinner Blake's law firm group is hosting. As for my other options, Adam is probably still spiraling and I don't want to go to my more superficial friendships to help me process Nia's bomb.

Sometimes I swear adulthood is staring at your phone and wondering which of your friends has enough time to deal with your latest emotional meltdown, then realizing none of them do.

Luckily, I'm used to dealing with the messes in my life alone. I collapse onto the gray couch Jamie left behind (along with the enduring mold of her ass on the middle cushion), and pull up my Notes app so I can start a list of pros and cons.

After ten minutes, I have this:

1. I'm moving to Seattle again (pro/con?)

2. For good (con)

3. If I don't, then I'm unemployed (CON)

4. If I do, my friends will probably forget I exist (don't even have to say it)

Oh god. I *can't* move to Seattle.

Even as I think it, though, I remember my time there: those first weeks that I feared would turn into overwhelming loneliness, but instead blossomed into happy hours and weekend explorations with coworkers who turned into friends; the relentless green of it, the way it felt calmer than San Francisco, hushing a vibration in my blood. In New York, there was static noise I could never turn off. I loved Seattle so much I invited Adam and Jamie up to visit, though that never came to fruition.

I suspect I loved it so enthusiastically because I knew I'd come back home. But now San Francisco doesn't feel like home, so how do I know where I actually belong?

Anxiety starts closing its hands around my throat, humming through my body like—

Wait, no, that's my phone underneath my ass. When I grab it, there's a FaceTime request from Adam.

Right, the DJ disaster, aka a problem I can actually fix.

Purpose replaces panic. I can't wrap my head around a life-changing move with everything else going on, which means I can push Seattle away and deal with it when the wedding is over. For now, Adam needs me.

I sit up, flipping on the nearest lamp before wiping under my eyes, then accept the call.

"Hi!" I chirp.

Adam's dark brown hair is a disaster, a harbinger of an imminent meltdown. There are shadows smudged under his hazel eyes, but relief passes over his tan, freckle-dusted face when our eyes meet.

"Hey, are you busy?"

"Not at all." My voice echoes in the empty apartment. "How are we doing?"

He rubs at his jaw. "We're terrible, but slightly less terrible than earlier."

Grace pops onto the screen, resting her chin on Adam's shoulder. She blows a lock of shampoo-commercial-worthy black hair off her exhausted face.

"Hi, Gracie," I say gently. "I'm going to work on a DJ list tonight, someone who'll play the raddest shit."

"Thank you so much." Her brown eyes fill with uncharacteristic tears as Adam pulls her closer. "Okay, no, I'm *not* crying over a DJ, I swear."

"You're more than allowed to cry over a DJ. I've cried over worse, believe me."

This gets me a wet laugh. Adam shoots me a grateful look, then says, "If anyone should be crying over a DJ, it's me. You know I spent *months* finding Stevie."

"I know," I say indulgently. This is a man with meticulously created Spotify playlists. Good music at his wedding is non-negotiable. "What's the latest?"

He sighs. "Grace's brother's friend knows a DJ who might be available. We have a Zoom call with him tomorrow afternoon, but keep that list ready to go."

"I'm on it. See?" I tap the phone screen like I would his chest if we were in the same room. "You're already on the other side of this fiasco."

He runs a palm across his jaw, appraising me. "The other thing is, we need two favors."

"Anything."

"My grandma and grandpa are flying in from Dallas tomorrow and I was supposed to pick them up. Is there any chance—"

I hold up a hand. "I've got them. I love your grandparents, so you're basically doing *me* a favor."

"All right." He gives me a wary look. "Before I ask you for the other one, I want to talk about Eli."

It takes me several beats to digest the sharp turn in conversation. Finally, I get out "oh?" with an evenness I've perfected over the last five years.

Logically, I understand. We have to talk about Eli because he's been Adam's best friend since our sophomore year of high school and he's the best man at his wedding, an imminently approaching event. I've been watching the appointment on my calendar that reads *E here* for weeks with a sense of steely doom.

I only have to look at it for another day. He's flying in from JFK tomorrow.

But whenever Eli is involved, my logic flies out the window, middle finger extended. He's the last person I want to talk about. He's Adam's best friend, yes, but he's been *everything* to me: a stranger when he walked into our lives thirteen years ago. A friend. My best friend. My boyfriend, college and then live-in when he asked me to move to New York with him. Then, fifteen months later, a stranger again.

I have an Eli Mora list that's pages long, but Adam doesn't know that, because Adam thinks Eli and I found a way to be friends after the most cataclysmic breakup of our lives.

That's what we've made him believe.

Eli and I have never explicitly talked about it, but protecting Adam from the aftershocks of our breakup was mandatory. We came to a silent understanding about how things would work between us in order to keep our collective friendship at status quo, and the first time we saw each other after we broke up, a year later, we fell into it like we'd written the list of rules together.

In my weaker moments, I think about what a fucked-up testament it is to the way we knew each other before: bone-deep, down to the marrow. And I think about how utterly heartbreaking it is that we're using the same connection that allowed us to conduct a wordless conversation across the room to know each other in such a clinical way now. Like strangers who've seen each other naked in every way that counts, in all the ways that wreck you.

But after five years and plenty of practice, my weak moments are few and far between, aided by Eli's distant participation.

It helps that Adam's always been careful not to wade into the fray. There was only one time, when he was helping me move into Jamie's apartment, where he asked me, grave-faced, if I was going to be okay, and then if *we* were. For a second, I couldn't breathe. When Eli and I got together, it was easy to promise Adam that nothing would come between the three of us; anything less than forever was just a monster in the closet. Something that would never get us.

I was sick seeing him so worried over a promise we'd broken, and further terrified to think of what would happen if I got as messy on the outside as I felt on the inside. Adam had never given me any indication he had plans to cut me loose, but I knew, thanks to my mom's disappearing act and the transient friendships of my youth, that these things could happen anytime and for less legitimate reasons.

I assured him we were okay and after that, anytime he nudged the subject I repeated my line: *it's fine.*

And it is. But I don't want to talk about Eli. It's bad enough I have to *see* him.

I clear my throat. "Okay. Are you planning to leave me in suspense?"

"Listen," Adam begins. It's not his Jamie's Apartment voice, but it's not neutral either, and my brain sighs out, *shit.*

Grace stands. "I have a sudden hankering for the hand flex in *Pride & Prejudice*, so I'm going to leave you two to it. I'll see you tomorrow, Georgia."

I blow her a kiss, then fix my attention on Adam. He watches his fiancée leave, his eyes turning heart-shaped. "She's so going to fall asleep."

I love that he's in love, but sometimes watching Adam be soft is like observing an alien life-form. "Yes, adorable, please focus."

"Right. Okay." He lets out a breath. "It's just that . . . sometimes I wonder if you and Eli are really okay."

In the ensuing silence, my anxiety crests. "You have to give me more than that."

"Remember Nick and Miriam's wedding last year?"

At the mention of the Lake Tahoe wedding of our high school

friends, my heart lurches. I might be messy on the inside, but I'm pathologically good at keeping it locked up tight.

Except, unfortunately, when I'm not.

I was shocked Eli even came to the wedding. In the last five years, he's missed more events than he's made. I was even more shocked that he was bringing someone, and it was fine, it was okay, because I was bringing someone, too, a guy I'd been dating for a marathon period of three months. He'd just moved to LA but was coming back for the long weekend.

Only, it turned out he had a severe lack of object permanence. He hooked up with his ex two weeks after moving, apparently having forgotten about me back in San Francisco. I went to Tahoe alone.

It was a blow to my iron-clad plan to endure the weekend. I knew Eli and I would keep our distance, but we'd never been around each other with people we were dating. Even before we got together, I rarely integrated anyone into my friendship with Adam and Eli. No one was worth disrupting our dynamic, and it always did—Adam would turn blandly nice, and Eli would turn quiet. I sensed Eli felt the same way; I heard rare romantic rumblings about him, but he never brought anyone around. The entirety of our relationship, from friendship to everything to nothing, was a consistent stretch of not allowing anyone else into our bubble.

Nick and Miriam's wedding popped it, and I had no one to buffer the experience.

No human buffer could have prepared me for existing in the same space as Eli and another woman, anyway, and the raw flash of shock on Eli's face when he saw I was alone felt like an additional detonation in my chest. I looked away before it could turn into pity, then spent the night bending my own rules. I faked fine in front of everyone, but I got sloppy otherwise, splitting my time between drinking myself into oblivion and crying in the bathroom.

Eli got food poisoning and left before the night was over. We barely said a word to each other in front of other people. Another rule broken, flagrantly this time.

I didn't see him the next morning. Adam said he'd gotten on the road early for his flight back, and weeks later, mentioned Eli and his date weren't seeing each other anymore. Apparently his job had gotten in the way. It took everything in me not to laugh, or scream. His job got in the way of every relationship he'd ever had. Ours most of all.

"That night felt weird," Adam says, breaking into my thoughts. "Every other time we've been together you and Eli have been fine, but that night you were . . . not. Lately I've been wondering if you've been *too* fine and that night was closer to the truth."

"Adam, Eli got sick from the salmon and I was drunk. That was the mess."

"Grace saw you crying."

My heart falls out of my chest. "I— because I'd just gotten cheated on."

"I'm not convinced you even liked that asshole. Plus, his name was Julian. You know my theory on J names."

I rub at the pain blooming in my temple. "Yes, that all J names are inherently untrustworthy. Regardless, I did actually like him."

Mostly.

We stay locked in a silent standoff before Adam breaks it. "I stopped asking you and Eli about the specifics of your breakup because whenever I brought it up, you both brushed it off and said it was fine, and I respected that. I still do." Concern and suspicion crease the corners of his eyes. "But are you two really cool with each other? Or has this all been fake?"

I avert my eyes to the FaceTime square I'm contained in so I can monitor my expression. It *is* fake and it's necessary. What happened with Eli is the messiest thing I've ever experienced. I've never wanted to expose Adam to it. Giving him *any* glimpse into how I really feel a week before his wedding, when he's already a disaster, would be tragicomic timing.

"It's not fake," I manage calmly. "Why are you even bringing this up? Nick and Miriam's wedding was thirteen months ago."

"Yeah, and my wedding is next weekend, and you and Eli are about to spend nine days together, not your normal one or two."

I've never been more deeply aware of something in my life.

"I'm holding on to the crumbling corners of this wedding with two hands," Adam continues, "and I'm fucked up with anxiety, except it's mixed with intense joy and all these other weird emotions and Grace—"

He stops with a flinch, then gives me a pleading look. "I need my best people to be okay, mostly because I love you both, but also because *I'm* not okay. So this is like a speak-now-or-forever-hold-your-peace moment. If you need an out, tell me and I'll do whatever you need. Help you figure out how to do the best-people stuff separately, let someone else take over, whatever."

All I hear is, *you won't be around if you're too much.* It's an old fear, refreshed on an endless spin cycle.

I exhale to calm my racing mind and heart, then lean forward, wishing there wasn't a phone screen between us. Wishing there wasn't any distance at all, physical or otherwise. "Things have been going wrong and now you're looking for the next disaster. I get it. But that isn't me and Eli, Adam."

I should get a goddamn Oscar for this performance—my voice is steady, eyes wide and earnest, the color of a cloudless blue sky. I can already see him shifting this from *potential problem* to *not an issue*.

And that's exactly why the rules on my Eli Mora list exist. I can't let it crumble now, especially with Adam sniffing around the truth: I'm not over what happened between Eli and me. Not even close.

"You're *sure*," he says, inspecting me so closely I shrink back from it.

I hold up my hands, palms forward. "We're better than we've ever been."

That's laying it on thick, but I have faith the dynamic Eli and I created will see us through, just like it has every other time, Nick and Miriam's wedding aside.

It'll go like this: we'll greet each other when he gets here, a casual *hey* and *hello*. Our eye contact will be long enough to look normal, but not so lengthy that it clicks like a lock, the way it used to. We'll engage in friendly banter, will only touch if it sells the story. We'll reminisce if the memory includes other people, but otherwise never bring up the past. We'll be the Georgia and Eli Adam knew before we wrecked each other. We'll do that every day until we have to stand side by side while Adam marries Grace, mirroring the vows I thought I'd say to Eli someday. We'll be breezy, chill. Whatever Adam needs.

And when it's over, I'll let out the breath I've been holding. I'll wave from afar as Eli hops on a plane to New York and disappears back into his job.

Not long before I potentially hop on a plane to mine.

"All right," Adam says, oblivious to my two-pronged spiral. "If you and Eli both say it's fine, then it's fine."

I narrow my eyes. "What do you mean if *Eli* says it's fine?"

"I talked to him, too." He lifts an eyebrow at my gaping expression. "C'mon, I wasn't going to ask one of you but not the other."

That our responses mirrored one another's bodes well, but I can't help groaning, "You are a disaster."

"One less thing to worry about." He grins, and relief coils around my spine. "Now, back to the other favor."

"Anything."

"E's flight gets in tomorrow afternoon, right around when my grandparents land—"

No, no, no, my brain chants. I stare at my face on the screen, forcing my expression to stay in a Botox-wishes-it-was-this-frozen look.

"Can you pick him up, too?"

Chapter Three

"Absolutely *not*."

"I'm sorry, I didn't quite—"

"No!" I yell.

"—get that."

"Siri, stop," I shout at my phone on the passenger seat, which is eavesdropping on my shit-talking. I turn back to the task at hand: trying to exert dominance over the ticket machine at the entrance to San Francisco International's short-term parking lot. Even though I've repeatedly pushed the button, it refuses to cough up a ticket, and now there's a restless line of cars snaked behind me.

"You are *not* going to do this to me," I growl at the machine.

"Please take your ticket," is its snotty reply.

"I'm trying!"

Suddenly, an attendant materializes out of the ether. "You need help?"

"You have no idea," I mutter, but I temper it with a sunny, grateful smile. "I can't seem to get a ticket."

"Let's see here . . ." She pushes the button and a ticket slides out, middle fingers raised at me.

It takes every iota of self-control not to scream as I take it from her. "Thank you so much."

"You enjoy your day," she says, and moseys off.

We're way past that, I fear. I'm twenty minutes late, stress-sweating through my seasonally inappropriate sweater, and deeply wishing I could snatch back the "sure!" I threw at Adam's request; in mere minutes, I'm seeing Eli for the first time since Nick and Miriam's wedding.

"It's not like I could've said no, though," I huff, lurching up the ramp.

Arguing out loud with myself is a bad sign, but I'm right. After yesterday's performance, what excuse would I have? The next week is devoted to catering to Adam and Grace's every whim. More importantly, Eli and I are great, as far as our mutual best friend is concerned.

But now my plan to survive the next nine days without anyone knowing I've labeled it *surviving* has officially gone off the rails. I expected the first time I saw Eli to be at Adam's house for dinner tonight, with witnesses. We'd say hello like the old friends we aren't. Maybe I'd tease him about something—his hair and clothes being predictably perfect despite a transcontinental flight, or the junk food he inevitably has stuffed in his backpack. He's an annoyingly healthy eater except when he's flying; he used to assure me, with a mouth full of Snickers, that the lawlessness of air travel meant empty calories didn't count.

After tonight, I'd spend the week too "busy" to be around Eli before floating up to Napa County next Friday for the festivities.

Instead, we have to play Awkward Uber. Eli's flight gets in at the same time as Adam's grandparents', but he has a ground-eating stride he adopted in New York to maximize his six a.m. efficiency from apartment door to office. He'll get to baggage claim way before Adam's grandparents, which will leave us alone together.

One of the golden rules on my Eli Mora list: we don't spend time alone together.

"*Shit.*" I slam my door shut, hustling toward the elevator bay. I think back to the list I dragged out from its hiding spot in a box under my bed at one a.m., reciting it as I hop onto the elevator, and a minute later, rush off of it toward baggage claim.

"Don't make too much eye contact. Ten seconds, max. Don't stand too close. Don't touch. Obviously." I snort at the absurdity of the thought. I haven't felt that man's hands on me for anything but show in five years.

Baggage claim is a well-choreographed dance of chaos when I rush through the automatic doors. I wipe my hands on my jeans, the material abrading my palms. It brings me back into my body; my heart beats in time with my hurried steps as my eyes dart over the crowd. It would be amazing if Adam's grandparents suddenly had the need for speed and beat Eli.

"Don't say anything meaningful," I mutter. "Don't talk about anything more consequential than how great the weather is. Are there clouds in the sky? Well, there aren't now. The sun is shining, the sky is blue, everything is fine."

I repeat my mantra until it's in a cadence as easy as breathing, until I'm sure I've committed every item to memory. It's one thing for me to know I stumbled at Nick and Miriam's wedding last year; it's another to know Adam and Grace saw it. If this week is going to go smoothly, that list has to be ingrained in my mind. I have to play it to the letter.

And so does Eli.

I weave through the crowd, keeping my eye out for Adam's grandparents. Eli can handle himself. The nape of my neck prickles with anxiety when I make another lap and still don't see them. Am I so late that they think I forgot to pick them up? Did they jump in a cab or something? Do they even know how to do that?

What if I *lose* Adam's grandparents?

At least this new spiral is distracting me from my Eli-shaped thoughts, but now I'm turning in a frantic circle, searching for two septuagenarians who've likely peaced out because—

The crowd parts. It sounds ridiculous, but it's true. It's like a dance number in a movie, where everyone spins away to make room for the star to step into the spotlight.

That person is Eli, stepping off the escalator, using those ridiculously long legs to make his way toward me.

The first thing I notice is that he's gorgeous. A head taller than most people, with wide shoulders, dark hair that's slightly overgrown and rumpled, and aggressive stubble that's encroaching on beard territory. His jeans and T-shirt, though clearly in love with his body, are as disheveled as his hair.

That's wrong. Eli gets a haircut every six weeks. Eli's clothes don't wrinkle, and he's always clean-shaven because once his managing director stopped dead in his tracks, stared at the two-day growth on his jaw, and scoffed, "Come on." I exclusively called that man Luce (short for Lucifer).

Thinking about his boss makes me think about his job, which leads me to the second realization: he has a garment bag slung over his arm, but his hands are empty.

Eli is grind culture's poster child, the golden boy of Phillips Preston & Co, an investment bank where he's a Tech, Media & Telecom (or TMT) Associate. His phone is an appendage. No, his lungs—he can't breathe easily if it's not within reach. He should have it in his hand right now, answering a pls fix text from Luce or shooting off an email that can't wait, because they never can. His eyes should be bouncing to me to track my location, but then away. The ten-second rule.

That brings me to the third thing I notice, the reason my stomach spirals out of my body.

Eli's gaze is laser-focused on me. And he's not looking away.

I never forgot what his most concentrated attention felt like, but now as he's fifty feet away, then forty, then twenty, I feel the full force of it for the first time in years.

Even months before we broke up, we were shutting down, diluting a love that had once been so intense I felt it in every fragile system of my body. We stopped talking, were rarely alone together (thanks, Luce), and at the very end, tried not to touch. Maybe we thought it would be easier to let go of a relationship we knew was dead.

Now, for every second we go beyond the threshold of looking, I feel that old connection in my belly, the secret thread I haven't been able to cut all the way through.

I blink away from his attention, my gaze snagging on the thin gold chain laying against his skin, a necklace handed down from his dad, Marcus, who acquired it from *his* dad after visiting distant relatives in Spain years ago. Marcus used to joke that it's the most Spanish thing about their family, and Eli always keeps it close. It disappears under his collar now, unadorned because he only wears the St. Christopher medal that goes with it when he's with his parents. He doesn't have the heart to tell them he's been agnostic since he was seventeen.

My eyes reach the ground just as he comes to a stop in front of me and I watch as the toes of his old black Converse nearly kiss the toes of my Vejas. I last saw them stuffed at the back of our shared closet.

Don't stand too close. It's a neon sign in my brain, my handwriting on a piece of paper. Eli's initials are next to it, a five-year-old silent acceptance.

Now, he slashes a line through it.

Something grips me by the ribs—panic, confusion, an anger I have to control. I inhale, gathering each emotion in tight fists.

"Hey."

Eli's breath is mint and chocolate; it stirs the hairs at my temple. Soap lingers on his skin, layered under recirculated air. Beneath that is the spice of his cologne. I used to spray it on my finger and press it behind his ears, drag the scent down his throat while he watched me with hooded eyes.

"Georgia." That snaps me out of my shock, him saying my name, rare when we're alone.

My gaze jumps to his face. I'm so close that I can see his pupils dilate, the intensity of his expression. It's the polar opposite of our usual vacant coolness.

"Hello," I say, spreading a thick layer of unspoken *what the hell are you doing* over the words so I don't say it, because we don't say the messy stuff out loud. It's what wrecked our relationship, and what's saved us since.

If he heard the hidden message, he doesn't acknowledge it, just lets his eyes roam my face, like he's drinking me in. "Long time, no see."

I know how long, down to the day. "Has it been?"

"You look . . ." His pause is a millisecond long, interrupted by a catch in his breath, but it feels like forever waiting for him to land on, "Good."

What a stupid word. I want to look devastating.

"You look . . ." I try to get out the same word, because he does look good—devastating—but instead I say, "Wrinkled."

A shadow of a smile curls his mouth. "Yeah, well. A six-hour flight with nothing but my thoughts will do that."

My eyes dart around the baggage claim area. Save me from whatever this is. "Must've been some thoughts."

"You have no idea." Our gazes catch again, and my heart flips when he holds me there. "Sorry I'm late. Got caught behind a group of slow walkers."

He says it with a curl of familiarity, like he knows I know that slow walkers are to him what battery acid is to skin. Like he isn't standing too close and looking too long and saying my name.

What the hell are you doing?

It nearly slips out, but I grab my breezy veneer by the neck at the last second. "I was running late, too, so it's only three percent unforgivable. You still beat Adam's grandparents. Do you have a bag?"

This all gets tossed at him rapid-fire while I whirl around, pretending I'm looking for Mr. and Mrs. Kim.

"I checked a suitcase," he says behind me, closer now.

I look at him over my shoulder. Eli is the most efficient packer on earth, but apparently nine days' worth of clothes in a carry-on can fell even the most buttoned-up man.

My eyes land on a wrinkle in his shirt, right over the flat of his stomach.

"You should check which carousel it's coming out of, then." I turn back around, pointing toward a bank of televisions. "You can find it"—way—"over there."

"It's carousel five," Eli volleys back, taking a minuscule step toward me that might as well be a leap. I dance back, pasting a distant smile on my face. "Listen—"

No way. He's taking a page out of both Nia's and Adam's playbooks with that *listen*, and neither of the conversations that followed were in my favor.

A buzzing siren goes off. A carousel starting up. I crane around him to check. Six. *Dammit.* "I bet your bag's coming out soon. Your flight landed, what, twenty minutes ago? Twenty-five? Why don't you go check while I track down Adam's grandparents? We'll meet back here."

I'm mid-flee when I feel his fingers. He doesn't grab me; it's a brush against my arm, not even substantial enough to make me stop. But it sends a bolt of electricity through me and like that, I'm frozen.

When I look at him, I know everything is written on my face: shock, irritation, anxiety. The last thing is reflected in Eli's eyes, the shadow that's always there, but in that swirl of browns and golds is another emotion sparking, too. It's determination.

"Can we talk real quick?" he asks, voice low. "There's something—"

The rest of his sentence is lost to the roar in my ears. We don't ask to talk. There's so much we need to say to each other, which means there's nothing we *can* say to each other. It's been mere hours since Adam gave me his speech, and one *whiff* of something between Eli and me will send him into space.

Absolutely not, I don't say. I don't have to. Like a glorious mirage, Mr. and Mrs. Kim appear in the crowd.

"Ah, there they are!" I push past Eli, but I don't give myself enough room to pass him and my shoulder clips his arm.

I'm falling apart. I'm normally aware of the distance between us, but he's not being careful and suddenly neither am I.

It's the curse, Adam's voice intones in my head.

"Shut up," I mutter as I rush over to his grandparents. I refuse to believe this isn't just a temporary blip.

"Annyeonghaseyo!" I embrace Adam's grandfather, repeating the Korean greeting with the inflection they've drilled into our brains over the years.

Mr. Kim laughs. "It gets better every time we see you."

"It's been so long!" Mrs. Kim exclaims, pulling me into a L'Occitane-scented hug I sink into as Eli and Mr. Kim exchange a hug, too. "How many years, do you think?"

"Two, if you can believe it."

She grips me by the arms, assessing me. "You're more beautiful than ever. Isn't she, Eli?"

I let out what's supposed to be a carefree laugh; it sounds like I'm choking. "Oh, he doesn't—"

"Yes." Eli's response is immediate. His ear flushes a delicate pink as his gaze flicks to mine, and I swear something raw flashes in his eyes. But then I blink and it's gone, if it was ever even there. "She is."

A mechanical buzz rips through the air, and a crowd starts moving toward carousel five.

"Your bag," I get out.

"Yep, my bag," he says, one corner of his mouth twitching out, not up. Something like frustration works across his face, but then he blanks it out. It reminds me of the Eli he was those months before we broke up. The Eli he's been since I left him in New York.

But it's impossible to feel any momentary relief. He tosses me one last look over his shoulder as he walks away, and I don't miss the leftover gleam of determination still there.

Chapter Four

Eli and I are going to be alone for seven and a half minutes.

I was so busy obsessing over his *can we talk* that I didn't think about what came after the airport. Instead, I spent the car ride making small talk with Adam's grandparents while internally I screamed, *can we talk about what?!*

One possible option tightened my stomach with dread: Nick and Miriam's wedding. It's the subject du jour, but if he wants to talk about that, I'm running. He barely looked at me that night, but there's still a chance he saw the cracks in my cheerful laughter and wide smile.

Adam's parents call me and Eli their free-range kids, and when we get there, they sweep us into their adopted parental web. Eli disappears with David, probably so they can bond over the latest puzzle David's in the middle of. I let Laurie's hug recharge my Absent Mom battery, pressing my face into her cloud of blond curls, then raid my designated snack shelf in the pantry while we chat. Eli's old shelf is stuffed with canned goods, save for a fresh bag of Doritos.

It's not until we finally peel ourselves away that I remember we're leaving Adam's grandparents here.

Which means Eli and I are going to be alone for the drive to Adam's house.

I follow him down the driveway with my feet dragging, that *can we talk* squeezing my throat, his *yes, she is* like fingers pinching my chin, demanding my attention for a landslide of memories.

Look.

"You're beautiful," he says when I show up at Adam's house for prom junior year, where we're meeting up with a group of friends—

When his parents get divorced senior year after constant fights about money and jobs, and he cries, so I do, too, apologizing afterward for the makeup that's smeared on my face and his shirt—

When he kisses me for the first time on my twenty-first birthday, just after I blow out the candle on the cupcake he bought me, seconds after I wish for him—

Right before he tells me he loves me a week later—

When I ask him if the dress I'm wearing for his coworker's engagement dinner is okay as he types out a text to Luce, his stress-tight eyes flitting from his phone to me.

I'm so focused on the memories flying out of their usually padlocked box that I don't realize I've followed Eli to the passenger door until I crash into his back.

He turns, hand hovering over the door handle. His eyes are stress-tight again—still, maybe—but recognition sparks in them.

"Oh. You want me to drive?"

The question is absurdly personal coming out of his mouth. I hate driving and he never minded getting behind the wheel for me. He wouldn't know that if we were strangers.

"No!" I grip my keys like a lifeline, repeating less intensely, "No, I'm good. I love to drive, actually."

It's a stupid thing to say, but I don't expect him to call me on it.

So when one corner of his mouth lifts, my stomach clenches. And when he leans back against the car, forearms honest-to-god flexing as he crosses them over his chest, it falls out of my body entirely.

"You do, huh?" he says. "That's new."

As of five seconds ago, his raised eyebrows add, very unnecessarily.

"It's not that new," I reply. Now it's been *ten* seconds. "And I can handle a seven-minute drive regardless."

I'm proud of myself for hacking off thirty seconds. It's not like anything can happen in that timeframe anyway.

Eli clearly takes that as a challenge. Everything about him straightens—his body pushing away from the car, those shoulders, his mouth.

"Listen—"

"We should go. Adam's probably shot off four iterations of a 'where are you?' text," I interrupt, my heart leaping. I start to back up, but he hooks a finger through the belt loop of my jeans, stopping me in my tracks.

I stare down at his finger just as he releases his hold. He's not even really touching me—not the way he used to, with greedy hands—and yet it's impossibly intimate.

My eyes dart up to his throat, where his Adam's apple presses against goose-bumped skin. I imagine I can feel the vibration of his voice there with my mouth when he states, "I'll drive."

Our gazes clash. "I can do it."

"Of course you can," he says, an old mix of wry and weary. "But it's only seven minutes. Right?"

Right. Just fourteen thirty-second intervals where anything could happen, if this weird, determined Eli has his way. "Knock yourself out."

He circles the front of the car and I fumble to get the passenger door open, cursing under my breath.

Thankfully, he forgot to take the key, so I slide into my seat before he's in the car, jamming it into the ignition. The stereo comes to life and I spin the volume dial to an ear-splitting level, where *listens* and *can we talks* go to die.

It takes me three beats to recognize the song. I once cried to it in the bathroom of a dingy bar thinking about, to quote the lyrics, Eli's body being with somebody else.

I'm being trolled. I'm in the seventh circle of hell. I'll never roll my eyes at Adam's belief in curses again.

Maybe it's not his wedding that's cursed. Maybe it's *me*.

Eli slides into the driver's seat and stares at the stereo, then at me, unimpressed.

"Let's go."

My words are buried under the sound, but his eyes drop to my mouth, reading my impatience. He drags his gaze back up to my eyes as he presses the stereo dial, plunging us into silence.

I hear it coming, whatever he wanted to say outside, at the airport, maybe since we saw each other thirteen months ago. So I keep *his* gaze as I press the dial again, filling the space with that terrible song.

That's right, I think as frustration blooms over his face. *I'd rather listen to a song that makes me think about you having sex with someone else than discover the cliffhanger on the other end of your* can we talk?

He reaches for the stereo. I grab his thumb. We stare at each other for five seconds, indie pop serving as our standoff music, and I see his next move in the narrowing of his eyes. He must see something in mine, too, because we lunge at the same time, our fingers tangling on our way to the dial. My nerve endings sing with the contact of our skin; I get there first, slapping my palm over the button.

"Georgia," he says, with more emotion than we've given each other in years. It's half exasperation, half request, with a pinch of amusement, because Eli always gives 110 percent.

In it, I hear every way he's ever said my name, though: affectionately, through tears, in the middle of pleasure. Not the way he has in our post-breakup world, like air, something I can walk through without resistance.

"You can't just commandeer my stereo because you're driving," I yell over the music.

"You know that's not what I'm trying to do." He leans in to say it; I feel every word against my cheek.

"Just *go*."

His hand covers mine, his palm spooning the back of my hand. And then, with his eyes fixed on our connection, he presses down. Hard.

In the sudden silence, our separate heavy breaths sound like gasps.

"What are you doing?" What I really want to say is, *stop forgetting how we do this*. But I have to be unruffled Georgia. Easy Georgia.

"I need to talk to you."

"Since when?" I can't help my incredulous tone. He's never asked to talk post-breakup. He's never *wanted* to, same as me; that's why we've been able to go five years like this.

"Since f—" Eli's eyes widen and then close briefly. His next words are chosen carefully. "I want to talk before we get to Adam's. *About* Adam."

That doesn't soothe me, considering the conversation I had with Adam last night, and the fact that I know he had it with Eli, too. "What about him?"

Eli's hand slides from mine, his fingers moving over every bump of my knuckles. It lingers only to ensure I'm not going to attempt to destroy our hearing again, but it still sends an unwanted thrill through me.

Not ideal.

When it's clear I'm not going to stop him, he sinks against the seat, running a hand through his hair. "I've been . . . a catastrophically bad best man the past eight months, and a not-great best friend for longer. My job wa— is— I've had a lot of—"

When he's not looking at me, I can look at him—at the bunch of his jaw as he cuts himself off, how his mouth stretches into a grimace, the slight shake of his head. He's censoring himself. It's strange to know his tells but no longer be privy to what they're about.

He begins again. "He hasn't relied on me for any wedding-related thing, for good reason. And neither have you, despite the fact that we were supposed to share the duties. I mean, Jesus," he says, letting out a humorless laugh, "I couldn't even make it to the bachelor party I planned five percent of."

I lean back, startled.

Adam's Tahoe bachelor party three months ago was a joint effort in name only—Eli and I exchanged a few absurdly formal emails. I assigned him some tasks so he wouldn't feel shitty about it, but gave myself the brunt of the work, not trusting that the job that's gotten in the way of everything else wouldn't do it again.

I shouldn't be surprised that he recognized it. It wasn't the first time I played that game with him, nor the first time I was right to do it.

It wasn't his fault he missed the party, though. He was supposed to fly directly to Reno from his work's mandatory retreat in Miami, then drive to the cabin we rented. But he never made it, thanks to a tropical storm that blew in.

Truthfully, he hasn't been a catastrophically *bad* best man, but he hasn't been a good one. Even from thousands of miles away, I could see how much more he wanted to be involved, and how incapable he was of doing so.

And now, I can see how desperately he wants to change that. The fact that he's here nine days before the wedding is nearly unbelievable. Not only that, but he hasn't pulled his phone out once, not even when I was chatting with Adam's grandparents. He stared out the window, fingers fidgeting in his lap.

He's doing that now, except he's picked up the gum wrapper from my cup holder.

"You can't blame yourself for bad weather," I say finally.

His attention stays on the wrapper, shaping it. "I can blame myself for everything else. Not being there for him, not responding to texts in the group chat on time when shit's hit the fan. Adam texted me about the DJ thing and you know what he said when I asked if I could help?"

I press my lips together.

One corner of his mouth picks up grimly. "'We're all good, buddy. Georgia's on it.'"

I'm an asshole for the warm streak that sends through my chest, but I've got my own hang-ups.

Eli's long fingers continue to work in a familiar pattern, his thumb smoothing over the outside, turning it around his index finger. Forming a ring.

I look away. It's a talent he honed years ago at his sisters' request, and continued even after they stopped asking for them. I have dozens of my own in a Converse shoebox under my bed, all of them given to me first as a friend and then as a promise.

"I have so much to make up for." The crack in Eli's voice brings me back; the devastation on his face shocks me. Not that he's so torn up about it, but that he's letting me see it. "I need to make a dent this week in fixing what a shitty friend and best man I've been."

"What do you mean?"

"I mean, you've been Adam's right-hand woman in all of this. Every time I've talked to him, he's mentioning something you've helped with, how they'd be lost without you."

The praise sings through me so strongly it feels like relief. God, I need to be needed. To be held on to any way I can get it.

"You're a very good friend, Georgia," Eli says, and there's a tiny blade to his tone. Not enough to cut me, but enough that I know it's cut him to hear it. "I haven't been, and I have no one to blame but myself, but I want to change that. If anything else goes sideways, I need you to let him lean on me. Let me take care of things, run errands, whatever wedding shit he and Grace need."

"'Whatever wedding shit' doesn't inspire a lot of confidence."

His eyes flash, both with humor and stubbornness. "You know what I mean."

I want to say no, that he'll have to fight me for space, because I need it, too. If I go to Seattle, I won't have it anymore.

But Eli's had less for longer and we both know it. It's not just that he's been lost in his career; I'm the one who came back home. I've had the power of proximity on my side for the last five years. Letting Eli take on a few things to assuage his guilt won't kill me. More importantly, it'll make Adam happy.

"I promise you can rely on me," Eli says quietly, a tiny shiver to it.

I glance at him to find his attention on the ring pinched between his fingers. He turns it like he's appraising a diamond, his lashes sweeping across the faint purple hollows beneath his eyes.

I hear what he doesn't say: *you can rely on me this time.* We both feel the specter of missed dinners and weekend trips canceled, of feelings I didn't share and plans I made without him, of nights where I fell asleep alone in an apartment it felt like we shared in name only.

His addiction to his job is so indelibly tied to his anxiety, and I know the cause—the instability of his dad's career has always felt like the catalyst for his previously perfect family falling apart. He's been starving for something solid half his life. But that knowledge has never made it hurt less.

My throat is thick when I say, "I'm sure there's enough to go around."

"Okay." His gaze lingers on me, something indecipherable playing under the relief. "Thank you."

"Is that all?"

His mouth parts, his thumb moving absently over the ring he's made. Finally, he places it in the cup holder before his eyes meet mine. "Unless there's something on your mind."

It's not a challenge exactly, but I don't like the probing curve of his voice. "Nope," I say, sinking deeper into my seat. "I'm great."

Just *wonderful.*

Chapter Five

"Party's here!" I call as I open the bright blue door of Adam and Grace's shingled Craftsman, ignoring the gallery wall displayed above the entry table where I dump my purse. Last time I was here I noticed all the new pictures taken while I was in Seattle, including a group photo of Adam and Grace with their married Marin friends.

I peek into the cozy living room, which is empty but not quiet; a Mac Miller song is pumping through the sound system displayed on a fancy Scandinavian-style media unit.

It's a much nicer version of the TV stand Eli and I bought for our Upper West Side apartment, a thought I can usually squash before it turns into a memory. But today it splashes out in Technicolor: Eli kneeling on the creaky hardwood floor in front of the brick wall I fell in love with at first sight, muttering to himself while he assembled it. Me cross-legged on the mattress we hadn't bothered to push into the bedroom yet; the view was better from the living room. I watched him instead of reading the intimidating orientation email from my new company, then laughed when he tackled me, sweat dripping down his nose because we didn't have an A/C unit yet.

"Look," he whispered, his mouth grazing mine. "Our first piece of furniture."

Distantly, I wonder if he still has it, or if he sold it when he moved out.

Eli steps up behind me, pulling me from the memory.

"I'm going to drop my stuff in the guest room." His proximity pushes me into the past again before I shove it away.

"Great," I chirp, already prepping for the show we'll put on for Adam.

Eli's careful not to touch me as he brushes past, which feels unnecessary considering the myriad times he's already made contact since the airport, but whatever.

I watch him disappear down the hallway. He's staying at Adam and Grace's until we go up to Napa next Friday, and I try not to feel lonely that he's here while I'm flung away in the city by myself. He's alone all the time.

And you aren't?

With a sigh, I make my way to the backyard. Adam's cul-de-sac with like-minded homes is tucked against a densely forested hillside, so his yard is bordered by mature pine and oak trees, which are shimmying in the early evening breeze. A cream sectional and firepit take up most of the patio, and the lawn beyond it is choppily mowed—Adam's novice craftsmanship. In the city, the only outdoor space they had was a shared, sloping rooftop.

Adam's frowning down at the grill, but double-takes when he sees me.

"Dude, it's about time," he says, reaching out for a fist bump. "I thought you ditched me."

"When you're cooking Korean barbecue? Never." I sidle up to him, peeking at strips of sizzling galbi, then elbow him. "Hey, stranger."

"Hey, you." He wraps an arm around my shoulders, squeezing. "How're things?"

"Great." A word that doesn't fit, but the one I use most often. "I almost forgot what your face looked like, though."

He grimaces, flipping the meat. "I know, it's been, what, two weeks since we've seen you? Three?"

"Five," I say lightly.

"No way." His head tilts as he mentally calculates. "Shit, you're right. Well, you'll get tired of my face by the time this wedding is done, believe me."

I let out a hum. "Yours, definitely, but not Grace's. Where is she?"

"Had to run to pick up a prescription real quick," he says, poking at the galbi. "She'll be back."

I'm about to ask if everything is okay when a voice calls out, "Hey, Kiz, heard there's a wedding coming up. Thought I'd crash it."

When I look over my shoulder, Eli is framed by the French doors leading into the kitchen. My heart leaps, even though I just saw him. His gray T-shirt shows off the tantalizing curve of his biceps and the broadness of his chest, highlighting the way I'd fit right there.

They haven't seen each other since Adam visited him right after New Year's, which means I should step out of the way before—

Yep, there they go. Adam pushes around me with a whoop of joy, nearly hurdling over the sectional to wrap his best friend up in a hug. Eli lets out an *oof*, then a laugh. His eyes close as he claps Adam on the back, something grief-like tightening his features.

Adam's shoulders drop as he crows happily, swaying Eli back and forth. It's obvious he needed this. Not just me, but *us*. It's moments like this that I'm grateful for the work Eli and I have put into protecting our collective friendship, even though it's torturous at times. The thought of losing this is worse.

"I'm so glad you're here," Adam says.

Eli's exhale is shaky. "I'm sorry I wasn't here before. For the bach—"

"Don't start that shit again." Adam pulls back with a frown, smacking his cheek not-so-softly. "Not kidding, I will smother you in your sleep."

My heart pings at the expression on Eli's face, a replica of when he made the speech he must've practiced during his six-hour flight. Those wrinkles make sense now.

I saunter closer. "You know it's legit when Adam threatens murder."

"Exactly," Adam says, shaking Eli by the shoulders. "Besides, you covered my buy-in for our fantasy football league this season. We're good."

Eli gives him a droll look. "Sure, sounds even."

"It is," Adam insists. "Your robot brain wins that shit every year and it's infuriating when it's my money. You're saving me the high blood pressure *and* two hundred dollars. I can put that toward grill accoutrements or something."

"Or a neighborhood kid who knows how to mow a lawn," I say.

Adam shoots me a glare. "It's harder than it looks, you dick."

"To be fair, you make it look impossible," Eli says, rubbing a hand across his jaw as he slides me a conspiratorial look. I bite back a grin.

"Okay, you know wh—" Adam sighs, keeping one arm around Eli's shoulders and extending the other toward me, waving his hand. "Shut up and let's hug it out."

As I close the distance, I try to assess whether Eli will play along. He's been so intent on bucking our rules that a wild fear he'll do it in front of Adam grabs me by the throat.

But I should know better. He'll do anything for Adam, the same way I will. He lifts his arm, exposing that Georgia-shaped spot. One corner of his mouth quirks into the easy smile I haven't seen in private for years, executed perfectly.

"Come on in," he says, like he's inviting me into his home.

The hug doesn't last long, but I can feel every point where Eli and I are connected, the way his fingers tighten around my ribs. I swear I feel his breath stutter against my hair, but maybe it's the breeze. I breathe out slowly, not wanting to inhale any piece of him.

I'm the first to let go, and take two healthy steps back. "How was the DJ call?"

Eli raises an eyebrow at Adam's groan. "That good, huh?"

"Fucking weird." Adam shivers. "I don't want to talk about it. George, any luck on your end?"

"Got a potential list on my phone."

"I can hel—" Eli starts, but Adam waves him off.

"Nah, let's put a pin in it. No wedding talk tonight. Grace should be back soon, and Jamie and Blake are on their way."

Eli's mouth tightens, then flexes into the approximation of a smile. "Sure."

"Don't know what I'd do without you two," Adam says, shaking his head. "And I don't want to think about it."

I know Eli's response would echo mine: we don't want to think about it either.

"Your *hair*! Very dark, luxurious, sex-kitten vibes," Jamie yelps as she Kool-Aid Mans into the backyard, cinnamon curls shimmying against her fair-skinned cheeks.

"Thanks, suction cup," I tease as she launches herself at me. My arms go around her waist, squeezing hard so she can't let me go.

Just like that first time I met Eli, I felt an immediate sense of belonging when I met Jamie. A close high school friend of Grace's, she'd recently relocated from LA and was looking for a roommate, a welcome coincidence since I'd moved home with nowhere to go. I didn't want to stay with my dad, even temporarily; I'd just left a workaholic who largely forgot that I lived with him. Thankfully, Jamie opened her door without hesitation.

I miss her so much it aches in my bones.

She pulls back, wide brown eyes fixed on my hair. "You colored it! When?"

"Last month," I say as Blake Williams, Jamie's girlfriend, greets Adam and Eli in the background. It startles me to realize this is the first time she and Eli are meeting. Blake melted into our group so seamlessly that sometimes I forget she and Jamie only started dating eight months ago. Eli's wearing a contemplative smile as she and Adam laugh. Probably drawing up nickname options.

"Unacceptable," Jamie sputters. "First, that I haven't seen you in that long, and second, that you wouldn't send me a selfie."

I hold up my hands in defense. "I took a few, but the color difference didn't show in photos."

She's so tied up these days, and I tend to be a mirror anyway; whatever time someone has to give me is what I give back in an attempt to be unobtrusive. I still send her the most important bits of my life, but dyeing my hair two shades darker doesn't rank.

She presses a finger into my sternum, clearly not in agreement. "Send them anyway. Ten, minimum, from all angles."

I swat her hand away with a laugh. "You're ridiculous."

"She won't let up until you do, you know," Blake says as she saunters over. Her locs are pulled back from her architecturally perfect face, and an intricate collection of tattoos decorates the rich brown skin of her arms. She winds one around my waist, adding in her melting Tennessee twang, "Hey, honey. We miss you."

"Miss you, too," I say. My heart squeezes at the *we*, even though I love seeing Jamie so blissful. It's just hard to get used to her having another Person, especially because I didn't get to say a proper goodbye to what had essentially become our long-term platonic partnership. "I'll send her twelve, just to be safe."

"I want some commotion for the hair, that's all," Jamie says. "It looks amazing."

I shoot a meaningful look at Adam and Eli. "No one else noticed."

"It looks brown." Adam holds his hands up, eyes widening. "Was it not brown before?"

"I noticed," Eli says, moving closer.

"Okay, ass kisser," Adam mutters.

Eli laughs. "It *was* brown before, genius." His finger barely touches my neck as he separates a lock of hair from the rest, but it sets off fireworks in my stomach as if he palmed my throat. I freeze, watch him wind it briefly around his forefinger, then tug, his gaze intent on it. "Now it's a browner brown."

Wow. There's no way he's noticed my hair despite his oddly avid attention, which means he's really selling it tonight. His enthusiasm for our show runs on a curve—he's just as likely to be interrupted by a call or otherwise stressed into distraction.

But right now he's very present. Maybe Adam's speech spooked him, too.

I hook a finger over the lock he's holding, disconnecting us. "Way to nail the technical name of the color." My gaze flicks up to his hair. "Is that what you asked for, too?"

He rocks back on his heels, putting some space between us. "I went with brownest brown, actually."

I hum. "A bold move."

"It looks good." His eyes make a hard stop where my hair rests at the top slope of my breasts, then rebound.

Good. That word again. He says it now like it means something else, but I don't know what. What I *do* know is he's doing it for the proverbial cameras.

I grant him a sunny smile, saying, "*Thank* you," before sliding Adam a teasing glare.

"Oh, Christ," he mutters. "Can you two please cut me a break on my *wedding week?*"

"No," we say in unison.

"Hey."

We turn at the sound of Grace's voice. She's standing in the doorway, a CVS bag dangling from her fingers. She looks stunning in vintage Levi's and a white tank top that offsets her skin, her black hair waterfalling down her back. Not for the first time, I think about how lucky Adam is. Grace is gorgeous and smart, but she's also warm and almost supernaturally calm. Tonight she's glowing, even if her expression is curiously blank.

Come to think of it, so's the tone of her voice.

"*Whatisitareyouokay?*" Adam streaks past us, his freckles

standing out in stark relief on his suddenly pale face. His eyes move frantically over her. "Is it the—"

"Meadowcrest Ranch called. There was a fire."

"A fire," Adam repeats incredulously and with a confusing amount of relief.

"Adam," Grace says, exasperation weaving through her tone like a stiff breeze. "Our wedding venue caught on fire. It's *gone*."

Chapter Six

"It's impossible."

"It's not."

"It has to be."

"It's *not*," Grace insists. "They called me on my way home from the pharmacy, remember?"

There's a long pause before Adam whispers, "Gracie. It's the fucking curse."

They've cycled through this exchange three times, angled toward each other on their living room couch. They're in their own miserable world while Eli and I hover anxiously. Jamie and Blake are on an emergency In-N-Out run—in a moment of unfortunate irony, we all forgot about the galbi on the grill and it burned to a crisp.

Adam runs an agitated hand through his hair. "I understand that the worst part of all this is that Meadowcrest is damaged. My uncles have been managing the Blue Yonder renovation and it's been a fucking nightmare, and that was planned, not something catastrophic."

The three of us acknowledge his PR statement with murmurs of assent. Blue Yonder Winery has belonged to Adam's mom's family for fifty years; it's a gorgeous sixty-acre estate in

Rutherford that's been undergoing an expansion, their event space in particular. They're one of the few wineries in Napa County that can host weddings, having been grandfathered in before a law prohibited them on winery grounds, and want to capitalize on it. When Adam and Grace got engaged, the renovation was already underway. They chose Meadowcrest instead, a family friend's ranch with an outdoor ceremony space and a beautiful, remodeled barn.

Grace squeezes Adam's thigh. His gaze moves over her face, expression softening, until a spark of panic reignites. "*Fuck*. We're supposed to get married in nine days."

Grace is always the calm in the storm, the one who laughs off disasters and brings Adam down from the ceiling. So I'm wholly unprepared for the way she bursts into tears.

For a second, Adam looks stricken. But then he adjusts to the shift, wrapping his arms around her with a crooning "Honey."

"Everything is screwed," Grace says, pressing her face against his neck. "Why can't one thing go right?"

"It's my fault," Adam says. "I knew we shouldn't have gotten married in Napa if we weren't doing it at Blue Yonder. Everyone in my family has gotten married there since its inception. I was asking for this."

Grace pulls back, wiping at her cheeks with the heel of her hand. "Okay, no. The chances of it being ready in time for our wedding were slim. No one blinked when we chose Meadowcrest."

Adam groans. "I know, I know. I just need something to blame this on, other than a fucking feral animal chewing through wiring and sparking a fire."

She lets out a wet laugh. "God. Only us."

I pull my phone out of the back pocket of my jean shorts, tapping my Notes app icon. "I'll start a to-do list."

Adam and Grace don't hear me, but Eli sure does. He's across the room in seconds, hovering over my shoulder. His body heat against my back is a wall I could lean into. Instead, I take a step forward, craning my neck to look up at him. His gaze is trained on my phone screen. I angle it away.

If I weren't so close, I wouldn't see the tightening of his eyes as they bounce up to meet mine. But I am close. *He* is, so I see that tick of frustration.

"Maybe let him burn through his panic before you go full cruise director," he says, his breath fanning over my cheek.

"Definitely too soon for a burn reference," I volley back, tamping down a shiver. "I'm starting a list of ways to fix this, that's all."

"Why don't I do that?"

I raise an eyebrow. "Five seconds ago you wanted to let him burn through his panic."

His mouth twitches. "That was five seconds ago. I've moved on."

"Awesome, then you can put together your own list on your own phone."

"I . . ." Eli trails off. "I don't have it with me."

I blink. "In California?"

He gives me a look, like I should know better. I should. I do. "On me. It's in my room."

My brain inspects that from several angles. *Wrong*, it says, but I can't put the picture together.

"Okay, well, feel free to go get it. I'm not going to solve world peace, much less the Mount Everest that is this issue, in the next two minutes."

He crosses his arms, staring me down. In a friendly way, because we're still in Adam's sight line. "Don't forget what we talked about in the car."

"That was two hours ago. I didn't forget."

I haven't forgotten the conversations we had five *years* ago. The ones we didn't have, too.

I swear Eli sees that thought written on my face. I expect him to drop the subject and put distance between us like I'm trying to do. Go get his phone so he can disappear into it. It's a routine we completed many times when we were together and things got tense—both of us would walk away.

He steps closer instead. "They're going to need help."

"I know."

"Adam's going to need us."

That *us* hits me straight in the heart. I want to push at the word with both hands, right out of this house. Out of my life. "I *know*."

"Then let me—"

"George, you okay?"

Adam's voice cuts through the tension growing between me and Eli. I whip around, a questioning smile ready to go. "Yes?"

"Your face just looked—"

"Careful."

"Troubled."

"That's her making-a-list face," Eli interjects.

I can't help rolling my eyes. "I don't have a making-a-list face."

"You do," he says with a small affectionate smile, like this is real. "It's one of your many faces."

"What, are you counting my faces?"

"Got a whole list of them."

"Very meta," Adam jokes.

"Please, I did *not* give you permission to encroach on my dedicated list space," I say.

It's a veiled warning but he just grins, the easy one. I miss when that smile was real and just for me.

"We were about to start brainstorming." He says this to Adam, but his attention stays trained on me.

I don't miss his carefully placed *we*, but it's not like I can call him on it, so instead I turn and give Adam a mock salute. "Put us in, Coach."

"Actually, you may not need the list," Adam says.

Huh? A list is always needed. "Why? Are you postponing?"

"No," Adam says, exchanging a look with Grace. "There are, uh, a lot of reasons we can't, but the biggest one is that I'm not throwing away thousands of dollars without a fight."

"What Adam's saying is he might have a solution," Grace says.

"Perfect." I perk up, even though a tiny piece of me wishes I thought of whatever Adam dreamed up. My gaze darts to Eli, my unremorseful list-blocker.

"Could be a long shot, but it's the best one we have." Adam blows out a breath. "I'm going to see if we can have the wedding at Blue Yonder after all."

❧

If the house I grew up in was my first home and Adam's parents' was my second, Blue Yonder was my third. I spent every summer in high school there, working odd jobs with Adam, and Eli, too, when he joined us from junior year on. We continued the tradition into college, though that ended the summer before our senior year when Eli got an internship with a bank in New York, a necessary step on his path to becoming an analyst once he graduated.

"It's fine, I don't want to hang around you two while you're all in love and horny for each other anyway," Adam had said, but it was a half-truth. Those summers meant so much to the three of us. They meant *everything* to Eli and me. Especially our last one.

It was moonlit swims and lingering touches and a different kind of tension growing between us. A stomach-swooping knowledge that our friendship was changing its shape, and that Eli would be at Cal Poly with me come fall. Logically I knew he'd chosen it because he'd gotten the best financial aid package there. But in a way it felt like he was choosing me, too, and it made belonging sing through my blood. Possibility and fear and wanting stretched out in front of us that whole summer, as vast as the sky above us, and as untouchable with Adam around.

Eli and I never went back there together. Without new memories to layer over it, that last summer is preserved in amber. It's the only thing I think about when I'm there. How wrapped up my heart was in Eli. How much I wanted it, the *us* we already were but set on fire. How terrified I was to step into it because I didn't want to lose him as my best friend. I had so few of those.

It's why I was so relieved when Adam and Grace decided to book Meadowcrest. And it's why my heart drops out of my body as I gasp, "That would be *great*!"

Things happen in a blur. Jamie and Blake return with the food. My stomach turns at the thought of it, and also at the thought of having to stand next to Eli while Adam gets married in front of the massive oak tree Eli and I would take breaks under, my head propped on the hard pillow of his thigh. At the thought of dancing on the sprawling lawn overlooking the vineyard during the reception, where I watched Eli play tag with Adam's little cousins, grinning beautifully at me when he collapsed as they "caught" him.

Eli disappears into his room for a stretch of time and then comes back, but his hands are still empty. Neither one of us is making that list. Maybe that's why everything feels like quicksand.

Meanwhile, Adam paces from the kitchen to the living room and back again, phone pressed to his ear.

When he returns, we're all gathered, holding our breath.

I'm a villain for the *please, no* that goes through my head. Adam and Grace deserve a break. I just wish it wasn't a break that included Blue Yonder.

"My uncles think we can make it happen. The indoor reception space won't be ready, but the lawn's fine," Adam says, flopping down onto the couch next to Grace. "We need someone up there, though, and Grace and I can't go until next week because—"

He stops, glancing at Grace with wide, apologetic eyes.

"It's okay," she says. "They should know, given everything that's happened."

Adam turns to us, lit up, and blurts, "Okay, thank god, I hate secrets. Grace is pregnant."

There's a beat where we're all frozen, but then the room explodes with sound. My tear ducts figure it out before my brain does—I'm crying seconds before I say "Oh my *god*." A hand goes to my back as I stand. I assume it's Jamie or Blake, but no, wait, they're already hugging Adam and Grace.

It's Eli beside me. For a beat I think he's getting me out of the way, but his hand doesn't leave that tingling space between my shoulder blades.

He's pushing me toward Adam, into his arms.

My best friend pulls me into the tightest hug, nearly shaking, and I hold on, too. I close my eyes, willing the fist in my throat to loosen. It's amazing and surreal; their lives are going to change again.

And I might be in Seattle.

My heart takes off as I let Eli slide into my place and take

in the scene before me. It's been so long since we've all been together like this and I wonder if, after the wedding, we'll be like
this again.

My emotions are never simple, but tonight they're especially
knotted: happiness and fear and guilt for being afraid of what
might change. A sense that this is a goodbye to an era that shaped
me. The fear, again, that maybe it's a bigger goodbye, too.

Grace is answering questions being thrown at her as we sit—
she's only seven weeks; they found out two weeks ago; no one
but their parents and Grace's brother and best friend know. It's the
biggest reason they don't want to postpone.

She looks at Adam, threading her fingers with his. "I also don't
want to wait until after the baby comes. I'm ready to be your wife
right now."

"I'm ready to be your husband," he says, his entire heart in
his eyes.

"Oh my god, the serotonin," Jamie cries, winding her arms
around Blake's neck.

Eli wipes at his eyes and leans forward in the cream linen
lounge chair across from mine. I watch him exchange a proud look
with Adam, his expression flooded with an emotion that looks like
relief.

"What do you need?" I ask Grace. "Can we do anything?"

"Right now I'm trying to get through the day without puking.
Zofran is going to be my best friend." She points at the CVS bag on
the coffee table. "And, in the worst timing in history, I have an OB
appointment on Thursday for our pregnancy confirmation. We
can't get up to Blue Yonder before Friday morning."

"There's so much to do," Adam says. "Meadowcrest was all-
inclusive for food, including cake, so we need a fix for that. And
the fucking DJ. We can do the research, but it'd be life-saving

to have someone there to vet local vendors and help with winery-related stuff." His gaze goes to Eli, who straightens, before landing on me. "I know it's a lot to ask to get someone there right away, but . . ."

Jamie's working until Wednesday and Blake has a deposition on Thursday, which means she won't be able to get up to Napa until Friday. They're out.

Even if they were available, though, it's obvious who should do this. Adam's got his pleading eyes activated on me.

Sorry, Eli, I think with a twinge of guilt. I make a mental note to tell Adam to give him something to do here. Maybe he can help research bakeries on the phone he's so suddenly allergic to.

I open my mouth, just to make it official, but another voice overlaps with mine.

It's been years since we've said what we wanted out loud and had it be the same thing.

Now, as Eli's eyes lock with mine, we say together, "I'll do it."

Chapter Seven

What?

I can't say it out loud, not when Adam's looking between Eli and me, his expression lit up like it's Christmas and the A's winning the World Series and the day the three of us met and any moment with Grace all smashed together—a thrilling hope that's been solidified into reality.

I want to scream.

Instead, my eyes find Jamie's. She knows more about my and Eli's history than anyone. I was careful with my heartbreak at first, but like me, Jamie doesn't keep strangers. As we became closer, I realized she wouldn't retreat from my messy feelings, that in fact she welcomed them—"Baby, I'm a Pisces, I wallow in feelings," she said one night when she caught me sobbing over a pint of Ben & Jerry's—so I gave her the CliffsNotes version of what happened.

But five years is a long time to hold a . . . whatever this is. Not a grudge, but something equally heavy. Over time, I've finessed my message even with her, framed it as discomfort over orbiting in the same sphere as my ex rather than try to explain all the confusing messiness that I still carry around.

Judging by the wide-eyed look she gives me, it's not discomfort on my face right now. It's a concerning slip of my chill-girl-no-that's-totally-fine mask I glue over my perma-scream when Eli's in the mix.

I'm not chill. And it's not totally fine.

I wrestle my expression into submission, my eyes darting from Jamie to Eli, who's pointedly focused on Adam. After an entire afternoon of him looking at me, *now* he won't?

The curve of his jaw is carved out obstinately, his arms crossed over his chest. I'm so unused to this version of Eli; we never fought each other for anything, not even our relationship, but it's clear he won't let this go.

One thing is clear: no way are we going up to Blue Yonder together, of all places. The rising color in Eli's cheeks confirms we agree.

"I mean, it would be incredible to have you up there, E, but are you sure you'd be able to go?" Adam asks, his mouth pulling down with concern. "I know you technically have the time off, but do you *really* have the time off? I don't want you dealing with this shit and your usual shit on top of it."

I straighten. Oh, thank god, an out. "That's a great p—"

"Work isn't going to distract me," Eli says.

A short huff of laughter escapes me before I can stop it. Eli looks over at me, his mouth pressing into a thin line.

"It won't," he promises, his voice too confident, and too shadowed with our history. I swallow, looking away. "Work is the last thing on my mind. I'm here for you, for whatever you need."

He's talking to Adam, but if I close my eyes, I can imagine some parallel universe version of him saying it to an alternate universe version of me. With the real Eli, work always comes first. And with the real me, showing people I need them comes last.

I don't understand what his endgame is; Eli is many things, but a liar isn't one of them. Still, I can see his earnest words are softening Adam up—his shoulders drop, his frown lifting into appeasement.

"I'm here for you, too," I argue. *And I've* been *here for you*, I add silently. I *was the one you were giving please-help-me eyes to two minutes ago.*

Adam appraises us, head tilted, an emotion I can't identify passing through his eyes. Then his expression melts into something soft and happy. "This is perfect."

"What?" My confusion is perfectly synced with Eli's.

"It'll be great to have you both up there," Adam says. A lightning flash of what looks like pure panic crosses Eli's face before he shuts it down. "I mean, it makes sense, right? My best people, helping save the big day together."

The sound that escapes Eli's mouth is quiet. Mine is a honk.

"Wait. You want us to go up together? Me and Eli?"

I put the barest emphasis on his name, just a sprinkle, like Salt Bae with immense restraint. But I never make a fuss so I might as well have yelled, "You want me to go with *Eli*, the man who took a sledgehammer to my heart? *That* Eli?"

Jamie's looking at me, silently asking, *do you want me to step in?* I transmit back a deceptively calm *no*, scrambling to figure out how to do this when I promised Adam yesterday Eli and I were better than ever. When I told Eli he could hip check me to the side in order to assuage his guilt for being an absentee everything.

Blake flicks a quick look at me. "You really need two people up there? There must be plenty to do down here, too."

I want to hug her for stepping in, but Jamie does it for me, a little hand squeeze and a smile Blake returns with a wink.

"My parents and brother are getting in tomorrow from LA and will probably hover unless I give them something to do,"

Grace says. "And we have a bunch of other people around, including you and Blake. We should be good. But only if you really don't mind."

"You don't, right?" Adam asks.

He's looking at me like I hold the key to his happiness in the palm of my hands. I've never been able to resist a look like that. It reminds me of the way Eli looked at me when he asked me to move to New York with him.

It was a mistake to say yes then, and it'll be a mistake to say yes now.

But I don't get a chance to say anything at all, because Eli speaks up. "We're in."

"We're *in*?" I echo.

"Sure are." His eyes flick to me before looking at Adam. "See? We're already ready to go." I wonder if anyone else notices the imperceptible tightness in Eli's smile. "We'll get up there tomorrow and hit the ground running."

I wrap eye daggers in cotton candy clouds, shooting them his way. His gaze snaps back to me like he feels the slice of my secret frustration. Like he knows exactly what I'm thinking.

And maybe he does. Maybe he's wondering, too, what'll happen if we're together for the next week in a place where so many of our best memories live.

I wish that gave me any comfort. Instead, it only validates the feeling that *I'm* the cursed one.

I make it another hour before I announce I'm heading home. Nearly everyone groans their disapproval, and my secret praise kink purrs at the thought of being missed.

Jamie follows me to the front door. She gives me a bone-crunching squeeze, whispering, "We need a huddle. Lots to discuss."

I hum noncommittally, smacking a kiss on her forehead. The thought of picking up the phone exhausts me to my bones. I wish she were coming back to our—well, *my* apartment. I could lie in bed, stare at the ceiling while she played with my hair, unravel it all slowly because we had time for it. Fall asleep next to her like I used to all the time. But she has somewhere else to be, and truthfully, I can't handle another conversation tonight. It's time to disconnect my brain.

Which is why when I hear footsteps crunching down the driveway behind me, my soul lets out a deep sigh.

And when I hear a familiar voice call out, "Georgia," it gives up entirely, sinking to the ground in protest.

I slow to a stop. It takes eight seconds for me to buff away the edges Eli's been whittling into my patience all afternoon. Two seconds for me to turn around. Another three to watch him finish his swift lope down the driveway, his hands in his pockets.

He could be the sixteen-year-old version of himself right now. He used to follow me out of Adam's parents' house when I couldn't put off going home to silence any longer and he was crashing in Adam's guest room to avoid his pull-out-sofa-bed fate. He'd jog out with a little smile on his face and keep me there until I'd caught him up on the parts of my day he hadn't seen.

I thought a lot about his attention when things disintegrated between us. When we were friends, and especially after we became more, I felt like the only person in the world. Like I belonged to someone. He picked up every detail of my life like he was ravenous for it. I wondered a lot, alone in our bed while he pulled another all-nighter, when he stopped being hungry for me.

Now, as he stops two feet away, his gaze piercing in a way it's been all day and not for years, I feel the phantom pang in my stomach.

After a beat he says, "Quite a pickle you got us into."

My mouth drops open. "*Me?*"

"You agreed in the car that you'd step aside." Even in the semi-darkness, frustration is clearly written across his face. "You said you'd let me take care of anything else that came up."

"I didn't know that 'anything else' would be their wedding venue burning to the ground, Eli. I'm not going to sit there and say, 'Sucks for you, good luck with that.'"

I could mention the way Adam silently pleaded for my help, but that would be a dick move. A dagger right in Eli's chest. I don't want to hurt him; I just want him to go away.

"You wouldn't have to say that," he says. "I was there."

"But you *haven't* been." It's not a snap, but it's close.

The street light above us crackles, then extinguishes, plunging us into an intimate darkness that's barely softened by Adam's front porch light.

Lovely.

"That's the point, Georgia." Eli's voice is quiet. Edgy. "That's why I spoke up. But you spoke up, too, and now we both have to go."

"You don't have to," I say quickly.

"Yes, I do," he replies with an authority that sends goose bumps skittering up my arms. "I am."

"Grace said they'll have help, but there's still plenty to—"

"I know Adam gave you the same speech he gave me," Eli interrupts.

Even as he steps closer, his face is in shadow. He looks like the stranger I wish he was, pushing conversations I don't want to have.

My heart starts to beat faster. "He did."

"And I'm guessing our message was united, since he's so hyped about us going to Blue Yonder together."

In my mind, our list blows open to its well-worn pages and I see it: *never talk about the past or how we handle it now.* I see Eli's pen hovering, ready to cross it out.

"You don't need to recap," I say, as calmly as my rioting body will allow. "We're on the same page."

"Are we?" he asks with a searching quality I don't understand. "I mean, is there a reason you don't want to be up at Blue Yonder together, beyond awkwardness?"

"*Awkwardness?*" I blurt out.

In the smudged, inky night, the shape of his face is merely a suggestion, only known to me because I've traced every curve and angle of him. His expression is a mystery, and his tone is careful when he replies, "Would you call it something else?"

On the list of words I'd use to describe the way I feel about Eli, *awkward* is near the end, but every other one would expose too much.

"No," I lie.

He doesn't reply immediately, the air thick with a disappointment I know is mine. I hope he can't feel it.

"Adam will see through any excuse we make to stay behind, and it'll send him on a mental bender," he says finally.

"I know." Deep down, I knew as soon as we said *I'll do it* together that I was stuck.

"Part of me knew you'd volunteer," he says, his voice as quiet as the night cocooning us. The only other noise is the breath I'm trying to regulate, a pocket of crickets chirping nearby, a burst of laughter from inside. A lonely sound when I'm not in the middle of it. "Of course you would. You'd do anything for the people you love." The way he says it is rough and nearly affectionate, a fuzzy approximation of the tone he'd whisper in my ear, press into the side of my neck. Against my mouth.

I don't know why that ties a knot in my throat, but suddenly it's hard to swallow. I *would* do anything for the people I love: move to New York. Pretend to be friends afterward. Save a wedding.

"But I will, too," Eli continues. "So we're going to have to do this together. We can split up the tasks, but I'm not staying behind."

"Work really isn't going to get in the way? I'm not going to have to take over halfway through because there's some pitch emergency with Luce?"

It's not so dark I don't see the flicker in his expression. A brief devastation. "No. You won't be doing it by yourself. I don't even have my laptop with me." At my dubious expression, he says, "I won't go anywhere, Georgia."

The knot's in my chest now. I'm afraid for him to keep his promise just as sure as I am he'll break it. But he's right; we don't have any choice. We can't give Adam one more thing to worry about.

"Fine." I say it like the F-word it is, try not to notice the way Eli's shoulders get even tenser. "I'll pick you up tomorrow at nine."

"Fine," he echoes in a low, resonant rumble.

When I pull away from the curb a minute later, I can't help looking in the rearview mirror.

He's standing there, watching me drive away, the way he always used to do.

Chapter Eight

As soon as Jamie picks up the phone the next morning, I blurt, "Eli's been bodysnatched."

"Well, hello," she says cheerfully. "I nearly brained myself on the shower door trying to get to the phone. Clearly the injury would've been worth it."

"It's one of those mornings." I groan this, my hands slick on the steering wheel. I'm racing up to Adam's house to pick up Eli and I'm flustered and anxious and late. The rusted red metal of the Golden Gate Bridge blurs past as Highway 101 spits me into Marin County's rolling green hills.

"Tell me about it. I'm in tornado mode because Blake and I have an appointment with a financial planner this morning and I've been told I have twenty minutes."

"Fifteen," comes Blake's drawl.

"*Fifteen?*" Jamie wails. Her dresser drawers open and close frantically, a clatter I used to hear through our shared wall.

"Do you want me to call you—"

"No!" she yells. "Don't you dare hang up. I was expecting you to call me last night anyway and now you've gripped me with this conspiracy theory. I'll get ready while we talk."

What a perfect example of the ways our schedules repel each other. "Sorry for not calling, I passed out early."

In reality, I lay in bed for hours, my roaring thoughts too loud for *New Girl* to drown out, replaying every moment between me and Eli. When I did close my eyes, all I could see was him standing on the knife's edge of Adam's curb until I turned the corner, his tall, familiar body stamped onto the backs of my eyelids like I'd been staring at something too bright for too long.

"Let's focus," Jamie says. "Why has Eli been bodysnatched?"

"He's been acting super weird since I picked him up." I swear even now I can feel the snare of his eyes, laser-focused on me.

"Really? He seemed pretty normal when I saw him last night."

"He's being normal in front of Adam—"

"Because Adam will turn into a rabid raccoon if anyone even breathes wrong?"

"Exactly. But with me, he's been . . ." I search for the word, then groan. "I don't know. Bodysnatched."

Jamie, ever the emotional bloodhound, hears the anxiety pulling the strings of my voice taut. "Okay, tell me."

As I pass under the rainbow arch of the Robin Williams Tunnel, I give her a truncated rundown of Eli's behavior, from the airport to the driveway conversation last night. I tell her about his absent phone and his newfound dedication to being present for Adam, the way he's been just . . . *looking* at me. I even tell her about his wrinkles and his too-long hair and that beard.

When I'm done, she asks, voice enveloped in concern, "Are you sure about doing this?"

"It doesn't matter if I'm sure," I say. "Eli's desperate to prove himself, and Adam wants me up there to make sure everything goes smoothly. So it's happening."

"And how do you feel about that?"

I take Adam's exit on two wheels, gritting my teeth. "It'll be fine. Eli will do his thing and play hero, I'll do my thing, we'll get everything rebooked easily and then it'll be done."

"Georgia. None of those words were feelings."

I sigh. "I feel fine. I mean, mostly fine. It's weird. Not weird like I can't handle it—"

"No, of course."

"But weird. Objectively."

"Of course," Jamie repeats. "Objectively, having to hang out with your ex-Person for any length of time, never mind—"

"Eight *days.*"

"Very quick reflexes, thank you," she says, her voice full of amusement, but also care and empathy. Her classic trifecta. "Eight days with your ex-Person is objectively not the easiest thing, and this is a lot of time to be spending together for the first time in forever. You normally see each other in bite-sized pieces, you know?"

"Oh, I know," I say grimly.

"This is the man you loved helping you save your mutual best friend's wedding. It's okay to not be fine about it. If he's as determined to integrate himself into it as you're saying, it could get uncomfortable being around each other so much."

I groan as I get stuck at a red light, my heart beating hard and fast. "Okay, but what if we skip the discomfort and stay out of each other's way instead?"

For a beat, I listen to the *click-clack* of Jamie's makeup bag as she digs through it, the steady cadence of her breath. And then she asks, "*Is* it discomfort? Or is it something else?"

"Like what?" I ask, mashing the gas pedal when the light turns green.

"Fear, maybe?"

It's not a feeling I've allowed myself to consider, but Jamie's gentle probe unlocks the cage door of my emotions. Despite my best efforts, I feel it—fear, yes, but also a dangerous kernel of longing. One I recognize from thirteen months ago, and before that, too.

Eli and I had very little closure at the end of our relationship. When I left, that was it. We didn't pursue any follow-up conversations, and the relief of not having to dissect what we'd each done wrong superseded the hurt. Because the truth is, I did things wrong, too. I just didn't want to face them with him.

Over the years, I grew more careful with my closest friendships. I'd learned from Heather and Mya, where I'd been too eager, too needy for their time and attention. I tempered myself, never asked for too much, made sure I gave more than I took.

I was most careful with Eli, maybe because deep down I knew a fracture between us would shatter me. When we fell in love, I hesitated before I took the leap, even though I was sure about him. I'd have more to lose—not just a best friend, but everything: my Person, now my boyfriend, someone who could give me forever, a thing I craved so deeply, but only if I played my cards right.

In hindsight, I see how easy the first two years of our relationship were, how effortless it was to not ask for too much, because Eli was giving me everything anyway—attention, love, time. It wasn't needy if I didn't request it, right?

We moved to New York with so much hope and enthusiasm, had been planning and talking about it for months. We spent the first three weeks before Eli started his analyst training program setting up our apartment, exploring our city, falling deeper in love with it and each other.

The six-week training program was intense, but by that time

I'd started as an HR coordinator at a beauty company so both of our days were full, and most of his evenings were still free for me. Even when Eli joined his team in September, we managed to eke out time together—a quick breakfast in the morning, though most dinners were out now, and many of our weekends. He was so *good* at what he did. He loved that, felt exhilarated by it, and I was right there beside him.

And then he was still good at what he did, the gold-star analyst of his team, but a more senior analyst left and Eli had to step up to run the model on a mandate they'd won. What little time we had together disappeared. The expectations placed on him were another gold star; they doubled his stress, tripled it. He couldn't fail, because he was so good at his job and it was safe and he *needed* that. As the months went by and the demands grew, his anxiety grew beside it, monster-like. I watched him disappear under those expectations, locked in misery he was sure he could get out of in a year, maybe. Two, max, when he reached associate and he could start looking for a role that didn't have such a power-tripping managing director.

But somewhere in there I disappeared, too. I'd been happy those first couple months with Eli, but as his availability waned and then went away altogether, I recognized that I didn't really have my own place in New York, that my happiness was only tied to *him*. My job turned out to be a terrible fit, my boss a micromanager, the culture toxic. I had very few friends, none of them deep-rooted. Every type of loneliness I'd ever felt coalesced, an anxiety spiral come true. I repressed the ugly feelings that ballooned: the shame of needing Eli more as he drifted further away, the embarrassment of being so dependent on him. What was I going to do, ask him to quit his job because I *needed* him? Please.

Needing people like that had only ever hurt me in the past. It was easier to shut down. Over the course of months, our singular, intertwining life turned plural and parallel, until the night it cracked under the pressure of everything we weren't saying. Everything we still haven't said.

I've spent the last five years numbing myself to every feeling I had for him, good and bad. But what if that's only been possible because of our agreed-upon silence? Our distance?

"I'm not afraid," I say, and it's not a lie exactly. It's a wish that this bodysnatched Eli will turn back into the Eli I know. That the emotions he's been kicking up like insidious little dust motes will settle, and I'll successfully white-knuckle it through this week. "I just want everything to be easy."

Jamie sighs sadly. "I know you do."

In the background, Blake calls her name. Time's up.

I turn into Adam's cul-de-sac. "It'll be fine. He'll probably revert back to his old ways any minute, and then we can live totally separate lives up there."

After all, it's what we do best.

"I'm not going to mention that you're late," Adam says as he throws open his front door. "Mostly because you brought me Bob's Donuts."

"Fair trade," I reply, shoving the grease-splotched box at his chest as I push past him.

"It's a good thing, actually," Adam continues, flipping the lid. "When I went into Eli's room twenty minutes ago, he was knocked out cold. He's getting his shit together right now, literally and figuratively."

I stop short. "He was still sleeping?"

Eli's always been an early riser, even before his job demanded it. In college, I'd stay the night at the apartment he shared with three other guys and wake up with him wrapped around me, absently stroking my hair while he gazed up at the ceiling or out the window with soft, sleepy eyes.

Really, the only time he ever slept in was after a rare extra-late weekend date, or when his anxiety got the best of him and he'd spend the night—

"Pacing around the living room."

I whip around to Adam. "What?"

"I said, I got up at three because Grace needed water, and he was pacing around the living room." Adam pushes the front door shut with his foot, nudging me into the living room with his shoulder. "He was tapping away on his phone. He never lets himself have a break." He looks up as he settles onto the couch and does a double-take. "What's that look?"

I wipe my expression clean. "What look?"

"*That* look. Like something's up." He straightens. "Do you think something's wrong with Eli?"

Of course something's wrong with Eli. Something's been wrong with him since he got that godforsaken job. I was with him that day senior year when he found out Phillips Preston wanted him, a larger and more prestigious bank than the one he'd interned for the summer before. I saw the flare of relief and triumph in his eyes.

It was stupid of me not to see it coming, how his job would swallow him whole and give him everything he wanted: rock-solid stability, control over the trajectory of his own life, and a place to call home, one that wouldn't get taken away. He'd make sure of it.

Knowing he's still caught up in that cycle of late-night anxiety that often morphed into panic attacks underscores the need to keep my distance. Underneath Bodysnatched Eli is the *same* Eli.

"Nothing's wrong with him," I say, swallowing the irritation crawling up my throat. For better or worse, we're partners now, and Adam looks like he's two seconds away from adding Eli's behavior to *his* list of worries. "The time difference was probably messing with him. Maybe he was trolling Hinge or taking down a puzzle."

Adam laughs. "Funny you say that, because there's a half-finished Brooklyn Bridge puzzle on his floor. You know our boy."

Eli told me once how oddly soothing the practice was. "I like that if I work hard and long enough at it, it looks the way it's supposed to," he said. We were cross-legged on the floor in Adam's den sometime in high school, focused on finishing one of David's works-in-progress. Adam wasn't home, but Laurie told us to hang out until he was so we could all have dinner together.

Something hot flared in my chest watching the pink creep over Eli's cheeks when he said that, hearing the breath snake out from between his lips as he pressed a piece into place. When he got to Cal Poly, Sunday become our designated puzzle-making night, a tradition we carried with us to New York. Our hallway closet was filled with boxes of them, half of them forever unopened.

You know our boy.

I do, and god, I wish I didn't still. It's a gift to know someone when you're in love with them, and a curse when you're out of it.

I perch on the arm of the chair nearest Adam, swallowing hard. "Mystery solved, then. Eli Mora was up to his puzzle-making ways."

"Ah, that's why my ears were burning," a deep voice says just behind me.

I yelp, nearly toppling off the chair, but a pair of hands curl around my arms. For a string of unbearable seconds, the solidity of Eli's body presses against my back, a stabilizing wall until I can find my balance.

I want to linger; that's why I don't. Instead I twist around to appraise him. He must've just rolled out of the shower—his hair is wet and combed back from his forehead. A drop of water hangs off a lock curling at the nape of his neck, and a fresh soap scent clings to his skin, magnified by the warmth of it.

Despite the purple smudges under his eyes, he looks so handsome it hurts. So familiar it pulls at the space in my chest that's never forgotten what he meant to me.

Focus, Georgia. "Warn a girl next time you're going to scare the hell out of her."

His tired mouth makes a tiny improvement upward. "Doesn't that defeat the purpose of scaring the hell out of you?"

"He has a point," Adam says around a cruller before staring balefully down at the rest of the donuts. "Shit, I gotta save a couple of these for Grace, huh?"

"Where is she, anyway?" I ask.

"Yoga," he sighs, closing the box.

It's not until Eli's hands brush down my arms that I realize he's been holding on to me. That I sank into it. I sway like a loose-rooted tree when he finishes his lingering release.

"Sorry for cracking into your brand-new puzzle box, Kiz," Eli says.

"No, you're not," Adam replies cheerfully.

"No, I'm not." Eli's mouth pulls up affectionately as his eyes find mine and stay. The curve of his lips soften. "And sorry I'm late."

"All good. I was, too," I say with a sunshine smile. He blinks. I stare at his lashes, still spiked with moisture. We hang like that for one second. Two.

Tearing myself away, I point to the pastry box Adam's bear-hugging. "I brought donuts if you're hungry."

"I had a protein bar," he says. "We should get going."

His no-nonsense tone pulls at my spine. We have a job to do, and that job isn't staring at his unfairly thick eyelashes. "Yes. Absolutely."

Adam talks a mile a minute as we make our way outside, reminding us that his uncles and aunt will get us settled in the guest cottages once we're at Blue Yonder and going over the details of the bakery appointment we're driving directly to.

"Grace's appetite has been terrible the past couple weeks, but she's really excited about this bakery," he says, watching Eli as he tries to stuff his luggage into the packed trunk. "Apparently the woman's a genius, but she was terrifying on the phone."

"Terrifying?" I echo.

"Just . . . strangely intense about baked goods, but I guess that's her job, right?" He shrugs, scratching at his cheek. "She didn't even give us confirmation that she'd bake our cake. She just said, 'We'll see.'"

Eli peeks around the trunk. "What does that mean?"

"Hell if I know. But cake is the only thing Grace'll be able to eat at the wedding without puking and revealing our surprise baby, and I want her to have something she loves." Adam splits a pleading look between us. "We have to get this lady. Like seriously, do anything."

"That sounds potentially illegal, but sure, adding it to my list," I say.

"Speaking of lists, Grace and I put all your to-dos for the week together." Adam hitches a thumb at Eli as he shuts the trunk. "Eli transcribed for us, so you should be all set, but if you have questions you know where we are."

"Great," I say, looking over at Eli. "I can take that off your hands."

"It's on my phone," he says, his small grin bordering on karmic. "You told me to put together my own list last night, right?"

"Once again encroaching on my dedicated list space?" I tsk. "It's becoming a nasty habit, Mora."

"There's no 'I' in team, Georgia. We'll share it."

I smile serenely. "I'm not a good sharer."

"I believe in you." And then this man honest-to-god *winks*.

Adam watches us with a twinkle in his eye, unaware of the very real tug-of-war happening underneath our role-play.

Once we're all packed up, Eli and I take turns giving Adam a hug. He steps back onto the lawn, turning into the heart-eye emoji right before our eyes. "My best people. If we get out of this week in one piece, it'll be because of you two."

"We've got you," Eli and I say in unison, then exchange a look.

It's going to be a long eight days.

Chapter Nine

Eli is passed out hard in the passenger seat when I parallel park in front of Sucre Bakery in Yountville, a picturesque town halfway between Napa and Blue Yonder. He doesn't even stir when I turn off the engine.

I sigh, unbuckling my seatbelt.

Good thing I didn't let him drive; he offered when we stopped for gas near Adam's house, and I stared at the purple moons under his eyes as he topped off the gas tank, hip propped against the car.

"I'd rather not crash," I said, then blurted, "You're really not going to give me the list?"

He straightened, appraising me like he knew I'd been stewing. "We really can't share?"

"We agreed to split up the tasks."

"Okay." It was nearly a sigh, his gaze latched on to me. "I'll send you half of it. Fifty-fifty's fair."

He pulled out his phone as soon as we got in the car and my heart spiked seeing his name on my screen moments later, separate from the group thread we've shared. I expected him to fall headlong into his digital world after that, but instead he dropped his phone in his lap and turned on the radio, glancing at me. I took it for what it was—a silent promise that he'd be on his best behavior.

And he was, because he was unconscious five minutes later.

I should be grateful for it, but this scenario might be worse than a fully awake Eli Mora in my car for two and a half hours, including the hour-long standstill traffic he slept through. If he doesn't wake himself up organically, he's going to emerge from sleep in another dimension. I've encountered the full breadth of that experience, from gibberish conversations to sleepwalking, from happy, sleepy smiles to blank stares, like I'm a stranger.

It's silly to be scared, but that's the feeling pooling in my stomach. I stare at him, because maybe if I do it hard enough, he'll wake up on his own. And also because, quite honestly, he's beautiful.

His knees are spread, arms folded over his chest, hands tucked under his biceps. In his lap are his phone and the ring boxes Adam handed over with a declarative "I can't be responsible for anything significant right now." His lashes are fanned out over his skin, his brows cinched together in a familiar, Manhattan-shaped frown.

I glance at the clock. *Dammit.* Our appointment is in five minutes.

"Eli," I say, but it's more like a whisper.

His lashes flutter, then still.

"Eli," I try again.

Nothing, just his fingers twitching, a tell that he's still deep in his dream world, busy even in his sleep.

With a frustrated groan, I lean on the console, getting as close as I dare. *"Eli."*

His eyes fly open and lock immediately with mine, like he knew where I was down to the millimeter.

I can tell right away he's here, but not. His mouth tilts up, his eyes sun-touched and calm. I'm frozen in that look. It's a memory, hundreds of them: the first time we met; the first time we kissed, and the thousandth; our two years at Cal Poly and the thirtieth day we lived together. He's looking at me the way he hasn't for so long. I stretch toward it on instinct, that forever-needy girl inside me wanting its warmth.

He shifts in his seat, angling toward me. In a flash, his palm is shaping my cheek, then palming the back of my neck to bring me closer. And it's not warmth now, it's heat. Something that will burn me if I don't pull away.

But I can't.

"There you are." A smile melts across his face, slow and sleepy. "Hey, Peach."

It's been more than five years since Eli's called me that. Since he's sounded like he cares. Maybe that's what wakes him up, that he sounds so unlike himself.

Or maybe it's the way my hand flies up to his wrist in an iron grip.

Awareness snaps into his eyes and we hold like that, an inch apart, straddling the line between past and present before we both jerk back like we're on fire.

My elbow cracks into the horn, which honks in unison with Eli's head cracking against the window behind him.

"*Fuck*," he gasps, curling in on himself as he cradles the back of his skull.

"Are you okay?" I yelp, my heart flying. This car is unbearably small right now. Between me and Eli, there have to be fourteen arms and legs in here.

He groans again, still folded over. I can't tell if it's in pain. The shells of his ears are bright red.

"I was asleep," comes his muffled voice.

I swallow hard. "Yes, obviously."

He sits up slowly, rubbing at his head. "I didn't mean to—"

"I know. You're Ambien's side effects in human form when you're woken up." I lean back as far as I can, my shoulders pressed against the window. "I shouldn't have gotten so close. You—you weren't waking up and our appointment is in five minutes."

Rubbing the back of his head, he rips his gaze from my face and blinks out the window. People meander lazily along the wide sidewalk, drifting in and out of the various upscale storefronts along the street. The sun hangs high above us, laying its late summer rays onto Sucre's glossy black door fifty feet away.

Eli inhales as his eyes find mine again, seeming to shake off the last vestiges of his sleep. I don't know what I expect him to say, but it's not, "You parallel parked on your own?"

It took me four tries, but he doesn't need to know that. Let him believe I've improved over the years.

I pop my keys out of the ignition with shaky fingers, throwing open my door. "Yes. Are you good? 'Cause we need to go. Adam said we can't be late."

"Yeah, sorry," he says, his voice hoarse from disuse. "I—"

His phone dings. I stop, looking down on instinct, the sound vibrating down my spine. His screen is angled just enough that I see a calendar reminder before he picks it up and lets loose a low, foreboding, and all-too-familiar, "Shit."

"What?"

My tone is carefully blank. It's not the first time I've been handed a *shit* sponsored by Eli's phone, so I hate myself for the spike of disappointment I feel. I know better.

"I forgot I have a thing right now." Eli scrubs a hand through his hair, gripping the ends in frustration. "*Shit*."

"A thing that doesn't involve you eating cake?"

"It's a phone . . . thing. An appointment."

I manage to hold back a very inflammatory *of course it is*. It's probably some last-minute emergency for Luce. I *knew* he'd drop the ball. I just didn't know it was going to drop so soon, or that he'd look so tortured as he watched it roll away.

It takes me back to a few months after he started his job, when that same ball began dropping with regularity.

I still remember the first big thing he missed—the fancy birthday dinner of Rory, a woman I worked with who technically fit the definition of "friend" in that she seemed to generally, if not enthusiastically, enjoy my company. Luce needed Eli to work late and I got it: he couldn't say no. But my stomach still clenched when I told a table full of friends who barely fit the definition that my boyfriend couldn't make it after all. It was the first of many times, until them questioning whether he actually existed became a caustic running joke that I laughed off, that wrapped a resentful vine around my heart.

He made it out rarely, missed more nights than he made, and I understood, understood, understood. His exhausted relief made me feel like I was good, I was easy. I'd done this before.

But my understanding was a rope, and it got cut by the blade of his career expectations and the panic it put him in until it frayed completely. It made us numb. He'd come to me with his latest scheduling conflict, his expression defeated. I was vindicated because I called it. I'd pretend that it didn't matter, that I was fine, that I wasn't essentially a broken heart in a trench coat. He watched me push myself away from him and pushed back at first—asked me if I was okay, would I tell him if I wasn't? But I couldn't. I remembered telling my dad I wasn't okay at eight, at eleven, remembered him trying to find me a therapist and then outsourcing the search to a family friend because he didn't have enough hours in the day. I remembered how that wrecked him.

Eventually Eli stopped asking and I stopped inviting him places. I hid those ugly emotions to protect myself. And him, too.

I tried to pull him in one last time, though—that night in December is etched into my memory. I was back in San Francisco by New Year's.

Wordlessly, I climb out of the car.

Eli meets me at the front bumper. "Georgia—"

"It's fine," I say, striding toward the bakery. "We don't both need to be there anyway. I'll let you know how it goes."

I only get two steps in before his hand curls around my arm, towing me to a stop.

When I turn, I expect him to be apologetic or impassive, one of two emotions on this familiar spectrum. Instead, his eyes flash, an electric current that zips into me. There's nothing numb or defeated about him right now.

"I do need to be there," he insists. "I just—"

"You don't owe me an explanation. Do what you need to do."

His mouth firms. "Go in without me while I figure it out, but I *will* figure it out."

I swallow, thrown off. An Eli who's willing to toss aside his work interruptions is so alien-like, but of course. He's devoted to fixing this for Adam.

"I have to go inside right now or this woman is going to flambé me." I'm very aware that his hands are still on me, and even more aware that I can't pull myself away. Without an audience to reassure, there's no reason to let him touch me.

I don't move.

Eli's gaze sweeps over my face, his brows pushing into a furrow. I used to rub my thumb right there until it went away. My hand twitches, wanting it now.

NO, Georgia.

Finally, he says, "It's not what you think it is."

"It doesn't matter what I think."

"It actually does," he says, his voice low. "Very much."

My heart does something painful, a quick, shock-like pulse. I remind myself again that this isn't about me. It's about him proving something to Adam while I bear witness to it.

I can't let that hurt.

Eli's phone starts buzzing. His eyes close briefly. Another perfect reminder, right on time.

I extricate myself from his grasp. "Let's just chalk this one up to being on my half of the list. Take care of your thing, okay? I've got it."

Chapter Ten

Despite my assurances, Eli hovers outside the bakery as I step inside, phone in hand and eyes on me.

I shut the door, inhaling for a crumb of peace, and am immediately hit with the hypnotic scent of sugar. Like that, all my irritated thoughts disappear.

This place is perfect.

It's large, chic, and gleaming. The centerpiece is a display case stacked with immaculately decorated cakes and artisanal sweets, and the walls are a spotless white, the floors a pale marble so polished I can practically see my own reflection. The door behind the counter is painted the green of new growth, matching the crawling rose bush that takes up half the white stucco wall just outside.

"Welcome in!"

The Indian woman who greets me looks like a baker from the movies, with dark twinkling eyes and a bright smile glowing against golden brown skin, her black hair pulled into a perky ponytail.

This is the woman who spooked Adam? She looks like she should have cupcake emojis perpetually swirling over her head. She looks like my next best friend.

"Hey there," I reply with equal enthusiasm. "I'm here for—"

The green door swings open and a storm cloud of a human hustles out. Her lightning-strike eyes zero in on me.

"You're late," she barks, wiping her hands on the black apron tied around her waist. She's a tiny white woman, five feet if she's lying, with curly gray hair. She could be anywhere from fifty to seventy-five, based on her lemon-sucking expression.

I split a look between my new friend and this other woman who could take me in a street fight. "I— no?"

"You're my 12:30, right?"

I smile in relief. "Yes."

"Then you're late." She points to the clock on the wall. "It's 12:32."

"Oh, but she got here at 12:30," the other woman says. I throw her a grateful look.

"If you're early, you're on time, and if you're on time, you're late," the baker states, eyeing me from head to toe. She looks wholly unimpressed and I get it: I'm wearing a cropped black linen tank top and matching shorts, but clearly I should've shown up wrapped in tinfoil, because I'm getting grilled.

I scramble for something that will appease her. "I will . . . definitely write that down for the future. Uh, I appreciate your wisdom."

"This is Margot," the younger woman says. "And I'm Sarika. We didn't get your name."

I paste on my HR smile. "I'm Georgia. I really appreciate you taking us on last min—"

"Who's us?" Margot interrupts, pointing out the window. "Are you with him? Because he's taking off."

I turn to see Eli pacing down the sidewalk, phone pressed to his ear, mouth moving quickly. "Oh. He's with me, but he's not coming to the appointment. He's got a thing."

Her eyes narrow. "A thing?"

"A thing?" Sarika echoes, disappointed.

I wave a hand in the air. "A thing. It's fine, I can do it on my own."

Margot huffs out, "The point of a wedding is to do it together. No offense, but your fiancé doesn't understand the concept."

It's a truth universally acknowledged that people who use the phrase *no offense, but* are the most offensive people on the planet. More than that, I'm sure Margot *does* mean offense.

And then I realize what she's called him.

"Oh, god no, he's not—"

"No need to defend him," she mutters. "I'm not going to believe you anyway."

"Well, *I* saw the way he was looking at you when you came in." Sarika shoots me an encouraging smile. "It was like you were the only person on the planet."

My heart skips a beat, imagining that. Remembering the way he looked at me in the car.

When he was Ambien Eli, I remind myself. "There's a bit of a mix-up here—"

"He abandoned her for a 'thing.' He was all over the place on the phone, too," Margot says, shaking her head. "I don't understand you kids these days. You'll settle for crumbs."

Oh god, I haven't had a situation run away from me like this since spring break my freshman year of college.

Margot clearly misunderstood Adam when he called to set up the appointment, thinking Eli and I were the couple she'd be seeing. She loathes Eli for being an absentee fiancé and me for accepting it, which actually couldn't be further from the truth. I *didn't*.

Adrenaline hits me like a Mack truck. "He's not my fiancé. We're not in love. We're just the best woman and best man and our best friends' wedding venue burned down and we're replanning the whole thing and the bride desperately wants one of your cakes and I'm very sorry for being on time and also somehow late, but this is extremely important to her, which means it's extremely important to me, so if we could just get started, that would be fantastic."

I'm embarrassingly out of breath by the time I finish. Sarika has taken to dusting the immaculate countertop, eyes pinned to Margot.

If my speech moves Margot, she doesn't show it. I bet she kills it in poker. "I appreciate your friends' unfortunate issue. God knows every local has a soft spot for people impacted by fire. It's the reason I took this appointment. But my time is precious and I'm very discerning." Her gaze flicks down, then back up again. "So far, I'm not convinced."

Panic could easily overtake me right now, but I'll make this work, because I always make things work. And I'll do it alone, because I always do it alone.

"Can I have the opportunity to convince you?" I ask. "My friends deserve the best cake they can get, especially after what they've gone through. As far as I'm concerned, that's yours."

She tilts her head, and maybe I'm hallucinating, but I swear I see the faintest glimmer of satisfaction.

"All right," she sighs. "Come into the back. Let's get started."

I beam at her. "Perfect."

And then I text Eli: Do NOT come in here. I'll meet you at the car.

I settle into my chair in the tasting area, eyeing the spread in front of me. A tall, chic bottle of Italian spring water sits with two glasses, and Sarika's just set a tray of dainty cake slices in front of me.

My heart sings as I snap a few pictures and shoot them off to the group thread. About to pick out your cake!

"Okay," Sarika says cheerfully, sliding into the seat next to Margot, who's across from me wearing an inscrutable expression. "There are six options, and each slice has a card in front of it with the flavor descriptions."

I lean forward, taking in the beautiful handwritten placards with delicious-sounding combinations. "They look amazing."

"Do you know your friends' preferences?" Margot asks. "Sarika emailed them a list of our options yesterday, but we didn't hear back. These are our most popular flavors."

My heart drops at how deeply unimpressed she looks, and how unprepared I am to change her mind. I have zero idea what Grace and Adam want.

"That is," I say as I pick my phone up from my lap and start to sightlessly text a lowkey SOS beneath the table, "such a smart, great question."

"Start with the vanilla buttercream," Margot demands, pointing at the plate. "Everyone likes vanilla."

Does pregnant Grace like vanilla? I have no idea and don't want to be the one to send her stomach into turmoil. The fetus she's growing seems extraordinarily picky.

But I also don't want to say no to Margot, even though the exception to her declaration is sitting right in front of her, distress-sweating through her top.

With a fortifying breath, I pick up my fork and cut off a chunk, then shove it into my mouth. The familiar nausea that hits me whenever I taste anything intensely vanilla blooms, and my tongue goes Sahara-dry.

I block my mouth with my hand, croaking out, "It's delicious. A great option."

Maybe I'm a good actress when it comes to anything Eli related, but I'm clearly a terrible one when it comes to my vanilla aversion. Margot's expression turns to stone.

"Are you *sick*?"

Oh my god. "N—"

"Sorry I'm late," comes a deep voice from the doorway.

The silence is immediate and absolute as Sarika and Margot's attention flies over my shoulder. Margot's eyes narrow in irritation. Sarika's widen in awe.

I whirl in my seat, my gaze colliding with Eli's. And yeah, I get it. He's fairly awe-inspiring standing in the doorway, his minky hair cresting into anxious-finger waves, his eyes dark like the richest chocolate ganache. He's leaning an obscenely broad shoulder against the doorframe, one hand in his pocket, the other holding his phone.

He's beautiful. And I'm going to strangle him.

"What are you doing here?" I blurt, cake hitting my stomach like a rock.

"We're in the middle of our appointment." Margot sighs. "If you can call it that."

"I apologize for interrupting." Eli directs that at Margot before turning his attention to me. "My call ended early. Thankfully."

My smile is so plastic it cracks. "Love that, but I told you I had it."

"You definitely had something," he mutters, tilting his phone screen my way as he slides into the seat next to mine. I nearly swallow my tongue at the text there—mine, from a few minutes ago.

> WHAT CAKE FLAV DO U WAN??1 I
> NEED TO KOW RN LLOK AT THE LIST

All right. Not as lowkey as I thought.

His voice drops to a reassuring caress. "Thought you could use some backup."

My emotions tangle at Mach speed: irritation that he reacted to that text instead of the one telling him not to come in; confusion that he's here at all; and most distressing, relief that I'm not doing this alone. That he showed up. It's a tiny dust mote of an emotion.

I mentally blow it away. It matters least—it's the first one I need to focus on, because he didn't listen.

She is a beast, I transmit silently. *You just undid all of the goodwill I built.*

What goodwill? He flits a look at Margot, who's watching us with her arms crossed. *She looks like she's about to eat you.*

Then his eyes slide to the tray of cake, straight to the slice that's been touched. He frowns. "Did you eat the van—"

My hand slams down on his thigh. On instinct, I slide up to squeeze the thick, hard arch of muscle. My animal brain remembers exactly what kind of touch robs him of speech and I need him to shut. Up.

But my animal brain forgot *why* it robs him of speech, and so my heart leaps into my throat when his pupils blow wide with shock and heat, when his palm covers the back of my hand, fingers wrapping around mine. He holds us there for an unbearable smattering of seconds, his jaw flexing. And then he moves my hand down to his knee; it's a slow scrape until I hit the warm skin just below his gray shorts.

Goose bumps explode over every square inch of my body.

"The vanilla is very good," I say hoarsely, adding a silent, *she can't know vanilla makes me sick, we are* ruining *this*. "You should try it, too."

"Right." It's a wisp of a word before Eli seems to gather himself, turning back to Margot and Sarika. I yank my hand back, curling it into a fist in my lap. "Grace, the bride, loves tropical flavors like passion fruit. Do you have anything like that?"

Margot stares at him, her lip curling up. "I—"

"Wait, how do you know that?" I interrupt. Did they talk about it after I left last night?

He glances at me. "It's on our lists."

"It's not on my list. Is it on the full list you have?"

"I put it on your list, too."

"You did not."

"Excuse me," Margot huffs out, stepping forward.

"Georgia," Eli says, nodding his chin to my phone. "Check your list. It's there."

"This is why I need the full list," I tell him as I pull up his text, scrolling down impatiently. "See, it's not on—"

Cake flavors: passion fruit, orange, pineapple, chocolate with raspberry or other tart, vanilla

Well. Okay, so she *does* like vanilla.

"I told you we'd do fifty-fifty," Eli says quietly. "Everything you need to know is there. But if you want it all, I'll give it to you."

"Excuse me."

I rip myself away from the clutch of Eli's attention to find Margot standing at her full height. She looks seven feet tall.

She addresses Eli first. "Young man, this is not a Burger King. You can't just order what you want and expect me to whip it up. My assistant, Sarika, sent your friends a list so they could give us notice of their preferences, which they didn't do. Between that, the lateness"—at this, her gaze lands on me—"and whatever lovers' spat this is, you've wasted my time."

Eli starts to speak, but I rush out, "It's not a lo— Margot, I'm very sorry for this mix-up, but—"

She holds up her hand, silencing me. Beside me, Eli stiffens. When I spare him a look, he's watching Margot with a stony expression that rivals her own.

She smooths down her apron, then drops her chin to level me with a look. "Sorry or not, this isn't going to work. You'll have to find someone else to bake your friends' wedding cake. It's not going to be me."

An apparition of the cake of Adam and Grace's dreams grows wings and flies away. Somewhere, that old Sarah McLachlan song starts to play. And the check mark I'd already mentally placed alongside our very first item on the Fix Adam and Grace's Wedding list?

Erased.

Chapter Eleven

Eli and I don't talk for the duration of the drive to Blue Yonder.

The familiarity of it is as grating as it is comforting, because it's us: we'd sit in similar, tense silence in Ubers after bad nights, the city lights playing over our faces angled toward the windows.

But it's mixed with the memories of turning off this same highway to the winery, laughter bursting out of the open windows of Adam's decrepit Volvo, Eli smiling at me from the back seat.

That's us, too, and the way they tangle together makes me want to scream.

I clench my jaw as I catch sight of the rustic white fence that separates the beginning of the vineyard from Highway 29 and turn left, passing by the pale stone and wrought-iron Blue Yonder sign. Beside me, Eli is a pillar of silence, his arms crossed over his chest as he looks out the window. His knee bounces with just enough emphasis to join the sway of the car. He's stewing, which only increases the nails on my internal chalkboard. I know why I'm annoyed; why is *he*?

I force the view to distract me, letting it unwind my tension like the road unwinds ahead of us. The oak trees on each side reach for each other, creating a sun-dappled tunnel. As we drive the final short distance, the main building comes into view. It's what the Coopers call the Big House—a gorgeous white farmhouse on steroids that holds the visitors' center and offices, set on a gentle slope of land plunked in the middle of sixty acres of vineyards. The area around it is expertly landscaped with native plants, bright explosions of wildflowers, lavender bushes, and glossy-leaved trees. Behind it, the rolling green height of the Mayacamas mountain range stretches toward the sky.

Even before I stepped foot inside for the first time, I knew it would be a place that held laughter and conversation on tap; I'd never have to go looking for those things I craved so much. The quiet was different, too, weightless and content.

It's no wonder Eli and I loved this place so much. It was the sanctuary we both needed, the roots that tethered us to what felt like a permanent place. And each other.

I want to turn this car around and drive back to San Francisco. The cake is screwed. Nothing is going right. The last thing I want to do is keep failing *and* live alongside all the memories of Eli and I at our happiest while he's acting so strange.

Unfortunately, we're stuck in this situation, but I'm ready to fling myself as far away from him as possible until Saturday comes.

I pull into a parking spot to the left of the house, the engine barely off before I'm throwing open the door. I'm already at the trunk by the time Eli unfolds himself from the passenger seat, giving me a look so full of awareness that I feel momentarily naked.

But then he glances back toward the Big House, scanning the emerald lawn that wraps around toward the wine cellars and the building that holds the tasting rooms, along with the still unfinished indoor reception area, which is a stunning white building with floor-to-ceiling windows. I follow his gaze to the edge of the property where the familiar black-trimmed white cottages we'll be staying in are, the pool tucked into the courtyard. The air is still, mild for August, and filled with birdsong.

Our old stomping grounds. The place where my dad could send me for ten weeks, knowing I was in the best hands. Where Eli felt like he could breathe because he didn't have to listen to a soundtrack of grown-up arguments or worry about money and his future plans.

The place where we had that last, idyllic summer. Where Adam and Grace are going to get married. Where we're all going to be together for what could realistically be the last time in a long while, if recent patterns continue and I move to Seattle.

I want it to be perfect—the wedding, the whole night, my part in it. If I'm going to leave, I want to plant that memory deep in the soil here, keep my roots to this place and these people.

But if we can't even get a cake secured, I have my doubts about the rest of it.

Eli's sigh winds around my neck. I wait for the wide spread of his shoulders to drop the way they used to here, but they stay tense.

"Have you been here lately?" he asks without turning around.

I squint up at a puffy cloud drifting across the endless sky. The real blue yonder. "Not since Adam's grandparents' fiftieth anniversary."

Eli doesn't react except to let out a slow breath. He was invited to the party two years ago but couldn't make it. Jamie and I got drunk on a bottle of Cabernet Sauvignon produced the last summer Adam, Eli, and I were here. Adam and Grace were loved up on each other the entire night, which made Jamie weepy since she was fresh off a terrible breakup. I was trying to push away memories. Same shit, different day.

Eli tilts his chin up toward the sky. The sun touches his face in a pattern my fingers used to take. "It looks the same."

My chest twists at the wistfulness he can't hide, but I don't bother with a response. Instead, I blink away, popping the trunk.

Eli packed it like our bags were Tetris blocks, so despite the mighty yank I give my suitcase, it doesn't budge. It doesn't help that he's in my periphery, giving off Beautiful, Lonely Man Stares at Nature vibes as he inhales deeply, then exhales slowly. Out of the corner of my eye, I watch his mouth move minutely, like he's counting.

And then he turns on his heel and our gazes collide. My hand slips from the suitcase handle, feet skidding on the pavement.

He braces one hand against my back to steady me, wrapping the other around the handle.

I resist the urge to smack his hand away, hooking my finger around the inch of space he's left. "I've got it."

He slides me a look as we both yank the suitcase, levering it up a quarter of the way. "You don't."

"I do," I grunt, yanking again, just as he does. We get another inch.

"Just let me—"

"What if you just let *me*?" I shoot back with faux pleasantry. "And while we're at it, what if you had just let me deal with the bakery like I asked you, instead of barging in?"

We're smashed together, neither of us willing to let go, our noses inches apart. I can smell the cinnamon on Eli's breath from the gum he popped in the car, can feel his frustrated exhale against my mouth.

"I came to help you."

"I told you I had it." God, it feels good to get mad out loud. "I texted you not to come in and you didn't listen."

He huffs out a short, irritated laugh. "Your text to me and your text to the group told two different stories. You were flustered, so I read between the lines and took a risk, okay?"

"And we got kicked out of the bakery of Grace's dreams." I let that sink in before throwing the dagger. "*And* we have no cake."

"First of all, this is not all on me. That woman was annoyed before I stepped foot in that shop, and I put the flavors they wanted on your list. You just didn't look at it."

I let out an indignant noise that he steamrolls over.

"Second of all, Adam and Grace own some of this, too. They didn't follow up on what they wanted."

He pauses, an invitation to insert my rebuttal. Unfortunately, he's making good points. I let the muscle-memoried irritation over Eli's work call throw me off my game, then let the panic of trying to win over an unwinnable Margot lose it completely. I don't own the full scope of this disaster, but I do own some of it.

Eli's eyes move over my face, his expression softening. "That doesn't really matter, though. I don't think she had any real intention of helping us out. She was just getting off on some weird power trip."

"She would've helped me," I say petulantly, yanking on the suitcase again. It doesn't give.

He gives me a look as he readjusts his hold on the handle. When he pulls, I do, and it slides halfway out. "You wouldn't have been able to let's-be-best-friends your way into her good graces. Sorry."

He doesn't sound sorry at all, actually.

"You should've stayed outside," I repeat. "And FYI, there'll be plenty of opportunities for you to prove to Adam that you've changed, but charging in late to an appointment he told us not to be late for because you were on a work call probably isn't going to do it."

He lets out the most exasperated sound ever recorded from a human. "It wasn't a work call, okay? I had a therapy appointment. On the count of three, pull so we can get this fucking thing out."

He counts, but I barely hear it over the roar in my ears. His words ping-pong against my rebooting brain as he demands "go" in a low, tight voice.

The suitcase springs free with our shared yank, nearly decapitating me on the way to the ground. Eli stares down at it, hands on his hips, his ears bright pink.

I stare at him. "Am I hallucinating or did you just say you're going to therapy?"

He rubs at the stubble on his cheek; it abrades his palm, a soft burr that tickles *my* skin. "I did. I've been going weekly for nearly a year."

He tried when we were still together but had to cancel more often than not until he stopped going altogether. That he's been regularly seeing someone for this long is a miracle.

It's hard to identify all my emotions. There's shock and confusion and a tiny ache I can't push away for both of us. There are others, too: pride that he's doing this for himself, finally. An unfurling curiosity at the impetus for this. A heart punch that his anxiety and our crumbling relationship years ago wasn't enough.

And, of course, disbelief that he bailed on his therapist to white knight for Adam's cake when I *had* it.

"God, Eli," I breathe out. "You should've stayed on the phone with your therapist. One misspelled all-caps text didn't warrant you bailing on something so important."

"I didn't bail. I explained the situation and he actually encouraged me to show up for—" His mouth presses into a firm line, before he continues carefully, "He told me what we were doing was important. He told me to go."

"You must not have mentioned the *other* text I sent, then."

His eyes latch with mine. "I don't regret going in there. I knew if you'd looked at the list, you would've seen what the flavors were. The fact that you didn't told me you were spinning out. You live by your lists." I open my mouth to argue, but he holds up a hand. "I made the right choice, Georgia. You're not good at communicating your needs, especially when you're drowning."

It's a direct press on an old, painful bruise. "I didn't need—"

I cut myself off before I say *you*, but Eli hears it anyway. He huffs out a short, humorless laugh. "Yeah, I got that loud and clear."

Swallowing hard, I turn away, focusing my suddenly blurry eyes on the nearest oak tree while I settle my emotions.

My pathological refusal to, as Eli so therapeutically put it, communicate my needs is something I've tried to move past with the help of my own (neglected, as of late) therapist. But in times of stress or triggers, it's the first coping mechanism I cling to. I learned so young that other people's needs were default, that mine had to be scheduled to be met, or, more easily, taken care of myself. It was reinforced by my dad, who did his best while juggling a demanding career but only dropped the balls with my name on them; by my mom, who walked away because my mere existence was too much to handle; by the friends who didn't stick like Adam and Jamie and Eli, who were cool until I needed things or felt too much.

Eventually Eli did it to me, too, but first he made sure I never had to say what I needed out loud; somehow, when we were best friends and even in the first couple years of our relationship, he just *got me*. It's why things were so much harder when it all went bad; I could measure it against when things were good. Easy. Perfect, in some ways.

"Georgia." Eli says my name softly, with regret, like I've said all this out loud. It's a glimmer of the way he could read me before I stopped letting him.

"I didn't mean it like that," I say, rubbing at my forehead. "Not that it matters."

"Of course it matters." His voice is closer now, a low murmur near my ear.

I don't want to feel any of these feelings bubbling up and I don't want to rehash this old argument—not ever, but especially here and now.

I need to focus, make sure next Saturday goes off without a hitch, and I can't do that if Eli's around. He can do his part, too, but it has to be away from me.

"Listen." I shift my expression into neutral as I turn around. "It's been an intense couple of days and we're not used to being around each other this much, especially unsupervised."

Eli's eyebrows arch up. "Unsupervised?"

I arch mine back. "Can you think of a better word for it?"

After a beat, he says, "Not at the moment, no."

"I don't want to blow this, and neither do you, so it's probably in our—and, more importantly, Adam's—best interest if we stay out of each other's way."

"You're not in my way," he says with an edge of frustration.

I press my lips together so I don't say, *well, you're in mine.*

"I didn't mean to snap at you," he continues, mistaking my silence for doubt.

"It's not about that. It's not about you or me or—" I careen around the nearly blurted *us*. "I don't want to turn Adam and Grace's disaster into an even bigger disaster because we can't get our shit together, so let's take our split-up lists as our to-dos for the week. No hard feelings."

Eli stares at me, his eyes clouded with emotions I can't identify and don't want to. His jaw tightens, releasing as he looks over toward the Big House.

"All right. No hard feelings," he echoes. "Why don't you take your stuff inside? I'm sure everyone's anxious to see you."

I watch, confused, as he rights my suitcase, then pulls out my garment bag. When I don't move, he cups my elbow, making a hook out of my arm so he can drape the bag over it.

"Are you not coming inside?" I ask, trying and failing to ignore the sparks that fly over my skin at his touch.

"I'm going to call Adam first and let him know what happened with the bakery."

I nearly drop the garment bag. *"Now?"*

"You know it's just a matter of time before he's stalker-calling us."

"Well, yeah, but—" I hadn't even thought about having that conversation. "What are you going to tell him?"

"I'm going to give him some shit for not getting back to Margot and play up what a beast she was so he isn't as disappointed." Eli scratches at his jaw, eyeing me. "I'm not going to say anything bad about you. Or myself, honestly. Margot can take the fall for us."

"I wasn't worried about you saying something bad about me,"

I say, insulted on behalf of both of us. Despite our history, he's never come close to criticizing me. "I'm just wondering why you're willing to take that conversation on alone."

"Because I know it'll kill you to disappoint him." He gives me a small, wooden smile as he pulls his phone from the pocket of his backpack, nestled next to his suitcase. "And because I'm used to it."

Chapter Twelve

"Sorry, like I just told your fiancé, we're booked until the end of the year. You might want to try the Bake House."

"I already tried them," I sigh. "And he's not my fia—"

The line goes dead. I jab at my phone screen with a frustrated groan that echoes around my cottage living room.

That's the fourth bakery I've called within a fifty-mile radius, and every time they've mentioned a fiancé. It took two very confusing conversations and peering out my window at Eli seated on a poolside chaise, his phone glued to his ear and a Post-it pad balanced on his knee, to realize he's been calling every bakery within a fifty-mile radius, too. Apparently he's claimed the task, even though it's on my portion of the list.

Kind of. I took some creative license, but the cake flavors are on my list, which basically means finding a new one is, too.

I punch in the number of the last bakery, my gaze pinned on Eli while the line rings. He's off his phone now, so he's either beat me to this one or didn't find it. His attention is fixed on something neon pinched between his fingers—a Post-it note, folded into one of his paper rings.

It's a moment of familiarity, but since we got to Blue Yonder twenty-six hours ago, there's little else that's been familiar about him. Bodysnatched Eli Mora is thriving.

And he's messing with my head.

Though I have plenty of legitimate things to think about, I've instead spent the past day trying to figure out what's with him. Alien abduction? Demon possession? Some of it fits the profile, among it that moment in the car yesterday and the way he called me Peach, like I was still that person to him.

But I don't think demonically possessed people have weekly therapy appointments, or go on what I'm starting to think of as The Adam Apology Tour, or throw therapy-speak at their ex-girlfriends about their hyper-independence issues when they've spent the past five years *not* talking about anything that mattered to or hurt them.

I size him up as he tips his head back toward the sun, eyes closed. Maybe he's been exorcized. Maybe he's *lost* a demon. Did Luce move on and get replaced by a human being? Did Eli get a coveted VP promotion, one he's been striving for, or—least likely—has he decided to find some work/life balance?

Whatever it is, it's terrible timing for him to be so present and so *incredibly* in my way, despite our agreement yesterday to do the opposite. He's quite literally been everywhere I am: accepting hugs from Laurie's four siblings and their various progeny yesterday; a looming presence behind me while we toured the grounds to review the week's work with Adam's aunt, Julia, who's taking on the role of site coordinator; walking up the steps of his cottage, within inches of mine because the other two are still being renovated, because of course they are; brushing past me on the main patio outside the tasting room where we gathered for dinner last night, his hand a quick but indelible press on my back; passing down my favorite bottle of Chardonnay not five seconds after I'd sipped the last dregs of my glass.

And now, beating me to every Napa County bakery.

After five years as a ghost, these twenty-six hours of Eli's potent awareness of me and the world around him feels like a solid wall I keep running into. The newness of this Eli, how closely it echoes the *old* Eli, is so disorienting that I can't focus.

But I have to.

"Icing on the Cake, how can I help you?"

The chipper voice on the other end of the line sucks me out of my Eli haze. I'm proving my own damn point.

"Hi!" I say, matching their tone. "This is a long shot, but I need a cake for a wedding next Saturday and I was wondering if you could help me out."

"Ooh, yes." The person on the other end sounds delighted, a positive sign, until they continue, "Your fiancé called a few minutes ago. I'm so sorry for your trouble."

"He's not my— you know what, that doesn't matter." I force a breezy laugh. "Do you think you might be able to help?"

"I'm hoping so. My boss is out today, but I texted her your situation and she asked me to set up an appointment for you on Tuesday. You're all set for two p.m."

Relief and irritation tangle together. "Thank you so much. We'll see you Tuesday."

I hang up and rise to my knees, leaning over the arm of the loveseat to press my face against the window screen. I stare at Eli, strategizing ways to calmly tell him to back off my list and honor our agreement.

But then he stands and my thoughts fall off a cliff. I absorb that he's wearing light blue swim trunks seconds before he pulls off his black T-shirt, revealing acres of golden skin, a flash of gold against the nape of his neck.

My mouth instantly parches. I haven't seen him shirtless for years; he's filled out, especially since Nick and Miriam's wedding. He looks good. Gorgeous.

I used to be so well acquainted with that body that sometimes it felt like mine. I knew every blunt curve of it, every hard plane. I knew where his skin would shiver from a ticklish spot, where it would shiver from pleasure. His shoulders look even broader bare, the wings of his shoulder blades flaring as he tosses his shirt aside. I used to dig my fingers into that spot right there, run them in soft, whirled patterns as he fell asleep.

A face pops into my line of vision. "Great view, right?"

I scream and roll off the loveseat, my ass hitting the hardwood floor so violently that my teeth rattle. "Jesus, Cole!"

His cackle rolls in through the window as I crawl over. "You obviously think so, at least."

I push my hair out of my face, giving him an incendiary look. If you looked up the definition of *asshole*, Cole Cooper's handsome face would be plastered there. Adam's older cousin and the director of sales at Blue Yonder is a tall and rangy white guy, with a wide smile and deep brown eyes that trick everyone into thinking he's a puppy. In reality, he's a barracuda. He's responsible for ninety-nine percent of the trouble we got into here, and likely one hundred percent of the Cooper family's collective heartburn.

"I wasn't staring at him. I was *glaring* at him because he's being a shithead."

Oh dammit, my mouth formed words before my Eli filter could catch it. Even here, where our relationship is known in the most sanitized way—we dated, we broke up, we're friends—Eli and I know to play up the friendship angle. It's especially important now, when anyone could shoot off a text to Adam saying Eli and I are rumbling.

I'd place Cole at the top of that Most Likely To list.

On cue, his eyes light up. He glances over his shoulder, dark blond hair ruffling in the breeze. "What's our boy done now?"

I bite back a groan. "It's nothing. We both have tasks for the week and he took over one of mine."

"Ah," he says with a sage nod. We stare at each other before his face breaks into that switchblade smile of his. "Well, let's go ask him about it."

"*No.*"

But it's too late; he's already striding away with an infuriating spring in his step.

I scramble after him. The courtyard is nestled in the U-shaped space between the four cottages, with the pool and a collection of navy-cushioned chaises serving as the central gathering spot. Beyond a border of lavender plants, an old picnic table sits at the perimeter of the vineyard. I don't have to look to know my initials are still carved into the tabletop alongside Eli's and Adam's.

Cole's already at the edge of the shimmering pool, hands in the pockets of his khaki pants. Eli's gaze moves from Cole to me, some of the understandable Cole-related irritation bleeding out of his expression.

"Georgia thinks you're being a shithead, E," Cole says.

Eli's eyebrows fly up. "Oh?"

I let out a sigh that comes from the depths of hell. "I didn't say that."

Cole's eyes sparkle with mirth. "You absolutely said that."

"Well, I didn't mean it."

"You said it but you don't mean it?" Eli asks.

"I *meant* it," I amend, "as a term of endearment."

A grin curls at his mouth as he squints up at me. "Yeah, I've heard that's a real up-and-comer for endearments."

I give him a pleasant smile in return, with lots of teeth. "Right up there with *buddy*."

"And what did I do to deserve *shithead* over *buddy*?" He stands to his full height, pushing his hair back from his face, and for a second I'm fully bamboozled by the water running down his chest.

"Tuesday," is all I can say.

"Tuesday?" he repeats, oblivious to the sexual riot he's causing inside me.

I grasp for two brain cells to rub together. "We have a bakery appointment on Tuesday."

His eyes flash with surprise. "We do. How'd you know?"

"Because I was calling bakeries, too." I keep my voice even, well aware Cole is avidly watching our conversation. "Or getting all your sloppy seconds, more accurately. I just got off the phone with the one we have an appointment with."

"Okay," he says slowly. "Is that a bad thing?"

I cross my arms. "Is doing double work ever a *good* thing, especially on our timeline? We agreed we'd stick to our lists. The bakery was on my list."

He frowns. "No, it wasn't."

"Yes, it was."

"Your list said *find new bakery since the other one blew up in our faces*?" he replies, running a hand over his mouth, leaving it damp. "That would be very psychic of me."

"That revisionist history is very *adorable* of you," I volley back cheerfully. "My list has the cake flavors on it, which is nearly the same thing."

Now I get a flash of teeth, a tiny, triumphant grin. "It sure does."

"*Hey.*"

His grin turns wide and intensely beautiful. "You walked right into it." After a beat, he adds a silky, "Buddy."

Cole's been watching this exchange with a growing smile. Now he gestures between us. "Hold on, is this really about a bakery, or is this an ex-lovers' quarrel? Did one of you slip up and fall into the other's bed last night and expectations weren't met?" He widens his eyes at Eli. "Did you not give Georgia the good D?"

"*Hello?*" I exclaim. "You can't say that."

"I'm going to get out of this pool and kill you," Eli states, propping his elbows on the concrete currently burning the soles of my bare feet.

Maybe this is hell.

"So you did give her bad D," Cole says triumphantly.

"He never gave me bad—" I cut myself off so suddenly my body sways, my cheeks flaming at the choked sound Eli makes and the laugh Cole lets out. My gaze clashes with Eli's and it's sparks, memories that are quick and molten.

I whirl on Cole. "Speaking of *dicks*, you can't talk like that. Eli and I are friends."

Cole's attention stays on Eli. "Who are also exes."

"Years ago," I insist. "We're good friends. We're great."

Cole raises an eyebrow at Eli. "That's your assessment, too? You're great friends?"

His tone is oddly knowing, and I glance at Eli, whose expression stays blank when he says, "The greatest."

Cole's "hmm" is amused.

"Glad we got that settled." I turn to Cole. "We haven't seen you in years, Cooper. Maybe give us a minute to reassimilate ourselves to your personality before you start acting familiar, okay?"

"But I *am* familiar," he says, rocking back on his heels with a smirk as he gestures to Eli. "At least with that one. I've seen Eli several times over the last year and a half, in fact."

I blink. "You have?"

Cole strolls over to a chaise, tossing aside Eli's towel and shirt so he can stretch out, ankles crossed. "Yep. First time was when I was in New York for a conference last year, then back again to visit a friend. Not long before that wedding you came out for, right, E?"

"Why ask me when you clearly know the timeline?" Eli says evenly, backstroking away.

"For the drama," Cole replies, grinning. "Anyway, I went back this past April for the same conference and this kid managed to find time in a schedule that seems fucking lonely and ultimately meaningless, but hey, what do I know?"

He's not wrong, but my hackles go up anyway. Eli must've given him some indication of his unforgiving schedule when they met up, and his heart's in the right place, but Cole has the delivery of a swift punch to the face.

"Are you arriving at a point sometime soon?" I ask, clocking Eli's mutinous look.

Cole's eyes narrow, looking at me like the protectiveness bubbling in my chest has flooded my expression, too. Lifting a shoulder, he plucks up the paper ring sitting on the table, inspecting it. "The point is, I *am* familiar with our favorite shithead. Eli's a good listener. Hell, so am I." At this, his gaze sharpens, finding me. "Guess that means me and E are great friends, too."

"That's very precious," I say. "But that doesn't mean you get to say sensationally inappropriate things."

"That's, like, seventy percent of my personality."

Eli swims over to the edge of the pool, his gaze fixed on Cole. "Did you just come over here to be a pain in the ass or was there a point to your visit?"

"Yes," Cole replies.

"Which *one*?"

"Both, and speaking of precious—" Cole flicks the paper ring into the air, right at me. I reach for it on instinct, letting out a breath when it lands in my palm, whisper-light. "Did you make that?"

I close my hand around the ring. I won't be sharing *that* history with him. "No."

Cole's gaze drifts from me to Eli, staying on him. He offers a soft, "Ah."

Eli pinches the bridge of his nose. "Approach your point swiftly."

"Right," Cole says, snapping his fingers. "Georgia, my mom wanted to get your eyes on her big-ass checklist if you have a minute. She's up in the office."

"I'm on it," I say, grateful for a reason to extricate myself from the torture of a half-naked Eli and Cole, full stop.

He grins, folding his hands behind his head. "Don't worry, I'll keep your boy company."

"I wasn't worried."

"And I'm fully planning on drowning you," Eli adds. Cole just laughs.

That's a situation for those two to figure out. "See you, shithead."

"Endearment?" Cole calls.

"Derogatory," I call back. Eli's laughter follows me up the path before it's cut off by Cole's low murmur.

I force my curiosity away. Whatever's happening between them isn't my business. I can't get distracted by the overwhelmingness of this brand-new Eli Mora. It's already wrapping around me like a vine, and there's nothing I want less than to get caught up in it, especially on land where vines are meant to grow.

Chapter Thirteen

On Sunday, Adam calls when the sun has barely popped into the sky.

I swipe my phone off the coffee table, settling back onto the loveseat. "Do you know what time it is?"

"What are you doing?" he asks in lieu of a hello.

"It's 8:05, Adam, what do you think I'm doing?"

"Sleeping?" he guesses without remorse.

"Very recently."

Actually, I've been up for more than an hour toggling between TikTok, where I regularly stalk an old high school upperclassman who's now a professional photographer and married to the second-hottest man to come out of Glenlake High, and LinkedIn, where I've been panic-scrolling through job listings.

I should've kept my vow not to think about my dilemma, though; the findings weren't positive. There are options, but none of them can touch what I have now. I love my job, and I know from personal experience how rare that is. The only imperfect thing about it is that they want to send me back to Seattle for good.

". . . Eli?"

Adam's voice snaps me back into the moment, and I shove my spiral into a mental drawer.

"What about Eli?"

"Where is he?"

"Well, he's not *here* at 8:05," I say, wandering to the kitchenette. It's gorgeous now, with gleaming navy cabinetry and gold hardware, the countertops a pretty white marble with blue veining.

I miss the old version, with its lovingly worn maple wood and grapevine wallpaper.

The first two summers I spent here—in this cottage, actually, rooming with a lazy Susan's rotation of Adam's cousins—I didn't know how important this place would become to me. I was too overwhelmed by excitement and homesickness. I loved Blue Yonder, but it didn't belong to me yet, and that feeling always left me anxious. It wasn't until Eli joined us the following summer that I started to truly feel the homelike shape of it; then it became rooted in my veins.

I glance out the window, homesick again, standing in the middle of the place I miss. I take in the tall, swaying trees and the long stretch of land, its precise rows of vines laid out so carefully. The courtyard is silent and empty, save for birds hopping in the dewy grass, and the pool ripples quietly, as if vibrating with the memory of Eli's body slicing through it yesterday. It's peaceful, but I don't feel any of that.

"I assume he's in his cottage," I say, blinking away from the view.

Probably doing one of his new Eli things or filching something else off my list. Or maybe burying Cole's body. Despite the time I spent ruminating over yesterday's conversation and then admonishing myself for ruminating, I couldn't put the pieces together.

Once I'd formed my pillows into a human shape so my bed didn't feel so empty, I tossed and turned, replaying the way Cole almost seemed like he was challenging Eli. About what, though?

"Possession," I mutter.

"What?"

"Uh . . ." My gaze lands on the ring boxes nestled in the back corner of the counter, their rich red a stark contrast to the white marble. They look like two bleeding hearts. "I am in *possession* of your rings."

There's a short pause before Adam draws out, "Yes, I know that. I gave them to you." Another pause, this one more suspicious. "Why are you telling me that? Are you okay? Are you being held hostage? Is this some weird code? Because I wouldn't be surprised at this point, given everything else that's hap—"

"I'm not being held hostage, but thanks for making my theoretical traumatic experience about you and your curse." I lean a hip against the counter. "Which doesn't exist, by the way. Everything is going great. All the venue setup stuff is on track and we have a bakery appointment on Tuesday."

"Nice," he says. "Get it nailed down this time, okay?"

My heart drops into my stomach. "I'm sor—"

"ADAM," Grace yells in the background.

"I'm joking!" he exclaims, voice muffled before it clears again. "George, I was joking. I'm sorry, that was too soon."

I sigh. "Just tell me why you called."

Adam happily moves on; he has the attention span of a fruit fly. "Oh, because we set up a DJ appointment for you tomorrow. Gracie and I wanted to Zoom with the guy, but he was insistent that someone come in to vet the 'experience.' That's literally what he called it. An 'experience.'"

"Sounds epic." I pick up a ring box, flipping the top to find

Adam's gold band nestled there, same as it was last night when I checked. And yesterday morning, when I also checked.

As I start to slide the box back, I catch a flash of neon pink behind Grace's box—the paper ring Cole flicked at me yesterday. The one I should've tossed, but instead stuck behind real, actual rings that are real, actual symbols of forever.

I set my phone on the counter as Adam chatters on, picking up the ring. The paper is smooth and thick, layers folded meticulously by Eli's attentive fingers. When he used to give me these, I'd be so careful slipping it onto my finger—my index or middle, or, after we started dating, my ring finger, but the right one. He'd trace a path behind it, help me push it down, then look up at me through his lashes, grinning. Sometimes his happiest smiles were his smallest ones, and his paper ring smiles were just the gentle upward curve of his mouth.

"Looks good, Peach," he'd murmur, bringing my finger up to his mouth. He'd bite down on my knuckle, hard and messy until I laughed, then softer, just the scrape of his teeth, until I shivered.

"—thinking you can FaceTime me in. I want to see if this guy is legit. I swear, only the stone-cold weirdos are left," Adam is saying. "Is that a bad sign?"

I shake out of the haze so real I swear I can feel Eli's mouth on my skin.

"It's not a bad sign," Grace calls.

"It's not a bad sign," I repeat. "It's normal to have limited options a week before your wedding."

"Don't remind me," he replies darkly.

"Don't worry too much. All of my and Eli's combined brain cells are devoted to working this out."

And not one brain cell should be devoted to Eli.

I set the ring down on the counter, only it's more of a frustrated fling, and my wrist knocks into the ring box with Adam's band. It topples onto its side with a loud *thwack*—

And the ring bounces out, taking off down the counter.

"Oh, my *god*." I lunge toward it, but it's too late. It's rolled over the edge of the sink.

Straight into the drain.

"What? What?" Adam shouts.

"No, it's nothing!" I shriek, bending over the sink to peer into the dark abyss. "A bird ran into the window and scared me. I think it's dead."

"Sick," he says with dismay. "Isn't *that* a bad sign?"

"It's not a bad sign," I practically wail. His wedding band flying down the sink sure is, though.

"Well, if it's dead, make Eli take care of it. You're gonna cry."

I'm definitely going to cry, but I'm not going to make Eli take care of anything. This is all me.

"Uh-huh, sure." I lean farther over the sink, ramming my forehead into the lever handle in the process, which sends a violent spray of water all over the front of me. "Oh fu— Adam, I think the bird is moving. I gotta go, noted on the DJ appointment, *seeyougoodbye*."

"George—"

I hang up, then clap both hands over my mouth to muffle a moan.

Oh, hell.

I'm wetter, significantly more panicked, and three minutes down a YouTube rabbit hole when footsteps pound up the porch steps.

There's a brisk knock. "Georgia?"

No, no, no. I briefly consider not answering; Eli is the last person on earth I want witnessing this moment.

"Georgia," he repeats, his voice louder, more urgent. "Let me in."

"Good morning! No, thank you, everything is fine."

"I'm going to break down the door."

"Well, that's dramatic," I huff, stomping to the front door. I inch it open so I can stick my head through the gap.

Eli's standing there in gym shorts, his thin gold chain, and nothing else. There are sheet lines running across his stomach and chest, his hair standing up in the back. I'm trying so hard to be strong, but I'm only human and he looks beautiful and vulnerable, his skin still sleep-warm, probably, eyes hooded and mouth puffy.

"Sorry, but I abide by the no shirt, no service rule," I manage, ripping my eyes from the solid expanse of his torso.

"Apologies for the break in protocol," he says pleasantly, though there's an intensity in his eyes as he inspects me. "I ran over from a dead sleep."

Without the door serving as a barrier, I can hear the fine texture in his voice, the sandpaper he only gets first thing in the morning. I want to rub it between my fingers, feel it all over my skin.

Down, girl.

"That seems very unnecessary." Behind me, the sink ticks like a bomb.

"Debatable. Adam called saying something about you screaming and a dead bird and a bad omen."

"There's no dead bird."

He visibly deflates. "Okay, good. I would've taken care of it for you, but I would've cried."

"Who wouldn't?" I exclaim. This is why we didn't have glue traps for the mice in our apartment. Our neighbor across the hall used to catch and release for us.

"So, if there's no dead bird," Eli says, raising an eyebrow as a silent acknowledgment of my fib, "what's wrong?"

"Nothing. Everything is good."

The continuation of my lie fully awakens him. He places a broad palm on the door, his knuckles grazing my cheek. He exerts only the lightest pressure, a request I want to deny. But my body has defected from my brain and instead I rock back on my heels as the door creaks open.

Eli's careful gaze moves over my face, starting at what is surely now a welt on my forehead. My hair is a mess, the rest of me a wreck.

His eyes flicker lower, then widen, and I watch, mesmerized, as his Adam's apple undulates against his throat. "You . . . are wet."

I look down. "*Oh.*"

My sleep shirt isn't white, but this is a bad time to discover that if white's winning the wet T-shirt contest, lavender's a fierce contender. It doesn't fully reveal the shade of things, but it certainly details the shape.

Eli flushes, swallowing hard again as he looks away, scratching at his stubbled cheek.

We used to see each other naked every day, in mundane moments and intensely pleasurable ones. He's perched on the closed toilet seat to talk to me while I showered; I've watched him strip out of his work clothes while I recited a grocery list. He's had the nipples that are making his ears flush red now in his mouth hundreds of times. He's touched my breasts, kissed them, given them ridiculous pet names and fucked them. I could draw this man's dick by memory, have had my hands and body all over it, and yet catching a glimpse of his chest this close makes my face bloom fire-hot. We're both embarrassed, as if all that knowledge doesn't sit between us.

Or maybe it's because it does, because we're really looking at each other for the first time in so long, remembering things together in the same space.

Somewhere, my self-preservation instincts yell, *don't get pulled under. No more disasters.*

Right. Especially when I've already got one on my hands. I cross my arms over my chest, forcing a smile.

But Eli sees right through it and takes a step forward. "What's going on?"

"Nothing. I'm good." My voice wobbles. "I promise."

I expect that to be the last of it. I expect him to nod or clench his jaw or sigh, the way he would when I'd regurgitate that line when I was very clearly not good. I expect him to walk away.

But he's not that Eli right now, and god, that's terrifying. He stands there, his palm pressed to the door. It's the same spot he stood morning after morning, summer after summer, waiting for me.

It's so disorienting that he's doing it again. It's a homesickness of its own.

"What's going on?" he repeats.

The gentleness of the question twists with every other overwhelming emotion, and a knot forms in my throat. There's a quiet to his voice, some silent reassurance that whatever I need he'll take care of.

I shouldn't trust that, because I've leaned on people before and they've let me fall. *He* has.

But I don't want to be alone. I need someone here, even if it's Eli.

"I accidentally dropped Adam's wedding band down the sink and I don't know how to get it back and I'm fully freaking out because he's going to unfriend me and kick me out of the wedding," I burst out.

A hot tear rolls down my cheek. Eli's expression morphs from confusion to surprise to intense tenderness so fast it hurts, right beneath my ribs.

He steps closer, over the threshold, and for a second I think he's going to take me into his arms. For a second, I want it so badly I can hardly breathe.

Instead, his fingers graze mine, gone before I can really feel them. "Okay. Let's go figure it out."

Chapter Fourteen

I nearly forgot how hot Eli being ultra-competent is, a misstep on my part because he's the most competent person I know.

He's already gathered tools and turned off the water supply, and is now crouched in front of the sink, eyeing the pipes underneath.

"It probably got stuck in the P trap. I have to loosen these connectors and remove the pipe." He looks over his shoulder at me, a solid six feet away. I don't trust myself to be closer. "Do you mind shining a light in here so I can see?"

There goes that idea. "No problem."

I reach for my phone, stopping when I see the chaos-causing paper ring on the counter. *Shit.* Did Eli see it?

Picking up my phone with one hand, I flick the ring with the other, trying to scoot it behind Grace's ring box.

Instead, it ricochets against the backsplash, careening off the counter like Thelma and Louise's car. It swan dives onto Eli's naked back, then arcs away, landing on the floor next to his knee.

Eli looks down at it. I look down at it. Then we look at each other and the thirteen years of memories that silly little paper ring holds settle between us.

"Cole threw it at me yesterday," I explain, like he wasn't there to see it. Like that's an excuse for why I kept it afterward. "He's an asshole."

"Yeah, well," he says, "we all have our strengths."

Eli grins when I laugh, a full one that shoots heat through me, but it fades as he looks back at the ring.

He could ask questions. This version of Eli might, a realization that makes my heart skip. But instead he picks it up, pinching it between his fingers. He sits back on his haunches, not quite on his knees, but the effect makes my stomach freefall anyway. At one point, I wished for this.

His gaze flicks up to me. "I think this is my best work yet."

My breath leaves in a soft huff. "Give your medium some credit. That paper is much more luxurious than a straw wrapper."

"Not as good as a gum wrapper, though," he muses. "Less flexibility."

"You've always been passionate about your craft."

"Sure have," he murmurs. He looks at it for a beat longer before placing it on the counter. Then he clears his throat and rubs the back of his neck, turning to the sink. "Did you have the water running when the ring fell?"

"Oh," I stutter, disoriented by the shift in conversation. "Um, for a minute. That's how I got wet."

His eyes dart to my drying shirt. "Okay. It still should've stopped in the P trap."

I kneel at his hip, close enough to feel the heat from his skin. With my flashlight shining, he takes the tool and starts loosening the connector. I try to keep my attention on his work, but soon enough I'm following the trail of undulating muscles in his forearms up to the bunch and release of his biceps, the shift of his shoulders and the flex of his back.

Then, torturously, he lets out a soft grunt of exertion. My body recognizes it immediately as the sound he'd make when he'd watch me take him inside, and every erogenous zone I have lights up like a pinball machine.

I'm not going to survive this.

"I forgot how good you are at fixing random things." My voice is loud and wild in the quiet of the room, and Eli looks over, his eyebrows jumping.

"Guess I absorbed all that handiwork my dad did after he got laid off," he says, setting aside the wrench so he can shimmy the pipe. It wiggles, but doesn't separate, and he picks up the wrench again. "I liked going on jobs with him sometimes to keep him company."

An old ache is threaded through his voice. I know how it hurt him to watch his parents' previously solid marriage fall apart, how out of control it made eldest, responsible Eli feel to see everyone in his family suffer, himself included. His adult belief system grew from that disaster: financial stability that *he* controlled meant he'd never have to feel that way again.

No matter what other feelings I had, I never judged him for falling victim to the wounds of his adolescence. God knows I did the same thing. But while he was trying to fix what was broken in his past, he was breaking something that was right in front of him.

That thought is a splash of cold water. An addition to the list of reasons I need to keep my distance.

It's just hard when he keeps getting *closer*. Like now, as his shoulder presses into mine.

I scooch over. "How's your dad doing?"

"He's great," he says, pride rumbling through his voice. "He just bought a house in Pasadena, and he's got a carpentry business going."

I know. I follow him on Instagram, press a little heart onto every picture he posts of his work—beautiful furniture made of reclaimed wood that gets hundreds of likes and dozens of comments.

A few months ago, Marcus DMed me, said he appreciated every post I liked, and that he hoped I was doing well. He signed off with, *miss you, kiddo*.

I cried for three days, read it obsessively until I forced myself to delete it.

"And your mom and sisters are good?" I ask. Nina and Zoe are as ghostlike on social media as Eli, so they don't have accounts I can stealthily stalk, but I know via his dad's account that they're about to start their junior and senior years of college, respectively. Eli's mom texts me happy birthday every year, though I doubt he knows it.

I miss them all, but Kelly especially; I used to dream about calling her Mom someday. Now I keep my distance, but I've never been able to let go completely.

"Yep, they're all good. Mom's in Denver," Eli says, breaking that thought apart. "Her partner proposed a few months ago."

"That's amazing."

"Yeah. It was a long time coming. Everything falling into place like that, I mean." He pauses, darting a quick glance at me before returning to loosening the pipe. "For a long time I thought if my family didn't look like it did before all our shit went down, then how could we ever be happy like that again?" His attention shifts back to me, and this time his gaze is a lingering trace. "They really are, though. It's different, but that's okay."

I don't miss that he's talking about them, not himself, and I have the urge to ask him if *he's* happy. But it's not my place to ask. Softly, I say, "Well, that makes me happy, too."

Something warm and sad passes through his eyes. "What about your dad? He's good? Slowing down, I hope?"

"No, still working hard." I shrug. "Probably until the day he dies."

For a moment he's quiet, jaw flexing. And then he says, "He'll regret that someday. Having a daughter like you and not taking advantage of every minute."

My throat clogs. "It's—"

"Don't say it's fine." His eyes are locked on me, his voice strangely hoarse. "It's not."

It isn't, but it doesn't change the reality of it, and talking about it now won't either. It's too tender, and we're too close, and Eli's looking at me too fiercely. I could dissolve under his attention, but I *can't*.

I look away. "Adam's ring is probably screaming for us in that pipe."

I can *feel* his appraisal. His desire to push. Finally, he murmurs, "Okay."

The room quiets as Eli lays the wrench down again and wiggles the pipe. This time it pulls off, and he empties the standing water into the bucket.

"Hmm."

"What?"

"It's not here. It's either stuck in the pipe above, or it could've moved further this way." He leans in, squinting at the opening of the pipe that goes into the wall. I crawl closer, shining my light. We're basically under the sink together now, bodies connected from knee to shoulder. It's torture where our bare skin grazes.

His breath hitches, echoing around us. He tips his chin, the barest movement that still brings our mouths within inches of each other.

"If it moved further, we're going to have to call someone," he says.

"Fuck," I whisper.

His eyes flare, even as his tone turns soothing. "Let's try the other way first. Have you seen anything made of wire around here? A hanger, maybe?"

The conversation is neutral, but the air between us is thick. I can smell the mint toothpaste on his breath, see the beating pulse in his neck. "My dress is still on its dry-cleaning hanger."

"All right, go get that, please."

It's a quiet demand that lights me up, reminds me of the way he'd sometimes get bossy and greedy during sex, this same man who I feared didn't need me in the secret, desperate way I craved. It made our connection strip itself to the bones, turned it honest and real in a way I wouldn't fully allow in the rest of our life.

Everything is suddenly too much—the past, the present, Eli— and I lurch back. His hand curls around the back of my head just before it smashes against the cabinet.

"Careful," he rumbles, fingers tightening in my hair.

God, I'm trying to be.

"I'll be right back," I babble, scrambling out of our tight space.

After three hundred cleansing breaths and a stern, whispered lecture to myself, I return from the bedroom with the wire hanger. Eli molds it straight, then hands it back to me.

"Stick that down the drain and wiggle it. I'll stay down here in case it falls."

He crawls under the sink while I wiggle the hanger as directed. I have no idea what I'm doing, and my heart starts beating fast at the thought of having to call a plumber in.

As if he hears me spiraling, Eli says, "You're doing great."

"*Please*," I whisper, peering down into the drain.

And then a triumphant, "I got it."

"You got it?" I throw the hanger to the side as he scoots out. The ring is on his middle finger, sitting above his knuckle. "Oh my god, you got it!"

It's like someone's plucked me by the back of the shirt and dropped me over the edge of a cliff. The relief is that visceral. It's the excuse I'll use later for why, when Eli stands, I throw my arms around his neck.

I don't know the last time Eli and I hugged for real, because of a shared happiness. If I could pinpoint that moment, I probably would've spent the last five years torturing myself with it, so maybe it's for the best. I just know that when Eli wraps his arms around my waist following a brief hesitation, it feels like coming home after the longest time away.

He lets out a shattered breath, pulling me closer, crushing my breasts against his chest. His heart hammers with mine. Through the thin material of my T-shirt, I feel the cold metal of Adam's wedding band and I close my eyes, trying to remember it's about him and Grace, not this. Trying to remember I'm supposed to keep my distance.

But, fuck it. If this is the actual last time we hug like this—for real, in happiness—then I'm going to revel in it. I have enough memories that hurt; what's one more?

I should say something. Instead, I press my face into the curve where his shoulder and neck meet, biting my lip so I won't put my mouth on him. It's how I rationalize it: *at least I'm not going that far. It's just this. Just for a minute.*

Eli's nose brushes against my cheek, his stubble scratching at my skin. An accident the first time, I think, until he does it again. I pull back until the corners of our mouths are nearly aligned.

This is a bad, very horrible idea, my brain screams, but my body presses closer. Eli's arms tighten, fingers digging into the small of my back.

"Georgia," he whispers, and I hate my past self for writing on our list that we should avoid saying each other's names. I hate that I forced myself to be so careful, even as I recognize that I need it right now more than ever.

I scrawl out all the reasons in my mind: that Eli and I didn't work the first time. That trying again would hurt, likely in the same ways. It would ruin whatever modicum of ability we have to keep things bearable for the sake of our friendship with Adam. That this new Eli, who looks so much like the old one I loved, can't be here to stay. That I don't want this. Can't have it, or else it'll ruin me again, and this time I'll become the mess I refused to be before.

I'll remember all that in a second.

I pull back another millimeter. Two, until I'm looking at the deep, warm starburst of his eyes, filled with gold and sparking heat. His nose grazes mine and his lashes flutter down, press hard against his skin.

His hands drop to my hips. Shape them, and then grip them.

"You're not going to want this," he whispers.

I told myself the same thing seconds ago, but hearing him say it out loud scrambles my brain. "What?"

"In thirty seconds, you're not going to want this, and I can't pull away, so you're the one who has to."

My arms drop like his skin is on fire and I stumble back, my hip connecting with the tiny island behind me. With a ragged exhale, he turns around, snagging the ring box. I watch him press it back into the velvet. Shut the box. Lower his head and rub a hand over his face.

"I'm sorry," I croak out.

"It's okay," he says.

"I was excited."

"Me, too."

"About the ring, I mean."

He huffs out a laugh. "Yeah."

This was just us remembering. The memories of our last summer and what came after are everywhere, too easy to step into, and we both slipped like I feared. But with as much history as Eli and I have and how physically close we got after years of distance, it would actually be weirder if we *hadn't*.

It's a paper-thin excuse, but I grab it anyway.

"That was . . ." I scramble for a description that won't throw us right back into danger. "Surprisingly good teamwork."

He gives me an incredulous look over his shoulder.

"The *ring*, Eli."

Amusement replaces the heat in his eyes. "It's almost like we work really well toward a common goal when we're not fighting each other."

"Is that passive aggressive commentary about the bakery?"

He turns. "And the split-up list."

"That was equally your idea."

"I did it for you."

"What do you mean?"

He lifts a shoulder, leaning against the counter. "You clearly want as little to do with me as possible. I know you'd rather be alone here, or with Jamie or something."

Of course I'd love to be with Jamie. But if Jamie were here, Blake would be, too, and while I adore Blake and love hanging out with them, sometimes listening to the couple shorthand they developed while I was in Seattle makes me feel lonely. Less belonged to by Jamie. It's not something I'd ever admit out loud, though.

And it's easier to be alone, but that doesn't mean it's what I want.

That's not something I'd admit out loud either.

"It's not as awkward as I thought it'd be." *Awkward* is now my emotional support word for this, apparently.

Something passes over his face, a shadow of the way I felt when he said it. "Great."

"And you just saved the day, so I can't exactly say I don't want you here."

"Hey," he admonishes. "We did that together."

We let the realization sink in. It's a warm thing, familiar and foreign.

"What if we tackle the big stuff together?" he asks. "It'll make Adam happy and get Cole to stop heckling us."

"What's up with him, anyway? He was being so weird yesterday."

His gaze bounces away. "Maybe he just can't fathom having any interactions with his exes because they all hate him."

I laugh. "A solid theory."

"Anyway," he says, meeting my eyes again, "most importantly, we're clearly better at mitigating disasters when we're not doing it separately."

He's right—when we actually cooperate with one another, shit gets done. It's exactly what we need as we get down to the wire. Adam will get up here on Friday and be blown away.

But it means that I'll be living alongside Eli and this rebuilding awareness. I'll have to be so careful.

Eli braces his hands behind him. Watching me. Waiting.

"Adam did inform me he set up a DJ appointment for tomorrow, so we could try the teamwork thing out then." His gaze warms and so does my chest. Ugh. "He wants to FaceTime in anyway, so it's a good idea to go together."

"Done. And we'll do the bakery appointment on Tuesday together, too?"

"Yes, on our best behavior."

He draws an X over his chest with a somber, "Cross my heart."

I roll my eyes, but can't fully bite back a smile. He grins softly in return and for a second we get caught in it. He looks like twenty-year-old Eli, the summer version of himself when that spark was heating inside me, the version of him in subsequent years when I was fully in love.

Oh my god, stop, the peanut-sized logic in my brain sighs.

He shakes his head as if rousing himself and pushes off the counter. "I should go. I'm helping with the deck this morning."

"Right, yes, I need to get ready, too," I say. "I'm helping unload a bunch of stuff into the shed to hold for the reception."

I trail him to the door after we put the tools away, feeling an unsettling reluctance to let him go.

"Thanks again for digging me out of that mess," I say, leaning against the door as he strides down the steps.

He turns, shielding his eyes against the quickly rising sun. "Anytime."

"Well, hopefully never again." I say it lightly, but I'm not joking.

"Anytime," he repeats, with emphasis.

It's not until he's gone and I'm in the shower, replaying our charged moment, that I realize he told me I wasn't going to want this.

But he didn't say that *he* wouldn't.

Chapter Fifteen

"Our first foray into teamwork is off to a bumpy start," I hiss, cha-cha-ing real smooth as instructed.

Eli slides me a look as he hitch-steps. "Don't judge our abilities on this. Remember the ring yesterday?"

How could I forget? I've been playing it on an endless loop, minus the ring-saving—how it felt to have his arms around me again, the way his lips nearly—

"It's not us," Eli continues, reaching out to steady me as I stumble. "It's him."

"And then usually I transition right into 'Cotton Eye Joe' from the 'Cha-Cha Slide,'" Danny Diamond calls out, adjusting the fedora perched on his head. A sequin leaps poetically from his red vest, landing near the toe of his saddle shoe.

I had a sinking feeling when the address we entered into Google Maps led us to a dilapidated Napa strip mall, but I forced myself not to judge a book by its cover.

Turns out, I should have. Adam and Grace's potential DJ for the biggest day of their lives bears an uncanny resemblance to the principal from *She's the Man*, a thought that's distracted me every second of the thirty-three minutes he's walked us through "the experience"—a live demonstration of his typical wedding set, where participation is required.

"I love 'Cotton Eye Joe,' Danny," Adam's voice rings out. "Great vision there."

I glance at Eli's phone propped up on a rickety coffee table in the "lobby," which is the table squeezed between two sagging, puke-green couches on the other side of the room.

We dialed in Adam and Grace when we got here and since then I've watched as Adam has moved through the five stages of grief. Grace dipped while Danny was in the middle of explaining why "The Chicken Dance" is still relevant, claiming nausea (same), but Adam's been with us for the entire debacle.

That fifth stage of grief? Trolling.

Out of the corner of my eye, I see Eli roll his. I'm almost certain Adam's never even heard that song; he doesn't acknowledge nineties pop music.

Eli nods his chin toward the phone. "It's intervention time. We've got three minutes before he loses it."

The first notes of "Cotton Eye Joe" hit like the beginnings of food poisoning, as a rumble in my gut. I hold a finger up toward Danny. "We need a quick intermission to chat with the groom. Be back in a sec."

He throws me a dazzling smile. "No problem, I'll keep the music pumping."

Thanks to my enthusiastic participation, I've managed to do what I couldn't with Margot: capture Danny Diamond's undying adoration. Unfortunately, it's useless to me.

I drag Eli off the scuffed dance floor and over to Adam. We crouch down, scooching closer to fit onscreen, which puts Eli's thigh against mine from knee to hip. A waft of his pheromone-laced, spicy scent drifts right up my nose. It might as well be going straight into my veins; my mind goes blank, caught up in an Eli Mora sensorial storm.

I've tried my damnedest to forget what happened yesterday, but every time Eli gets within six feet of me, it's like we're back in that kitchen. I'm hearing the tortured breath he let out when he pulled me tight to his body, feeling the raging beat of his heart, hearing him tell me to pull away, because he couldn't.

Maybe it was all muscle memory and nostalgia, but certain parts of me aren't getting the message.

"Hey, bud." Eli's greeting to Adam is low. It rumbles through me, shaking me out of my haze.

"Uh, yeah, what the fuck?" Adam hisses back. "Are we seriously getting stuck with the 'Chicken Dance' man?"

I grimace. "There's no one else?"

"Not within a mile of our budget." He runs a hand over his face, groaning. "I *am* cursed. This is karma for stealing that car senior year."

"Wasn't that an accident?" I ask.

"Yes!" he exclaims, throwing up his hands. "Doesn't mean it isn't the reason for my curse."

Eli leans in. "Adam, you've done so many more curse-worthy things in your life."

"Between the two of us, we could come up with a much stronger list," I agree.

He raises an eyebrow at me. "Ten things, at least."

"Twenty, probably," I muse, sliding him a look. "Starting with the—"

"The *thing*, right," Eli catches on immediately, dipping his chin as a tiny, conspiratorial grin pulls at the corner of his mouth.

We've teased Adam like this a hundred times since we broke up. But this is the first time in over five years it's felt natural, not like a performance.

It should scare me—and it does. But it also feeds something I've shut away for so long.

"What would you put that one at, curse-worthy wise?" he asks, shifting on the balls of his feet. His knee presses more firmly against mine and I let it.

"Has to be number one."

"Really? I was going to say three, because of the *other* thing—"

I let out a low whistle, glancing at Adam, who's watching us with his arms crossed, his expression bemused. "I forgot about that. Extremely curse-worthy. Definitely number-one material."

"Good thing you have us to keep you honest, Kiz," Eli says. "Accidental grand theft auto doesn't even—"

"Okay, you dickheads," Adam says, laughter finally breaking free. "Instead of doing your banter-attack thing, why don't you take care of me emotionally? Save the roasts for your best people speech."

"I'm not going to roast you," I assure him, picturing the handwritten speech I completed weeks ago. "It's the perfect mix of charming and touching, actually. Which is exactly what the rest of your wedding will be."

"Yeah, and it's going to be musically backed by the fucking 'Hokey Pokey,'" Adam says, but his mouth twists into an easier smile. We're turning a corner.

Eli leans in to close the sale. "Listen, you're not getting anything out of watching this. Georgia and I will take care of the rest of the appointment. Go hang out with your wife."

Adam wags a finger. "Not my wife yet."

"In five days, though," Eli says, and his voice drops into a sweet, cajoling timbre that whispers across the back of my neck. "And it's going to be awesome, I promise."

Adam sighs. "Right. I need to focus on that."

"Yes, and we'll focus on this. We won't walk out of here without a plan, okay?" Eli holds a fist up to the screen. Adam does, too, with a smile that's less anxious than it was two minutes ago.

His eyes dart to me and I nod, tucking away every trace of my doubt. "We've got this."

"Love you, squad, thanks for always having my back." On a dime, his fond smile turns into a smirk. "George, don't end up on any tables if he plays Lil Wayne, okay?"

I let out an indignant gasp as Eli's shoulder shakes against mine. "That happened *one* time—"

The call ends.

"Little asshole," I mutter.

"I mean, *I* won't stop you," Eli says, "if that's where the music takes you."

When I glance at him, he runs a hand over his mouth, wiping away a smug grin.

"The music will *not* take me."

What a good night, though. The weekend before we left for New York, Eli, Adam, Grace—his newish girlfriend at the time—and I went out in the city to celebrate the grown-up phase we were moving into. I was hopped up on vodka sodas, adrenaline, and the anticipation of a future that stretched on and on. Of *course* I climbed on the table and danced, while Eli watched me from below like I was ridiculous, like he wanted to devour me. He made good on it later when he carried me into the hotel room we'd splurged on, handsy and laughing, stripping me down, telling me he loved me, he was so fucking happy, our life was going to be so good.

Our gazes collide and my heart takes off. We both look away simultaneously.

Eli clears his throat as we stand. "That joke was a good sign. He seemed calmer."

"That makes one of us." When Eli gives me a questioning look, I surreptitiously gesture to our surroundings. "This is abysmal, and there aren't any other options. He and Grace have trusted us to get everything on track and so far the only thing that's on track is the reno work."

"Hey," he says with a frown, stepping closer. "We're doing this together now, right? We've got five days left. Everything's going to get done."

I swallow hard against the trepidation climbing my throat. "And what if it doesn't?"

His eyes trace my face, something almost protective flashing in them. "Why don't we—"

A loud clap echoes in the room, and Eli and I startle, looking over at Danny. I let out a breath, forcing myself to shift away from my rising panic.

"Ready to go again?" he asks hopefully.

"Absolutely," I sing.

"Perfect. Now, I try to keep things upbeat because the only acceptable Danny Diamond dance floor is a packed one." He grins. "But I do like to throw in a slow jam every once in a while. Let's check that out."

"Oh, uh . . ." The last thing in this world I need is to be pressed up against Eli while some love song plays. "I think we understand how that works. Actually—"

"That's great," Eli speaks up, walking back to the dance floor.

He turns to me as the overhead light dims, holding out a hand, his gaze intent. *Get over here*, is the message.

I go.

The music starts as I step into the cradle of his body. It's an old Norah Jones song, but still shockingly modern compared to anything else Danny's played. I wrap one arm around Eli's neck, letting him take my right hand in his. It feels like that hug yesterday, but with intention.

I know exactly what I'm doing and I'm doing it anyway, because Eli asked me to.

The cutout in my pale blue summer dress is suddenly a liability. It's at my lower back, exactly where Eli lays his hand, and it's like being electrocuted, like being liquefied from the inside out. I'm barely human, just a wildly beating heart and spiraling attraction.

"Why are we doing this?" I croak out.

It takes him a beat to respond. "Because we're rallying right now. We're going to come up with an idea and when this song is over, we're going to pitch it to Danny and get the fuck outta here, then drink an entire bottle of wine in celebration."

I manage a laugh, my mouth nearly at his neck. His skin turns textured right there, tiny hairs standing on end, and I huff out another breath to watch it happen again. "All right, let's rally. Before Danny interrupted us, you said, 'Why don't we . . .'"

"I—" He pauses. His fingers graze up my spine, then still, remembering we don't do that anymore. "No idea. I think I was about to say something terrible so you could riff off it with something genius."

I squeeze my eyes shut. "You overestimate me."

"You underestimate yourself."

The compliment does its job, as he probably intended. My

brain kicks into fix-it mode, writing out options, crossing each one out as I get to them.

But then—

"A list."

"A list," he repeats, a low murmur across my cheek.

"We'll give him a list of songs he can play, and tell him he can't deviate from it. We'll pay him extra for it if we have to. Adam has about five hundred Spotify playlists we can pilfer from to make sure it's what he wants."

Eli pulls back, a smile blooming. "See? Genius."

"It could work, right?"

"It's our best shot by far. We have nothing to lose except 'Cotton Eye Joe.'"

I start to extricate myself. "Great, let's—"

"Finish the song." Eli's palm is warm pressure at the small of my back, and it brings a flash of memory with it—his hand right there, pressing me down onto our bed. "I don't want to insult his 'experience' before we ask for a deviation from it."

"Sure," I whisper. "Okay."

We keep dancing. It feels incredible. Like torture. I finesse it in my mind until I can rationalize why we don't have to stop: this is teamwork. Our new dynamic is an inarguable improvement from what we've been doing the last five years. If I can live in this space without slipping further into one that might hurt me, this week will be a success.

It's just that I've only ever fully fallen into things with him: friendship, love, turning him into a stranger. I have to be careful to keep myself right here—in his arms, fine, but only for this moment.

When the song is over, I nearly fling myself out of Eli's hold.

My hip catches on his still-curled fingers, and he looks at me, dazed.

"Danny," I say, unable to tear my gaze away from Eli's for one second, then another. Finally, his expression clears, and he nods, a silent *the floor is yours.*

I turn to Danny, hands clasped in front of me. "We'd like to make you a deal."

I'm curled up in bed, my pillow person at my back, mindlessly scrolling on my phone.

I can't sleep. I got close earlier when Eli was in the pool and the sound of his measured strokes lulled me into a sort of trance.

But it's silent now, well after midnight, and my brain is on an acid trip of thought patterns. Everything is either Eli-shaped—familiar and heated and somehow also completely different—or disaster-shaped—a list of the things that refuse to get checked off.

Danny Diamond wasn't too keen on our idea.

"Now, Georgia, I like you, but I've been doing this for nearly thirty years. I know what works and what doesn't." His mouth pulled into a disappointed line. "You can take me or leave me, and by the sounds of this request, you're going to have to leave me."

It was my idea, and my fault he rejected us. It doesn't matter that we wouldn't have been able to hire him otherwise. All I can see is another thing that's gone wrong.

I toggle back to my text messages with Jamie. She's been checking in every day and I've been responding, but tonight she wrote, Okay, your text messages are a) too bubbly and b) way too infrequent. Is everything good up there??

My response was a paragraph just to prove her wrong, but the message boiled down to the same as all the others. I can't tell her that the curse is alive and well: Everything is good. We're making progress! Miss you, can't wait to see you Friday. Xo

I didn't hear from her after that, so I assume the text did its job.

I close my eyes, manifesting a lobotomy, a win. Some sign that everything is going to be okay, that things will at some point turn the corner from mindfuck to the way I need my life to be: compartmentalized and controlled.

What feels like seconds later, I wake with a start.

Was that—?

Yes, a knock at my window. The ceiling swirls above me while I figure out what year I'm in, if I'm sixteen-year-old Georgia and I'm going to sit up and find sixteen-year-old Eli at my window, beckoning me outside like he used to.

I sit up, my eyes flying to the window. There *is* someone there, covered in white. A ghost.

My mouth opens to scream.

"*Georgia*," the ghost says, exasperated.

But it's not a ghost. It's twenty-eight-year-old Eli, asking me to let him in.

Chapter Sixteen

Eli steps back as I throw open the front door, white dust swirling around his shoulders.

"Why do you look like a powdered donut?" I exclaim.

"The ceiling fell," he coughs out.

Oh god, of course it did. "I'm going to need way more details than that."

"Can you hose me off first?" he asks, running a hand through his white-streaked hair.

"Oh." I pause, making a quick sweep of his body. He's not wearing a shirt, but I'm becoming immune to that. Or at least comfortable with how not immune I am to that. "Sure."

He starts to turn, but I stop him, placing a hand on his chest. His skin is hot beneath my palm, heart flying.

"Are you okay?"

The moon isn't providing much light tonight, barely touching her fingers onto the world around us, but even in the darkness I can see how blown Eli's pupils are. His mouth is a tense, flat line.

"Yeah," he says, voice pitched low. I don't believe him. He raises his hand and for a second it hovers over mine, still pressed to his skin, before he drops it. "I was awake. I dodged most of it."

I caught the time as I was coming to the door—it's half past one. I get out a wobbly "Thank goodness" and I mean it; it's not like I want him squished. But why was he up?

"Are *you* okay?" he volleys back, dipping his chin to keep my gaze. He's not asking outright, probably knowing I won't admit to it anyway, even though all the signs of my disappointment are glaring: I had him drive home, holed up in my cottage after telling him I was fine but tired, not hungry even though my stomach rumbled the entire ride back.

"Yeah." I can tell he doesn't believe me either. My mind flashes back to his soft knock earlier, the stack of to-go boxes and sweating iced tea sitting on the porch when I opened the door a few minutes later. "Thanks for dropping off that food."

"Your stomach sounded like a haunted house," he replies, and when I roll my eyes, his mouth hooks into a tiny smile. It hooks me, too, sways my body closer to his, even when his mouth straightens, parts slightly.

I can't pull away, so you're the one who has to.

There's a twitch against my fingers. A muscle in Eli's chest. I still have my hand on him.

"Sorry," I gasp, dropping it like his skin is on fire. Which it is, kind of. "Let's go take care of this."

I uncoil the hose hooked up to the side of my cottage, the one we used to wash the dirt off our legs after the near-nightly walks he'd beckon me out for in the vineyard blocks. It wasn't just vines growing out there—it was our awareness of each other, the knowledge that our dynamic was shifting, as undeniable then as it is now.

Suddenly I don't know if I'm in the past or the present. The darkness, my memories, everything that's happened between

Eli and I the past few days—they soften the divide of time, making it liquid like the pool shimmering around the corner.

"It's going to be cold," I warn.

"I remember," he says, eyes on me. The most dangerous phrase when it comes to us.

I turn the hose on him. It's like ice. An incidental spray falls onto my bare feet, and I flinch when he does.

He tells me what happened while I clean him off: that he noticed a crack in the ceiling in his bedroom almost immediately. That tonight the ceiling looked bowed, but he didn't trust his eyes because it'd been a long day. He was planning to show it to Adam's uncle Cal in the morning, but then it crumbled.

I stare at my handprint on his chest while he talks. I trace the skin it exposes with my eyes, the streaks at the bottom of my palm where I couldn't quite pull away. His heart is under there.

The mark looks indelible, like a tattoo. It's the last thing I wash away. I just want to be there for a second longer, but once we lapse into silence and the rest of the dust has been washed away, I don't have a choice. It'll expose what I want: his body, exactly like this. My touch, closer to the heart he's tucked away for the last five years.

I aim the stream at his left pec. Eli dips his chin, watching the cloudy mixture run down his stomach, into the waistband of his shorts.

My handprint is gone in seconds. I drop the hose at my feet, a surge running into my veins when he looks up at me through his lashes, running a hand over his chest.

We're here. It's now. It's a reminder. A warning, too.

"I think we're good." My heart takes off in anticipation of my next words, knowing he has nowhere else to go. "Come on in."

It's been an hour and a half since I said good night to Eli. He insisted on setting up a makeshift bed on the loveseat, a piece of furniture that fits a medium-sized child lying in the fetal position, but what was the alternative? Have him share the bed I'm currently tossing and turning in? It's huge, big enough that we could both sleep in it without ever touching. God knows we've slept in a bed together hundreds of times before.

It's why I let him take the loveseat instead—because we've slept in a bed together hundreds of times before. It wouldn't have meant the same thing tonight, but the times that it did mean something would've taken up residence as a third body between us.

I also let him take the loveseat because some not inconsequential part of me wanted him here, and I don't have a valid reason for wanting that. Not one that will keep me in the halfway space I need to be in, anyway.

So instead, I have my pillow person, and Eli's actual presence in the living room is a phantom presence right next to me.

I squeeze my eyes shut, trying to count sheep. But I can only picture my handprint on Eli's chest, so I count the fingers spread out there instead. *One, two, three, four, fi—*

There's a sound on the other side of my closed door. I sit up, holding my breath, waiting.

A floorboard creaks, and time bends again. I'm back in our Manhattan apartment, waking up at three a.m. in an empty bed, listening to the sounds of the city that sleeps just as often as Eli— rarely. Even before I get out of bed and pad to the door, turn the knob, and inch it open, I know what I'll find: Eli pacing the room, his face illuminated by his phone screen.

Except this time there's no phone. It's probably buried in his cottage.

Maybe that's why he's on the loveseat, head cradled in his hands, his mouth moving almost silently.

He's counting, too.

When this first started happening, I'd go to him, wrap my arms around him from behind and press my hand over his heart to make sure it slowed. I'd toss his phone out of reach. But soon enough, going out there only made things worse. I knew why he was spiraling, knew the only thing that would eventually calm him down was to pick the phone back up. My awareness of it and the way I not-so-secretly hated it only made him more anxious, which he tried to hide. In return, being useless *and* exacerbating the problem made me retreat. I'd lay in bed, thinking, *you were too much*, staring at the ceiling until he slipped in next to me, a million miles away.

Now, I take a step back, unsure.

The floorboard creaks under my heel. Eli's head whips around, his wild eyes finding me. He inhales sharply, straightening.

"I'm sorry," we gasp out at the same time.

I hesitate. "Are you okay?"

It's the same question I asked earlier, and now I see that his expression is a more potent version of what it was before. He was panicking when the ceiling fell. It must've felt like the entire world was caving in on him.

There's no reasonable way he can say he's okay, but I expect him to anyway.

Instead, he says, "Actually, I'm having a panic attack."

My chest tightens. "Okay. Should I go?"

"No!" His voice comes out high and curt. He shakes his head

with a long exhale. "Don't go, I just— my therapist gave me a few ways to get calm, but they work best when I'm lying down."

Well. It's certainly a valid reason to have him in my bed.

"Come in here."

That he doesn't hesitate underscores how panicked he must be; he was clinging hard to that loveseat earlier. I step back as he brushes past me, curling my fingers around the hem of my T-shirt so I don't reach for him.

He sinks onto the left side of the bed on instinct, his shoulder brushing against my pillow person. My heart jumps. I used to text pictures of them on nights we weren't together at Cal Poly, or, in the earlier New York days, when he was stuck at work late. I'd always send one word along with it: lonely. Eli's text back would always be, Good thing you have Sammy to keep my spot warm 'til I'm back. The name would change every time: Tom, Milo, Diego. Each of the Golden Girls.

He's the only one who could look at it and know what it means. I'd rip it up if he wasn't practically draped all over it. Instead, I circle to my side of the bed, clicking on the lamp before sitting down.

At first, I just watch as he closes his eyes, resting his hands on his stomach. His pulse beats hard and fast under the fine coil of his chain, his cheeks and ears flushed. He takes one measured breath, then another.

"What's one of the ways you calm yourself down?" I ask after his tenth breath, eyes glued to his throbbing pulse.

Eli's eyes flutter open, landing on me. "There's this grounding technique called five-four-three-two-one. Amari, my therapist, taught me in one of our first sessions. You focus on five things you can see, four things you can touch, three things you can hear, two things you can smell, and one thing you can taste."

"And that works for you?"

He nods, releasing a shaky breath.

I lower my voice. "Okay, what do you see?"

Eli's eyes bounce around the room wildly. "A painting of Blue Yonder. A perfume bottle. A white dresser. Your overpacked suitcase exploded all over the floor." He meets my gaze when I laugh quietly. His mouth twitches, even as his pulse continues to beat heavily in his throat. "You."

For a second, my heartbeat matches his. "Okay. Four things you can touch."

He closes his eyes. "The sheets. This pillow under my head. The breeze coming in from the window. Myself."

"That's a little personal, Mora," I tease, trying not to imagine that. Or remember it. I know exactly what it looks like.

Focus, Georgia. His pulse is slowing already.

He squints an eye open. "My hand on my stomach, I mean. My hand is resting on my stomach, and I can feel that."

"Specificity is your friend."

"I'll work on my entendres," he mutters, closing his eyes again. "I'm not used to an audience."

It hits me in such a tender spot that he's letting me see him like this when no one else has, not even past me. It feels more intimate than anything we've ever done.

I clear my throat. "What's next?"

"Three things you can hear."

"And?"

He sighs, his shoulders sinking further into the bed, hips settling, knees falling slightly open. His unraveling is mine, too. "Crickets outside. An owl somewhere." He pauses. Swallows. Quietly, he says, "Your voice."

"Two things you can smell?" I whisper.

"You're going to start noticing a trend." A slow smile melts across his mouth. "But you're right there, so I smell you. That coconut lotion. Whatever's left of your perfume."

There's recognition in his voice; it's the one I've always worn. "And one thing you can taste."

For this I get a flash of teeth. "Iced tea. I stole a sip when I dropped yours off earlier."

"Ex*cuse* you."

He laughs, shoulders shaking. "Delivery fee."

The tension that's left his body has suffused into mine. I'm turned inside out by his callouts, the awareness he had of me as he was pulling himself out of his spiral.

"Did that help?" I ask, rubbing a hand across my racing heart. I'd try to play the game myself, but right now every answer would be Eli, and none of them should be.

His eyes open under heavy lids, drifting to me. "It did. Thank you."

I hesitate. "Do you want to talk about it?"

This time, it's Eli who hesitates. Some of the anxiety pulls back into his eyes and I mentally kick myself.

"Sorry, forget I said that."

The silence pulls between us. The longer I look at him, the further I feel myself slipping from that halfway space. He's in my bed. We've had a solid twenty-four hours of interaction that feels like nothing we've done in the past five years, but an echo of everything before that. I just helped him walk through a grounding technique he learned in *therapy*. He's the same and totally different. The fifteen-year-old boy I liked and the twenty-year-old man I loved, and the twenty-eight-year-old I have to keep right here, because at one point he was the twenty-three-year-old man who broke my heart.

I'm so busy staring at him, seeing all the iterations of him like I'm hurtling through time and space, that I miss his answer.

"Georgia," he says.

I snap into focus. "What?"

"Did you hear me?"

"No, I— no."

He lets out a breath. "I said, I quit my job."

Chapter Seventeen

It's like Eli's pushed me off a cliff and my brain got stuck behind. My body floods with adrenaline, and then seconds later it actually sinks in.

Every moment since he's stepped off the plane plays like a movie in hyper speed: his phone allergy, his determination to be present for Adam, how he insisted on coming to Blue Yonder and his assurance that work wouldn't get in the way. Everything about him broke open because his job was the thing that kept him tightly bound.

"You quit your job," I repeat.

"I did." He exhales sharply, like it's hitting him anew. "Seven weeks ago, actually."

My jaw drops. "*Seven* we— what? Why?"

He sits up, rubbing a hand across his jaw. "That's a loaded question."

There's a question in *his* voice, and I get the message loud and clear: *do you want to hear the answer?*

The truth is yes, I'm desperate to, and also no, because what difference does it make? Whatever reason he did it is for him, not me.

The flash of grief I feel is real, though. The part of me that I

sealed off when I left New York feels the pain acutely, wishes that
we were having this conversation sitting in the bed we bought, in
the apartment we rented. What would we be doing right now instead of this if we hadn't barricaded ourselves from each other?

It's a useless thought, though.

"Well. Wow. Are you starting a new job when you get back
to New York, then? One with a hopefully less Luce-like managing
director?"

At my obvious conversational swerve, disappointment settles into the crease between his brows. "No."

"No what?"

"No to all of those things."

"The new job or New York or Lucifer?"

"Correct," he says, his mouth twitching.

I narrow my eyes, turning his non-answer over, until I realize
he's answered everything: no to a new job. No to a boss, Lucifer-
adjacent or not.

And no to New York.

My heart flips over. "You're not going back to New York."

"I'm not going back to New York," he confirms.

"You're coming ho—" I stop myself from saying *home*. San
Francisco doesn't belong to us; it won't belong to *me* soon enough.
"Here?"

He nods, eyes fixed on me. "Do you have any thoughts about
that?"

There are just two: *thank god we're in a better place now* and
STAY in that place however you can. Even if I go to Seattle, Eli will
be closer, more present by default. Having him nearly three thousand miles away as a ghost was safe; this is not.

"Should I?"

His response is quiet, a small confession. "I'd like you to."

I side-stepped the heavy turn before, but with those four words, Eli brings us right back. I'm not prepared to talk at length about what this is doing to me. I have no interest in unpacking messy baggage with Eli right now; it'd probably make things worse and that's the last thing we need. We're supposed to be cleaning *up* messes, keeping things easy.

I have to give him something, though—he'll keep prodding otherwise.

I pick at a thread on the comforter, twist it around my fingers. Pull until it snaps. "I think, as disastrous as things have been, you and I have reached . . . an understanding." When I meet his eyes, he raises an acknowledging eyebrow. "And anyway, I would never begrudge you wanting to be closer to your family and friends."

"Our friends," he corrects.

"Right." It's a word of belonging. It hurts and sings through my blood. It fits and feels too small, all at the same time. "So, you'll be back in the city as of Sunday?"

He leans back on his hands. "When I say I'm coming back here, I mean to California. I'm flying down to LA on Sunday. I've been working with a recruiter for the past few weeks, and she got me hooked up with a really strong lead for a strategy director role at a media company down there. I've had two phone interviews with that place, and have two other interviews set up in the coming weeks just in case."

"A strategy director role?" I echo, confused. "You're leaving banking?"

"Yes," he says, and there's so much finality in that word that my spine straightens.

Years ago, when we were still together, he talked about eventually transitioning over to the client side. It's one of the reasons he was eager to work in the TMT sector—he'd have more flexibility to get us back to the West Coast, where you can fling a dart with your eyes closed and hit a tech or media position.

But that was his plan after he'd made VP. *Long* after.

". . . sent me over a few options in tech up in the Bay Area," he's saying, "but with all the layoffs, I'm not eager to go in that direction. The LA position seems more stable, and I really need to find something soon."

I look over just as a spark of panic returns to Eli's expression. In a strange way, it makes me feel safe to see it, to know he's so diligently looking for a replacement. To know that even if he's closer, he'll still be wrapped up in his career to some extent.

"I'd been thinking about quitting," he continues. "A lot, actually. I just didn't expect to do it when I did. It was sort of . . . impulsive."

"That's not a word I'd *ever* use to describe you with your career," I say without thinking, and in my voice I hear the weight of our history, the pain of it.

His gaze lands on me; he hears it, too. It feels like he looks for hours, days. Forever.

We have to get out of this. "I just mean—"

"It was a long time coming regardless," he interrupts, his words careful, his attention intent. "Missing Adam's bachelor party wasn't the only thing that brought me to my decision, not by a mile, but it was the catalyst. In the car on Friday, you said it wasn't my fault that I missed it, but storm or not, it *was*. I should've told them no, but my anxiety wouldn't let me and my priorities were . . ." His eyes glitter in the low light. He looks furious and devastated, but also determined, that same emotion he stepped off the plane with. "That job came first at a time when it shouldn't have, and I paid the price for it."

A fissure cracks my heart before I can stop it. He's not talking about us, but in another life, that sentiment would fit perfectly. A puzzle piece we've been missing for years.

If we were talking about us.

God, now we *really* have to get out of this. "Does Adam know?"

Something flashes in his eyes—that disappointment again, maybe. "You're the only person I've told, other than my family. I'll tell him once they're back from the honeymoon."

I nod, then say softly, "Wow. You really blew up your life."

Our gazes catch and hold. I feel so many things—confusion wondering why now and not five years ago, sadness knowing the answer would likely devastate me, fear and pride and such an intense, unwelcome wanting—and I hope he doesn't see any of that. I hope he sees a Georgia who's surprised but unruffled by this news. Who's unruffled by him in her bed at three in the morning on a Tuesday, in the place where we started to tip into love years ago.

After an unbearable beat, he looks down, his ears turning pink. "Belatedly. But yeah, I did."

"Hey, stop worrying about the bachelor party." I nudge his ankle and he points a private, mirthless smile at the bed. "Seriously, Eli, you're here for the most important part. You're literally saving their wedding."

He looks up. "So are you."

I hum noncommittally, ignoring the narrow-eyed stare he gives me. I can see him ready to circle back to his earlier *are you okay?* But now that the adrenaline has drained from my body, I'm about to fall over.

"I should go," Eli says quietly, sensing the shift. "Thank you for . . . well, Jesus. Everything. Sorry I fell apart on you."

"Don't be sorry."

I nearly blurt out what it meant to see him like that, to have him trust me. Eli Mora doesn't let himself come undone; for a secretly messy person like me, it was like seeing my reflection. It's not something I'd ever run away from. It's something I crave.

Maybe that's why I say, "You don't have to go."

Eli's already swung his legs over the side of the bed, but he freezes. "What?"

"That loveseat is for toddlers. Just stay here tonight."

He gazes at me, and in those seconds, I think five times about snatching my words back. But then he says, voice pitched low and rough, "I can't."

"Why?" A stupid question. I can think of a million reasons we shouldn't, and yet the single reason we should wipes all of that away: this bed isn't either of ours. Sharing it tonight doesn't have to count.

"I—" He grimaces, then lets out a helpless, pained sound.

"What if you have another panic attack?" I want to smack myself for pushing. "I don't wa— you shouldn't have to be alone."

I don't want you to be alone. He hears the words I didn't even say, and some of his hesitation dissolves.

"It's fine," I say, swallowing hard. "This bed is more than big enough for both of us."

"But is it big enough for the three of us?"

"What?"

He glances down between us. "Nick Miller here."

Dammit. I yank one of the pillows up, whipping it at him. He catches it with a laugh.

"No judgments for my pillow person, please. Are you staying or going?"

Eli looks at the bed, at the pillows, at me. A word floats between us, a text sent through space and memory: lonely.

Maybe we both are, and have been.

"Okay," he says, "I'll stay."

Outside, time was liquid, but it solidifies here. It's now and he's sliding back into the bed. It carries no memories. Nothing can pull us under.

Still, I hold my breath as I click off the lamp, plunging us into a darkness that immediately pulls us closer, in tension if not in body. The moon peeks in through the window, slicing across Eli's face as he turns toward me when I lie down.

"Night," he murmurs.

"Good night," I whisper back before turning away from him.

I send a silent threat to Nick Miller to keep us on our sides, and then, exhausted, I fall into a deep, black sleep.

Awareness comes in pieces. At first it's warmth, increasing to a heat that works its way under my skin so deliciously I arch toward it.

And then it's a naked back under my skimming palms, a solid thigh pressed between mine, the brief chill of metal and then warm skin as my mouth traverses the column of a throat. I sigh against the rumble that vibrates my skin.

It's the kind of vivid, early morning memory-dream that used to torture me, but now I sink into it, remember the hands that would—

"*Yes*," I sigh as a broad palm cups my ass, cinching me tight to the body I'm wrapped around. Fingers graze the waistband of my sleep shorts, moving under my shirt to trace the column of my spine until they curl around my ribs, digging into the underside of my breast. There's a neediness to the touch that makes my stomach spiral.

I squeeze my eyes shut, blocking out the weak sunshine trying to get in, any reality that will break this apart. I want to live in this liminal space where there's a heart beating hard against mine, someone who reaches for me first. It's why I've always loved early-morning sex. There's an instinct to it that no other time allows, just bodies and hearts doing what they want more than anything else.

I crave a mouth against my throat the second before it's there—teeth scraping my skin, almost biting, a burn that dissolves into throbbing pressure. A deep groan echoes mine. Someone desperate for me.

No, not someone. Eli.

His sleep-slurred, "Fuck, Georgia," is pressed against my cheek as I'm gently pushed onto my back.

My eyes pop open.

It's not a memory or a dream. It's now, time as twisted around us as the sheets. Eli's hovering over me, his chain dangling in the bare space between us. His pupils are wide, mouth parted and swollen from sleep. I want them swollen from me.

It's a fully coherent thought and a terrible idea, and yet—

My hands move up his sides with a mind of their own. He shivers, his eyes falling shut, and my body gets heavy again, not with sleep but something hazy and warm like it. I search for telltale signs that Eli's in one of his dream states.

"Where are you?" I whisper.

His Adam's apple bobs in his throat. Huskily, he says, "With you."

"Are you awake?"

His eyes are wild and hot, not because he isn't here. Because he *is*. "Do you want me to be?"

It's an offer, an escape from liability, and I'm not strong enough to deny it. This is real, but close enough to what we've done before that we could slot it into another memory once it's done. It wouldn't count against my list of reasons not to get wrapped up in him.

And god, I miss it so much. I miss *him* so much.

"Can you be awake in three minutes instead?"

His expression slackens in relief, and he lets some of his weight settle onto me, slotting in right where I need him. "You're in charge of the timer."

"Why?" I gasp, arching my hips against his.

"Because I won't be able to stop," he murmurs. "And we have to. Right?"

"Yes," I start to say, but he dissolves the word when his mouth slants over mine.

There's no easing into it. Eli knows exactly what I like—a teasing tongue sliding against mine at first, an overwhelmed groan as he takes it deeper and then pulls back to bite at my lower lip. The reality of kissing him again is a shock I couldn't have prepared myself for, like finding something I thought I'd lost forever sitting on my top shelf. Within reach the whole time, back in my hands again.

I know I have to put it away, and I will. I will. In three minutes.

His hand slides under my shirt, resting at the base of my ribs, and I arch, wanting him to touch me like he used to.

"You can," I say against his jaw.

He does. Puts me into the palm of his hand, pinches my nipple between his thumb and forefinger. The teasing is done.

"Fuck, you feel so good," he breathes. "I didn't think—"

He groans, a frustrated sound that matches his fractured thoughts. I dig my fingers into his back, urging him closer.

His breath stutters, fanning over my mouth as he pulls back to take me in, something disbelieving in his eyes just before he kisses me again. It's deep and slow, an assurance that he won't be rushed despite our ticking clock. *Time is nothing*, he tells me. It's a demand for me to follow, and I do, because we're here, it's now. It's a memory, a dream, something real.

We hold on wherever we can—me gripping the hair at the nape of his neck, him pulling my thigh over his hip to make our connection tighter.

"I could make you come in three minutes," he murmurs, pulsing against me in tiny, unbearable waves. He's so hard it's close to pain, but I like it.

"One," I gasp out.

His smile curls against my mouth, because he could do that, too, and I lick at his bottom lip, take it between my teeth. It snaps him out of his amusement—or maybe it's the reminder that we're running out of time. He tangles a hand in my hair, grips it while he kisses me, holding me right there for him, for his warm, pleading mouth and his soft, wild sounds.

I could make any sound in return, say anything, beg him and be good for him and he'd take it all. He'd ask for more. It'd break him open, and god, I want it. Eli is so contained, can't bear to relinquish that tight fist of control. He doesn't know how beautiful he is when he falls apart, when his hair is wild and his neck is flushed, when there are bite marks on his chest and he's telling me everything he wants, how much he needs me.

I know we're out of time, but he's moving against me like it's fucking, even though it can't be. He's brushing his thumb over the high plane of my cheek like it's tender and timeless, even though it can't be that either.

"I dreamed about this," he whispers as he starts kissing down my neck. "Touching you like this. Tasting you."

I lace my fingers through his hair, staring up at the ever-lightening ceiling before I close my eyes to shut it out. "Last night?"

He only hums into my skin, sucking at my throat. He pulls back to appraise the mark he leaves, then looks at me with possessive, hungry eyes.

"Georgia," he breathes. "I—"

A burst of laughter echoes outside. Cole and someone else. A few other someones, maybe. They're not close enough to know what Eli and I are doing, but close enough to burst through that liminal space and let reality slide in.

They're getting ready for another day of bringing Adam and Grace's wedding to life. That's why we're here, too, not to roll around in bed.

With a frustrated groan, I slither out from underneath the beautiful weight of Eli's body. My heart is pushing at my ribs, desperate to get back to him, but logic is finally kicking in.

"Time's up," I croak out.

Eli's sprawled out on the bed, hard and flushed, his gaze raking over me from head to toe. I can't imagine what I look like right now—a total mess. He's looking at me as if he likes me messy. As if he wants it.

No. I don't have to say it out loud to make that clear for both of us.

He levers into a seated position and wipes a hand over his mouth. "Yeah, I know."

Panic rushes through me, wondering if we've ruined our tenuous truce, if slipping back into the past for even three minutes is going to send us back to the way we were days ago. Bizarrely, that option is now the worst-case scenario.

God, we shouldn't have done this.

Eli opens his mouth, and my heart drops to my feet.

"What the hell happened to the cottage?" I hear.

He closes his eyes. "I'm . . . going to go take care of that."

"Okay."

"Okay." He stands up and I look away as he adjusts himself, my entire body flushing. "I'll see you for the bakery appointment, yeah?"

"Yeah. Of course," I say, but he's already halfway out the door.

Chapter Eighteen

"This is our last chance."

My eyes roam over Icing on the Cake, hands on my hips. We're loitering just outside the faded brick building on a quiet, tree-lined street near the main drag of downtown Napa. The noontime sun is perched high above us, bleaching the sky around it.

This place isn't as fancy as Sucre, but the cheerful yellow door, matching awning, and sweet display of desserts in the window have raised my hopes despite attempts to claw them back down to earth. The disasters that have befallen us this week put our odds somewhere in the gutter, but I can't give up with Adam and Grace's eternal happiness on the line.

Eli's standing a few feet away with his hands in his pockets, wearing an indulgent look.

"What's that face?"

His expression turns innocent. "It's not a face."

"It's a face. You're making a face."

"It was just a good line, that's all," he says. "Extremely dramatic, but solid."

"I'm serious," I groan, removing the clip holding my hair in a messy updo. "We're going to have to do whatever it takes to get this cake."

Eli watches avidly as I throw the clip into my bag and rake my fingers through my hair. "I'm drawing the line at sexual favors, but I'm down for almost anything else."

I give him a look, and he flashes a little smile in return. "We're out of options, Eli. If you need to get on your knees, so be it."

His smile turns into a full grin. "I love Adam and would do anything for him, but I won't do that."

"Okay, Meat Loaf," I mutter.

"That's not to say I'm opposed to the position under other circumstances," he continues. "Just not for Adam."

I don't dare look at Eli, but my mind immediately flashes with memories: him pressing me against our front door, kneeling in the foyer as he pushed up the hem of my dress, laying open-mouthed kisses up my thighs while I wound my fingers into his hair; the way he'd drag me to the end of the bed by my ankle, laughing, so that my legs dangled over the edge and he could insinuate himself between them to pepper sweet kisses on my stomach.

The way he would've knelt for me this morning if I asked him to. If I'd let that timer spin out of control, if Cole and Cal hadn't interrupted us and then pulled Eli away to survey the damaged cottage.

We spent the morning apart after that, and I was so busy with Aunt Julia that I didn't see him until it was time to go. The distance felt necessary, a bucket of cold water over my head and a chance for me to remember the list of reasons I can't put my hands on him again:

1. Because we did this before and broke it

2. Because after five years of barely talking, we're finally in a better place and I need to protect that

3. Relatedly, because of Adam and our inextricably tied friendship

4. Because, yes, Eli quit his job, but he's already got his sights on something new, and old habits die hard

5. Because even if something were to happen, I'm likely leaving for Seattle

6. Most importantly, because I can't afford to be distracted this week

And I am distracted, torturously. My body's been edgy since he left my bed, a feeling that only got worse during the car ride over here, which was filled with surface-level conversation—nothing about what we did this morning or Eli's confession last night. Our back and forth still managed to feel like the weight of his body on mine, and now I'm stuck with the sexual version of a held-in sneeze. I desperately need relief.

But that relief would come in the form of an Eli-gifted orgasm, and I can't. No matter how much I want it.

And god, I do.

I bite back a groan at my circular thoughts, nodding toward the bakery. "We should go in."

"We're twelve minutes early," Eli says, dodging a stroller-pushing dad as he follows me to the door.

"I'm not taking any chances."

He stops me, his gaze assessing, and then amused. "Margot traumatized you."

"You've got some burn marks from the dragon, too, buddy," I say, flicking a finger at him.

"Buddy, huh?" he murmurs, fighting a smile. "What happened to *shithead*?"

"You've graduated since you've been such a good boy," I say dryly.

"I thought *my* shithead was an endearment."

"Derogatory, I'm sorry to tell you."

The smile wins as he reaches past me for the door handle, putting our bodies in torturous proximity. "I knew it."

I tip my chin back, adjusting to the way he looms over me. If I pressed up on my tiptoes, I'd be tasting him right now. "Don't be smug about it."

"Not smug." His mouth softens into a tender little curve. "I just like that I knew."

The moment quiets and stretches out, and I hold my breath, not wanting to break this spell. Knowing we have to for so many reasons.

His gaze skims my face before landing with intention on my mouth. "I . . ."

When he doesn't continue, I whisper, "What?"

His eyes find mine again and he lets out a breath that touches my lips the way I wish his mouth would. The way I know it can't.

"This isn't our last chance," he says, and for a second I think he's talking about us, until I remember: we're at the bakery. For the cake. Because Adam and Grace need a *cake* for their *wedding*. "But I recognize that it's our best one, so if this place is up to your standards we'll make it work. Even if I have to get on my knees."

"I thought you crossed that option off the list."

The corners of his eyes crinkle. I have to curl my hands into fists to stop from touching those time-worn lines. "I will if it comes down to it, for you."

He's teasing, of course, but it still makes my heart drop into my stomach. "Don't tell Adam that. You know he gets sensitive about being our number one."

Adam has always claimed the number one best friend spot in both my and Eli's brackets; to this day he jokingly refuses to acknowledge a lower spot. I've held on to that small token of belonging, but I can't help wondering where we all honestly sit now. Grace is his Person, and he's introduced other friends into his life, too. Soon they're going to have an infant to focus on. The more phases he leapfrogs ahead of us into, the further away the number one days feel.

"If Adam finds out about this hypothetical and bizarre sexual-favor scenario, you can support my lie and tell him it was for him," Eli says, interrupting my thoughts.

I exhale as he finally opens the door, nudging me inside. "Deal. Let's hope we won't have to pull that lever, though."

"Afternoon!"

We turn as a tall Asian woman with close-cropped salt-and-pepper hair steps out from behind the L-shaped counter. The space doesn't gleam like Margot's shop, but it's much warmer. The front room is small and crowded with a few other customers roaming around, the floor a slightly faded black-and-white checkerboard. One wall is full of floating shelves holding trailing Pothos plants and stacks of love-worn baking cookbooks.

"Are you my two o'clock?" the woman asks as she reaches us.

"We are." I take her offered hand, stepping aside while Eli does the same. "I'm Georgia and this is Eli."

"Hey, you two, I'm Tai." She runs her palms down the white smock tied around her waist, splitting her gaze between the two of us. "Usually I like to meet with the couple for—"

She keeps talking, but my brain blanks out. All I can think of is Margot kicking us out of her bakery because we were on time instead of early and because she hated our vibes. Grace and Baby Song-Kim not having a cake to enjoy on Saturday. My spot in that bracket.

"That's us," I blurt out. "We're the couple."

Eli turns to me, eyes wide, and I hold out my hand. He stares at it, then at me. I wiggle my fingers. *This is your kneeling moment, dude.*

After a beat, he takes my hand. It's tentative at first, like we haven't done this a million times. But when his fingers wind through mine, it's with a confident pressure. Tendrils of attraction and an old, familiar comfort wind through my blood. Our eyes meet. It's that lock-click, even under false pretenses.

"That's us," he echoes, eyes on me.

I smile, adrenaline pouring through me as I turn to Tai. "Thank you for taking us on such short notice."

"That's perfect, then," Tai says. "Let's get started."

Eli gives me a look I can't decipher, but follows me without a word.

"I like getting to know my couples as we're doing the tasting, but tell me if I get too nosy," Tai says as she sets two square white plates in front of Eli and me. There are six slices on each, delectable little triangles of flour and sugar my roiling stomach can't handle right now.

"Sounds good," Eli says beside me. His knee bobs underneath the wood table, his bare skin brushing up against mine over and over.

I wish we hadn't both worn shorts. I wish I could read any thought or emotion on his face to determine if he wants to strangle me for this latest pickle I've gotten us into, but it's blank. He held my hand until we sat down, then placed it on my leg, his palm grazing my thigh as he let go. Now his hands are clasped between his legs, his fingers tangling and untangling.

Tai describes each of the flavors to us as she takes a seat in the chair across the table. "Why don't you try the vanilla first?"

"I've got this one, just to check it off our list," Eli says, giving me a pointed look. "Georgia has a vanilla allergy."

My response is immediate, exasperated, and years old. "It's not an allergy, I just sometimes can't tolerate it."

"Every time she eats it," he says.

"Not *every* time."

"It's every time," Eli whispers to Tai conspiratorially. She raises a questioning eyebrow at me.

"I— okay, that's true, but it's an *intolerance*." I nudge Eli's knee. "Why don't you and your mouth do something more productive than spreading slander?"

His amusement turns heated. "Sure, I'm taking requests."

"Noted for later," I play along, and god, I wish. His eyes spark, like a true fiancé's would. "But for now I mean the cake."

"This is fun," Tai says, splitting a smile between us.

Eli grins over at her. "I agree."

Unfortunately, I do, too.

"So, how'd you two meet?" Tai asks.

My brain goes offline as I unfold a napkin in my lap. For a second, I forgot we're supposed to be faking. "Uh . . ."

"At a Halloween party," Eli steps in, pressing his fork into the slice. I watch as he takes a bite, licking his lips with a soft, satisfied hum that sounds like the noise I licked off his tongue this morning. It buzzes through my body like a sugar high. "Georgia was singing karaoke and tripped over the tip of her pepperoni pizza costume as I was passing by. Knocked me flat on my ass." He glances at me. "Literally and figuratively."

I blink at him, my mouth parting. In return, his mouth curls around his fork as he takes another bite.

Ohh-kay. He's not going to strangle me, but he is going to play with me as payback. Amusement and something smokier curl through me.

"Thankfully you were wearing that blow-up T-Rex costume, so it broke our fall," I say.

He lifts an eyebrow, cutting into the next slice, which is passion fruit. "Yeah, until your crust punctured one of my arms."

I lift an unapologetic shoulder. "Hazard of the costume, I'm afraid."

Tai laughs. "What song were you singing?"

"It was—"

"Celine Dion," Eli says. "'It's All Coming Back to Me Now.' I thought someone was playing a clip of a dying cat on the speaker system until I turned the corner and saw her standing on the coffee table."

"I don't stand on tables!" I cut in with a defensive laugh.

The gold in his eyes is lit up like stars. "Anymore. But you did as a pepperoni pizza."

I take a bite of cake. "Also, my singing isn't that bad."

This is a patent lie, and the dying-cat comparison is Eli being generous. He used to sneak into the bathroom when I was performing shower concerts; I'd find him leaning against the counter when I pulled back the curtain, wearing a tender grin.

"Buddy, come on," he laughs quietly and the curve of it makes it sound like he's calling me Peach. There's so much affection in it. If I didn't have five years' worth of evidence that he's good at playing roles, I'd sink so deep into this that I'd never come out.

This isn't our old role-playing, though. It's softer, like we're doing this in support of one another, not in defense of ourselves. There's a heat, too, though it's surely just left over from our slip-up this morning.

"The passion fruit is good," I say, nodding at his nearly gone slice.

"Delicious," he agrees, eyes on me.

"It's funny," Tai muses, "I've been doing this for twenty-three years and I've discovered it's usually the imperfections that make people fall in love. Bad singers, would-be chefs who burn every meal. My partner snores like a freight train, but when they travel for work, I can't sleep. Go figure, right?" She gestures between us. "Now back to you two. Are we talking love at first sight?"

"No," I say in unison with Eli's, "Yes."

I gape at him, shocked he's weaving such an integral part of our story into this moment. He must be saying it because it's familiar, which makes it more believable.

Tai clocks my reaction and leans in. "Very juicy. Try the peach bourbon next and then tell me all about that."

The cake might as well be cardboard in my mouth. Every sense is locked on Eli, waiting for his answer.

"She had fake pepperonis all over her face, and she was still the most beautiful person in the room. She rearranged everything in my body when she ran into me. Again, literally and figuratively." His voice is quiet, eyes on Tai, but I can feel his awareness of me like a tether between us. One corner of his mouth picks up as he takes a bite of cake. "Mmm. This one's my favorite."

Tai beams. "I'm so glad you love it. I have a bias toward peaches."

"Me, too," Eli says with a brilliant smile. "That wa— it's my nickname for Georgia. Peach. I called her that the night we met, and she called me Ninety-Nine because I was the ninety-ninth person to try that nickname on her. I wasn't very original."

The line between real and play is blurring, and I scramble to keep up. "Not original, but far superior to Pepperoni Face."

His laugh is soft in volume and rough in tone; it feels like his palms moving over me this morning.

"And for you it was later?" Tai asks me.

I can't find my words at first, too busy thinking about Eli's. I watch him fiddle with a long strip of paper he must've peeled from his napkin. False scenarios float through my mind, but in the end, there are some things you can't fake.

"We were best friends for a long time and that felt like winning the lottery to me, so I was scared to mess with it." Eli's devoted attention is a touch, like fingers framing my face. "We used to work at our friend's family's winery every year and the last summer we were there, things changed. We were going to be at the same school after a couple years of distance, and once we were there, I just . . ." I stare down at Eli's fingers, frozen on that strip of paper. "He bought me a cupcake for my twenty-first birthday in October. Chocolate, of course."

Tai laughs, but is otherwise rapt, and I think back to that night two months into the school year. I watched Eli climb the steps to my off-campus apartment, a familiar blue box from a local bakery in one hand, his other palm moving down the thigh of his jeans. He looked at the door, not knowing that I was looking at him, taking in every detail of his face because I knew I'd want to remember what he looked like the moment before we tipped over. We'd been dancing around it, him tentative and me terrified, even though I knew it was inevitable. The previous weekend we'd nearly kissed in the dark hallway of a frat party, the tang of beer burning my nostrils, his breath on my mouth. Someone had interrupted us, and I'd lived in that suspended moment the entire week, my heart somewhere in my throat. In his hands.

I still remember how carefully he lit the single candle, his palm curved protectively around it afterward. I wanted his hand exactly like that against my neck, cradling it before he kissed me. He sang "Happy Birthday," eyes on me, that deep, beautiful brown lit up with flame. I was so scared. I wanted it so much.

"I wished for him," I admit, my heart in my throat again. "Then I blew out the candle and the wish came true. That's how it's been ever since."

Eli's eyes finally meet mine, dark and sparking, and he keeps me there. He remembers, too. The memory is so alive between us it's touchable.

Maybe I didn't give him all of me, but I gave him more than I ever gave anyone else, and instead of taking it back I locked it up. Now saying anything about how we used to be, how much I loved him, feels like unlocking it again. I'm scared he's going to see what was left over when we broke up. What's starting to spark again with a little bit of oxygen.

It's that thought that straightens my spine. "I love the peach, too, but passion fruit might be the winner." I raise an eyebrow at Eli. "Don't you think?"

Remember it's Grace's favorite and we're here for her and Adam, not us? Remember that we're playing a role?

He straightens, too, as if I've yelled it at both of us. The strip of napkin wrapped around his fingers is nearly dissolved, too flimsy to keep any kind of shape, if that's what he was trying to do.

"Right," he says. "The peach bourbon is my personal favorite, but passion fruit's the winner."

Tai nods with a smile. "It's a great decision, though there's not a bad decision you could make in the bunch. My cakes are delicious."

"They're incredible," I say. "We would be so grateful if—"

She waves me off. "Say no more. The cake is yours."

A flash of guilt hits me knowing we're getting it under false pretenses, but it's quickly replaced by relief. "I'm not going to, but just know that I could seriously kiss you right now. You have no idea what this means to us."

"It's my pleasure," she says. "Let's talk through the rest of the details and then we'll be all set."

The rest of the appointment flies by, and by the time we're finished I'm an exhausted, elated mess.

Once we get outside, I pull up Venmo so I can send Adam a payment request, just so he can see we've crossed an item off the list.

"A win, finally," I say, darting a glance at Eli.

He's watching me, hands in his pockets, his expression unfathomable, but he flashes me a smile when our eyes meet. "Quick thinking with the fake-fiancé thing."

I groan. "I'm sorry. That was a very impulsive thing to do."

"I mean . . ." He lifts his shoulders and a thousand unsaid words fill the silence. In another life, it could've been real and we both know it. "It worked, right?"

"Thank god she didn't ask for a proposal story," I joke, and he laughs, but it's soft and strange. He wipes a hand across his rough jaw.

"Yeah, well. I probably could've come up with something," he says faintly.

Our gazes tangle. We played a dangerous game in there, and I only realize it now with my heart still racing. With Eli looking at me the way he is, full of memories.

He opens his mouth to speak, but his phone starts ringing in his back pocket. It's a flick on my forehead, a reminder made more urgent when he smiles wryly and says, "It's the boss."

"The boss?" I echo, confused.

"Adam. He's FaceTiming," he clarifies, and I get it, because *this* is our job. Not staring at each other thinking about the past, but staying firmly in the present to make sure Adam gets the best start to his future.

Right.

I go to Eli's side, making sure to keep enough distance between our bodies that I won't be tempted to curl into him. "Let's tell him the good news."

Chapter Nineteen

Adam and Grace are throwing a party.

Fine, they have people over to help put together wedding favors; it's practically an assembly line. But when Eli accepts the FaceTime and I see a familiar group of people sprawled out behind Adam in their living room, I'm suddenly back in Seattle, both in the past and what could be my future. I'm FaceTiming with my friends during my six months there, snagging them in parts and pieces when our schedules allow while they integrate themselves deeper into the lives of the same coupled-up friends behind them now, or their new Person, in Jamie's case. Saying "No big deal!" when they tell me they can't visit after all and deleting the list of places I wanted to take them. I'm FaceTiming them sometime next year from the apartment that only holds one body—mine—while Grace holds Baby Song-Kim.

Will their kid know me, or will some friend who lives down the street with a similarly tiny potato person become the godparent?

God. *Am* I going to be one of the godparents? Is there a test I have to take to prove myself? Can godparents be long distance?

"Come back," a voice murmurs.

Eli. His hand presses into the dip of my lower back, and all of my present senses slam back into me.

"Dude, where were you just now, the moon?" Adam asks, rapping the screen with his knuckles.

I point at my ear with my middle finger. "No, it's just hard to hear with the rager you're throwing." I glance at Eli, who bites back a smile. "Replay the last thirty seconds for me?"

"I was just telling Adam how charming and persuasive we were, and how they now have a kickass cake," Eli says. His fingers are still notched between the bumps in my spine. On screen, we're standing close with the bakery just behind us, shoulders barely brushing. No one would know he's got his hand on me.

"You have a cake!" I exclaim.

"We have a cake," Adam crows. "I'm so relieved that I'm not even going to freak out about the number I just saw on Venmo."

Grace pops up behind Adam, a long strand of ribbon looped around her neck. "Hi, hello. I love you both always, but I love you extra hard today. I'm going to take down half of that cake on Saturday." Her eyes fill with tears and she throws up her hands, exasperated. "Oh no, I'm crying just thinking about it."

"Seriously, thank you." Adam places a hand over his heart as Grace gets pulled back into the fray. "I was worried we wouldn't land it today. The appointment was taking so long, I thought maybe something had gone wrong again, like at the other place."

"It was nothing like the other place," Eli says, a protective note in his voice. "Georgia killed it. She had Tai in the palm of her hand."

I elbow him. "We both did, and it helps that Tai was an angel. Plus, you're the one who found the bakery in the first place."

"You would've found it if I didn't."

"Well, yeah, because the bakery was on *my* list."

He grins. "We're doing this again, huh?"

I roll my eyes. "My point is, don't give me all the credit. You killed it, too."

"It's that gold standard teamwork," he says with a smile and soft eyes, and it's true. We're an amazing team right now. We need to keep it that way.

"Hello, can we focus on me for a sec?" comes a grating voice.

Eli's amused huff brushes against my cheek. When I glance back at the phone, Adam's looking between me and Eli with an inscrutable expression. "Damn, you two are really vibing today. What's up?"

Just a minor morning dry hump and a mountain of confusing feelings, I think, my cheeks heating.

Eli's answer is more PR-friendly. "We have the ultimate motivation of not fucking up your wedding, and a ticking clock as the cherry on top. There's still work to do."

Adam sighs. "Right, the DJ. In brighter news, Aunt Julia got dinner squared away. One of her friends owns a catering business and he apparently owes her for something that sounded too sexual for me to dig into, so we're set. And everything is really going okay at Blue Yonder?"

"Everything's on track," I tell him. It's a miracle, honestly, how smoothly everything's gone on site. We'll be done by the time they get up here on Friday, no problem.

"That's great." He sags back against the couch, his relief evident as he looks between us. "You two are my curse-breakers, I swear."

We wave him off, but he leans in, expression earnest. "Seriously, whatever you're doing?" He points between me and Eli. "Keep it up, because it's working."

"**You're sure you're okay with me staying here again?**" Eli asks when we get to the cottage after dinner.

He's hovering in the doorway with an air mattress tucked under his arm and the moon at his back. I forgot to leave lights on, so his face is bathed in shadow, making his expression unreadable.

"It's fine," I say, kicking off my sandals. My heart beats hard against my ribs.

The walk back to the cottages was quiet, all the conversations we haven't had keeping stride with us: what happened this morning; the memories we handed over at the bakery to sell our story, when realistically we didn't need to; the way we both patently ignored Adam's *keep doing what you're doing* after he hung up.

And most importantly, tonight's sleep situation.

At dinner, Cole told us that Cal had tried taping up the holes in the ceiling of Eli's cottage earlier, but that it was "pretty fucked."

"I figured," Eli said, running a hand over his jaw. "With everything we had going on today, I didn't think about finding somewhere to stay."

"Just crash at Georgia's again. It's the path of least resistance," Cole said, flicking a wrist at me with so much nonchalance that it could only be calculated. Sure enough, he continued, "Unless it would be too weird, what with your previous intimate knowledge of each other's nighttime habits."

Eli sighed. "From the bottom of my heart, please shut the fuck up."

Julia leaned past Cole's shoulder, pushing back her halo of curly blond hair. "My darling son, stop being a dick."

"What a thing for a mother to say," Cole said, feigning insult, but the emotion was lost in the sharp curve of his smirk.

Julia hooked her arm around Cole's neck. "Eli, there's an air mattress somewhere in the Big House. Want us to dig it up for you?"

Eli and I exchanged a look that transmitted mutual agreement. If we said no, it would look weirder than saying yes. And anyway, by that point it was approaching nine. It had been a long day. I had no energy to come up with an alternate plan, especially when, unfortunately, Cole was right—it was the easiest option.

Just not the safest, I think as Eli brushes past me now, toeing off his sneakers by the door and setting the air mattress down next to them. I want to strangle the not-insignificant part of me that hopes there's a hole in it.

After I click on the living room lamp, I straighten to find Eli with his gaze pinned to me.

"You okay?"

I frown. "I just told you it's fine."

"Not about that," he says, his eyes moving over my face. "You've been quiet since we talked to Adam earlier."

I raise an eyebrow. "Keeping tabs on me?"

"Always," he says with a grin that fades quickly. "Just making sure, that's all. Adam is good at communicating his gratitude, but he's also good at saying shit without thinking. When he brought up Margot—"

"Oh, that didn't bother me." Adam bringing up the disaster at Sucre doesn't make the list of things I'm thinking about.

What *is* on the list is Adam's *keep doing what you're doing* and all that implies.

"Something did," Eli says with the confidence of someone who's known me for more than a decade. It lights me up; I can't help it. "What's up?"

I hesitate before admitting, "That group at his house tonight was the one he and Grace got close to while I was in Seattle. It's weird seeing your friends have other friends, and it made me feel far away again, you know?"

"I've lived three thousand miles away from everyone I love for years," he says, his eyes steady on me. "So yes, I know."

There's an understanding in his voice that's heavier than mine, and it unravels a realization: he must've sat on FaceTime calls where we were all here, seen pictures of events he couldn't make it to, and felt like he was holding on to the people he cared about by a thread. All this time I've assumed that his job has kept him occupied, fulfilled in a way we couldn't touch, that he was too busy to miss what he never came back to, but it's clear it didn't. Or that it lost its shine somewhere along the way.

What happened?

"So, is that why you've been so feral about making all this work?" Eli's teasing voice interrupts my thoughts.

"Feral?"

He laughs. "You know what I mean."

"You've been feral, too," I say, pushing at his bicep with a fingertip.

"Yeah, but you know why. I have something to prove."

Maybe I do, too.

I don't say it out loud; it sounds ridiculous. But more importantly, I think he hears it anyway. The compassion in his eyes tells me so, reminding me that even though this new Eli isn't like any other version I've known, all the other Elis are layered underneath it, including the one who was my best friend. That version of him *knows* me, and knows exactly what bruise it pokes.

I sigh. "When I got back to San Francisco a few months ago, a lot had changed. Adam and Grace were in Glenlake, Jamie was all wifed up in Oakland. It's become a lot harder to find time for each other. Before last Friday, I hadn't seen anyone in over a month. And it's not like I want to tell them to stop what they're doing; I love that they're all in love. I don't begrudge Adam or Jamie for having their own lives and being busy, or for things shifting when I was away."

"Upheaval is kind of a shitty rite of passage in your twenties," Eli agrees.

"Right, but . . ." I shrug, staring down into the space between my and Eli's bodies. Our knees are nearly brushing.

"But it hurts all the same to feel far away," he says, and I hear it again, that heart-deep understanding.

I nod, imagining all the miles stretching between San Francisco and Seattle. Wondering how I'll bridge them. "Maybe I am a little feral, but just because I want to stay in Adam's life. And Jamie's, too, of course. I don't want them to leave me."

It's such an old fear, sprouted from my mom walking away. It's a memory I can't even remember, but something that's shaped my entire life all the same. Even now I can't shake it off, and I hate that. I should be okay on my own, but I can't help searching for that feeling of belonging. It's so hard for me to find my place— when I do, maybe I hold on too hard, but it's only because I know what it's like to lose it.

Eli's silent. I feel naked in all the wrong ways. "That sounds incredibly dramatic now that I've said it out loud—"

Suddenly, his hand wraps around my wrist. I blink up at him, my breath catching when I see his expression. It's a fierceness that catches the Eli-shaped spark in my chest. A sadness that's five years old.

It collars me around the throat, holds me in place as surely as his actual touch.

"Georgia." He breathes my name, then stops.

"You don't have to—"

"I do," he says, stepping closer. "Anyone who could leave you doesn't deserve you in the first place." He swallows hard, his eyes searching mine. "And I know for a fact that Adam and Jamie are smart enough to never let you go."

It's clear Eli isn't just talking about them. It's us, too, the way we left each other long before I left New York. It's an apology without having to say it, maybe, and it softens some jagged thing inside me.

There's a question in his eyes now. A spark of resolve, like he's going to open the box where our mess lay.

Keep doing what you're doing, Adam's voice yells in my ear, and it's like being shoved in the back.

Eli inhales and I do, too, cutting him off. "I might go for a swim."

That spark banks itself at my graceless subject change. "A swim."

"Yeah, a swim. The thing you've been doing nonstop in the pool out there, unless you've laid some claim to it."

"You've had an open invitation every time," he says, voice low. My stomach spirals. "You want some company?"

My knee-jerk reaction is to say no, only because of how badly I want to say yes. But then I hear it again: *keep doing what you're doing*. This time it's a suggestion, an item added to Adam and Grace's wedding list.

We can exist in our halfway space that way, can't we? Go for a dip together, celebrate our win and figure out how we're going to tackle finding a DJ. Lean into the tentative friendship we're rebuilding without stepping into the shadowed spaces of our past. Clearly we *are* onto something and Adam can tell. The superstitious part of me doesn't want to mess with that.

And the other part of me is just hungry.

"Sure," I say. Eli's relieved-sounding exhale wraps around me. "Let me get changed."

"I'm going to grab my suit from next door," Eli replies. "I'll see you in a few."

Chapter Twenty

Our last summer at Blue Yonder, Eli swam whenever we weren't working. He'd done the same thing every year before, but I'd never allowed myself to look at him. Or at least *look* at him, not like I did that summer, tracing the curves of his biceps, the soft arc that belied the immovable solidness underneath, and the bare taper of his hips. I mapped the thick swell of his thighs, the way his swim trunks plastered to them when he got out, revealing the paler, vulnerable skin where his tan faded away. I'd watched his body grow into itself year after year, and my awareness grew with it, peaking when every beautiful plane and limb of him met its full potential.

I didn't do anything with that potential then and can't do anything with it now, but as I make my way across the grass, I also can't help but feel what I did then—anticipation. Unbearable awareness. My body remembers everything that happened here, and wants everything that didn't.

Eli's already in the deep end, his chin tipped up toward the sky. He looks over his shoulder when my feet meet cement, then turns completely as I halt next to a chaise. The water ripples around him, limned with the moonlight above and the pool lights below, casting him in a captivating mix of shadow and light.

Time is bending again and I don't know which version of my-self I am. I can't pick out which version Eli is either, and I don't know if that thrills me or scares me.

"Hey," I say stupidly, like we didn't just see each other five min-utes ago. I hug my towel to my stomach.

"Hey," he replies, his eyes tracing the curves my red one-piece exposes. His hands have taken every path imaginable, and he looks at me like he's remembering that. He clears his throat, drift-ing backward. "The water's perfect."

It's the invitation I need. I toss my towel onto the chaise and make my way to the deep end, nearly on top of where Eli's tread-ing water. He looks up at me. I look down at him.

I'm pretty sure he's holding his breath, so I hold mine, too.

And then I jump.

When I come up for air, Eli has water running down his face.

"What," he says, blowing out a wet, laughing breath, "was that?"

I slick back my hair. "A cannonball."

"Uh-huh." It's a silky acknowledgement that's more texture than sound; it slides over my skin like water. "Don't act like that wasn't a declaration of war."

"I can't help that you were in my splash zone."

"You made *me* your splash zone."

"That's very self-important of you to think so."

He grins. It's sharklike, sharp-toothed and focused. My heart starts beating fast, latching on to anticipation of something I can't name.

Eli drifts close. Droplets of water cling to his eyelashes and the thick stubble along his jaw, glide down the pillow of his bottom lip and the length of his throat, settling into the grooves of his thin gold chain. He stops mere inches from me, then dodges left suddenly, circling to my back. The water ripples around us, his chest grazing my shoulder blades.

"You want to rumble, Georgia?" he murmurs, nearly in my ear.

It's an old, familiar question, one he used to ask whenever I'd jump in after him. It gave me the perfect excuse to put my hands all over his slick skin under the guise of roughhousing, so I always said yes.

I want to say yes again. To get him messy. It's safe here, right? At least it's not in my bed.

Maybe he hears that, or maybe he makes the decision for us. Suddenly his arms are wrapped around my waist and he's lifting me out of the water, lobbing me like a beach ball.

I go down screaming and come up sputtering. "Okay. You're *dead.*"

His eyes light up and then darken with intent when I advance on him, his broad shoulders shaking with suppressed laughter at my awkward leap-shuffle. I give up, diving underwater to get to him quicker. My eyes are going to burn later from keeping them open, but I want to see the body I'm about to conquer.

But my suit is a red flag, so of course he sees me coming. His hands shoot beneath the water, fingers wide and palms out as he twists his hips away from me.

I get my hands on them anyway, pushing to get him off balance, but in seconds he's got his fingers around my arms, yanking me to the surface. I come up gasping, using his body as leverage to get on his back by planting a foot on his thigh and curling over him. It's messy business—my boob smashes into his cheek and his fingers dig into my ass—but I manage to plaster myself against him with a triumphant shout.

He's laughing out loud, a beautiful sound I missed so much it momentarily stops me. But then his hands cup my thighs, hitching me up. I band one arm around his shoulder, curve my free hand around his throat.

"Now what?" I whisper in his ear, and suddenly neither of us are laughing.

There's a vibration against my palm, the kind of groan he'd feed into my mouth, but held back. His voice is low and even when he says, "You tell me."

I hook my legs around his waist and my heel brushes against him. I realize then that he's hard, and I stop breathing. He has to feel my heart racing against his back. He groans for real, a bitten-away sound that echoes into the silent air as his hands come around my ankles, tight. I think he's going to push me away, but he holds me there. Waiting.

I could stop. I should. But this anticipation is desperate to go somewhere finally. The last time we were here it was straightforward—he wanted me and I wanted him, but we didn't let ourselves have it. There was no history between us, though, no heartbreak, and now I feel myself craving the ability to go back there. To play it out a different way and keep doing what we're doing in the simplest terms: wanting each other here. Now. While we have the excuse to. Letting that be enough and then letting it go.

Exhaling, I focus on the nape of his neck. So vulnerable. The perfect place for my mouth.

"Are you giving up?" I murmur, and I almost hope he says yes. I'm scared of what I want.

His response is immediate. "No."

There's something immovable in his voice and a spark flares in my stomach, setting fire to any leftover doubt. He's not going anywhere.

"Put your hands on me, then," I say, leaning to the side like that'll topple him. It doesn't. "It's not a real rumble if you aren't even trying."

Eli's hands move fast from my ankles to my thighs and suddenly I'm being pulled around his body. He boosts me until we're nose-to-nose. Until we're lined up in a way that confirms how much he wants this.

"I *am* trying," he breathes out. "You have no idea how hard I'm trying."

My head tips back at the urgent press of him between my legs, but his thumb notches into the divot below my bottom lip, his fingers holding me in place for the unrelenting latch of his gaze.

A handful of seconds extend between us, the water putting its hands on each of our backs to sway us closer together. His nose grazes mine, and in the total silence surrounding us, his soft groan sounds like a sonic boom.

It's such a needy sound, a thing I crave with a perpetually empty stomach. I chase his mouth and after a hesitant second, he gives it to me. There's water on his lips and mine, and it makes for a perfect slide in tandem with his desperate tongue. He makes another sound, like it hurts but it's *good*. Our kisses get harder, needier, his whiskers burning my skin as his mouth traces my jaw, moves down my neck.

He asks, "Do you remember our last summer here?"

"Wh—what?"

"Do you?" His fingers dig into my thighs, pulling me closer.

"Yes." It's a sigh, then a groan as he bites gently at my throat.

"There were so many things I wanted with you. So many ways I just *wanted* you. It's how I feel now," he murmurs, and my heart takes off. "I knew as soon as Adam asked us to come up here that it would happen and I still did it because I—" He stops, and time does, too. I'm terrified of what he could say.

Please keep it simple, I think. I tip my head back, make eye contact with a star. Wish for it.

Eli lets out a breath. "Because deep down I wanted it to. But I don't know how *you* feel. What *you* want. And every time I start to ask, you change the subject."

My tongue is slow to form a sentence. It wants Eli, not conversation. "I want to keep doing what we're doing."

He pulls back, even when I grip his hair in protest, his eyes wandering over my face. That glimmer of determination is back. "Try a line you didn't steal from Adam."

"Don't you see his point? This time last week we weren't even talking to each other, and now we're kicking ass together, and that was just because of a half-asleep makeout this morning."

"I wasn't asleep," he says stubbornly. "Not even five percent."

"I'm just saying, imagine what we could accomplish if we—"

His eyebrows drop, his voice a warning rumble. "Don't say it right now when I'm trying to have a conversation with you."

"Your fingers are currently digging into my ass, so you're picking a terrible time to want a conversation."

"We've been dancing around this for days," he says, unmoved. "Not to therapize you, but I need you to communicate your needs. I need to know where your head's at before we do anything else, no matter how much I want it. Whatever this is, it has to be honest, because last time—"

"Okay, okay," I interrupt. I don't want to talk about last time. Simple. Clean. No mess.

"I *do* want to keep doing what we're doing, even though a week ago I couldn't have fathomed I'd be in a position to accept it,"

I say. "But I also recognize that we're here to help fix Adam and Grace's wedding, and that we need to concentrate on that." I swallow hard, tracing the slash of Eli's collarbones with my eyes, watching goose bumps raise on his skin. "It's just hard when I'm . . ."

He stays silent.

"When I'm wanting this," I say, frustrated. I watch his pupils dilate, his eyes turning hungry. "Wanting you again, like that summer, like—" *Always.* "I don't know what to do with it."

"It's all I can think about," he breathes out.

"Me, too."

"So tell me what you want."

"I *did.*"

"Say it again," he demands.

"*You.*" It's out of my mouth before I can stop it, an echo of last night when Eli was in my bed for the first time in five years, telling me with a racing heart that I was all he saw, felt, heard, tasted. I'm compelled by the low, rough texture of his voice and the way he's looking at me, like he's starving.

I lick my lips just to watch him chase the movement. "I don't want to complicate things, especially in the middle of saving Adam and Grace's wedding. There's so much in my head and it's so messy—"

"That's okay," he insists, and I can hear how much he believes it. But I don't.

"I just know I want this right now, at least until everyone shows up. I need it to be that simple," I press on. "And I think we're becoming friends again, and I . . ."

I trail off as his eyes flutter shut. Uncertainty draws a hand around my throat. "Or I don't know, maybe—"

His eyes pop open, latching on to mine, clear of any emotion. "No, we are," he says quietly. "We are."

"I don't want this to mess with that, or with fixing the wedding. So if you're not in agreement, please get your hands off my ass, because—"

He does take his hand off my ass, but just one, and only so he can wind it through my hair to keep me steady as he sucks at my bottom lip, teeth scraping. A second later, he seems to find himself again, and places the softest kiss on my top lip, then my bottom, his eyes open and searching mine, so deep and warm from beneath heavy, wet lashes.

"I'm in agreement," he murmurs against my mouth. "We'll do this, keep it simple."

My relief is drug-like. "Okay."

He pulls back. "But when we leave, if we're really friends, we're not going back to the way we were before."

A curl of pleasure works through me, knowing I'll have him in some way. "I know."

"I hated it," he says, voice low.

"I did, too."

He takes my response for the confession it is and resolve darkens his eyes. It's coupled with an X-ray-like awareness, like he sees the wanting in me. The fear. Like by agreeing to this, he's letting me get away with something.

Sure enough, he says, "You and I are going to have a reckoning, Georgia. It doesn't have to be this week, but it's going to happen."

"Fine." I say it quickly, like the F-word it is, not like a promise. Reckonings are messy. They ruin things. I can't deal with that future possibility right now, and under the terms of this new agreement, I don't need to.

It's now, not the future. A blissful thought. A boundary we won't cross, no matter what Eli says.

He's still watching me. "This is going to mean something to me."

It's a last warning, but I don't need it.

"It's going to mean something to me, too." His expression slackens with relief, then tightens with a need I feel between my legs. I reach up to frame his jaw, pressing my thumb to the corner of his mouth. It lifts beneath my touch, just a millimeter. Enough to count. "I mean, of course it is. We're not strangers. We're . . ."

"Us."

That single word fuses me to him. A tiny voice whispers, *oh hell*, but I push it away. "We're us."

He lets out a soft, slow breath. And then he says, "Then that's enough."

Chapter Twenty-One

We fall through the cottage door, hands everywhere.

Eli's already peeling off my bathing suit straps and my palms are coasting over his skin as I reach up to catch his mouth. It's so familiar that time slides away and suddenly I'm in my apartment bedroom at twenty-one, being stripped down by him for the first time, inhaling the birthday candle smoke fresh on his skin. I'm thinking, *this is Eli, I have him. Look at the way he needs me; look how it matches mine.* What a revelation it is.

And then I'm back here, it's now, and he's pressing a murmured, laughing apology to my chin as I trip over his discarded sneakers. It's now and it's tongue and teeth and Eli's deep groans, it's my breasts against his chest when he gets my bathing suit down to my waist.

We're kissing and it's now, but the feel of our bare skin sliding together for the first time in five years holds the echo of the first time ever. It's in the way Eli exhales *"oh"* in surprise and relief. In memory.

How strange it is to have a first for the second time. How lucky and messy and perfect. It makes my eyes sting, even though all of this is temporary.

We make it to the bedroom, kissing the entire way. His hands traverse my body as we stop at the foot of the bed, a slow slide upward until he's cupping my face. It's like he's revisiting every piece of me that belonged to him before.

"Hi." The word rides out on a sigh as he presses a kiss to my forehead.

My laugh is quiet so it doesn't break the moment apart. "Hi."

"What're we doing tonight?"

"Everything," I whisper. "If that's what you want."

There's a beat of silence, then his hoarse, "It is."

The room is dark, but the moon slices in through the window and so I see his expression like there's a spotlight shining on it. The raw need there, an old affection, the shadowed thing I can't quite make out. His eyes move over my face, thumbs brushing along the high planes of my cheeks before moving down to trace the seam of my lips. When I part them against his skin, he lets out a soft, pained exhale.

The frantic pace from a moment ago softens. He leans in to kiss me, no tongue, just his lips against mine. His palms are so careful on my jaw, like he doesn't want to break the moment apart either. I can *feel* how overwhelmed he is. How easy it would be for second thoughts to sneak in to turn us back.

But I want him, everything, right now, so I cup his neck to bring him to me. I part my lips against his, make a needy sound I know will undo him, and it does. He groans, sliding his tongue against mine, sealing my body to his with a firm hand to my lower back.

"Fuck, you feel so good," he breathes. "Thank god I jerked off earlier."

His admission pierces my sex fog, then intensifies it. "*What?*"

He sucks a path down my neck. "Before we went swimming."

I pull back. "It took me, like, five minutes to get changed, and you were already in the pool when I got out there."

He raises his head, his lust-drunk expression turning sheepish. "Yeah, well, it took *me* like five seconds."

I let out a cackle that pulls his swollen mouth into a wide grin, and he bends, dissolving into soft laughter as he scrapes his teeth against my collarbone.

"What were you thinking about?"

"You." He presses the word into my skin; it goes straight to my veins. "This. The way you taste and your sounds and your laugh. How well you fill my hands. What it would feel like to have you again." A pause as his fingers flex into my back. He inhales, and then stops. "Several other things I'll keep in the vault."

"That depraved?"

He hums, a private sound. "Something like that."

Pushing his hips into mine, he tips me back onto the bed, then follows me down. The looming spread of his shoulders blot everything else out. Nothing can touch us.

"Are we stupid for doing this?" he asks, voice low.

I swallow, wondering what answer will allow for this to continue. Probably not what I actually say, which is, "A little bit."

There's a flash of relief in his eyes, a release of the tension line between his eyebrows. It's not an answer that'll fit into a neat box, but god knows it's real, and he looks at me as if he likes that.

I do, too. We won't hurt each other when we've said out loud what this is.

And maybe it's not stupid, I think as he presses me into the mattress in a way that feels vital, like I'm being consumed by him. Maybe it's just like going back to visit a home that isn't yours anymore. Maybe you don't have the key, but someone lets you in anyway, and you stay awhile, and it feels so good just to be somewhere you once belonged.

Eli's mouth fits over mine, bringing the feeling full circle. I get lost in the beautiful, familiar cadence of his tongue winding with mine, of the way his palm drifts down my body. He loves to take his time with me, and I sink into every second that's mine.

Eventually he moves lower, pressing open-mouthed kisses down my neck, his teeth grazing skin until he reaches my nipple. His breath is warm just before his tongue is wet and swirling, centering the need that's been suffusing my entire body into that one point he's licking, sucking at, drawing into his mouth.

"Do you remember when we got together . . ." He shifts over to my other breast, murmuring, "And I told you about the things I wanted to do our last summer here?"

Hazily, I recall Eli handing me confessions:

I wanted to get my hands all over you in the pool so you'd feel me when you went to bed, he whispered at the corner store one night.

Wanted to put you on your knees in your cottage living room, he murmured against my ear at a party, his body curling over me from behind.

Wanted to kiss you in the middle of a vineyard block. Tell you I love you at breakfast, while we were working, in the middle of the night—

Just because I could.

The last thing winds itself around me. It pulls fear and exhilaration into my veins, even though I know he's talking about what we're doing now—finally getting to act out the way we wanted each other then.

"I remember," I sigh.

"I've still got my list," he says, his hand curving over my thigh. "I know how you love those."

"Mmm," I murmur as he drags his quietly grinning mouth down my ribs.

I *need* them and the thought that we're building a new one makes me feel simultaneously bound and free. I can let it be exactly what it is within the boundaries of the week and the items we check off together. Our old list is largely dead, but this—this will keep me safe.

"Let's get through as much of it as we can," Eli says, rising to his knees and curling his fingers into the bathing suit bunched at my waist. He asks "okay?" to stripping me down and having me this week and I breathe out a desperate "*yes*" to both things.

I watch, rapt, as he peels my suit down my legs, tossing it over his shoulder. For a second, he looks flattened.

His eyes move up to mine, his throat working before he speaks. "Goddamn. My memory never does you justice."

"Get up here."

He does, carefully levering his body over mine. "*Very* glad I jerked off earlier," he groans as I get my hands between us to unlace the front of his swim trunks.

"Why, so it doesn't take five seconds?"

He laughs, even as he squeezes my thigh in warning. "I'll last as long as it takes for you to beg me to make you come."

I groan. Eli is the living embodiment of *it's always the quiet ones.*

His mouth drifts to my ear. "I love it when you beg, Georgia. You never ask for anything."

His voice is dark and low, but there's a pleading note there, too, and it breaks me apart, especially when he kicks his trunks off and presses against me fully naked. He's so stiff between my legs, so exactly what I need. Our mingled gasps rise up toward the ceiling like steam.

"Please get inside me," I whisper.

"Not yet," he whispers back.

I grip his hair, bring him back for a kiss that's hard and messy, but too soon he's leaving me, making his way down my body, his chain a tickling drag along my skin. He pushes my thighs apart with his shoulders, then places a wet kiss on each one, licking me there instead of where I need him.

"I forgot what a tease you are," I complain, lifting my hips. "You're in the wrong spot."

He grins, sucking a mark right near the crease of my thigh. "Show me where you want me. It's been a while, not sure I remember how it goes."

I tsk. "Losing your touch?"

"Maybe yours will inspire me," he says silkily, then repeats a rumbling, "Show me."

With a sigh that's half exasperation and half desperation, I slip my hand a bare inch from his mouth, spreading the wetness he's created. I make it easy for him to taste me when he gets tired of this game. And he will, soon.

"Fuck." His voice is strangled. "That's—that's very inspiring."

I run a wet finger along the seam of his lips, gasping when he catches it with his teeth and sucks at my skin. His groan vibrates through every part of me, setting me on a delicious edge I need him to push me over.

"Mm." He shackles a hand around my wrist, licking my fingers before he looks at me with a sweet smile. "Peach. It really is my favorite flavor."

I pull myself from his grip, heart flying as I trace exactly where I want him. "Is my showing portion of this over?"

He noses my hand out of the way, places a soft, almost chaste kiss on me, then licks his lips.

"I remember now," he says, gripping my thigh, pushing it further open. "I never forgot. I just wanted to see you."

When he puts his mouth on me, the sound he makes is utterly wrecked, his fingers digging hard into my thigh. He doesn't have to say the words for me to know it's good, but he does anyway because he knows the praise will make me mindless. He whispers, "You taste incredible, you're so fucking good, Georgia, look at what you do to me," as he wraps a hand around himself, stroking slowly while he licks me so well.

It's like a spark catches fire minutes later when my orgasm hits—it's heat and licking flames, Eli's wild groans and the way he pins my twitching hips down to keep me on his mouth. I'm done, but *he's* not, not until I'm begging, pulling at his hair.

He rises to his knees, his eyes glittering in the darkness, still stroking himself. "Jesus."

"Are you joking?" I nearly slur. "How did you get better at that?"

"Not with practice," he assures me. "It's just you."

"We're not done, right?"

"No," he says. "We're not."

He crawls to the bedside table, letting out a relieved breath when he finds condoms there. It's Aunt Julia's touch—as a former high school counselor, she has a deeply pragmatic view of sex, so condoms are littered everywhere like prophylactic Pokémon. When I was a teenager, opening the drawer made me blush. Now I want to collect them all.

Eli rolls the condom on, situating himself against the headboard. It's my favorite position and it occurs to me that he remembers that. That he remembers a lot of things.

It should scare me, how seen that makes me feel. I remind myself that some bits of the past will bleed in, but it's okay. It's now.

"C'mere." His features are carved out with a severe need, but there's something infinitely soft there, too, as I crawl onto his lap. His hand wraps around my hip, holding me above him, while his other cups my face. He pulls me in for a quick, quiet kiss. "You good?"

"I will be when you let me get on you."

He groans, then laughs softly. "I'm just trying to prepare myself for it."

"Me, too. But I want you right now."

It feels like a mutual admission and he looks at me like it is one. We haven't done this in years, and it *does* mean something to be back like this.

He positions himself for me and I finally sink down, watching his expression melt from anticipation to shock to a pleasure that looks like pain. Soft, helpless sounds fall out of his mouth as his head falls against the headboard. I lean in to run my tongue over the salt of his skin, working him all the way into my body until my ass rests on his thighs.

It's so intensely deep. I feel like I'm full of him to my throat, like he's consuming me.

"Fuck." Eli lets loose a short, disbelieving laugh, gripping my hips. "Georgia, please don't move yet."

"I *have* to."

He wraps one arm around my waist, takes a handful of my ass, then burrows his face into the curve where my neck meets my shoulder. I feel the shake of his thighs underneath me, in his hands holding me tight to him, in his back beneath my palms. "God, you feel so good. I missed you so much."

His voice breaks in the middle of the confession, cracking a tiny fissure into my heart. Soothing a missingness I've carried with me since I left New York.

Careful, I whisper to myself.

He whispers something, too, but the words are pushed against my neck, lost to me. Whatever it is heats my blood, some alchemic reaction to the needy arch of his voice.

I start to move in earnest and he accepts it with a pleading groan, his fingers digging into every part of me he can access. It's so good, so scary, so *much* and he's showing me that he wants it—

"Exactly like that," he pants against my cheek. "I'll take it all."

I groan, sliding my mouth over his as he curls his arm around my waist. And then he tips us sideways, rolling me onto my back without sliding out, his thighs pushing mine apart, hips holding me down. I love his weight on me, the way he anchors my body with his own. I've felt so adrift, before and now—sometimes I think I've been adrift always—but he's keeping me right here.

His name rides out on a plea and I don't even know what I'm begging for—his body or his heart, to be held on to again and forever this time, even though I know we can't. But I say it again anyway, and he hisses out a "*yes*" that spirals through me.

"It's so good," he pants, his eyes moving over my body, from my breasts bouncing with his thrusts down to where we're connected. He's wet with me, and it's an easy, deep glide now. I swear he dissolves right in front of me, his eyes falling shut, cheeks flagged red, the delicate chain of his necklace swaying between us as his pace increases. "Oh fuck, you have no idea how much I . . ."

He dips down with a low groan, slides his tongue into my mouth, his body into mine again and again.

"Please," I breathe out after minutes of riding the edge with him. I can feel how close he is, and how much he doesn't want it to end.

His hips slow, his strokes getting longer but not as hard. "You want to come or you want me to make you come?"

"I want you—" I hiccup around a moan as pleasure twists down my spine. I'm so close, blissed-out and frustrated in equal, unbearable measure. A tear snakes from the corner of my eye. "I want it to be you."

He wipes his thumb through the moisture at my temple. "I can feel it, you're right there," he praises, voice tight, then whispers, "Let me help you."

Propping himself on an elbow, he slides his hand between us, pets his thumb over me right there—*right there*. I say it out loud, and he nods, leaning down to kiss me slow and deep, thrusting into me hard. It's all of it—the hard and fast and the deep and slow that winds me so tight it hurts and then drops me into wild relief.

Eli's ragged moan catches in his throat as he curls an arm underneath my shoulder, his hand cupping my neck. It's chaotic, me losing myself underneath him, Eli losing himself into me. He goes completely silent for a beat as he goes nearly too deep, then comes with a low, fractured noise.

He says my name, tunnels his fingers into my hair while his hips rock slowly, not ready to end it.

"Fuck me," he finally sighs, kissing up my throat, along my jaw.

"I think I did," I say, dazed, smiling up at the ceiling when he laughs.

It takes a solid sixty seconds for the bliss to wear off and reality to slide back in—I just had sex with Eli.

I did my best to cling to now, but those little flashes of further and future and forever snuck in, revealing what my deepest, messiest self wants: Eli, in every era.

You can't have it, I remind myself.

Time will run out once everyone descends on Friday and we get swept up in the real reason we're here. Selfishly, I want to grip it tight, not let it go.

It's why I let Eli lift himself off me with just the briefest lingering touch, so I can start exposing myself to what I'll have to do soon enough. It's why, when he returns to bed after we both take our turns in the bathroom, I let my eyes drift over his naked body, so I can remember what it looks like when I no longer have access to it.

He climbs over me, his eyes warmly assessing. I still feel his hands everywhere, the tender spots where his fingers dug in. The ache between my legs is a lovely bloom.

When he reaches my face, his eyebrows drop. "Are you freaking out?"

"No." It's almost the truth.

He dips his chin, pinning me with a look.

"Okay, yes, but just a little." I pause, running my thumb along his collarbone. "We had sex."

His voice lowers. "We did."

"And it was—" My brain trips over a word big enough for it, but there isn't one. "Really good."

At this, he grins. "It was."

"Are *you* freaking out?"

"Yes." He pauses. Something intense shines in his eyes—a photo flash, there and gone—before his expression turns teasing. "But just a little."

"We *are* kind of stupid," I say.

"But we're doing it together. Teamwork, right?"

"The teamwork was related to saving Adam's wedding, not me begging for your dick, but I mean . . ."

Eli barks out a laugh that triggers mine. "I *like* it."

"Clearly I do, too."

I get what I want—a smirk, his eyes wandering over every piece of me he's wrecked. But that look turns thoughtful quickly.

I pat his pillow, affecting a lightness I don't feel. "Lie down with me."

After a brief hesitation, he does. In the dark, we stare at each other for a stretch of seconds, and I beg him wordlessly not to let the future or the past burst through the door.

His eyes drop to my mouth, trace over my cheeks, my nose, memorizing me or this moment or both.

"Do we need Nick Miller tonight?" he whispers finally.

I let out a relieved breath. "No pillow person necessary. He was a terrible chaperone."

Eli grins, one that leaves as tenderly as it came. "Then come here."

He opens his arms and I don't hesitate; right now I don't have to. I scoot over, sighing when he pulls me close, humming against his throat when he kisses my temple, his mouth lingering there in a firm press.

And exactly like that, I fall asleep.

Chapter Twenty-Two

"Should we review our checklist?" Aunt Julia asks a small group of Coopers, along with Eli and me, in the courtyard the next afternoon. She raises a questioning brow at me and I nod cheerfully, praying my cheeks aren't flaming.

It's just that word. *List.* Something that used to be a cornerstone to my sanity is now loaded with horny meaning. All I can think about is Eli's list of things he wants to do with me, numbered with the things he did *to* me last night and again this morning, when daylight was just a strip of paler blue along the velvet horizon.

I can feel his attention from several feet away. Even now, at nearly four p.m., it's like I'm slogging through honey, captured in the sweetness of what we did.

". . . the tent's all set up and our oak tree, Big Daddy, is strung with all its lights again," Julia's saying.

I join in on the celebratory applause, shaking myself. I need to get my head in the game, not think about the way I woke up to Eli's racing heart under my hand, how instead of climbing out of bed to pace the panic out, he turned to me. How he pulled me closer when he came down from it, his mouth hungry and grateful.

"Cal did a bang-up job on the arch for the ceremony," Julia continues. "Tomorrow we'll weather-proof the deck and make sure all the ticky-tacky stuff is ready for Friday when the kids arrive."

Unbidden, my gaze drifts sideways again, only to find Eli's already watching me.

Caught you, he mouths.

You were looking first, I mouth back. His lips curve up and the warmth in his eyes is a spark that heats my blood. It's only Cole's murmured "Eye fucking? In front of my mother?" that tears my attention away.

That, and the frisson of anxiety remembering Eli and I haven't checked everything off *our* list yet.

The conversation wraps up minutes later and the group disperses. Except for Cole, of course. He turns to me and Eli, hands in his pockets. "How're the vendor searches going?"

"We're still working on the DJ," I admit. It's such a huge component of Adam's happiness, and getting stuck with the Danny Diamonds of the world is the albatross around our necks.

"My friend is the lead singer in a band, and they're playing tonight at a bar downtown," Cole says. "I don't know if they're available, but I could shoot her a text."

I grimace. "Adam really wants a DJ."

Cole lifts a shoulder. "Beggars, choosers, etcetera."

"He's going to be disappointed if we can't find a DJ, don't you think?" I ask Eli. "A band can't properly capture the spirit of 'Blow the Whistle.'"

"Let's check them out just in case," he says, running a hand over his stubbled jaw. "I really don't want to have to crawl back to Danny."

"Have dinner while you're at it. We're done for the day anyway and there's a new Peruvian place right next door to the bar." Cole says this with a strange amount of earnestness, his attention on Eli. "It's super chill. The band goes on at ten, so you have time."

Some wordless conversation passes between them; finally, Eli shakes his head with a small, rueful smile. Cole grins triumphantly, then hitches a thumb over his shoulder. "I have to get back to work, but seriously, go. Have fun. Don't do anything I wouldn't do."

"Okay, well that's nothing," I call to his retreating back.

"Exactly!" he returns over his shoulder.

Eli turns to me. "You up for making a night of it?"

My heart dips at the way he's looking at me, like he's being careful with his hope. It wraps another vine around me.

I remember my lists: the one I'm sharing with him that's allowing us to keep doing what we're doing—and the one that reminds me why I can't let it go past that.

"Yeah," I say, forcing myself not to hold on too tight to the way he lights up. "Let's do it."

The Peruvian restaurant is very chill. It's also deeply romantic—moodily lit, all soft, warm lamps hanging over each table, candles flickering, bathing everything in golden light. Out on the patio where we're seated, a musician plucks at a Spanish guitar. Jasmine climbs a trellis behind her, sweetening the heavy air.

Eli orders a bottle of wine and we exchange a wordless toast, our eyes catching over the rim of our glasses. From there, the conversation meanders, an easy mix of reminiscing about and roasting Adam. I tease him about reviewing the menu online beforehand; he teases me for taking eighteen years to pick something. We have a robust argument over the latest season of a Netflix show Eli swears is overrated and I'm obsessed with. Halfway through the meal, we switch entrées, an old, unconscious habit.

I find him watching my mouth often, eyes glittering from the candlelight. A few times I look up to catch him with a different expression on his face. Something more private.

It's not a date, but it feels like one, and instead of spiraling about how it can't be, I stay firmly in the moment. I keep his wineglass full, watch *his* mouth when he licks it after a particularly delicious bite of food. Lean in as he meticulously folds a receipt into a paper ring while he waits for me to finish the dregs of my wine once the bill is paid.

I rest my chin in my hand, watching him. His fingers are beautiful—long and lean, capable of all kinds of magic.

"I can't believe you still make those."

He gives me an inscrutable look. "Why would I ever stop?" He sets it on the table between us, nodding at it with a boyish smile. "I mean, look at that thing. Perfect."

It is, and when we're done, I furtively swipe it. Something to remember tonight by when it's long gone.

I hate to leave our sexy cocoon, but there's work to be done, so we make our way next door. The bar Cole's friend is playing at is small, but the high, arched ceiling gives it the illusion of spaciousness. One side is taken up by a chic jade green bar, which is backlit by a golden wall of liquor. Otherwise it's dim and absolutely teeming with people standing at bar tables or trying to flag down bartenders. On the far side of the room, instruments are being set up on a small stage, an equally small dance floor in front of it.

Eli steps closer, his chest pressed to my back, resting a light hand on my stomach. His pinky finger brushes the strip of skin between my cropped black top and my silk skirt. "You want a drink?"

I melt into the touch, leaning back against him. He hums happily. "Just a Coke. I have to drive us home in a few hours."

"Okay." His mouth grazes my ear. "I'm going to— is that *Cole*?"

Immediately I put three inches of space between us, looking around. Sure enough, he's near the stage, head bent while a stunning Asian woman in a skintight black dress talks to him.

As if he feels the sudden, undeniable urge to say something inappropriate, he finds us in the crowd. Brightening, he waves in a *come over* gesture.

"God forbid we have some peace," Eli grumbles.

Laughing, I reach for his hand under the guise of leading him through the crowd. Our fingers tangle, his thumb brushing against my wrist.

"I was just telling Isla about you two," Cole says when we get to him, his eyes dropping like a heat-seeking missile to where we're connected. Eli's hand moves to the small of my back as Cole raises an eyebrow, though he doesn't comment. Instead, he turns to the woman at his side. "Isla, this is Georgia and Eli. They're in need of a band."

"Well, our best friends are," Eli corrects, taking Isla's proffered hand. "It's the last big thing we need to check off our list before their wedding on Saturday."

"I heard about their bad luck," she says. Her sympathetic smile is electric, her black hair a sleek curtain down her back. "Our Saturday gig fell through, so if you think we'd be a good fit after listening to the set, we're available."

I'm so distracted by the razor-sharp perfection of her winged liner that it takes me a second to respond. "That'd be incredibly lucky for us."

"Santos, time," a lanky white guy calls from behind the drum kit.

She turns to us, going up on tiptoes to plant a kiss on Cole's cheek. "Duty calls. We'll connect after the set?"

"That sounds great," I say, waving as she struts off.

Cole splits an assessing look between Eli and me. "How was dinner?"

"Very chill, as promised," I say.

"Didn't know you were going to be here tonight," Eli adds.

"Isla invited me and I thought, why the hell not?" He tilts his head, smirking. "Don't tell me you're not happy to see me, Mora."

"Thrilled," he deadpans. "I'm going to go grab drinks. You want something, too?"

"An old fashioned would be great."

Just then, a bass line starts up, shaking into my ribs. A cheer ripples through the crowd. Eli turns toward the bar, but Cole follows, curling a hand around his shoulder so he can shout something in his ear. I assume it's a change in drink order, but Eli immediately looks hassled, shaking his head. Cole gives him a *come on* look that Eli returns before mouthing what looks like *drop it*. Cole holds his hands up before pushing his way back to me. When our eyes meet, he rolls his.

"What was that?" I ask, leaning in to be heard over the intro of a Doja Cat cover.

"Nothing, apparently."

I frown. "Did you say something weird to him?"

"No, just too commonsensical."

"Between you and Eli, I guarantee he has more common sense."

His eyebrows twitch up. "You'd be surprised."

I side-eye him, wondering again what's going on between them. They always got along the summers we were together at Blue Yonder, but their dynamic this trip is a strange mix of ultra-familiar and mutually exasperated.

Cole doesn't seem inclined to enlighten me, though, and Eli keeps brushing it off. Still, I level a stern look at Cole. "Are you going to behave tonight?"

"I wake up every morning dedicated to *not* behaving," he says, a grin working its way back onto his face. "So, no, probably not."

"You really haven't changed at all."

I mean it as an admonishment but he just laughs, his attention sliding over my shoulder before he steps closer. "Wanna dance?"

He does a little two-step that's actually decent, turning in place before holding out his hand. He's utterly ridiculous, but I can't help the nostalgic soft spot that's burrowed somewhere (deep) in my heart, so I take his hand.

He keeps a respectable distance between us, leading me around the dance floor. It takes me the span of the Doja song to realize that Isla's band is *really* good. There are eight of them up there—Isla and another lead singer, a Black guy whose voice is goose bump–inducing, with a full band behind them.

I turn to Cole, eyes wide. He just laughs. "You're welcome."

We dance through the majority of a Miley cover, yelling the lyrics when Isla points the mic at us. Cole spins me in a dizzying circle that ends with me facing the bar and I search the crowd for Eli, heart racing, hoping he's making his way back to me. But he's leaning against the bar, hands empty. Our eyes meet, that latch thing it's always been. It's never faded, no matter how hard I tried to shut it out, and now I let it hook into me.

He raises an eyebrow, his gaze flicking past me to Cole, like, *you're seriously dancing with him?*

Jealous? I mouth, teasing. My heart skips a beat when he nods, his eyes flashing and a smokelike grin drifting across his mouth.

"Be careful."

I startle, looking back at Cole. "What?"

His expression is more serious than I thought him capable of. He leans in, placing a hand on my back. "Listen, I don't care what story you're selling Adam, but it's very clear to me that you're not just friends. I never believed you were when you spent summers here either."

"We're—"

"You're fucking in that cottage, at the very least," he interrupts, and my stomach spirals. "And at the very most—"

"I'm struggling to understand how the least *or* most of it is your business."

"It isn't," he says plainly. "But you're Adam's best friends, which means you're my friends, too, whether you claim me or not, so I'd be remiss if I didn't tell you that shit like this can get real sticky, real fast."

I balk. "How do *you* know?"

"Because I've been there, done that, caught the therapy bill, and me and my ex didn't even have a best friend in common. If either of you gets hurt, it could get rough. Not just for you and Eli, but for your other musketeer, too. That's all I'm saying." His mouth lifts wryly. "It could be fine. Great, even. It's what I'm hoping for. But I also hope you're being honest with each other. And I *really* hope that you're being careful with your feelings—and his."

I swallow hard. He's just pinpointed every fear I've had and nailed it to the wall. But I'm not going to let either of us get hurt. We *are* being honest with each other about what we're doing.

And I'm being careful.

"Solid advice, but I don't need it," I say stiffly.

His eyes narrow. "You're not messing with him, right?"

Heat flares in my chest. "Disrespectfully, fuck off, Cole."

He appraises me as the song ends, and there's a beat where the absence of the music becomes its own sound. My ears roar with it. Finally, a bastardy smile curls over his mouth. "I see."

I blank out my expression, looking back toward the stage. "I promise you don't."

But he's not done, because he never is. "Weddings are weird things. They have a way of bringing out the truth, don't you think?"

I can't help flashing back to Nick and Miriam's wedding last year, the way it felt like the first measurable tear in the rules Eli and I shared. Cole's voice is knowing, but he can't know about that. Even Eli doesn't know the truth of that night, which means it really is obvious how wrapped up I am.

Great.

"The only thing this wedding is bringing out is the end of Adam's anxiety," I say.

Cole hums, then laughs when his eyes slip over my shoulder. "Incoming."

I turn as Eli pushes his way through the crowd, drinks in hand. His gaze jumps from Cole's hand, still lying between my shoulder blades, to my face. His eyebrows pinch and he mouths, *you okay?* I school my expression, force away the remaining annoyance lingering there, and mouth back, *get over here.* A proprietary glint enters his eyes and something curls through me—that narcotic feeling of belonging.

"I think he wants you back," Cole murmurs conspiratorially. Louder, he says, "Come get your girl, Mora. I'll hold your beer."

Eli ignores him, presenting the glasses to me. I carefully pluck my Coke out, then take his beer so he can hand Cole the old fashioned.

Suddenly, a familiar, wall-shaking beat starts up. The crowd immediately loses it, shouting the opening lyrics to Too $hort's "Blow the Whistle."

I whirl on Cole, who's nonchalantly sipping his drink. "Did you do this?"

"Have to sell the product," he says with a shrug, but he can't hide his small, proud grin.

Eli laughs incredulously. "Are you for real?"

"Cole," I venture as Eli pulls my phone out of my purse so he can take video, "are you . . . a sweetheart?"

He scoffs. "Okay, don't be disgusting. Are you sold or not?"

I look up at Eli, triumph burning in my chest when he nods, grinning. "I'll text the video to the happy couple for final approval, but it looks like we can check this off the list."

"Excellent. I'm going to make myself scarce until their set ends, but congrats on your final accomplishment." Cole nods his chin at us. "Don't tell Adam, but I think this wedding is going to be even better than the first attempt. Second time's a charm, right?"

And then, with a wink, he strolls away.

Chapter Twenty-Three

"Tonight was good, huh?"

Eli rarely drinks, anxiety aggravator that it is, but right now he's adorably tipsy and rosy-cheeked as we make our way down the path to our cottage, hands clasped, gravel crunching beneath our shoes.

"It was very good," I agree, still enveloped in the easy intimacy we shared all night: at dinner and on the dance floor after Cole left us, using the dense, undulating crowd as an excuse to dance impossibly close, and then on the quiet drive home when Eli leaned his head back, eyes closed, running his hand up and down my thigh in a soothing circuit.

Really, the only hiccup in the night was that weird interlude with Cole.

"Adam seemed stoked about the band," Eli continues.

I make an assenting noise. If the HOLY SHIT YES text I got after sending the video is any indication, we can give ourselves—and Cole—a big pat on the back.

Things are starting to go right, and not a minute too soon. Adam and Grace will be here in less than forty-eight hours.

My fingers tighten around Eli's reflexively at the reminder of our time limit.

The grounds around us are silent, the courtyard we're passing through cloaked in darkness. I can make out the shape of the wedding venue—the tent for the reception, the freshly finished deck, and the oak tree that will drape its shade over Adam and Grace on Saturday. It all looks like a promise. It's not the picture they painted when they planned their wedding the first time, but the one that's developing now looks beautiful in my imagination. I just hope they agree.

"They *are* way better than a DJ, right?" I ask. "I'm not just talking myself into it?"

Eli stops, tugging on my hand so that I'll turn to him. I do without hesitation, sinking against his body when his hand shifts to the small of my back.

"That band is a hundred times better than any DJ we could've found on such short notice," he says, pushing a loose strand of hair behind my ear. "It's probably ten times better than what we could've found on long notice. We owe Cole for this one, too, but it's time to admit that Geli is killing it."

"I'm . . . sorry." I blink. "Did you just mash our names together?"

He grins. "I did."

"Wow, that's—"

He presses a finger to my lips. "I'm going to be embarrassed about it tomorrow, but please let me get away with it for now."

It takes everything inside me not to laugh. "Okay."

"Adam's face is going to melt off on Saturday. He's going to wonder why he ever wanted a DJ in the first place." I can see the pleasure in his eyes, the need to prove himself turning into something triumphant. My heart expands; this Eli is a far cry from the one who sat in my car last week. "He's going to be indebted to us for the rest of his life."

I close my eyes and imagine that. Not him owing us, but knowing I've grown roots deep enough to stick for that long.

When I open my eyes, Eli's looking down at me, his face illuminated by the moonlight. Kissed by it, in all the places I want my mouth.

"You're the best best woman, Georgia," he says with a tenderness that takes the shape of adoration. Something intensified by alcohol, no doubt. It goes to my head like champagne all the same. "And I'm turning into a not-terrible best man."

"Drunk Eli gives himself a lot more credit than sober Eli, but not enough. You've been the best best man this week."

He runs his hand up and down my back, pleasure and amusement warring on his face. "I'm buzzed, not drunk. Drunk Eli would've forgotten that you gave Cole the first dance instead of me. Buzzed Eli remembers *very* clearly."

"I gave him the first three if we're being accurate." Eli spears me with a look so unimpressed that I laugh. "Do I need to remind you that you got every dance after that?"

"No," he says, a rough purr entering his voice. "You were grinding your ass into me for the better part of two hours. It's already permanently in my mental reel."

I give him a slinky smile. "See? And anyway, Cole talked about you the whole time, so you might as well have been there."

His hand stills. "He talked about *me*?"

"Well, you and me," I amend. "Turns out he's onto us."

"Onto us."

"He knows we're . . ." I struggle to find a word that isn't too big or small for what this is, the Goldilocks of It's Complicated, before landing on a very underwhelming, "Doing things."

He hums, his fingers starting to play up my spine. "What did he say?"

The decision is split-second: I won't divulge it all. Doing so would go against the agreement Eli and I made to keep things simple this week. Everything Cole laid out was about future things, not what we're doing right now, and none of that is going to come to pass.

I clear my throat. "Basically that. He's onto us. Specifically, he mentioned the unsavory things he thinks we're doing in the cottage—"

At this, Eli's expression clears. His grin is equal amounts lopsided and heated as his hand wanders down to palm my ass. "I think they're very savory."

"Easy, tiger," I laugh as he dips his mouth down my jaw, placing sweet, open-mouthed kisses there. "You don't seem surprised that he knows. Or concerned, for that matter."

After a beat, he says, voice muffled, "I'm not concerned."

"Do you think he's going to say something to Adam?"

"No." The word is a brush against my throat. "He can keep it to himself. And more importantly, he knows it's not his business."

"That's what I told him, but it didn't stop him from saying something anyway."

"It's probably my fault. Maybe I'm being extremely obvious about it," he murmurs. "Maybe he's been catching me staring at you when you're not looking, thinking about all the unchecked things on our list."

I move gratefully with the subject shift. I don't want to think about complicated past or future things. I want to be here, sinking into the simplicity of wanting each other then and wanting it again now. Acting on that, instead of thinking about all the hurt that happened between it.

"Still pretty long, huh?"

"You have no idea." His body sways into mine and he catches me around the waist, curving a hand around my neck. His thumb makes a soft path along my jaw as he says, quieter now, "This is on the list."

"What is?"

"Kissing you right here. I always loved being outside with you at night in the summer. You looked so beautiful that it made my heart ache." His voice drops. "And so happy. I loved seeing you like that."

There's an ache in his voice that becomes a twin feeling in my chest. "Well, here we are again."

"Yeah." The word is barely a sound, small and grateful. Eli pulls my hand to his chest, right over his pounding heart. "Will you give me your mouth now?"

It's so easy to say yes. He lets out a bare groan as soon as our lips touch, another one, hungrier now, when I give him my tongue, my taste, those quiet sounds that seem to wind his need so tight. He curls over me, hand still cradling my face, gentle despite the way our kiss turns deep and unrestrained.

"Fuck, the way I've wanted you," he breathes against my mouth. "I don't know how anyone can look at me and not see it."

He says something else, into my skin the way he did the other night. All I hear is the *you*, and I repeat it in my head in a rhythm that matches the beat of his heart: wild and fast, over and over and over again.

Eventually, his mouth turns patient. He gives me a tender kiss on my lips, in the middle and then at each corner. Up along my cheekbone, to the outer corner of my eye, my temple. For a handful of seconds he stays there, a kiss that doesn't end, and I close my eyes, holding on to him.

Right now *just keep doing what you're doing* feels like falling, and it makes me grip him tighter. I can't hit the ground.

"C'mon," he says finally. He puts his hand over mine, still pressed to his heart. "Let's go home."

I wake up to an empty bed. When I check my phone, there are a handful of texts that my eyes are too bleary to read, so I toss it aside after checking the time—nearly ten, dear god—and drag my tired body out of the bedroom.

Eli is sitting on the loveseat, shirtless, pulling absently at his necklace while he scrolls his phone. He looks up when I walk in, setting it on the table.

"There she is," he says, giving me a lengthy once-over.

He's clearly cataloging the signs of the way he wrecked me last night once he'd fully sobered up—the whisker burn he left on my thighs, the disaster he made of my hair when he turned me onto my stomach and tangled his fingers into it, pushed into me with hard, slow strokes while he murmured, "This is what you needed, isn't it?" He kept that pace for so long, telling me he could be so patient when he wanted to, he could wait forever for me, until I was a begging mess, whispering, "please," so ready to fall apart for him. Only then did he push me over the edge, groaning, "It's what I need, too. All the time."

"Here I am, in all my glory," I croak out.

The room is small enough that with just a few steps I'm close enough to reach, and Eli wastes no time reeling me between the V of his legs, gazing up at me. "You're beautiful."

And then he wraps his arms around my waist, resting his cheek against my stomach; his exhale takes the shape of relief. It's quietly intimate, so familiar, and for a second I can't breathe. I'm preemptively jealous of the Georgia who gets this now.

I curl over him, running my fingers through his hair, remembering how I wished for him on my birthday all those years ago. Remembering how it came true, and the bliss and mess that came after it. I know better than to wish for anything now, but it curls like smoke from a birthday candle anyway, still warm from the fire that burned it.

"Are you hungover?" I ask.

His breath puffs through my sleep shirt. "Not in the pounding headache way."

It takes me a second to get it. "In the racing thoughts way."

"Yeah. Probably why I ended up staring at my bank account this morning, and then switched over to LinkedIn."

"Oh." My heart dips and I start to step away, but his hold tightens stubbornly. "Anything new on the job front?"

"I got an email from my recruiter about that strategy role. They want me to come in a week from Monday to meet with the wider team. Should be a lock." His tone is a curious mix of relieved and weary.

"That's good, right?"

He groans, tilting his head back to look at me. "It is, but . . . I don't know. I vacillate between feeling so fucking burned-out that I can't imagine working right now and having panic attacks because it's been almost two months since I got a paycheck and I'm paying Amari out of pocket, among other things. Going to the client side means better hours, which is good because I don't want to work eighty hours a week anymore, but it's also less pay. And what if this doesn't work out and I'm still unemployed in another month?"

I can feel his body shaking, see the hard beat of his pulse in his neck. It reverberates through me, a physical manifestation of my shock at his confession: *I don't want to work eighty hours a week.* That admission alone is something I never thought I'd hear. Eli works so hard because he thinks he *has* to.

But then I hear the rest. How, even if it looks different, he still needs it. That anxiety is so deeply ingrained that he can't fathom taking real time off to repair the way his previous job broke him.

"Do you still have some savings?" I ask. *Some* is probably an understatement; Eli is meticulous with his money. After we broke up, he moved into a place with a friend on the Lower East Side, even though he could've afforded something on his own.

"I helped my dad with his down payment and had to use a chunk of it the past couple months, but yeah."

I consider my next words carefully. I told him he should quit, just once, after watching him work until one in the morning seven days straight. He was so busy he was skipping meals, so tired he fell asleep fully clothed. I said it on a Friday morning, ten months into our time in New York, after months of watching the way he'd transformed from someone familiar enough to love into just enough of a stranger for me to silently pull away from.

"I need to stay until I make associate. Another year, maybe a little longer," he said, looping his tie end through the knot at his throat, his exhausted eyes trained on his reflection in the mirror. He's always been his dad's twin, and I wondered if that's who he was seeing right then, some version of his dad who wasn't struggling, divorced, and alone. "Then I'll get something better."

Better, he said, but not *less soul-destroying*.

"What if you took a break?" I venture now. "A real one?"

He pulls back, running a hand through his hair. "Amari broached the same idea, but . . . this LA job seems fine. Better than what I was doing before, and I can bounce off of it if it doesn't work out."

It's a weak echo of what he said long ago, but I hear it anyway, and it presses against that old bruise.

"Well. Wherever you end up, I hope they treat you better than Luce did," I say.

His expression relaxes. "I won't accept anything less, I promise," he says. "I wish I could take a break, but this is a fair medium."

"All right."

He must hear the doubt in my voice. "I'm better since I started therapy, but that fear of not having stability is hard to shake."

His tone is imploring, a request for me to understand, and I do, even if it hurts.

"As childhood wounds often are," I murmur.

A wordless understanding passes between us. We've both fallen victim to it. God knows it shadowed all the corners of our relationship.

I shift backward, feeling more bare than I did when he got me naked last night. He clocks it, scoots to the edge of the love-seat. His pleading expression turns determined and he hooks his hands around my thighs. "Georgia—"

It's my turn to give him a pleading look. *No reckonings here. It's not what we agreed to.*

His mouth straightens as he tows me between his legs, propping his chin on my stomach. After a beat, he sighs. "Thanks for taking care of me last night. No hint of a headache."

I let out a grateful breath. "Thank Advil and H_2O, not me."

Instead of laughing, he gazes up at me. "You're always taking care of other people. Who's taking care of you?"

The question comes out of nowhere, hits me somewhere deep, even with the tender way he asks it. Maybe because of it.

"Oh, you know, good ol' me," I say in a tone two hundred miles away from casual.

He looks wrecked at that, and I feel the impact in my chest. "I thought I was. Before, I mean."

God, he's really hell-bent on dredging shit up this morning. I want to side-step it, but I can hear his self-censure and I find myself unable to deny him a response. He thought bringing me to New York was the start of something forever-shaped, that those thankless hours he worked were for us. All he could see was that he was building something stable for us to set our foundation on.

But I never wanted the foundation. I just wanted him.

"I know you did," I say, throat thick.

"Would you ever ask me to take care of you?" he asks quietly. "Right now, if you needed something, would you say it? Even if it's just a cup of coffee or breakfast, I'll do it for you."

There's so much I need, but it's tangled—old things and new, future ones that I can't give him. I can only give him right now.

"I do need something."

"Tell me."

I climb onto his lap. There's a flash of emotion in his eyes, something stormy, but when I trace his mouth with my fingertip, he melts under my touch.

"You."

It's too much and a crumb, and I'm gratified when he accepts it without digging deeper. He takes the slide of my tongue into his mouth with a pained sigh, holds on to me tight while he grows hard beneath me.

"Guess that's a no to coffee," he groans after a minute.

"Your coffee sucks anyway."

He huffs out a laugh. I love the way his happiness tastes; my favorite emotion, the easiest one.

Things have veered wildly off course with my shirt around my neck and my hand down Eli's boxer briefs when there's a knock on the door.

Eli rips his mouth from mine, his expression murderous. "I swear to fucking god, if that's Cole—"

But that's not the voice that drifts through the door. "Open the door, my elusive grapevine, and let your best friend in."

It's Jamie, a full day early.

Chapter Twenty-Four

"Oh my god."

Oh *my god*, I just said that out loud. *Loudly*. Eli shoots me an *are you serious?* look, pressing his hand over my mouth.

"Georgia?" Jamie calls. "Are you okay?"

I lean back, injecting my voice with the delight I would genuinely feel if I didn't currently have a hand around my ex-boyfriend's dick. "Yes! I'm great! I'm naked!"

"What are you doing?" Eli whispers, eyes wide.

"Uh, I—I just got out of the shower." I nearly tip backward scrambling off Eli's lap. "I'm putting on a shirt. I'll be right there!"

"Okay," Jamie says, dragging out the word.

"Get up," I hiss at Eli, sprawl-kneed on the couch, and gesture to his very obvious erection. "You have to get yourself together before I answer the door."

"You can't answer the door right now," he whispers back incredulously.

"I have to! Jamie's going to know something's up."

He stands, catching me around the waist. "Something *is* up. I'm hard from a hand job you were giving me ten seconds ago and you're wearing my Denver Nuggets shirt, which very clearly displays the beard burn on your thighs from riding my face last night."

My brain is busy tripping over forty different thoughts, so what comes out of my mouth is a defensive, "She won't know the *position*."

Eli stares at me, then grins. "I forgot how bad you are under this specific kind of pressure."

I shoot him an incendiary glare. This isn't the time to bring up when his college roommates came home early and found us on the couch, and I blurted out that Eli was inspecting a potentially cancerous mole on my boob.

Jamie knocks again. "Seriously, are you okay?"

I turn wide, pleading eyes on Eli. "What do I do?"

His eyes bounce back and forth between mine. "If you don't want her to know, I can climb out a window."

"Oh god, that's so dramatic." I bend over, resting my hands on my knees with a groan. We're trapped. "It won't matter anyway. She'll know."

He gives me a bitten-off grin. "Even if I climb out the window?"

"Yes," I whisper. "She's gonna know."

"How's she gonna know?"

"Because she knows *me*." I wave a panicked hand over my face. "She's going to read it all over this and my face-riding thighs!"

"I thought you said she wouldn't know the position."

"*Eli*."

His laugh is nearly soundless. "It's fine, I'll go. We'll figure something out when we're not panicking."

I stop him with a hand to his chest, my mind racing.

The truth is, Jamie already knows more about my history with Eli than anyone. She'll be shocked it happened, but it won't cause the ripple effects it would if it were Adam at the door. If anything, her sudden presence feels like a lifeline. Maybe I can try to untangle my complicated thoughts with someone other than myself.

"No," I say. "I can handle it now. I'd rather be honest than have you fall out a window."

Warmth passes through his expression, and after a beat, he pushes his shorts down his hips. "Take these. I'll go get dressed and—"

"Good idea." I grab his shorts, yanking them on. "Let me take care of it so we can prevent a jump scare."

"I was going to say I'll be back in a second. You're not doing this alone."

"I can," I insist.

"You're *not*," he insists back, and my heart squeezes. He pushes at my hip. "Go. I'll be right there."

I start to make my way to the front door, but then his hand is around my wrist with a startled "*Wait.*" When I turn, there's a flash of fear in his eyes before it turns searching.

"Our agreement . . ." He trails off and at first I don't understand. "The terms were until everyone shows up."

It hits me then, that with Jamie here unannounced and a day early, we're no longer alone. Everything could end right now. I'm unprepared for how that feels, like getting hit in the chest and having the air pulled all the way out of my lungs.

"I—" I can practically hear Jamie breathing on the other side of the door. My throat tightens with panic and an absolute, unwavering unwillingness to let Eli go just yet. "I'm not . . ."

"I'm not ready," he says. My heart dive-bombs into his hands.

"We could extend the terms," I say quickly, glancing at the door. "Until the wedding's over. We just have to be chill about it. We can't be a distraction."

Eli stares at me, his exhaled "yes" kissing my cheek.

My heart takes off. "Yes?"

"I do *not* remember it taking you this long to put clothes on when we lived together," Jamie calls.

I turn back to Eli, and I know I look wild, probably desperate, but I am. I don't want our time to be up. I know what's on the other side and can't face it yet.

"I've never been good at stopping when it comes to you," he whispers, his eyes moving over my face, a tiny pinch between his brows. He pushes at my hip again. "So, yes. Go."

It takes me a few deep breaths after he's disappeared into the bedroom to get myself together. I'm shaky with relief and left-over adrenaline and the knowledge that I have Eli for a little bit longer. And when I finally make my way to the door and open it to find my best friend there, the relief increases tenfold.

Jamie's contemplative look turns to sunshine as she leaps into my arms. "Helloooo, gorgeous."

"Hi," I say into her hair. "What's with the surprise visit? I thought you were coming up tomorrow."

"Didn't you get my texts? I sent a few this morning letting you know I was on my way."

I think back to my bleary notifications and bite back a groan. "Nope, missed those."

"Oh, I—" Her eyes slip past me. "Oh my god."

There's no need to look at what's snagged her attention, but I do anyway, simply because my eyes love to trace the shape of Eli. He's walking through the living room, a bashful but resolved tilt to his mouth.

I clear my throat, facing my best friend, who is now staring loudly at me. "That's the sentiment of the day."

"Morning, James." Eli's hand finds my lower back, fingers

notching against my spine. It's a gesture that feels so easy, like breathing. God, I'll miss it.

"Well, I guess that answers the question of whether you're okay," Jamie says, raising an eyebrow. "But I have about a million more."

"How many times?" she screeches.

"Four." I recalculate. "Wait, no. Five."

"Since *when*?"

I cover my face, groaning. "Tuesday."

We're sitting on the patio of a strip mall café nestled between a Jamba and a nail salon, downing iced lattes the size of our forearms. After a quick conversation with Eli, we left him at Blue Yonder so I could tell Jamie the real stuff: about Eli's behavior the past six days, how well we've been working together, how we slowly circled each other until finally giving in, and the terms of our agreement. I also told her about Eli's job situation, information that felt acceptable to divulge. She's my Person, not Eli's, and can keep a secret. Plus, it lends important context to the conversation.

Namely, that there's an end date. I sandwiched that in before all the sex confessions, though, a detail she's thankfully fully distracted by.

"Five times in two days," Jamie marvels. "You've had time to plan the wedding in between all that banging?"

At the next table, an older woman peeks over the top of her Beverly Jenkins book.

I kick Jamie in the ankle. "Yes, loudmouth. It's going to be perfect."

She grins mischievously, then leans forward in her seat, her expression straightening. "And it's not just sex. There are feelings."

My sigh is despairing. "Yes."

"First of all, that's to be expected, so stop acting like you've committed a crime. You two have history a mile long. Second of all, you're not exactly giving me late-breaking news. I always knew that there was still something between you two."

I frown. "What do you mean?"

"The things you care about most are what you talk about least." Her observation is quiet but hits hard. "And you never talk about him. Not before today, anyway."

It's impossible to argue against that, so I don't even try.

"Let's circle back to what happens after the wedding is over," she says, crossing her arms.

So much for the distraction. "When it ends, you mean."

"Right, when it ends. Tell me why it should."

I give her a look. "You know why it should."

She gives me one back. "Humor me."

"Well," I draw out, "beyond the obvious reasons of not wanting to get my heart obliterated again if it doesn't work out—again—or worrying about the impact to our friendship with Adam if we try and it goes to shit"—I raise an eyebrow—"ag—"

She rolls her eyes with a smile. "Again, yes, I see the pattern."

"He's leaving for LA on Sunday," I continue. *And then maybe I'll be making my way up to the top of the West Coast. Eight hundred miles from you.*

There's too much going on already to drop that news now. But it's strange to recognize that if we were still living together, Jamie would already know about Seattle. She would've seen it on my face as soon as I walked in the door. She would've brainstormed with me, scrolled through LinkedIn by my side. Maybe she'd already have tickets for some future visit.

I push that thought aside. "The point is, I'm not looking to repeat history with the same outcome."

"You said he was acting different, though," she says, swirling the ice in her cup.

"Yeah," I admit. "He's been amazing up here."

Actually, he's been exactly what I needed and never would've asked for. I wanted him out of my way at first, but now I'm grateful he refused, that he fought for the teamwork I now don't know how I'll live without. Because I *will* have to live without it.

"This week is a bubble with an end date, Jamie. He needs a job, and he's clearly going to do whatever he needs to in order to make LA happen." I squint up at the sky. It's blue, endless. So pretty it hurts. "He's changed, I can see it. I mean, god, he quit the job that was his entire life and he's in *therapy*. But that part of him that hurt me before . . ." My gaze rebounds to my hands clenched in my lap. "It's still there. I get *why* it is, but I can't put myself in the same position."

"And that's okay," Jamie says. "God knows it takes courage to give your heart to someone once, never mind again after they've broken it. You don't owe him a do-over." She tilts her head. "What about that reckoning you said he wanted, though?"

"Ugh." I mentioned it in a drive-by; I should've known she'd latch on to it.

Jamie cups a hand around my knee, her voice quiet. "Why don't *you* want that, too? A conversation just to get everything out in the open once and for all so you have some closure, at the very least?"

My throat grows too tight to speak. I don't want it because reckonings never do any good. I have solid evidence of that: how

I overheard my dad on the phone once, mentioning that he and my mom had had so many angry conversations in the six months before she left, talking in circles about how to make things better. How it still makes me question sometimes if he wishes he'd been the one to walk away, even though I know he loves me, that I made his life as easy as I could.

How Eli's parents had arguments that were endlessly rehashed, but never led to anywhere but the end.

How, even if Eli and I had talked ourselves hoarse when we lived together, even if I had begged him every night to take better care of himself, of me, he would've chosen his job. How I would've had to hear that out loud instead of living it silently. It wouldn't have made things better. It would've hurt *more*.

Jamie's fingers tighten around my leg, holding me in place. "What you've been doing the past five years hasn't brought you any peace, but six days together has pushed you two into some other space. What if what Eli wants does, too?"

"No," I say thickly. "It'll ruin everything."

"What if it doesn't?" she presses. "What if you get some answers that I *know* you've been craving?"

His job. Why he quit. Why I wasn't enough to make that same decision for.

Fear crawls up my throat. "I don't want to feel the bad things anymore, Jamie, and talking about everything we did wrong will hurt and be pointless. I don't need closure, I need to move forward, and I think when this is over we can be friends. I don't want to make things unnecessarily messy."

"And you probably didn't when you were together, but it did anyway, didn't it?" She lets that sink in before her tone softens. "It's not about not being messy, it's about being honest with your mess."

Yeah, that's rarely worked in my favor.

I don't have to say it. Jamie reads it all over my face and sighs. "Listen, I came up here because it seemed like you needed me, and I knew you wouldn't ask. But it's also because Blake and I are at each other's throats right now."

"*What?*" My eyes run over her face, looking for signs of misery, but she grins widely instead.

"Oh, yeah. She's an unholy disaster with her upcoming trial, and our financial planning meeting? Comically bad. We have such different ideas about money. I love her more than anything, but she's so stubbornly set in her ways and my tornado ass moving in with her upended all her little systems and processes."

"Well, I love your tornado ass."

"Don't worry, she loves my tornado ass, too. She's just a Capricorn." Jamie dips her chin, dark eyes pinning me in place. "Relationships are messy, but that's how you know they're real. Blake and I have shown each other every ugly piece of ourselves and she still loves me. She loves me more for it, in fact. Sometimes you have to cut yourself open, Georgia, and you hold yourself *so* tightly."

"I have to." I hate the way my voice breaks.

"You think so, and I understand it," she says. "You were shown that you weren't allowed to need things that inconvenienced people, and you learned to make yourself smaller. But why can everyone else be messy and you can't?"

I look at the blurred shape of her, blinking as a tear rolls down my cheek. "Because then I'm alone."

Jamie's hand envelops mine. Her skin is warm, the squeeze of her fingers the only thing keeping me from spiraling away.

"I know you're scared. I mean, fuck if that's not the human

experience," she says quietly. "But you deserve to let yourself feel whatever you need to. You can be messy. A disaster, if you need to. The people who love you will accept every single piece of it, I *promise* you."

I think about how hungry Eli's seemed for that this week, and I know it's real, that he wants it. But it's also just right now. We're cocooned in timelessness here, some belonging we left behind, and that'll end. I don't want to be left with nothing when it's over.

"I'll think about it," I tell her, focusing on a toddler running by on shaky legs. He doesn't even cry when he falls.

Jamie's assessing gaze is heavy on me. She leans forward, then brushes her fingers along my wet cheeks, cleaning up the mess. "I love you, Georgia, you silly girl."

"I love you, too," I say around my tight throat. I can't talk about this anymore. "God, how long's it been since we've had a marathon talk like that?"

She grins, one soft with remembering. "We used to have them on that little gray couch of ours all the time. I'd braid your hair and tell you about my latest terrible date, since you never had any."

"I never had any terrible dates?" I echo dubiously.

"You never had any dates, period." Her mouth purses in mock confusion. "Hmm, wonder why."

I pinch the back of her arm where it's most tender, and she lets out a laughing yelp. "I dated Julian."

"Oh, *one* guy in five years and it was Trader Joe's Beef Jerky Boy. What a record."

I roll my eyes. She was in the checkout line with me when I met Julian, who did have an ungodly amount of beef jerky in his basket. He never graduated to first-name status with her.

Jamie lets out a honking laugh. "Remember how we'd watch movies that would make us cry afterward? Usually because you didn't want me to cry alone?"

"*Little Women*," I sigh.

"God, *please*," she wails.

Our laughter twines, then fades away with the ease that's kept us bound to each other for five years. She rests her head on my shoulder, threading her arm through mine.

I want to tell her that missing her hurts, that I wish we had more time together. That I'll need her more than ever if I go to Seattle, even though it's going to be fifty times the distance between Oakland and San Francisco, a span we already can't seem to cross with regularity. But like all my most important words, they get stuck in my throat.

But then my eye catches on the storefront down the way and every troubled thought in my head disappears. It's a party supply store, and the window display shows an elaborate pink bachelorette party setup: streamers, a holographic banner, and an abundance of penis-shaped paraphernalia.

I straighten. "Jamie."

"Hmm?"

"Can we go to that store?"

She twists in her seat, squinting. "Party Depot? Why do we need to go there?"

An idea is forming so quickly that it makes my body feel like it's tipping over the peak of a roller coaster: dizzy and breathless, heart high in my chest, holding on for dear life.

Maybe I can't give myself a do-over with Eli, but I can give him one of his own.

Chapter Twenty-Five

I'm nearly finished taping silver streamers to the cottage living room wall the next night when I realize maybe I've overdone it.

Over the streamers, there's a balloon banner that says BACH THAT ASS UP, which Jamie and I almost peed our pants laughing over. The kitchen island is littered with top-shelf liquor, non-alcoholic drinks, and snacks, among them some of Eli's airport favorites. My phone is connected to the Bose wireless speaker Cole let me borrow, and I'm streaming one of Adam's playlists. I even got a disco light.

Adam's redone bachelor party is going to be all the things it was the first time in Tahoe, but better, because this time Eli will be here.

My heart dips at the thought of him. I stayed with Jamie at the hotel last night, partly because we never get sleepovers any-more and partly because the thought of sleeping without Eli felt strange. A dangerous feeling. In forty-eight hours, we'll both be gone.

The reality of all that was too much to think about, so I simply didn't.

I couldn't fully shake off my longing for him, though, so I let him follow me to the cottage after dinner under the guise of

helping me pack up my things since we're moving over to the hotel tonight, too. I swept up the paper rings he's made over the last
few days, stuffed them into my bag just before he came out of the
bedroom with my suitcase. I let him wrap his arms around my
waist and told him he could text or call me if he woke up panicky,
no matter the time. He said softly, "That's new," and I nodded,
thinking of the rings in my bag and his body against mine and the
bachelor party supplies in my trunk. Thinking about our list and
this whole week, how old and new and scary and thrilling it's felt,
how simultaneously borrowed and ours.

I let him press me against the counter and cover my mouth
with his, trying to squash thoughts of the future. He held me still
with his thumb notched against my chin so he could come back
to me over and over, stretching time so thin that while his mouth
was on mine, it felt like forever. But then time came back to us
when he pulled away with a wrecked sound and a grumbling, "We
have to go right now or we never will."

When we got back to the Big House and Jamie saw how undone we were, she laughed. "You're going to have to fake it if you
don't want Adam seeing right through you tomorrow."

Eli and I exchanged a look, and he scratched at his jaw wryly.
"Yeah. I think we can do that."

And when Adam and Grace descended on Blue Yonder this
morning at the same time Jamie and I pulled up, that's exactly
what we did. We traded casual *heys* and *hellos*, made eye contact
that was long enough to look normal, but not so lengthy it clicked
like a lock. We orbited one another while the chaos of the day
pulled us together and then pushed us apart like a tide: the pull
when we showed Adam and Grace how Blue Yonder had transformed, the push when I stepped away to double-confirm the
venue address with the vendors for Aunt Julia and Eli disappeared

for his therapy appointment. The pull again when he asked me if I wanted more wine at the rehearsal dinner. We went with it, like we always have.

But underneath it was the knowledge of what we've done this week, the twining of our old and new, and so all day I saw the cracks in his faking, felt them in my own. There was the slight hitch in his breath at the press of our shoulders when he poured my wine, the way I caught him staring at me during the rehearsal when no one else was looking. The ache I've felt all day wanting to be with him.

Just a little longer, I think, straightening a stubborn streamer.

But first, this party. I kept it a secret from Adam and Eli, snuck away from dinner early so I could set up, and told Jamie I'd text her when I was done so she could bring everyone over. Now, with a steadying breath, I shoot off a message: Ready.

I step back, taking everything in with a racing heart while my memory flashes to Eli's devastated expression in the car last Thursday when he talked about missing the bachelor party and his abysmal best man record. To Monday night after he told me he'd quit his job, when he called the party the catalyst for his decision. I know how much this will mean to him, and he'll know I know. I want to say I'm doing all of this for him because he's my friend, and he is, I am.

But there's a helium-like feeling that constantly presses at my ribs when he's around and when he's not. It's not as simple as friendship. It never was, and maybe he'll see that.

A cacophony of noise rattles the steps, matching the sudden thunder in my pulse. Cursing under my breath, I wipe my sweating palms down the front of my magenta eyelet dress.

I jump when the door flies open, then paste a smile on my face. "Happy bachelor party!"

Everyone files in, *oohing* and *ahhing* as they make a beeline for the liquor. I smile at the groomsmen, the bridesmaids, Cole and then Grace, who apologizes for crying once she sees what's happening. Blake steps in with Jamie, who smacks a loud kiss on my cheek and whispers, "He has no idea. You're going to flatten him." She doesn't mean Adam.

He and Eli come in last. They're nearly side by side, broad-shouldered with lines bracketing their mouths and the corners of their eyes. They're the boys I ran around every inch of this property with, now all grown up, and the nostalgia of it nearly knocks me over.

I measure Adam's expression first—confusion, then realization, his eyes meeting mine as his mouth falls open—then look at Eli.

He's staring at me. His face is totally blank at first, but then I see it—the way his eyes start to glisten, the shake of his hand as he rubs his mouth. The sweep of his lashes as he looks down, turns to Adam, and then pulls him in for a hug.

Everyone is setting up shots and singing to Mac Dre as I hear Adam say, "It's good, buddy. I didn't ditch you when you broke my PlayStation, right?" Eli murmurs something and Adam laughs, rubbing his back. "Stop pinning it on Pop-Tart, that poor dog's dead and can't defend himself." And then quieter, barely over the music, "Stop beating yourself up over it. I love you, you're here. That's all I need."

And I think, *this is what love is.* What I'm looking at, what I'm feeling, what's happening here this weekend. What I crave in every corner of my bones, and what I'm so scared of getting, because so often I lose it.

Eli runs a hand over his face, turning to close the door while he wrangles his emotions. It makes mine riot inside of me. I wish everyone would leave so I could wrap myself around him. We faked it for five years, but after twelve hours, I'm over it.

Adam approaches, a huge smile on his face, reminding me why our discretion and old fake rules are necessary. He's getting married tomorrow, a day he told me needs to be perfect after the litany of disasters. A day I want to be simple, undiluted joy for all of us. He never needs to know that Eli and I were . . . whatever we are right now.

I hand him the BACH THAT ASS UP sash. "Happy bachelor party. Again."

"You knew he needed this," he says, and a recognition that makes my nerves dance passes over his face. But then he blinks and it's gone as he pulls me into a crushing hug. "No one deserves you. You know that?"

I laugh around the lump in my throat. "Yeah. Keep me anyway."

"Duh." When he pulls back, the tender moment is over; he's shifted into party mode. "Want a shot?"

"Of Pellegrino, yes."

"Amateur." He squeezes my shoulder as he pushes past me, the faker. He'll take one shot for posterity and then switch to water.

I know Eli's there before I turn to confirm it, but it still startles me, the loom of him. How gorgeous he looks, red-eyed and dis-oriented.

"Oh. Hello," I say brilliantly.

"Hey." He swallows once, and then again. "I can't believe you did this."

I press my fingers to the base of my throat so I won't touch him, and his gaze drops there. "You deserved a do-over."

The tension pulls between us, tight and unbearable. I want to wallow in it, snap it in half with my mouth on his.

"I can't say what I really want to," Eli says hoarsely. "So right now I'm going to say thank you and hug you, because if I don't get my hands on you in some way I'm going to fucking lose it."

I get out a relieved, whooshing, "*Yesokay*" before he pulls me close. One hand curls around my shoulder to anchor me to him, the other wrapping around my back, his fingers digging in so hard it's pleasure-pain. He breathes out against my neck, not quite a sigh, almost a groan.

"So, hey," a voice says in my ear after a lingering moment. I wrench back to find Jamie standing there with a too-wide grin on her face. "The pelvis-to-pelvis-hug situation can only go on for a few seconds if you're going to pull this off. I'm just saying."

My cheeks erupt with color. "Right."

Eli coughs, ears flushed. "I'm gonna—"

"I'll go—" I say, stepping to the side. But I step to the same side as Eli, so we crash into each other. He exhales, gripping my arms, and bites back a small, frustrated smile.

"I'm going to the kitchen," he says. "Away from you."

"Right. I'm going . . . somewhere else." His fingers drift down the back of my biceps and I give him a warning look as I back away. "Away from you even more."

Even if all I want is to be closer.

For a while it works. I get lost in the din of conversation, the bumping music, the buzz of excitement.

But then there's a palm pressed into the small of my back when I'm chatting with a couple bridesmaids. A tug on the end of my ponytail as I'm straightening a stubborn streamer. Fingers tightening around my hip in the middle of an impromptu dance break, a thumb brushing up and down my hip bone, and then a body pressed up against me for half a second before it's cool air again.

Eli is circling me.

I shoot him a look and he grins, his gaze heavy. I feel it like his hands are all over me already.

It makes me want to play right back.

So later, when I see him sitting at the kitchen table with Adam and Grace, an empty seat beside him, I excuse myself from my conversation with Jamie and Blake.

"You're a mess," Jamie laughs as I sweep past her.

I am, and right now I don't care. The revelation is as startling as it is freeing.

Eli's back is to me, so he doesn't see me coming. My palm tingles even before I lay it on his shoulder, my thumb grazing up the nape of his neck. He looks up when Adam and Grace do. The light is low, but I still see the way his pupils dilate.

"What are we talking about?" I ask, sliding into the seat next to him. Our knees bump and I keep mine there, biting back a smile when Eli casually shifts in his seat, spreading his legs further. Now we're touching up to our thighs.

"The curse," Adam says around a pretzel stick.

Eli stretches his arm along the back of my chair; his forearm presses against my skin above the low back of my dress. "I was asking if the curse is in the room with us right now."

"Both of you knock it off," Grace replies, resting a hand absently on her stomach. I smile; yesterday, Adam texted an all-caps LIL' S-K IS ALREADY GORGEOUS to the group chat after their OB appointment and sent a picture of the sonogram, followed by THAT BEAN WILL BE MY CHILD.

Grace gives me a knowing look. "We were talking about how we're not going to talk about the curse anymore, because the curse is done."

"And *I* was about to say, gird your loins, because rain is fore-casted tomorrow," Adam volleys back. Under the table, Eli slowly sways his leg back and forth, pushing into my thigh again and again. The sensation of his gray slacks rubbing against my bare skin is unbearable. "Thank god we have a tent."

"It's a forty percent chance, which is basically nothing, accord-ing to my cousin," Grace says, then clarifies to me and Eli, "She's a meteorologist."

"That's being generous," Adam mutters.

"Just visualize yourself out on the deck that Eli helped build with his bare hands for the ceremony." I pat his thigh, tilting a smile in his direction, then trace the seam of his pants for one thrilling second.

Eli straightens on a cough, dropping his arm between us. Un-der the table, neither Adam nor Grace can see the way his palm slides up my leg, how his thumb traces the arc of my thigh.

"Your first dance under the stars," he adds, pressing his finger-print into my skin. "Because the sky, of course, is clear."

I hum, heart beating hard. "Of course. Because the weather's perfect."

"And everything else is perfect, too, because your best people knocked it out of the park." Eli's eyes stay on me under the guise of waiting for my response, his expression neutral even as his hand lands on my knee, tracing the cap.

Goose bumps explode on my skin. "How exactly did we do that?"

He lifts the pressure of his fingers until they're barely there. That focused, light attention is somehow worse. "Not the curse."

"Definitely not the curse," I say. Adam sighs, equally amused and aggrieved, but I ignore him, lifting an eyebrow at Eli.

He tilts his head, gaze moving over my face. "Hmm."

"Hmm," I agree.

"Maybe it was the—"

I snap my fingers. "I know. The teamwork."

That word is as Pavlovian as *list*, and the awareness of what we've done here together sinks into his eyes, heavy and hot.

His jaw flexes, like his fingers around my knee. "That's it."

"Yeah, yeah, point taken. Fuck the curse, it's going to be great," Adam says. He presses a kiss to Grace's forehead, then her mouth, pushing her hair back from her shoulders before glancing back at me. "And seriously, George, thanks for tonight. I mean, Tahoe was fun, but this second time around is special."

He and Eli exchange affectionate smiles before Eli looks at me. From the corner of my eye, I clock that Grace has snared Adam's attention back, but it scares me, how stripped away Eli's expression is right out in the open. I watch his mouth curve around a quiet, "It is."

I give a modest shrug, every nerve in my body reaching for him.

He wants to say more, I can tell, and when someone cranks the music, he snatches his opportunity. He leans close, tipping his chin so his mouth fits right at my ear. His stubble burns my cheek.

"I'm going to knock on your door later," he whispers. "Please answer it."

I don't hesitate. Our time is leaving us too fast. "I will."

Chapter Twenty-Six

The knock on my hotel door at two a.m. is patient and hushed. *I'm* not patient right now, though, so I dash to answer it. Every second Eli's not in my room is a second I resent.

I wish he'd fall through the door and grab me with needy hands, but that's not how it goes. Instead, he steps slowly inside when I wrench the door open and fall back to make space for him. He looks at me for what feels like hours but is only seconds. It's a lovely twist of time, extending the moment so I can take everything in: the warmth of his eyes, the way his hair crests back from his forehead, how his palm rubs a pattern over his chest, the hard press of his throat when he swallows.

His voice is low in the hush of the room. "Quite a party you threw there, Peach."

We've pulled so many things out of the memory box of our relationship—the pieces of ourselves we've shared, the sex, Blue Yonder itself. But it's the old nickname and the way he says it— tender, with a hook to it—that finally pulls me all the way back into the home-shaped space I left five years ago.

I love him, and I want to scream because I can't do anything about it.

"Oh, that old thing?" I breathe out, dancing back.

He steps closer, eyes fixed on me. "Don't be modest. I know those streamers were a pain in the ass."

"Half of them fell down by the end of the night," I huff as his hand wraps around my wrist.

"Ungrateful little assholes," he murmurs sympathetically, towing me closer.

My eyes flutter closed when our chests meet. "Completely defiant to my vision."

"I've heard that about streamers," he says, cradling my cheek with one hand, letting the other curl around my hip. "They're very willful, it's not your fault."

My breath winds around a soft, pleading sound as he finally puts his mouth on me—just at my jaw, open-mouthed, hungry.

"I knew I should've taken them down."

His mouth is at the corner of my lips now. "That would've been a shame, seeing as how you and your fifty-seven streamers completely took me apart tonight."

"Fifty-seven?" I turn my head microscopically, and he lets our mouths graze before pulling back. After hours of having to keep each other just out of reach, Eli isn't ready to let me have him.

"I counted. You were across the room with Adam and you laughed and I l—" His exhale is hard and shaky. "I wasn't going to be able to fake it. I had to face the wall and count streamers."

"God, it felt like four thousand," I gasp out as he presses a kiss at the hollow beneath my ear.

I can feel his smile against my skin, how it washes away with his next rough words. "You did that for me."

My body pulses with need, my heart with *everything*. "Yes."

"Why?"

Oh god. Even the diluted version is completely exposing, but it's like my mouth is disconnected from my brain. Words start pouring out.

"Because I care about you." It's such a weak version of my actual feelings, only enough to release the barest pressure in my chest. "Because I wanted you to have a second chance so you can stop trying so hard to prove yourself. Because you're good enough, even after you fall short."

Because some part of me wants to forgive him for that.

"I don't know if I deserve it. I've missed so much." His arms tighten around me; not even a sheet of paper could come between us. "I haven't been here, and it's all I've thought about for—for so long."

"But you're here now. That's enough." It's more than enough; it's all I ever wanted. "You didn't need to prove yourself, Eli. You just needed to show up."

It's an accidental slip into the past, and he recognizes it immediately. He pulls back, frames my face in his hands, his eyes wide and searching.

"Georgia." My name is a single-worded question, shaped like the reckoning he wants and I can't give.

I shake my head, whispering, "We have so little time." My heart is everywhere: in my throat, crawling away from him, in his hands. "Please."

His eyes flutter closed, frustration working across his beautiful face. "*Why?*"

"Because it's what we agreed to this week," I say. *Because this will end if we talk now.*

He sighs, then pulls me deeper into his arms. Suddenly I'm surrounded by a tight, lovely pressure that allows me to sink. To let go. We stay like that for one minute, for two, swaying, his frustration and my fear fading away into a feeling like peace.

But I know that if I keep holding on I'll want it too much, for longer.

I pull back just enough that our cheeks brush. Then our noses. Our lips.

"Kiss me," I whisper. "I want you."

Eli lets out a soft sound. We hold there for a delicious moment, and then the mood shifts to what I expected from the start—impatient and needy.

He covers my mouth in a hot press, like he's confirming I'm here, it's real, we're in this room together. Once he does, his teeth slide against my bottom lip, asking me to let him in. I do, inhaling his groan when our tongues meet, letting out a hungry sound when his hand tangles in my hair, tightening at my nape to hold me there. I'm captive for a kiss he takes deep and slow, and it feels like only seconds before he's hard.

"Tell me what you need," he whispers once I've divested him of his shirt and my dress is pooled at my waist. The demand, how much he wants that, opens me up. I can't say it all, but I can let some of it out. I want to take him apart like those stupid streamers did, but all the way. If we have to say goodbye to this soon, I want him *overwhelmed* by me.

"You had something on your list we haven't checked off, and we're not in the cottage, but we're close enough," I say. "I'd hate to waste an opportunity."

"What—" He inhales sharply as I lower to my knees. The memory unravels between us, his whisper from years before: *wanted to put you on your knees in your cottage living room.* "Fuck, Georgia."

There's a sharp edge of wonder in his voice, like he can't quite believe this is what I need, and he doesn't blink or breathe when I unbutton his dress pants and push the waistband down his hips, along with his boxer briefs.

When I brace my hands on his thighs, he comes back to himself, his expression turning severe. He takes himself in hand before I can, curls his other hand around the back of my neck. For a moment, he holds me there, stares so adoringly down at me as his fingers move restlessly in my hair, as his hand moves restlessly up and down the length of himself.

"Make it messy," he murmurs finally, and I hear what he's really saying: *make it real.* The two things can't exist without the other right now, and I lean in with a relieved sigh, replacing his hand with mine.

At the touch of my mouth, he breathes out my name, tells me how fucking good it is as I tease and lick until he's wet enough to take all the way in. His thighs go tense, his fingers framing my jaw as he feeds himself into my mouth. It's soft groans and unwinding praise—*just like that, god, look at you*—while he wipes away the tears that gather under my eyes from my effort, his thumbs such a tender brush along my skin. He lets his body take over, but just for a minute, fist tight in my hair. I can feel how close he is on my tongue, can taste it there, too.

"No more," he gasps out, pulling me off my knees.

Before I can take a breath, he slants his mouth over mine, nudges me backward until I'm falling onto the bed. But he's right there to catch me, crawling over me as he gets us naked. His mouth is starving and wet on my breasts, his fingers perfect and circling between my legs. I feel like I'm drowning underneath him and I want it—that complete, blissful obliteration.

"That made you wet," he murmurs before catching my nipple between his teeth.

"Mmm," I sigh.

"You like seeing me like that," he continues, soothing the

sting of his bite with a stroking lap of his tongue. "How much I need you."

"Yes," I groan as he slides one finger into me, then another.

"I don't think I could ever show you how much." He sounds so dismayed that I laugh, and he grins. "Can I try anyway?"

He doesn't wait for an answer, instead sucking at the slope of my breast, once, twice, again, creating a series of marks that'll be hidden beneath my dress tomorrow. The thought unravels me.

"Excuse me, you have a job to do, and it's me."

He laughs, grabbing for his pants, then freezes. "*Fuck.* I was in such a rush that I forgot to bring a condom over. Do you have one?"

"No," I groan. If he moves anywhere but into me, I may legitimately die.

His sigh mirrors my thoughts. "I can go—"

"Hold on, wait." I pull him over me again. His hips fall into the cradle of mine, putting him exactly where I need him. "I have an IUD."

"Georgia," he breathes out. "Hold on."

I don't know if we're saying it the same way, but after a second, he pulses forward, slipping barely inside. I groan, sliding my palms up his back. "I got tested last fall and everything was negative. I haven't been with anyone since then."

"Same for me, but longer."

Something about the timeline tugs at me, but then he says, "Is it okay?" in a sweet, hoarse voice. When I nod, he surges forward, just halfway. The feel of him is unreal. It's been so long since I've had him like this, and it's so intensely what I need: sex, the way only he can give it to me. Stripped down and needy and messy and perfect. I can ask for more and he'll give it to me.

Like now, when he slides all the way inside and I whisper, "Deeper." He gives me what I want, lips parted, an astonished sound escaping as his thighs push mine further apart, as he gets as deep as he can. He catches my mouth with his, and our eyes lock before his fall closed, overwhelmed.

And then he starts to move and I feel it, the way I let him into my body and my heart.

For now.

"Make it messy," I whisper in his ear, and he laughs, lifting up on his knees so he can watch the way my body takes him.

He's not gentle, but he's tender, and his eyes stay on mine while he reaches between us, stroking his thumb over me as he pushes into me over and over again.

His eyes spark as my groans become staccato pants. "You're so good for me," he murmurs. "God, I love you just like this, *look* at you. You're going to make me come."

My mind is fuzzy from my impending orgasm, but not so fuzzy that I don't grip on to his *I love you*, the following *just like this* fading away like vapor. He means in this moment—my needy sounds, my body giving his pleasure—but it still winds me tight.

I dig my nails into his back and he falls over me, bringing us so close that his necklace pools onto my throat, hot from his skin. I can tell by the way his breath hitches, the panting exhales he presses into my neck, that he needs it like this, too.

When he pulls back, I watch him fall apart—his expression is stark, drawn with need. He kisses me, but it's more sound than feel. An aching groan curled into my mouth, a panting sigh alongside his slick tongue against mine, and then finally, just his grazing lips.

"Go slow," I beg. "I don't want it to be over."

"It's okay," he whispers. He doesn't slow down. Somehow he knows exactly what I need: to fall fully with him like this, because I can't in any other way. "When it's done, we'll just start all over again."

And I whisper back *yes*, even though I know it's not true. I inhale it when my body tightens, and then on an exhale, let it go.

There are dark, ominous clouds on the horizon.

"They're not going to go away just because you're staring at them every five seconds."

"You're going to feel real foolish when I make it happen," I joke, looking over to where Eli's perched on the bed, leaning back on his hands.

"I believe in you, but even you can't control the weather."

His smile is small and affectionate, and he looks so indecently good that it pulls me away from my nervous thoughts—his knees are spread, his dark gray suit pants pulled tight to showcase the hard curve of his thighs, and his white dress shirt is unbuttoned just enough to reveal the hollow of his throat, a sliver of the gold chain lying against it. I rested my thumb there this morning while I shaved his face at his request, panted against it when he set me on the bathroom counter afterward and fucked me.

I've felt a restlessness I can't shake since I woke up to Eli gazing at the ceiling, his expression troubled. I wondered if he was replaying the molecule-rearranging sex we had, if he was as overwhelmed by it as I was, and in what way. Or maybe he was thinking about how tomorrow he'll be on a plane to LA, and how the next few weeks might determine the trajectory of his career.

When he saw I was awake, his expression cleared. He pulled

me into his arms, pressing a kiss against my messy hair. "Why are you staring at me?"

"Because you're very pretty," I croaked out.

His grin was tender, but since then he's been vacillating between inhaling like he wants to say something and watching me with a look I can't decipher.

With Adam and Grace spending the morning getting ready together, Eli and I decided to do the same. Even though I've been savoring every second of it, it's with a panicky flair; the real world beyond our hotel room door is knocking incessantly. Tomorrow we're going home, and that home is in different places, as it always was. He's in his head, I'm in mine.

And now, those goddamn clouds, the wet ground. Sometime overnight it must've rained.

"Do you think Adam's flipping out?" I ask as I make my way to the closet to change. My dress is a satin number with a slit that goes up to my thigh, in a rich green that matches the Blue Yonder vines.

"Odds are always high."

"He's probably making a voodoo doll of Grace's meteorologist cousin." Eli's laughter washes over me as I drop my robe and step into the dress, pulling the spaghetti straps over my shoulders. The zipper is going to be impossible to pull up on my own. "Do you mind—"

But he's already there, one hand holding the zipper at the base of my spine, the other pinching the fabric together mid-back. I shiver at how avid his touch is even in the middle of something so mundane.

"It's unreal," he says quietly, "that I love watching you get dressed as much as I love watching you get naked. I used to sit at the office when I was working late and think about how you were probably putting on your pajamas and I was missing it, and fucking hating myself. I never thought I'd get to watch you do it again." His exhale brushes over my neck, right below where I've fashioned my hair into a loose bun. "Don't think I'm taking this moment for granted, Georgia, or any moment you've given me this week."

My throat goes fist-tight at the mention of our past. He curls his hands around my shoulders and I catch the resolute press of his mouth in the mirror just before he turns me around.

It feels like I'm crashing into him for the first time again when our eyes meet; my breath is gone, and deep inside me, a lock clicks.

Oh, hell.

"Eli—"

"I know we have our agreement," he says, and panic blooms on me like a blush. "But I've spent all week—actually, fuck it—many years not saying things and regretting it. I'm done not saying them. I—"

There's an urgent knock at the door.

Eli's gaze slips over my shoulder, then lands back on me, fire flashing in his eyes.

Another knock, this one louder.

"I—I have to get that," I manage.

"Of course you do," he sighs.

I whirl, walking on numb legs to open the door, which sets off a series of unfortunate events. The first is that the handle catches on my dress seam and rips a healthy gash in it. The second is that I'm so busy gasping about my dress that I fling the door open wide enough that Adam—who's standing there with a storm-cloud expression—sees Eli in my room before I can formulate a reason he's here.

"Oh good, there you are," he says to Eli, releasing a sharp breath. "I knocked on your door but no one answered."

The level of unbothered in his voice coupled with what he just interrupted spirals me higher. "We— he was just—"

"She ripped her dress and I heard her yelling down the hall," Eli steps in. "She's freaking out."

I throw him a look over my shoulder, and he raises an eyebrow like, *aren't you?* That man and his damn double meanings and his damn inconvenient reckonings.

Adam waves that off, like he doesn't care. I'm baffled by it, until his distraction from the knife-cut tension in here becomes clear.

"Unless you've got something vital hanging out, you need to forget about your dress for now," he says grimly. "We need to get over to Blue Yonder. Everything's fucked."

Chapter Twenty-Seven

Adam was being dramatic when he said everything was fucked, but not by much.

We're a ragtag group, standing in the lobby of the Big House while people rush around us like water around river rocks. I'm pinching the gap in my dress. Jamie has her bridesmaid dress on, a floaty yellow number, but is bare-faced, her mass of curls pushed back by a terry-cloth headband with cat ears. Adam's mom, Laurie, who met us as we pulled into the parking lot with a placating, "Don't panic," has a blond head full of heatless rollers. And Grace, who hobbled down into the hotel lobby green-faced, looks stunning with her hair and makeup done, but she's wearing a pale pink satin sleep set and Adam's flannel shirt, her feet shoved into old Adidas slides. It's Party up top, Progressively Panicked the rest of the way down.

It's only Eli who's perfect in his suit. He looks calm and determined standing next to Adam, and it makes me feel that much more unraveled.

I'm done not saying them.

My stomach dips. Saying *what*?

"This is what we've got going on," Laurie says, wrapping an arm around my waist. "Last night, the wind pulled a Big Daddy branch down onto the deck. The damage is contained to a corner, so it's still usable. We've got people working on shifting the chair and aisle setup."

"Okay, well, that's not so bad," Adam says, shooting a hopeful look at Grace, who looks green again.

"I'm not done."

Adam sighs. "Right."

She goes on to say there's another storm system on the way that could hit during the ceremony, but Cole ran out to buy as many umbrellas as he can find for guests. The power has been going in and out all morning and the bakery's delivery van won't start, so they're scrambling to find an alternative vehicle to get the cake here.

"There was also a mix-up with the florist and they went to Meadowcrest instead. They're here now, but we probably lost about two hours of setup time."

My heart drops. *Shit.* That was a task I'd taken on despite Aunt Julia's offers to split the list. "I— no, I double-confirmed the address with all the vendors yesterday."

But even as I say it, I remember getting distracted when Jamie popped into the office to let me know she and Blake were back from their grocery run for the party, and I had to dig up the cottage keys so they could drop the bags off. And then again when Eli returned from his therapy call and he kept drifting past the open door, eyes locking with mine.

Seeing my stricken look, Laurie tightens her hold on me. "Hey, don't worry, sweetie. It might've been a wires-crossing situation."

No wires were crossed. This is all on me.

Adam runs a hand over his mouth. I can't read the expression on his face, whether he's angry or disappointed or numb. Any of the options make my head throb. "Are they going to be able to get everything done on time?"

"Yes."

Everyone's attention flies to Eli.

"It's going to be fine," he says, his eyes focused on me. It's a soothing thing on top of steel. "We have five hours and a dozen hands. We can make up a couple hours easily."

Adam eyes him for a beat, then raises an eyebrow, glancing at me again. "All right."

His tone is even, but I've known Adam for sixteen years and can sense some emotion underneath those two words. I feel naked, stripped down by Eli's words an hour ago, by the way I can still feel the phantom touch of his hands all over my body. And Eli is stripped down, too, unapologetically. It's not just a friend trying to soothe a friend; the timbre of his voice is heavy with a different kind of care.

So much for being discreet. Thankfully Adam seems too caught up in everything else to fully digest the tone, but anxiety ricochets through me.

Silently, I manifest an escape hatch.

"Blake and I can go see if the florist needs help," Jamie steps in smoothly, hooking her pinky through mine.

"Absolutely," Blake agrees. "We're happy to put ourselves to work."

"I should really fix my mis—"

Julia bustles in, looking harried. "Your officiant just called. She's got severe food poisoning and can't make it."

Adam blinks. "You mean the person who was going to *marry us*?" He turns on his heel to pace away from us. "Right, of course."

"Okay, that's bad," Grace whispers.

Julia holds up her hands. "Don't panic."

"Not listening to that, Aunt Jules," Adam calls back, chin up to the ceiling. "I told you all the curse was real, and this—" He releases a sharp breath. "Okay. We need to check on all of our necessities—make sure Grace's wedding dress isn't ripped to shreds, check on the caterer, call the band and confirm they haven't been swallowed by a sinkhole." His attention snaps to me. "You have our wedding bands, right? They haven't been snatched by some Gollum-looking dude?"

"Is this thirteen-year-old Adam who thinks *Lord of the Rings* is real speaking?" He gives me a flat look and I hold up my hands. "Kidding. Yes, I have them—"

The words die in my throat. I picture my Wedding Go Bag sitting on the desk in my hotel room. The one I meant to grab as we were rushing out the door, but got distracted from in the midst of my panic. It has my makeup bag in it for touch-ups, various toiletries in case of emergency, a pair of flip-flops for when my feet finally mutiny against these five-inch heels.

And Adam and Grace's wedding bands. Along with my best woman speech.

Oh shit. Oh *shit*.

Adam steps forward. "I don't like that look, Georgia, what is that look?"

"No look! I have them." It's not a lie; I *do* have them. Just not here.

"Great, well then, if that's all—"

Cal strides in, interrupting Adam's sarcastic quip. "The bakery just called and said it'll be faster if someone drives over to pick up the cake. One of the employees will ride along to make sure it stays stable in the car."

"Please. In curse-speak, that means the cake is getting fucked up," Adam groans.

In his eyes, it's one more problem, but in mine, it's a way to check three items off my list: I can jet over to the hotel and get my bag, make up for the vendor snafu by taking this task off everyone's plate, and put myself out of Eli's reach. God knows what he'll say if he gets me alone for a few minutes.

Escape hatch manifested. I'm already backing toward the lobby doors, calling out, "I've got it. I'll be back before you can even miss me."

The bag is sitting on the desk just as I left it, Adam's and Grace's rings nestled inside. The breath my throat refused to let go of the entire two-wheeled drive over expels in a relieved whoosh.

I look around, half expecting the room to look hurricane-struck. *I* feel wind-swept after Eli's cut-off declaration, so everything else should, too.

But it's quiet and still, calmly holding signs from our morning together—the razor and washcloth still on the countertop along-side the towel he laid down to set me on, the mussed-up bed and his cologne on the nightstand. I can smell the spice of him. Feel his breath on my neck when he confessed that he'd think of me alone in our apartment while he was alone at his office. It's a split-screen image in my mind: Eli at work, me at home. Both of us thinking of the other.

God, the absolute, heart-crushing *waste* of it.

Even feeling the phantom pain of that time hurts so badly I have to curl away from it. I don't ever want to feel the concen-trated version of that heartache again, yet Eli seemed determined to make us remember. To make us talk about it, when what good will it do?

I've spent all week—actually, fuck it—many years not saying things and regretting it. I'm done not saying them. I—

There's a list of declarations that could come after that, because if I wanted the reckoning, they'd be on my list, too: *I want to talk about New York. The night you told me you were done. Why we didn't fight for each other. Nick and Miriam's wedding. My job. This week. What we're doing. What are we doing?*

Suddenly, I don't know. When we made our agreement, I justified it. I was distracted by him and thought giving into it would satiate me in a way I could control. But my need has always been too big, too greedy, too capable of creating messes. Now I can see that the agreement was built with flimsy scaffolding, an excuse to live in a fantasy for a bit. To be, in our own words, a little bit stupid. What would've happened if Adam didn't interrupt earlier? Would I be wrecked right in the middle of the most important day of our best friends' lives? Would Eli?

It's safe to say the agreement is dead, and all I have left is the list of reasons I can't have him beyond this week. We'll leave Blue Yonder and the spell we wove there will be broken, and though my heart doesn't want that, my rational brain knows it's for the best. In reality, we aren't the twenty-year-olds who loved each other but hadn't said it yet. We're the twenty-eight-year-olds who said it hundreds of times and still broke each other's hearts.

Maybe he'll go to LA and let go of this determination. Once we're away from each other, maybe everything won't feel so consuming. I'll love him still, but my heart won't be as utterly exposed as it feels right now.

We just have to get through this day and tomorrow morning and then we can forget about agreements and lists and reckonings.

My phone trills, startling me.

"Get your head in the game, Georgia," I mutter, pulling my phone out of my bag.

I assume it's Adam with a well-deserved text asking where the hell I am, but that's not the message that greets me. It's from Eli.

Call me if you need me.

I do. I can't. I stare at it for a handful of seconds I can't spare. No more distractions. No more disasters. No more mess.

All good! I write. Be back soon.

And then I slip my phone into my bag, ignoring the tight squeeze of my heart. When the door closes behind me, it's with a near-silent snick, separating me from all the memories and wishes held in that room.

At Icing on the Cake, I'm presented with a gift from the universe: there's another baker in Tai's place, which means I don't have to face her and remember the tale Eli and I spun. I hold my breath while the box is loaded into the minivan I borrowed from one of Adam's cousins, only releasing it when they get it into the back seat without incident. The high school employee who's riding along with me snugs in next to it and then we're good to go.

It feels too easy given everything else that's happened, but I decide to take it without question.

You good??? Adam texts as I shut the door. You've been gone for a while. Nothing's wrong right?

NO, I text back with clammy fingers, running around to the

driver's side. My heels slip on the pavement, slick from a quick-moving shower while I was inside.

My phone buzzes in my hand again. Reassuring, is Adam's response.

"Shit, shit, shit," I mutter, turning the ignition and glancing at the dashboard clock, which broadcasts a very worrying time.

I spend the duration of the drive back to Blue Yonder cycling through a mantra of, *it's fine, it's fine, the cake is fine, you are fine, everything is fine and* will *be fine*. I picture myself gliding down the aisle, smiling at Adam and Grace as they get married under a miraculously materialized blue sky, dancing to Isla's band with the stars peeking through the tent-top, enjoying a slice of this cake. Having a perfect night and not thinking about anything that makes my heart ache.

I'm nearly calm by the time we pull into the parking lot. I sling my bag over my shoulder, then help get the box out of the van. I continue my mantra to the beat of my careful, staccato foot-steps as we make our way up the Big House stairs, balancing the cake. People give us a wide berth out into the courtyard, which is suddenly looking extremely wedding-like—the deck is set up for the ceremony, and the final touches are being put on the tables inside the tent. Grace and Adam wanted rustic, kaleido-scopic color, and it's everywhere—in the flowers, the table run-ners, the rainbow breadth of the bridesmaids' dresses, the green of the land.

Everything is fine. Everything is perfect.

But then I catch sight of Eli standing at the end of the path with Adam and my heart trips. He's nodding, but looking around distractedly, his eyes wandering—

Locking with mine. I feel his breath on my neck again, the heat of his body, hear those words: *I've spent all week—actually, fuck it—many years not saying things and regretting it. I'm done not saying them. I—*

STOP, I silently yell. I can hear all the words he didn't say unraveling behind it, and I *just* got them out of my head.

The box bobbles, and the bakery employee gasps.

"Sorry," I gasp back, my heart pounding. "We're good. It's fine."

But Adam's and Eli's eyes widen in tandem and then they're striding up the path, their broad shoulders bumping in their haste to get to me.

"I've got it," I call out. "Just tell us where to pu—"

Eli's close now, so I see the moment it hits him, seconds before it hits *me* that the sole of my shoe is sliding on the wet pavement. That my feet are slipping right out from beneath me.

And that I—and, more importantly, the cake—am falling.

Chapter Twenty-Eight

Eli wraps a hand around my arm just as my ass hits the ground. The cake tilts the same way my stomach does: fast and hard, with a sickening sense of doom.

But then Adam's there, righting the box before it can fall. He closes his eyes, exhaling a shaky, "Holy . . ."

"Is the cake okay?" I yelp.

"Are *you*?" Eli shoots back, his fingers tightening around my bicep.

"Yes." I clamber to my feet, eyes burning, my damn heels slipping again. "But the cake—"

"It's fine," Adam says, peering over the top of the box. "Well. The majority is fine. There's one side that's pretty smashed." A wounded sound escapes me and I move to inspect it, but he twists the box away. "It's *fine*, George, seriously, I could not give a shit about imperfect frosting right now."

"I give many shits." Mainly because I'm the reason for it.

"Are you okay?" Adam asks, ignoring that. "You really biffed it there."

I twist to inspect the damage. "Yeah, I'm f—" *Fucked.* At least, my dress is. There's a long streak of mud extending from my ass to the hem, dirt and grass clinging to the fabric. I look like I was rolling around in the vineyard blocks.

The burn in my eyes turns into a frustrated flood and I blink furiously, keeping my chin tucked to my chest to hide my imminent breakdown.

"I'm going to run to the bathroom and clean up," I get out.

Eli's attention is a weight between my shoulder blades all the way up to the Big House.

Once I'm inside, I slip into the bathroom, leaning against the door as soon as I shut it. The sudden silence makes my ears ring, sets off a low tremble in my body.

So much for no more disasters.

I try to breathe through it, using the same cadence Eli does for his panic attacks, as I set my bag on the counter. I grab the zippered pouch that holds the safety pins I'm looking for, along with a tin of Altoids, some tampons, and the notebook with my best woman speech.

Only it isn't there.

"What?" I whisper in confusion, dropping the pouch to dig frantically through the bag.

I pull every item out until it's impossible to deny: the fancy notebook I bought because I thought it would make an emotionally satisfying keepsake to remember a night of togetherness with my best friends—probably our last one for the foreseeable future—is nowhere to be found. The speech I worked on for weeks to create a perfect representation of my friendship with Adam and celebrate him moving into this next phase with Grace is gone.

It's weird that what grips me feels like grief, but that's it, some sort of loss that now I won't have the right words to explain what this era of my life has meant before it leaves. I've never been able to say real goodbyes to the things that have formed me—not my mom or my first defining best friendship, not my relationship with Eli or, thanks to our agreement ending unceremoniously, whatever this week has been. Not sharing a home and day-to-day closeness with Jamie or the inevitable shift in my friendship with Adam, the first best friend who stuck around. Nothing I've cared about most has been tied up with a pretty bow before it was given away. It's all been messy. It's made me wish and need and crave.

And it turns me into this—a girl in a broken dress, crying alone in a bathroom.

I don't hear the door open. Barely hear the measured footsteps that stop just behind me. But my body recognizes the person it loves most, so when I'm pulled against a solid chest, I know it's Eli.

"Take a breath," he murmurs into my hair.

What I really want to do is curl into him and never leave. I curl my hands around his ribs instead, pushing. "I can't do this with you."

"Why?" His arms stay wrapped around me, his hand a steady pressure between my shoulder blades.

"Because you're going to—" *Want to talk about it. I'm trapped here in this room with you and you could say anything,* every*thing, and I'll break down and I can't break down when everything's already falling apart.*

"I'm not going to," he says, frustration threaded through his voice. He wants to say it all, despite his promise. "But I'm not going anywhere either, so take a breath, Georgia."

It's not a request. It forces me to inhale and then let it go, to breathe in again in fragments. God, it feels good to be held up by him. And god, I want it for so much longer than this moment we're in.

"What do you see?" Eli asks quietly, his palm smoothing over my skin.

"What?"

"Five things," he says, and my pulse spikes with understanding. His calming exercise.

My voice comes out hoarse. "The sky." I stare at the gray patch framed by the window, wishing it was blue.

"Good." A soft praise. "What else?"

"Um, white tulips. This pretty jute rug. My bag spilled everywhere. Fancy hand soap."

I catch his eye in the mirror hanging over the sink. *You.*

"Four things you can touch," he says, his eyes dark, intense, unavoidable.

I close mine, let my fingertips wander. "My dress and my shoes. The counter against my hip." I reach out to trace the sink. "Cold porcelain."

You. I graze my cheek against his shoulder.

"Three things you can hear."

"Voices in the lobby. The string quartet practicing for the ceremony outside. Footsteps."

You. My own *I love you*, a thing I can't say out loud. It pulls relief into my veins to have it sit somewhere between us, unknown to him.

His voice is low and soothing. "Two things you can smell."

"Fresh grass," I say, inhaling deeply. "Rain."

You. The same spice he's worn for years. The specific alchemy of his skin that winds itself around my body and heart.

"And one thing you can taste."

I lick at my wet lips. "Salt."

You. I wish it was you.

"Georgia," he says, sounding pained. When I look up at him, I see it in his eyes. "Why are you crying?"

I shake my head. "It doesn't matter."

"It does," he says.

"It's not the time."

"It *is* the time, because you're feeling it right now. Why are you crying?"

He says that, but I hear: *right now, if you needed something, would you say it?*

I've spent so many moments denying him—and more importantly, myself—the answer. Right now, I don't have the ability to.

"I'm a fucking mess." Saying it out loud feels like getting the wind knocked out of me. All the air rushes out of my lungs before I'm ready, but the emptiness that follows brings weightlessness.

Eli tucks a loose, sweaty strand of hair behind my ear. "Hey, join the club."

"This club sucks."

"I know," he says sympathetically. "No free swag or anything."

My wet laugh turns into a fresh round of tears, and I cover my face. "God. I messed up with the flower vendor."

"Who's here and all set up," he says calmly.

"And the cake."

"Which is fine."

I peek through my fingers with a flat look. "It's smashed on one side."

"So they angle that side away from everyone." His eyebrow

tilts up when my expression doesn't change. "It's going to get eaten anyway."

"My dress is ruined," I say, dropping my hands. "I'm going to be the black mark in all the photos."

"That's not possible."

His eyes make a quick circuit of me, and it's not a heated look, but it warms me all the same.

"Sounds a little biased," I sniffle.

One corner of his mouth pulls up. "C'mon, Georgia. Not a little."

My breath catches low in my throat. I look down between us, at the bare inch of space between our bodies, searching for a way to claw us out of this quiet intimacy.

Eli's breath hitches, like some emotion is caught in his throat. Like he's pushing past it to say something.

"Hey, I brought you— oh."

Eli and I startle apart at the sound of Adam's voice in the doorway. He doesn't look surprised, nor does Jamie when she peeks around his shoulder. A knowing smile blooms on her face, but then her gaze tracks down my cheeks and it falls away.

It's her voice and Adam's in unison: "Are you *crying*?"

"No!" And it's true, I'm not currently crying, but it's still ridiculous. My face is streaked with mascara. "No, I just needed a few minutes to fix my dress."

Everyone is kind enough not to mention that my dress is, in fact, still not fixed.

"We were reviewing the list of things she thinks she messed up, actually," Eli replies.

I gape at him. "Thanks, *traitor*."

"Messed up?" Adam echoes, bewildered. "What do you mean?"

Now it's Adam's turn for my incredulous look. "Adam, I just nearly took out your cake. You know, the thing that Grace was most excited about?"

He winces. "I almost hate to tell you this because we were all emotionally attached to the cake, but this morning Grace literally threw up saying the words 'passion fruit,' so we can let that stress point go."

"I— oh." I blink as Jamie pushes Eli and Adam out of the way, coming over to swipe her thumbs under my eyes.

"What else?" Eli asks. He leans a shoulder against the wall, crossing his arms over his chest. He's so fucking beautiful. Unfair, when I resemble a disheveled hamster.

"What else what?"

His gaze is steady. "What else is on your list?"

My attention drifts back to Adam, a lump growing in my throat. He's watching me, hazel eyes wide, tall and handsome in his suit. But I can see the freckle-faced boy underneath the height and squared jaw, that kid I walked up to the day the loneliness of losing my best friends became something I had to let go of. I saw something in him, some kindred thing that came true, and knowing I don't have the words to properly convey what that's meant to me makes me want to cry.

Oh, but I am. What a surprise.

"I lost my best woman speech."

Adam frowns. "How do you lose a speech?"

"I wrote it in a notebook and I thought I put it in my bag, but it's not there," I say, and his mouth parts, his expression fading from confusion to realization, then sympathy. "I know how stupid it was to not put it on my phone instead. I just . . . I wanted it to be special." I bite my lip, looking at Jamie and Adam in turn. "We haven't had any time together the past three months, and before that I was in Seattle and no one could get up to visit, which trust me, I understand. Everyone's got their own lives and you're moving into new, exciting eras, and I'm so—"

My voice cracks. Around my waist, Jamie's arms tighten. "I'm so happy. And now you and Grace are having a baby, Adam, and, Jamie, you and Blake are, like, on the bullet train toward matrimony, which I swear I won't lose my speech for." She lets out a thick laugh. "But with all of that, and me potentially leaving, it feels like the wedding is the last time we'll all be like this before things really change, you know? It really is the end of *this* era. I wanted to properly memorialize it with a kickass speech that would make Adam weep."

I'm out of breath by the time I finish, and there's a beat of silence.

Then Adam says, "I'm going to digest all of that, but did you just say you're leaving?"

"Okay, because I thought I was the only one who heard it," Jamie replies.

My stomach drops as I meet Eli's wide eyes. "Sorry, no. I didn't mean to say that."

"You didn't mean to, but you *did*," Adam says.

"It's easy enough to pretend I *didn't*," I shoot back.

He laughs incredulously. "Yeah fucking right. Tell us."

I groan. "Can we wait? I didn't want to say anything until after the wedding, and there's so much going—"

"Let's deal with it now," Jamie interrupts gently.

I swallow, cornered. "I— my role got transferred up to Seattle. Well, actually, *my* role was dissolved. The role up in Seattle is director level, but they want me to take it. Nia told me right before I went on PTO."

Out of the corner of my eye, Eli straightens.

"You're moving?" Jamie gasps out.

"I don't know. I think—maybe." Helplessly, I repeat, "I don't know."

Adam runs a hand over his mouth. "Whoa."

Jamie circles me so that we're face-to-face. Her eyes are huge, overflowing with emotions. She whispers, "How do you feel? Are you happy about it?"

The question hits me sideways. I've been so caught up in the anticipatory fear of making the decision that I haven't given myself time to think of what it would feel like to be there. "I don't know. I mean, I love my job and a promotion is objectively a great thing, but . . ."

My gaze slides to a still-silent Eli. There's a kaleidoscope of emotions playing over his face, but I can't catch any of them.

"But I'm scared, too," I admit, caught in the magnetic clutch of his eyes, and there, I see one: understanding.

"Of what?" Adam asks.

I turn back to him, catching Jamie's gaze on the way. I shake my head, too afraid to let the words out.

"It's okay," she assures me. "We love you. We can take it."

It's an echo of the other day: *you can be messy. The people who love you will accept every single piece of it.*

"Because everything changed when I was up there for six months," I admit, and the pressure off my chest is almost instantaneous. "You moved out, and Adam and Grace moved away, and now we barely see each other. It feels like the fuller your lives get, the less space there is for me. If I leave, maybe that space will go away completely."

Eli's attention is a weight, like his hands on my back just minutes ago. It was like that with him, too. The bigger his job and anxiety got, the further it pushed me until I was crammed into a corner. Until I was so small there was no space at all.

"Georgia, no," Jamie breathes out. "There will *never* be less space for you."

"There's definitely less time. This is the most time we've spent together in . . ." I trail off, shaking my head. "Since way before I left for Seattle."

Adam's quiet. I can see him calculating. Digesting. His expression drops when he realizes it's true.

"I'm not asking you to change your lives, I'm just saying I don't know where I fit, and that's hard. I don't want to lose you. I don't want us to drift away without knowing it until we're too far to get back," I say, my voice breaking. "Growing up, I didn't have the true-friends thing, or the close-family thing, and then you came along and turned into both for me. And I'm sorry, I know it's so much to take, but I *need* you all. I don't want you to forget me if I move to Seattle and I don't want to miss you the way I have for the past nine months, and I'm scared I'm the only one who feels that way."

My gaze slips to Eli. He presses his lips together, blinking down to the ground.

Adam takes me by the shoulders, breaking my connection with Eli. "First of all, you needing us in your life isn't too much to take. Fuck anyone who ever told you that, and yes, that message goes straight to those assholes Heather and Mya, among others." His scowl softens when I choke out a laugh. "Second of all, why didn't you *say* anything?"

"Everyone's had so much going on and no one else seemed particularly bothered by it. And it's hard for me to . . . say things sometimes." I glance at Eli again and swear I see the shadow of a wry smile before turning back to Adam and Jamie. "I don't know, the timing never seemed right." My groaning laugh echoes around us. "Not that talking about it hours before your wedding is great timing."

"The ideal timing is when you're feeling it," Eli says with the softest edge only I catch.

"Exactly," Jamie says, wrapping me in a tight hug. "So first, let's cross out that we're going to forget you, because that's never happening. Things changed so fast and it happened while you were gone, so it was hard to process. Truth be told, it's been an adjustment for me, too, although I don't even think I wrapped my head around it until we spent the past couple days together. Life has been so busy, but I *miss* you. I need to do better."

"I do, too," I say against her shoulder. "I should've said something."

"Yes." She pulls back, tears in her eyes. "Please, if you ever need more than I'm giving you, or if you need me to hop on a plane, just tell me and I'll do it. I would do anything for you."

"I've been wrapped up in my life, too, and I'm sorry," Adam says, squeezing my arm. "I can get myopic about my own shit, especially when curses are involved."

"Oh my god," Jamie mutters over my "*Stop*" and Eli's "Here we go," but Adam just grins.

"Time's going to get scarce when Lil' S-K comes, but we're lifers. You're the best woman at my wedding. You're going to be my kid's godmother." My heart soars and he tugs on a hank of hair, his mouth twisting. "You think a few hundred miles would change that?"

"It sounds dumb when you say it," I admit. "Just not when I'm feeling it."

Jamie runs a finger under my eyes. "Forget about us for a second. Do you *want* to go to Seattle?"

I let out a shaky breath, setting aside all of my various fears—drifting away from them, failing at it the way I failed in New York, being lonely, forgotten.

The truth is, I've never had an opportunity like this. I've lived in Seattle before, but it was temporary, and I moved permanently before, but New York was for Eli, not me. I can't know what living in Seattle permanently will feel like unless I do it. That's the terrifying risk.

But maybe it could be the thrilling reward.

"I think I do," I admit. "I'm just scared."

"All the best things are scary," Jamie says, squeezing my hand.

"What if you make new best friends?" I ask.

"Fuck that," Adam says. Jamie's pointed look seconds that emotion.

"What if I hate it up there?"

"Then you come back to us," Jamie says, eyes luminous.

"What if I love it?" I ask thickly.

"Then we come to you for as long as you're there," Adam says. Over his shoulder, something flashes in Eli's eyes with that answer, a thing that shakes me.

I look at Jamie. "What if it's forever?"

"Then it's forever," she says simply.

My heart is growing with each answer, stretching in a way that feels like pain. "That's a lot of flights."

"I'm a slut for miles," Adam says. "I have an entire credit card devoted to getting miles."

The scene in front of me fades, replaced with a developing picture of my potential life in Seattle: doing a job that I love with people who appreciate and recognize me. Falling back into the cadence of happy hours and weekend adventures. Finding a place of belonging that *I* made, something I've never done. Letting my friends come see me, weaving them into that fabric. Saying goodbye to the era that shaped me, yes, but starting a new one that'll watch me grow.

Adam ducks into my line of sight, knuckling a tear from my cheek and wiping it on my shoulder. He grins when I roll my eyes with a laugh. "You're stuck with us, George. Got it?"

"Loud and very clearly."

I sneak a glance at Eli. He's been so quiet this entire conversation, but his silence is shaped like words, like a monster looming at my back. Everything is just starting to feel calm and controllable. I let my messiness out here, but this is a cup of water I can hold without spilling. The mess with Eli is the ocean; it'll drown me.

I beg him silently to let it be, but he just gazes back at me, only breaking our connection when Adam opens his arms wide and says, "Group hug time."

We all surge in. Eli pulls me close, and I end up halfway smashed onto his chest; his heart presses against mine, racing. I close my eyes, knowing I might not be able to touch him like this again this weekend. Not until we have some distance and that reckoning fades away.

"I love you all," Adam says, and for the first time today he's choked with emotion. "We haven't found an officiant yet, so I don't even know if Grace and I are going to be officially married today, but whatever happens, thank you for everything you did to make the good parts even better."

Everyone's arms tighten, and it's like being crushed. It's perfect. It's mine.

"Hate to interrupt whatever super weird shit is happening here," comes Cole's voice from the doorway. We turn as one and his mouth tips up sardonically before he focuses his attention on Adam. "I just heard you're looking for an officiant."

He perks up. "Yeah."

"That's great news," he says, "because I'm ordained. What do you say we go get you and Grace hitched?"

Chapter Twenty-Nine

It's a terrible day for a wedding.

The sky is dark, the air thick with the threat of rain and further disasters. The deck full of people seated on either side of the flower-strewn aisle looks almost insignificant underneath the relentless stretch of gray. Blue Yonder isn't earning its name today.

Adam doesn't care. For as high-strung as he's been this week, he's steady as he takes his parents' arms so they can escort him down the aisle. A tiny smile blossoms when his dad leans over to whisper something. He nods, eyes shining.

And then it's time to get going. Julia directs them to start down the aisle, and everyone turns in their seats as the string quartet plucks out the first notes of the processional song.

I stare at the broad stretch of Eli's shoulders in front of me, my heart tapping out a staccato beat. I did my best to salvage my dress—it's safety-pinned now, but still mud-spattered and wrinkled. The thought of walking down the aisle in front of one hundred pairs of eyes when I look this undone makes my stomach roll.

Eli goes and I start to follow, only to realize my heel's gotten caught in a loose thread at my hem.

Of course.

"Go ahead," I whisper to the three groomsmen behind me. Eli turns, hearing the quiet commotion, but I frantically wave him on as I hobble to the side. Jamie's already stepping out of the line of bridesmaids.

"Just rip it," I hiss as she lifts my leg to inspect the entanglement. "I'm burning it tomorrow anyway."

Jamie swallows a laugh, then yanks at the hem. It does rip, but at this point it's an enhancement. She rises, squeezes my hand, and then steps back into line with a wink and a mouthed, *love you.*

Though it's been seconds, it feels like everyone's been waiting for me to move for days. Time stretches out like a spotlight. When I start my walk down the aisle, my heartbeat drowns out the plucking strings.

I force myself to focus on what's in front of me. Cole's the most immediate focal point: he's standing at the end of the deck under a gorgeous arch that features an explosion of wildflowers in a breathtaking palette. Behind him, the massive oak tree looms, with the rich green sprawl of the vineyard stretching out from there. Adam is to his right, fidgety with anticipation. He gives me a brilliant smile and I smile back, feeling the inevitable tears prickling in my eyes.

And then my gaze drifts to Eli, and in reality I keep walking, but in my mind I'm frozen in the middle of the moment. It's not for us, but my heart aches imagining a parallel moment where it would've been. He's looking at me like he sees it, too, like it hurts him just as much.

I wish it didn't hurt still. I wish I knew what it would take to make it stop.

I slide into the space his body's left for mine, and the quick, warm press of his fingers against my back steadies me when I wobble.

"Those shoes are lethal," he murmurs in my ear. I pull back to see a trace of a smile on his lips, the storm clouds cleared from his eyes.

I grip my bouquet. "I'm throwing this entire outfit away when I get home. It's trying to kill me."

His Adam's apple presses hard against his throat, a transfixing undulation against his skin. "I think it's got a vendetta against me, too."

"Not another victim," I murmur.

"Sadly." He skims me from head to toe. It's quick, maybe three seconds, but it lingers on my skin. "You look so beautiful I can't feel my knees."

Shock and heat wind around me. I whisper, "I'm a mess."

"I know," he whispers back, his eyes deep and pleading.

The music fades, forcibly shifting the moment away from us. Eli exhales; I feel it in my chest. Everyone stands in one fluid motion, and the air thickens with the rustle of clothes, a throat clearing, a sniffle. Then silence settles around us, like a held breath before a thunderclap.

The violin draws out its first note. I look over at Adam, feel the brush of Eli's breath on my cheek as he does the same, and together we take in the way his expression transforms from anticipation to something so potent I couldn't give it one name. It's love and assurance and devotion, the most intense focus. Preternatural calm. I see him playing back every moment that got him and Grace to this point. I see how grateful he is that every second they've spent together—good, bad, cursed—has brought them here.

I press a hand over my burning heart.

The music swells, beautiful and bright. Grace turns the corner, gorgeous in an off-the-shoulder, wispy dream of a gown in delicate ivory, her hair falling down her bare back. When she meets his eyes, her face breaks into a smile that's sun-like, and Adam's eyes flood with tears.

They don't stop looking at one another, not even when her dad hugs her and then Adam. Their dizzy-looking smiles are identical as they face each other, clasping hands.

"Hello, wife," he whispers.

She gives him a radiant look. "Not yet."

"Hurry," Adam tells Cole without looking at him, drawing a ripple of laughter from the guests.

It's as if the sky heard and wanted to get the last word. It rips open, unleashing fat, warm raindrops onto us. There's a surge of surprised gasps as people scramble under their seats for umbrellas.

"*No,*" I whisper in dismay, drawing my shoulders up to my ears. Eli's mouth twitches up, rain caught in his lashes as he gazes at me.

And then there's laughter—Adam's and Grace's, chins tipped back toward the disaster raining down—as the ceremony begins.

Once they're married, Adam and Grace don't care about anything. Not the way we'll be immortalized as a bunch of drowned cats in the group photos taken around the Blue Yonder grounds. Not the way it starts raining again, nor the way the softly rolling hill we used for a series of shots turns into a small river that sends us all skidding onto our asses. When Grace stands, her dress is brown. It's the only time Adam looks concerned, but she grins and kisses him until his expression turns euphoric. The photographer circles them, getting every angle.

They don't care when they hear the tent has sprung a leak, turning the space underneath into a mini mud pit, which snapped a leg of the table holding—wait for it—the cake. Aunt Julia caught it before it fell, but now there are two destroyed sides, prominently displayed on Adam's grandpa's ancient poker table.

And when the power goes out as they're making their grand entrance into the reception, Adam and Grace just look at each other with amusement as the crowd chants "Kiss, kiss, kiss." Once they get to the dance floor, lit by battery-operated string lights, they do just that to raucous applause. I watch Adam's mouth form the words, *I love you* every time he presses a kiss to Grace's lips—once, twice, again and again—while Isla and her band huddle briefly onstage.

Finally, she and her bandmate come to the very edge of the stage.

"Can you hear me?" Isla calls out. The crowd hoots in response, a wolf whistle that could only come from Cole's loud mouth piercing the air. She grins. "Good. Leo and I are going to do this acoustically until the generator kicks in."

Silence falls and then Leo starts plucking out a melody on his guitar. Adam and Grace sway, lost in their own world.

It's hard to fully appreciate the way the night is marching on despite the universe's best efforts to thwart it, though. My brain is stuck on one last disaster as we get closer to dinner, and thus the speeches. Namely, that I don't have one. Today has been so chaotic I haven't had time to think about what I'm going to say.

When dinner is served, we make our way to the round table reserved for the wedding party. Eli ends up across from me, sandwiched between two groomsmen while Jamie and Blake flank me. I have a conversation with them. I'm pretty sure I eat my meal, though I taste nothing. I laugh—and cry—through both Grace's and Adam's parents' toasts.

But my brain has turned into a spin cycle of thoughts: snippets from my old speech, the milestones of my friendship with Adam and his relationship with Grace. Eli's breath on my neck this morning, the way he touched me, the things he said. The things he didn't, which are hanging around my neck just as heavily. The way I've been avoiding him since. I don't trust myself—not my fear *or* my need.

Jamie nudges me. "Julia is waving you up, tenderoni. I think it's almost your turn."

I glance toward the dance floor, noticing Eli's suddenly empty chair. Beyond it, Julia is indeed waving me up to the dance floor. Grace's maid of honor is wrapping up.

I stand, my heart beating out of my chest, fingers reaching instinctively for my notebook before I remember it's not there. With a groan, I turn—

And run right into Eli.

"Oh," I gasp out. "Hi."

"Hi," he says. "You good?"

"Mm-hmm," is all I can manage.

His eyebrows form an unimpressed line. "You've been green for the past hour."

"I'm . . ." I swallow around the easy words, forcing myself to choose the real one instead. "Okay, I'm scared. I don't want to mess up."

"That's not possible," he says, with so much conviction that some of it transfers to me. "It doesn't have to be perfect, Georgia. Just true."

And then he nudges me toward the dance floor, his fingers sweeping down my spine as I walk away.

I sincerely wish the power hadn't turned back on; looking out at the sea of faces makes my vision swim. I take the mic from Julia, nearly dropping it thanks to my sweating palms.

But when my wild eyes clash with Adam's and he leans forward, an encouraging smile on his face, I let out a breath.

It doesn't have to be perfect. Just true.

"Um, I had a speech prepared," I start shakily. "But in keeping with today's theme, I lost it, so you're going to get some cobbled-together thoughts instead."

"Who are you?" Adam calls, grinning.

My laugh echoes in the night air. "Oh, right. I'm Georgia, Adam's best friend for the last sixteen years. Actually, I'm basically the sister he'd never actually want, since he loves being the center of attention." I raise my eyebrows meaningfully. "As evidenced by the way he's already taking over my speech."

Adam boos over the ripple of knowing laughter.

"Love you," Laurie calls from her table.

I grin, feeling some of my tension release. "And if you're wondering why we've been friends for so long, the answer is yes, I'm using him for his amazing parents and unlimited access to Blue Yonder's incredible wine selection."

"I didn't pay her to say that," Adam's grandpa shouts, and laughter swells again.

"But honestly, Adam and I have been friends since the day in sixth grade when I complimented his Hannah Montana shirt. The truth is, I'd been crying because I really needed a friend, and I figured anyone who liked Miley Cyrus had to be trustworthy."

I look over at Adam again, whose amusement has buffed away into soft-focus affection. My throat tightens. "You had to have known I'd been crying, but you didn't even blink. You just said 'I know' when I told you your shirt was cool, asked what class I had, walked me to it, and then said you'd see me at lunch. It was the first time I felt like someone had seen me when I wasn't all together and didn't run away."

He puts a hand over his heart, eyes glistening, and I point at him menacingly, feeling mine flood in return before continuing.

"If there's one thing Adam won't do, it's run away from real emotions. It's all he knows how to feel, at their most keyed-up intensity." The crowd titters and Adam leans back in his seat, waving me off. Grace leans into him, laughing. "If he's mad, he'll say he's mad. If he's happy, he'll say that. If he's drowning in the anxiety of a cursed wedding, he'll say that, too. It's how I knew Grace was the one. He texted me and Eli at one a.m. our senior year of college, probably minutes after their first date ended, and all it said was 'I'm in love.' We knew that ending up here was inevitable."

My gaze darts to Eli before I realize I'm doing it. I remember that night, not just because of Adam's declaration, but because after we got the text, Eli and I speculated about which one of us would get married first. We'd been curled up in his bed, studying, cocooned in a quiet that soothed me.

Eli doesn't let me look away. I can see the same memory playing in his mind. I can see him thinking what he said that night, now in past tense: *it was going to be us.*

I turn back to Adam and Grace, heart beating fast. "Anyway, I know this wedding has been . . ."

"A shit show," Adam announces.

"A shit show," I confirm with a laugh. "But all it tells me is that you two will take anything on—the highs and the lows and the messes—and love each other through it all. You're not afraid of anything, because you know you've got one another. It's such an honor to witness." A knot forms in my throat; it's happiness for them, grief for me. "I love you both. Cheers to this beautiful new era."

I lift the glass Julia hands me as everyone yells out their cheers.

Grace gets to me first, pulling me into a breath-stealing hug. "Georgia," she whispers with a sniffle. "Please. You can't do that to a pregnant person on her wedding day."

"I'm sorry," I laugh.

She pulls back, her dark eyes wet. "*Thank* you. We love you."

I squeeze her hand. "I love you, too."

Adam wipes at his eyes with the heels of his hands before he steps around his wife, pulling me into his arms. "Okay, you *asshole.*"

I smile into his shoulder. "You're welcome."

He squeezes me until my ribs groan. "I don't know what your original speech was, but it couldn't have been better than that."

I don't remember it either. Whatever pieces of it that had been running through my mind are gone now. I said exactly what I needed to.

"I guess one of the many disasters this day has brought worked out okay."

Adam studies me, then turns us so that we're looking out at the scene before us. The dance floor is streaked with mud, the cake an abomination. Everyone looks waterlogged. The tent has seen better days.

But the din of noise is giddy, laughter swelling constantly. Laurie and David are dancing to the beat of it, gazing at each other with such proud smiles. Jamie's got her arms looped around Grace's waist a few feet away, cheek resting on her shoulder, as Blake talks with enthusiastically waving hands. Eli's listening carefully to Julia, head dipped and nodding, as she hands him the mic; his speech is next. Every table I look at is a snapshot of happiness.

Beyond the tent, the clouds are starting to clear, the black sky now littered with stars and a content, low-hanging moon. The air is heavy with humidity and the smell of the soil that's sustained Blue Yonder for over fifty years.

If you asked me to describe what love looked and felt like, I'd say this.

My throat crowds with tears. Adam tightens his hold on me.

"It's weird. I had this image of how today was going to go for months. And completely objectively, the reality is worse. I wanted it to be perfect, you know?"

"I know," I choke out. I did, too.

"But god, Georgia," he says, his voice growing thick. "I'm so fucking happy. We could've been doing this at Meadowcrest with perfect weather and, like, electricity." His wet laughter joins mine. "But this is my home, you know? Everything's a mess, but it *is* perfect in its weird way."

I nod, unable to get any words out.

"I don't know," he says, shaking his head. "I think it had to happen like this, where everything went wrong the first time so it could go right this time."

"I wouldn't say it's going right," I say dubiously.

"It's not going perfectly. Doesn't mean it's not right."

Something flickers in my chest. "Are we not hating the curse now?"

"Maybe not. It knew what I needed." Adam grins. "Still got married to the love of my life. Cole bought a Slip 'N Slide. It's going to be an epic night."

"I don't want it to end," I admit. I could spend ten more days here. One hundred, a lifetime tucked into that cottage down the path, suspended in a bubble that keeps my happiness so concentrated my heart feels heavy with it.

"Me neither," he says, then gives me a reassuring squeeze. "But we've got more nights like this on tap, George."

"Yeah," I say faintly, my gaze wandering to Eli.

But I know it won't ever be like this again, and that makes the goodbye even harder.

Chapter Thirty

I look up at the darkened cottage from the bottom step. It's
two a.m. and my feet ache. My back aches. My heart aches. The
euphoric sounds of the afterparty drift down the hill and I wrap
myself up in it. It'll be a memory soon.

I climb up another step of the cottage. *Our* cottage. I watched
Eli all night—holding the mic as he gave his wedding speech;
chatting with Nick and Miriam, who came up for the wedding;
watching me as *I* chatted with them; out on the dance floor as we
circled each other. I told myself not to get too close, but I ended up
in his arms anyway during the last song.

We didn't say anything; the music was astronomically loud,
and I said goodbye, watching the tiny hairs rise on his neck. He
couldn't hear me, but maybe his body understood the word. His
hold on me tightened, and I swear hours later I can still feel the
pressure of his fingertips.

My hand is on the door handle now and I'm thinking about
goodbyes. The one we'll all have to say tomorrow. The one I'll
have to say when I leave for Seattle. The one I gave Eli earlier, and
the ones we had before that wrecked me equally: when I left for

Cal Poly freshman year and it sunk in that I wouldn't see him every day. The goodbye he ripped out of me the night we called it done, and the one I left him on one of his Post-it notepads when I moved out because he didn't want to be there to watch me go.

I never want to say goodbye to him is the thing. That's the problem. It's why I'm here, because I don't want to hear him say it out loud, and yet I have to say goodbye to this week *somehow*— what we did, how we've shaped the word *us* into something that still hurts, but that I can at least touch.

Once inside, I sit on the loveseat and look around, not bothering to turn on the light. I know this place by heart. I see every corner Eli and I have inhabited—the kitchenette where we nearly kissed after rescuing Adam's ring, this loveseat where he had his panic attack and let me see it, the bed where we were messy and real. I go back further, turn over memories from the past five years. Longer than that. I think about hellos and goodbyes, beginnings and endings. I imagine an endless circle that brings me back to one feeling again and again and again: loving him.

Outside, a wood step creaks. My eyes fly open. I don't know how long I've been thinking about Eli, other than forever, but there are footsteps. They're steady and measured. My heart doesn't know whether to fly or dive.

Then the door opens and Eli's there. Tall, beautiful, rumpled. He wears moonlight like a crown; it traces its fingertips down his body, silhouetting him.

It's that circle. Time bending back to the last goodbye we had. He's still in the doorway, but it's our Upper West Side apartment. It's December five years ago, close to midnight. I'm wearing a dress, but this one is short and black with long sleeves. I'm sitting on our couch in the dark, hands folded in my lap. I walked home from my company's holiday party at the Empire Hotel because I had to burn off some of my emotions, but my legs aren't even cold anymore. That's how long I've been waiting.

"What are you doing here?" he asks then, breathlessly, with a potent mix of exasperation and fear.

Fear because it'd been fifty-eight days since I'd asked him to do anything with me other than grocery shop; I counted. My company's holiday party was tonight and I finally capitulated two days ago, asked him to find a way to make it because I didn't want to go alone. Five years ago me loathes my job by this point—my passive-aggressive boss, the friends who make that word mean something lonely, the sly jokes about how Eli must have a secret second family. I thought all night about how all he wants is one whole one. It's what he's working so hard toward, and it's what we're ruining in our pressure cooker of silence and anxiety and disappointment.

He's exasperated, probably, because it's clear by the way his dress shirt is clinging to his chest that he ran to the hotel, or back home when he saw I wasn't there. But I'd already been there for nearly three hours, alone in a ballroom full of people, staring at the fake Christmas tree and six-foot-tall menorah across the way, feeling the same way I did in kindergarten when my dad couldn't make it to that holiday concert. At six, I looked out into the audience and didn't have a touchstone. At twenty-three, it was the same. I sat through dinner, endured conversations with people I can't stand, ignoring those knowing looks, ignoring the single text he sent at 10:07.

I thought about the end until I got up and left without saying goodbye. I drafted my resignation email on the walk home.

And when I got home, I imagined a pile of bricks. Each brick was a time he'd fucked up or I had, a time when either one of us could've said what was on our mind and said nothing instead. It was endless tiny transgressions that didn't ruin us in the moment but added to the wall we built.

On this night in December five years ago, I see how tall it is. How unclimbable.

He's afraid because he sees the wall, too. He's exasperated because he's so tired that he thought today was Thursday, not Friday. He didn't *not* show up, he says, he just didn't realize. I never texted to ask where he was, and never responded to the one he sent saying he was coming.

He's afraid because I didn't wait. Because, on this night five years ago, I tell him, "I'm done. I can't do this anymore."

Five-years-ago Eli stares at me for a long moment. In my dreams sometimes it's hours. And then he says, devastated, "I know."

Now, as he steps over the threshold of our cottage, closing the door behind him, I think about how I could've yelled that night. I could've laid out every ugly thing that I was feeling. But I still would've walked away, and it would've been rubble instead of something that, five years later, can be rebuilt in a different way.

If we're careful.

"What are you doing here?" Eli asks now, but there's no fear, just that godforsaken determination.

I don't want a messy goodbye. I'm so tired of those. "What are *you* doing here?"

"I came to—" He cuts himself off with a wave of his hand. He's clutching his phone, along with a Post-it notepad and a pen. "You first."

I nod my chin at him. "Conducting some important business that couldn't wait?"

The joke lands flat; he's been so present here. Nothing has

been more important than what we've done this week. But I'm too caught in the web of our past and the fact that this whole thing is about to go pumpkin-shaped.

"Sorry," I murmur, wiping my sweating palms down my thighs as I stand up. "That was— I'm sorry."

He nods. Steps closer. "What are you doing here?"

"Came to say goodbye." It's the truth wrapped in an innocuous statement. "It's been quite the week and this cottage deserves a moment of silence, especially since I'm not sure when I'll be back."

"It has been quite the week." Another step. He's five feet away, close enough that I can smell the rain on his skin. "I hoped you'd be here. I lost you over by the Slip 'N Slide."

"Keeping tabs on me?" It's an echo of a few nights ago, right before we went swimming. Just before we gave in.

"Always," he says quietly, but this time it's not teasing.

"If you thought I'd be here, why'd you ask what I was doing here?"

"Just wanted to hear you say it."

"That's very tricky of you," I get out.

One corner of his mouth picks up, then straightens. I see the resolve there. I see what he wants. "Georgia—"

"I don't want to talk," I interrupt.

He moves closer, and there—there's the exasperation. "You don't even know what I want to say."

"Yes, I do," I state, circling the coffee table so I'm that much closer to the door.

I want to talk about New York. The night you told me you were done. Why we didn't fight for each other. Nick and Miriam's wedding. My job. This week and what we did.

It's all been sitting at the base of my throat for days, some of it for years, and I feel it rising in me like a wave.

He huffs out a breath. He doesn't even try to follow me; that lock-click gaze is enough to stop me. "Then just let me say it."

"First of all," I huff back, "you're breaking the agreement."

"With all due respect to the agreement, fuck the agreement. Also, the week is over." His voice lowers. It's nearly a caress. "I told you we were going to have a reckoning, Georgia. That I've spent too long not saying the things I want to say, and I'm done not saying them."

"God, *why?*" I burst out. "What good will it do?"

"A whole hell of a lot more good than not talking has done us."

I shake my head. "No."

He takes a step. "*Yes.*"

The wave is growing—need and fear and panic and anger. "We're just getting back to a good place after five years of hell. For me, at least."

Something ignites in his eyes and I realize it's the first time I've ever said anything like that out loud.

"For me, too," he says.

"Right," I implore. "Right, and now it feels okay, doesn't it? This week has been good, hasn't it?"

"It's been—" His voice breaks, and his expression does, too. Under the determination is an emotion I've seen flashes of all week: hunger. "It's been everything."

"*Yes*, and we're becoming friends again."

Eli paces away, scrubbing his hands over his face with a wild groan.

I push on, desperate. "I don't want to wreck that, so why are you pushing this so hard? Why does it matter?"

I thought I knew what the reckoning would be, but when he

turns on his heel and stalks back to me, I'm in no way prepared for what he actually says.

He stops just short of me, a flame in his eyes.

No, not a flame—a wildfire.

"It matters," he says, his voice breaking, "because I'm in love with you."

Chapter Thirty-One

Everything stops. Me. Time. Earth, probably.

"What?" I whisper, flattened.

"I'm in love with you," he repeats, calmer now.

For a flash we're back to the night he told me he loved me for the first time, a week after my birthday. We're at the grocery store, delirious from studying, and I'm blearily arguing with myself over whether Smucker's or Welch's has the more accurate grape flavor for the PB&J I plan to annihilate. I look over to find Eli watching me, the softest, most happy smile on his face. His paper-rings smile. In that moment, I say "What?" and he says, "I'm in love with you." That easy, like he's said it a hundred times before. It takes me a second to realize this is the first.

But it's now, not then. I get out a strangled, "Again?"

He's not smiling, but his mouth is soft, his eyes are soft, this word is soft: "Still."

A circle. Time bending.

"Oh my god, Eli." My voice shakes. "What does 'still' mean?" He inhales, but my imagination has spiraled. "Are you talking this week? A few months? Were you in love with me when you flew the woman you were dating across the country to go to Nick and Miriam's wedding?"

The hurt in my voice is clear; that she was there at all, and that he made so much effort because he wanted her there *that much*. He can hear it, and I have no right to feel it. I was bringing Julian, though those logistics were lazy, and then moot once he dicked down his ex. But this is what happens when I get messy—it's unfair and illogical and ugly.

Eli stares at me for a long stretch. Not like he's warring with whether he wants to answer; like he's preparing before he untethers it.

"She was Cole's girlfriend at the time," he says finally. "Well, as close to a girlfriend as Cole is capable of."

My jaw drops. "What the hell, Eli? You were dating Cole's *girlfriend*?"

"No," he says, a flash of tender amusement lighting his eyes. "Remember how Cole said that he'd been in New York a few times over the past eighteen months?"

I nod on instinct; my brain is busy trying to put all the puzzle pieces together.

Eli lets out a breath. "The first time he visited—to go to that conference, but also to see Emma—we met up. I got very drunk, and he asked how you were and I just . . . unleashed. I'd never *talked* about us, Georgia. I couldn't with Adam, and obviously I couldn't with you, and Cole was there." One corner of his mouth quirks up. "He is actually a really good listener, by the way."

I can only get out a squeak.

Eli runs a hand through his wrecked hair. "That's why he's been so weird all week. He knows how I feel about you and has been encouraging me to come clean. And by encouraging, I mean being fucking nonstop about it."

I think back to Cole telling me to be careful. To him asking if I was messing with Eli, and how he transformed when he saw the truth on my face.

Eli moves to stand just in front of me. I can't help the way I sway toward him.

His eyes bounce between mine, searching. "I wasn't sure if there was a point, because before this week you made it clear you wanted to keep me at a distance. And then, when things changed, I didn't—well, *don't* know how you feel or what it would do to this new dynamic between us. But then I realized that the point is being honest, Georgia. You get to do whatever you want with that information, but at least you *have* it."

I have no idea what to do with it. I can't even keep it in my hands long enough to inspect it; it keeps slipping away, silver-quick.

"Anyway," Eli continues, "when he came back to see Emma right before Nick and Miriam's wedding, I told him that you were going to be there with someone. I didn't want to miss the wedding, but the thought of going alone and seeing you with someone else, someone you'd been dating for *months*—"

He inhales sharply, like it hurts to even say it, and that pain radiates into me. We both dated so infrequently; I'm not sure Eli ever had a relationship, and I never wanted it confirmed. Nick and Miriam's wedding was the first time I knew he was seeing someone, and likely vice versa.

Even seeing him with someone for a few hours made me spiral. I spent all night imagining him touching her like he used to touch me. Needing her in *any* way when my need for him still had claws.

It doesn't matter that I dated Julian because I was tired of being stuck and lonely, and that in the end it only made me lonelier. It doesn't matter that I didn't give him any meaningful piece of me. Eli can't see my heart, and it's for the better because he'd see his name everywhere in it. But it's for the worse because he doesn't see that his name is *everywhere* in it, and that hurts him.

I hate that we're hurting each other again. Still. "I don't think we should—"

"I didn't want to go alone but I also didn't have anyone to go with," he interrupts. "My dating life was pretty much nonexistent because I didn't want anyone but you, so it's not like I had options. Emma ended up offering to be my date. Said she'd make a long weekend of it, go see Cole after the wedding."

I'm frozen, his *I didn't want anyone but you* banging around in my chest.

"But then I showed up." Eli's gaze holds me in place. "You were alone, Georgia, and somehow that was so much fucking worse, because it was someone else who'd let you down, and I had to see that on your face. I had to remember all the times I'd done that to you and the way you faked the same smile you did that night." His voice breaks as he searches my face. "I couldn't watch it again. I said I had food poisoning so I could leave."

He blurs until I can't see him. I spent that whole night so miserable thinking he wanted her, thinking he'd moved on when I couldn't, even if it looked like it from the outside. I spent the months after trying to shake it off, trying to pull myself back into the space where that old list kept me safe. But maybe it was dead even before he stepped off the plane last week.

"When I say I'm still in love with you," he says quietly, "I mean today and yesterday and this entire week. I mean at Nick and Miriam's wedding and I mean for the past five years." If possible, he gets even quieter, but now he's closer so I get every word. "When I say I'm still in love with you, I mean the first time I saw you and right now. I mean every second in between."

"No," I manage, even though it's true for me.

"*Yes*," Eli says. "That's why it matters. Because I'm so in love with you that I feel like I can't breathe. I think it every time I look at you, every time you let me in or you laugh or you look at me like I mean something to you. I know it's fucking messy, and I know you hate that, but it's also *true*."

I feel like I'm being pulled apart string by string, like everything that I've kept inside is being unraveled by him. I'm being methodically disassembled, all my tender parts exposed.

"I can't do this," I breathe.

His expression collapses. *"Why?"*

"Because I want to keep you!"

It bursts out of me before I can catch it and we both reel back, rocked from the shockwaves. Emotions play over his face—surprise and confusion and understanding and then, of course, a brand-new heartbreak—and suddenly I'm crying.

The truth is startling for me, too, but that's what it is. I've only ever wanted to keep him. All my lists are used for keeping things and people, because I'm so bad at it when I'm not holding myself in place. My Eli Mora lists are the most concentrated versions of that, even the one we used for five years. *Especially* that one.

His eyes glitter in the near darkness. "Georgia."

I back away, pressing up against the kitchenette island. "I lost you once, and I don't want to lose you again. You don't want to hear that I was so fucking miserable with you and without you. That I was so lonely in New York and after."

"I do," he says hoarsely, but I shake my head, pleading.

"I want to keep you because when we broke up, the first person I wanted to call to make it hurt less was *you*, my best friend, and it *killed me* to realize I didn't even have that anymore."

His eyes flutter shut.

"I needed you too much back then, and I still need you." I'm not sure I've ever said that out loud, and it cracks something down the middle of me. To admit it. To see him stand there and absorb it. "This week has shown me we can still have that, but if we keep doing this, I'm going to think about how you're in love with me and you've been in love with me this whole time— through *everything*—and yet you let me leave you without a fight. I'm going to think about how you quit your job *now* and how you're going to therapy *now* and how I wasn't enough for any of that five years ago."

Oh god, I didn't mean to say that. The silence is so absolute it's a sound. Eli stares at me, his face ashen.

"Is that what you think?" he asks finally. "That you weren't enough?"

I shake my head, panicked.

"Is that what you think?" he presses.

I grip the edge of the counter. "I think you chose keeping your job over keeping me."

It's the truth, plain and ugly, right there between us.

"No," he says, his eyes wet. "I didn't choose my job. I chose *you*, the same way you were choosing yourself. I chose to respect your decision to walk away from the misery we were both stuck in. I couldn't pull myself out of it, but you did. And I'm not saying I loved the way you did it, or the way *I* did it. If we'd just talked, if I'd pushed you . . ." He trails off, searches my face. "You said you needed me too much back then, but all I saw and heard from you was that you didn't at all."

"It wouldn't have made a difference if I told you," I say. "You were—"

I stop, and he presses, "What?"

"You were shut away in your own expectations and anxiety. I wouldn't have been able to get to you anyway."

"You didn't trust me enough to ever say it, though," he says. "And you didn't trust yourself enough to let it out."

He's right. I don't say it, but I doubt it hurts less when you already know the answer.

The room settles into silence except for the hard beat of my heart echoing in my ears. I want to be done. Want to run, but I can't move. All I can do is watch Eli while he gazes out the window, his expression far away, somewhere years ago, maybe.

Finally, he looks back at me. "I wish I had said all this a long time ago, but I wasn't okay when we broke up—before that, too, obviously—and I was very aware that I had no fucking clue how to be. Part of me wanted to beg you to stay. The amount of times I picked up the phone to call you, Georgia—" His voice cracks on my name. "But how would it have been fair to ask you to give me another chance when I couldn't give you what you deserved? I couldn't even give that to *myself*."

I close my eyes, imagining him in New York staring at his phone while I stared at mine in San Francisco, missing him so much my stomach was hollowed out.

"I'm not saying I'm fully okay now," he says quietly, and when I open my eyes, he's a looming, blurred shape before me. "But being in therapy this past year has helped me understand that things in my life have to change, that I *want* them to—with my job, with Adam . . ." He dips his chin, holding me in the crosshairs of his gaze. "And with you. You were always enough for me. I wasn't enough for myself. I had to get there, and I'm so fucking sorry I hurt you along the way."

My throat goes tight at his apology, even as something loosens in my chest. "I hurt you, too, and I'm sorry for that."

He nods, absorbing the moment. My words. Finally, he says, "I know you have very little evidence that I'm not the person you walked away from five years ago, but it's true. We were twenty-three, and I was a fucking mess who didn't know how to say it out loud or ask for help. Now I do. I'd like to believe there's a reason we're here like this again."

Or still, I think. That tendril of belonging tightens around my chest. Time is cruel and a miracle all in one swoop. It shows you what you had, and sometimes brings it back to you, but it's always different.

"Some of our twenty-three-year-old stuff is still there."

I think of his flight to LA tomorrow, the job he'll likely take. The anxiety that lingers. I recognize the ways he's changed, but I only know him in practice as the man who *did* choose his career, no matter what lens he wants to look at it through. My heart won't survive it a second time.

"It wouldn't be like before," he says.

I don't know that. I still don't know exactly why he quit his job and I'm too exhausted for this conversation to go on for another hour in order to find out.

And it doesn't matter. He's going back to it. Differently, yes, but our lives are about to be a thousand miles apart.

"Talk to me," he says quietly. "I can take it."

"It's too messy."

"I told you I want that." He moves closer and I see everything on his face: hunger and frustration and love, messiness of his own. He wants us to trust that.

But I can't. Not if it means there's even a one percent chance it changes things for the worse. I just got him back.

"You asked me if I'd ever tell you what I needed, if I'd ask for it," I say, swallowing hard. "This is me telling you: I need your friendship. I need that to be enough for us, at least for now."

For a long moment he just stares at me. His pulse works in

his neck, a quick, hard beat, and it dawns on me that he might not want that with me. That I might lose him anyway.

"I miss you," I rush on. "And I'm tired of missing you. I don't want to try something and have it ruined again and end up with crumbs. This week has been a fantasy. I fell in love with you here before, and I let myself do that again, but reality is different. The first two years of our relationship and even the first couple months in New York proved that we're really good at loving each other when it's easy, but nothing about our current situation is easy. We have history and you're going to LA and I'm going to Seattle. It makes it messy in a way that's terrifying for me."

"It's terrifying for me, too," he says, eyes flashing. "And it doesn't have to be LA."

"But it *is*. And maybe ultimately it doesn't have to be, but you have to figure that out for yourself, Eli. It has to be something you choose because *you're* choosing it, not your anxiety or me or anything else."

I won't trust it otherwise. I don't say it out loud, but maybe he hears it. His shoulders drop, and that argumentative furrow between his brow smooths out.

"Please," I say. "Let us leave this week with something we know we can have."

Slowly, he bridges the last inches between us. Takes my jaw in the cradle of his hands and lifts my chin. He looks down at me, thumbs moving over my cheeks, and I see the pain there. The love. Everything I feel.

"Is that not what you need?" I ask. "Or want?"

"Of course I want it," he says, his attention following the path of his touch. I can practically see the wheels in his mind turning over thoughts I can't begin to guess at. When our eyes finally meet, he looks freshly determined. "I want you any way I can have you. I want you *every* way I can have you. I just want it to be honest."

I nod, fear still pulling my chest tight. "It is."

Almost completely.

His lashes fan out over his skin just before he leans forward, pressing a kiss to my forehead. It's a lingering touch, but not nearly what I need from him. I need his body over mine, pushing inside. I need him falling apart and pleading, pulling marks into my skin so I can remember that we were here after we leave. That this was real. All of it.

I can't ask him for that, though. It's almost enough that he pulls me into his arms, pressing his body against mine.

"Okay," he whispers.

I nearly collapse with relief, gripping his damp shirt. "Okay."

"Are you going back to the party?" he asks against my hair. "Or the hotel, I guess, since it's two in the morning."

I shake my head. "I think I'm going to stay here. I'm not ready for it to be over."

It's a subtle invitation I don't expect him to accept. We've never stuck around after the hard parts.

But instead he runs a hand down the length of my back. My dress pulls taut at the waist before he exhales shakily. "I'm not either. But I can't be with you." His mouth skims over my ear. My cheek. Stops just shy of my mouth. I stay frozen, trapped under his touch. "Sex, I mean. I won't be able to let you go."

"I know," I whisper, aching. "Just lie with me."

In the bedroom, he unbuttons his shirt and hands it to me so I don't have to sleep in my dress. We turn our backs to each other while we undress, but the sounds and the memories in this room and others fill in the blanks for me. I get to keep him, in part, but I'll still miss him—the wide spread of his shoulders, the solid taper of his torso and the beautiful curve of his thighs. The shape of his mouth and how it broadcasts his emotions, the way his fingers trace every known path and new ones, too. The swift pound of his heart and its slower, calmer beat. The way I got to have all of him this week. It was a fantasy, but it was real, too.

When I slip his shirt on, it's still warm from his skin.

We crawl into bed. Lie down. Face each other. We touch, but only at the knees and where his fingers twine with mine.

"I'm proud of you," he says. "For taking the promotion in Seattle. You deserve all of that, and I know how much you love your job."

"You do?"

He lifts a shoulder. "It's easy to tell when you talk about it. Your eyes get all wide and happy."

I laugh softly. "That makes me sound feral."

"We've already established you are." In the darkness, his teeth flash. "A little bit."

I press my knee against his, both in admonishment and also because I like feeling his skin. "I do love it." My next thought catches in my throat, but I force the words out. "I'm scared, though."

"I know," he says, and I wonder if he knows I mean about *all* of this. "But you're doing it anyway. Sometimes I think it means more when you're scared. You know the risks, but trusting yourself ranks above all that."

"Is that how you felt when you quit your job?"

He shifts, his gaze moving to some point over my shoulder. The familiar sound of his skin sliding against the sheets is such a strange comfort. "Yeah, I was scared. Terrified, actually, and I still am, but I know I made the right decision." His eyes find mine, lock into place. "Now more than ever."

"I'm proud of you, too, you know. For quitting. I hope Luce fucking choked on your resignation." Eli's laugh is sharp and surprised before mellowing into something quiet, like gratitude. "I'm proud of you for going to therapy, too. I see the difference."

His eyes search mine. "Do you?"

Wordlessly, I nod. He brings my hand up to his mouth, presses his parted lips there, exhaling against my skin.

"What time are you leaving tomorrow?" I whisper.

"Ten. Cole's driving me to the airport. He has to go to San Francisco anyway." He pauses. "It would be too hard if you did it, I think. Plus, you got me on the way up."

It's the right call, but I hate it. "Yeah, one time's free of charge but twice is pushing it."

He grins, sweet and beautiful and sad.

In the darkness, my heart aching, I say, "If you wake up before me tomorrow, don't wake me up."

"Okay," Eli murmurs, tucking a hand under his cheek, eyes locked with mine.

He'll wake up before me and go, and we won't have to add this moment to the other times we said goodbye. Maybe it'll hurt less.

I don't know who falls asleep first, but when I wake up to brilliant mid-morning sunshine, his side of the bed is empty.

The only sign of him is a paper ring, placed carefully on my nightstand.

Chapter Thirty-Two

"Are you excited for your first day of work tomorrow?"

I abandon my wrestling match with an IKEA box to look at Jamie. She's standing in the middle of my brand-new living room in my brand-new apartment, hands on her sweatpants-clad hips. Over her shoulder, a fresh view peeks at me: the modern white apartment building across the street, the brilliant green treetops lining the sidewalks, and above it, a deep blue slice of cloudless sky. It's the blue yonder, right here to greet me for my first weekend in Seattle.

I pull up the last piece of tape on the box, pushing it flat. "I'm a very nausea-inducing mix of excited and nervous. Is that weird? I'm not the new kid. I mean, I recruited half the people in that office, so they know and should love me from a financial standpoint, at the very least."

"Bare minimum," Jamie agrees.

"But I don't know," I say, looking around my new space. "I still have that new-kid feeling."

She walks over, flopping down onto the floor next to me. "I know that pukey feeling well. I always get it when I'm about to do something badass. Usually reminding myself I'm about to do something badass sends it packing."

"*Am* I doing something badass, though?"

"Georgia." Jamie scoots until we're facing each other, knees pressed together. Her expression is fierce and admonishing and full of love. She looks like a prickly kitten. "You're so badass at your job they were like, 'Here's a promotion and more money and a relocation bonus because we love you so much, go be amazing.' You're starting over in a new state eight hundred miles"—she points a menacing finger at me—"but one phone call and plane ticket away from everything you've ever known. Hell yeah you're nervous, but you're excited because you know you're doing something amazing for yourself. You're excited because you *know* you can do this."

I nod, my throat thick.

"Does it feel right?" she asks.

I think about going into Nia's office the day after I got back from Blue Yonder last month, the slick of my palms against the Blue Bottle lattes I'd bought for us. The slight shake in my voice when I told her I was accepting the director position, and that I could go up as soon as they needed me, which turned out to be as soon as I could get up there. I remember the way the knot in my stomach unraveled once I said it.

Since I made that decision, I've vacillated wildly between excitement and nervousness. I've even questioned the decision a few times. I certainly would never classify moving up here as being badass.

But here I am, sitting in my apartment with Jamie, and underneath the excitement and anxiety is another emotion that feels like peace. It reminds me of my early summers at Blue Yonder; I knew it was special, but it didn't belong to me yet. I had to settle into the feeling over time, trust it slowly.

That's how this tiny one-bedroom in South Lake Union feels to me now.

"Yeah," I say. "It feels right."

"Then that's what matters," Jamie says, wrapping her arms around my waist.

I smack a kiss on her head. "Thank you."

"That was a good pep talk, right? Like, on a scale from one to ten, what am I looking at?"

"An easy twelve," I confirm.

"Twelve! Blake would chastise you for going off scale."

"But it's just us right now," I say. "So you get a twelve."

She hums, then tightens her hold on me. "God, I'm going to miss you."

For the thirtieth time this weekend, my eyes fill with tears. "Jamie, what the hell? You promised you wouldn't make me cry if I let you help me move up here."

"That's on you for not knowing I was lying," she says, pulling back just as a tear streaks down her cheek.

We stare at each other, faces still soggy from the last crying jag we went on, before dissolving into laughter. Our goodbye is imminent, and the thought of doing it hurts, even though we'll be fine. We'll do anything for each other, and I know more than ever that if either of us aren't doing enough, we'll say it out loud.

With a sigh, Jamie rests her cheek on my shoulder. We lapse into comfortable silence, soaking in our last hour together before I have to send her back home. It's strange that the same word can mean different places, and yet the feeling exists when we're together, too, no matter where we are geographically. What a comforting thought.

"Okay, enough sad-girl shit." Jamie straightens and wipes her palms down her wet cheeks. She does the same to me, grinning when I laugh. "What else can we knock off your very comprehensive to-do list before we have to go to the airport?"

I give her a sideways look, biting my lip. "Okay, I have a confession."

"What?"

"I lost my to-do-list notebook," I say, then clap my hands over my mouth.

Her eyes widen. "*What?*"

"I can't find it anywhere." There are pages and pages of items with all the things I need to do and buy, the companies I need to call for service setups, even local restaurants and shops I want to check out. I've been carrying it with me everywhere, but Jamie and I have been to practically every storefront in Seattle. There's no way I'll track it down.

"So, wait. Have you just been . . . winging it?"

"Kind of," I groan. "I've got a half-rewritten list on my Notes app, but it's not as comprehensive, and I've been too overwhelmed to panic about it. I'm running on gut instinct, mostly."

Jamie blinks at me, the surprised O of her mouth curling out until she's grinning. "Georgia, you don't even go to the corner store without a list. Are you telling me we went to Target yesterday and you dropped five hundred dollars on things you didn't need?"

"I needed most of them!"

"Those sweatpants?" she volleys back, pointing at the tie-dyed pair that match hers.

"They're a keepsake," I say defensively, curling my legs under me. "It's the leisure equivalent of us looking at the same stars at the same time when we're not together."

"And that rug you were arguing with yourself over for ten minutes?" Jamie continues.

I run my hand along the multicolored rug I now own, spread beneath me on the hardwood floor. My old neutral rug is currently in a moving truck on its way up to Seattle with the rest of my furniture; I didn't need this. But it felt like a requirement to help turn my blank slate of white walls, pale hardwood, and chrome appliances into a space that feels like mine. It's my favorite thing in the apartment.

"I knew it wasn't on my list," I admit. "I just wanted it."

Jamie shakes her head in wonder. "My baby's growing up. See what happens when you throw your lists in the fire? You end up with gorgeous rugs."

It's those two words—*list* and *fire*—that make my mind slip into its Eli-shaped space. I think about the list we followed for five years before he set it aflame, about the list we left back at Blue Yonder, the one that lit that dormant spark between us again, and about the much more nebulous one we're following now. The one that's keeping us friends.

It's been a month since I shut the cottage door behind me the morning after Adam's wedding, Eli's paper ring looped around my thumb and all of my emotions wrung out. Now that ring sits on top of the Converse box that maintained a place of honor in the back seat while Jamie and I road-tripped up a few days ago. I eye it on the bookshelf, my heart diving the way it does anytime I think of Eli these days.

Which is always.

Jamie follows my sight line, arching an eyebrow. She's well aware of the bombshell conversation Eli and I had the night of Adam and Grace's wedding. I unloaded it over drinks the following week, grateful she listened without voicing her opinion, though I could see the question in her eyes over the way we'd agreed to move forward.

We haven't talked about him this weekend, but I don't miss her sly awareness when he texts, which is regularly.

It started with a text the day he left for LA. Once I'd gotten home, I stress-cleaned while recounting every moment I'd spent with Eli in blissful, painful detail. Even though we hadn't said the word out loud, the feeling in my chest was as heavy as good-bye, and I had no idea what came next. We hadn't talked about what friendship looked like between us, what the rules were.

Then my phone dinged with a text from him.

Not saying goodbye or anything. Just
letting you know I landed safely earlier
and got picked up by this random guy

Right after that text was a picture of Eli and his dad. They looked like twins—golden skin, dark eyes and hair, lethal eye-lashes, the same quiet smiles. Even with the purple smudges un-der his eyes, Eli looked beautiful. God, I'd just seen him the night before, had fallen asleep with his hand in mine and woken up in the middle of the night with his face buried in my neck, and now we were hundreds of miles away.

Mooching off any ride you can get from the airport, huh? I replied so I wouldn't send a string of *I miss yous*.

His response was almost immediate: Besides preferring to be chauffeured by someone who knows my middle name, Ubers are expensive and I'm unemployed

Not for long, I wrote back.

For a few minutes he didn't respond. I stared at my phone in my dark, quiet apartment, waiting for him.

Sorry, my dad won't stop hassling me
to tell you he says hi. I had to lock

myself in the guest room to get away
from him

I thought back to his dad's DM months ago, the *miss you, kiddo* that nearly broke me. But this felt like a tether.

Tell him I say hi back and to hassle you
anytime

I'll pass on the first part of the
message, instigator

I laughed, then held my breath while the text bubble popped up and disappeared and popped up again.

Finally, a text appeared and my heart spiraled out of my body.

I miss you, it said, followed by a lightning-quick, as a friend.

The relief of being able to text back I miss you, followed by the frustration of the safe but inadequate add-on, also as a friend, was so strong that my eyes stung. I missed him in every way possible, but at least I could say it this way. It was a boundary I was grateful for, even though I simultaneously resented it.

He's been so steady with his communication since, and I soak up every morning message, every picture of his most recently completed puzzle (I know how hot this is, he texts, try to contain yourself) or a Georgia license plate he's seen in the wild (Found you). In return, I text the silliest, most mundane things. I just want to know he's there, and he always is. I didn't realize how much I missed it until I had it back—an Eli to rely on. An Eli who's present and diligent, who feels like mine in a way.

Just not in the way my heart wants.

"It's looking so good in here, Peach Pit," Jamie says, pulling me away from my thoughts. "Once your furniture's here, it's going to *really* be yours. I'll have to come back to see the finished product, of course."

"Of course," I agree, unhooking my claw clip from the hem of my ratty T-shirt. Twisting my hair up, I secure it with the clip, then take in my space. "I worried it would feel boring or empty, but even without all my stuff here, it feels familiar already." I lean back on my hands, looking over at her. "This is the first time I'm living somewhere that's just mine. Isn't that wild?"

Jamie's eyebrows shoot up. "Seriously?"

I nod. "Obviously I lived with my dad growing up, then had various roommates in college. Then I was living in New York with Eli." I barely trip over his name and the memory, and that feels like progress. Warmer things have replaced it. "And then you. But even after you moved out, it felt like *our* place, you know?"

"Always will be," Jamie says with authority. "And now this place gets to be yours. How's it feel?"

I inhale deeply, looking around. "It feels . . . right. Like it'll be home."

"Just remember you have another home to come back to," she says, taking my hand.

I squeeze her fingers in mine. "I know."

Her eyes fill again and I see her revisiting the same memories I am: packing up my stuff with Adam, Grace, and Blake, making a party out of it, saying an official goodbye to the space that saw so many of my highs and lows, that grew my friendship with Jamie into what it is right now. We even FaceTimed Eli, and for every second I heard his voice over the phone I wished that I was hearing it in person.

He's got his own thing going on, I told myself, though I still don't know what that thing is. He didn't end up taking the job he said was a lock—Didn't work out, he texted when I asked about it, but I've got other things lined up—and sidesteps the subject otherwise. It's the only thing we *don't* talk about, besides loving one another.

But I get to come back to him like I do Jamie and Adam and Grace and Blake, a home-shaped place. That's so much better than what we had for five years.

And if it's worse than what we had for eight days, I do my best not to think about it.

Chapter Thirty-Three

My first day in the office, I'm greeted with a surprise welcome breakfast, complete with a WE MISSED YOU banner, delicious pastries from Fresh Flours, and plastic champagne flutes for mimosas.

There's a gorgeous, glossy-leaved plant sitting on my desk when I get to it, and I frown, plucking the heavy cardstock from a metal card holder stuck in the soil.

As I read the card, my heart picks up speed:

> *I thought about sending flowers, but a plant will last longer for you. Keep in mind I know nothing about plants, so if this one is terrible, pretend to be impressed, okay?*
> *Good luck this week and every week after, Peach. You're going to do amazing. You already are.*
>
> *Love,*
> *E*

It takes a significant number of slow breaths to unwind the knot in my throat. I focus on each individual word, on that *love* written in someone else's handwriting but dictated by Eli. I hear his voice from that night at Blue Yonder, his *I love you* followed by the *still* that echoes in my mind when I have a hard time remembering that this is what's best.

And it *is* what's best. The fact that he's sending this from LA instead of New York is a testament to that. The fact that he's sending it at *all* is a testament to that.

I hold the card up in front of the plant and snap a picture, then text: Brave of you to get me a plant when you know my track record with them.

It's not until I glance at my photo that I notice a number written in the bottom right corner of the card: 212. It's probably just the way they keep track of deliveries or something, but it's a surprising oversight for an otherwise meticulously written card.

Eli's response pops up: I have faith in you.

Biting back a smile, I type, I'll take good care of it, I promise. You didn't have to do this but it's the best part of my day so far (coming from the girl who had a mimosa at 9 AM on a Monday).

My brain applies the brakes after that, but my heart keeps my thumbs moving. Only thing is it'll probably make me miss you every time I look at it. With a squeak of panic, I add, As a friend.

Maybe that was my master plan, he writes back immediately.

Oh god. I'll be sure to get you a massive ficus or something for YOUR first day as payback.

"Ooh," my coworker, Minh, says, popping up over the divider that separates our cubicles, her eyes locked on my plant.

I set my phone on the desk. "Are you having plant envy?"

"Um, yes. That's from this fancy place I've been dropping the most obvious hints to my wife about. No dice, though." She tilts her head, her long pink hair slipping over her shoulder. "What a gorgeous anthurium. Do you see how its leaves are heart-shaped?"

"Sure do," I say, running a thumb over the curve of one.

"So lovely," she sighs. "Is it from your partner?"

"No." I blink away, my chest aching. "It's from one of my best friends."

Saying it out loud makes me feel like I'm not just duping Minh, but myself. And when I check my phone a few minutes later and see Eli's response, that feeling doubles.

> You don't need to send me anything
> to make me miss you, Georgia. I
> already do.

A pattern emerges over the next few weeks, and slowly but surely, my new life simply becomes my life.

I fall into a rhythm of the job I love, supplementing nights and weekends with outings with friends from work. I even pick up running again as a questionable homage to my high school cross-country days, and text Adam a picture of me mid-run along Lake Union one evening, looking more like mid-*death*. He immediately FaceTimes me, silent with laughter for a solid thirty seconds, but stays on the phone for twenty minutes after that, cycling between roasting and encouragement.

I buy a calendar for my fridge and write out everything I have to look forward to over the next few months, including a visit from my dad, who's coming up the weekend after my birthday at the end of October. Even writing it out feels wildly improbable, but I watched him purchase the ticket the day I went over to tell him I was moving. He vacillated between pride—"Of course they gave you a promotion, kiddo, you're a star"—and concern—"You'll be careful up there right? Let me order you some pepper spray"—before landing on the logistics of having a daughter outside of arm's reach—"Will you be home for the holidays? Christmas, at least? I'll have to work through Thanksgiving."

Later, we unboxed the take-out Vietnamese I'd picked up. I watched while he strode around his kitchen, grabbing plates and utensils. My dad is tall and barrel-chested and looks a handful of years older than he is. But we've got the same dark brown hair and blue eyes, the same arch to our brows and our laughter has the same melody. I'd never paid much attention to our resemblance, but in that moment I was grateful for it. It reminded me that he's a person I belong to, too.

Maybe that's why I blurted out, "Do you want to come visit me?"

He stared at me, chopsticks suspended in his hand; at first I thought it was because he couldn't imagine taking time off. But when he circled the counter and pulled me into a hug, he said, "I'm sorry you have to ask like that."

"Like what?"

"Like you already know I'm going to say no."

That single moment won't turn our relationship into some picture-perfect postcard, but it's the seed of a realization planted: I can ask for things I need and allow the answer to surprise me.

I also get back in touch with my therapist.

"What made you decide to get started again?" she asks during our first appointment.

"I was inspired by a friend," I say, thinking of Eli. Always thinking of him. I turn my attention from the dusky evening sky out my window to my living room, now fully furnished. "And like

I mentioned, I just moved to Seattle this week. It's a pretty massive life change and I could use some guidance processing it all."

My sessions are weekly, partly because my health insurance actually covers it—a the-bar-is-in-hell American miracle—but also because I've spent months holding so much in. It feels good to let go. It's one of my first realizations after a few sessions.

I've spent so long hiding emotions away, but my confessions to Adam and Jamie, to Eli, even being vulnerable with my dad, has challenged the urge to. I'm seeing examples of the way my life improves when I deviate from my lists, when I ask for things that aren't easy, when I'm messy and people accept it.

When I mention this to my therapist, she's thoroughly impressed.

"I love this discovery for you, Georgia." The people pleaser in me sings. No amount of therapy will fully release the chokehold praise has on me. "I want to encourage you to keep pushing yourself. Keep doing it in small ways, because it's incredibly important to build that emotional muscle, but be open to it in higher-stakes situations as well. You did such a wonderful job of that with your dad, knowing that the risk of not getting the answer you needed was high. So keep at it, okay? And recognize how much easier you can breathe each time you do."

"I will," I say. "But holy shit it's scary, even afterward."

"Ah, but that's how you learn to trust yourself."

Her words are so similar to what Eli told me our last night at Blue Yonder when I admitted I was scared to go to Seattle: *sometimes I think it means more when you're scared. You know the risks, but trusting yourself ranks above all that.* It almost feels like looking back on a premonition, and looking ahead to a promise I need to make sure I see through. I dedicate myself to the work.

Sometimes when I get home, I don't turn on all the lights and flip on the TV before I take out my earbuds, because I'm too busy catching up with Jamie or Adam or I've got friends with me, or simply because the quiet doesn't bother me. Other times I have my music blasting even after I've fired up every sign of life in my apartment. There are times when I shut the box on my emotions, but often I can talk myself into believing it's okay to feel them, even if it means I end up crying. I usually go for a cleansing run after.

Sometimes I feel lonely. There are nights when I stare at the ceiling, watching the reflection of headlights crisscross my ceiling, when *New Girl* is my nighttime companion and the only way I can get to sleep. I remind myself that it's not a regression. That it's normal and okay. I start to believe it. Sometimes in those moments I call Jamie. Sometimes I text Eli, and our easy back-and-forth brings me back down to earth. Sometimes I handle it alone.

And sometimes I'm happy in a fully uncomplicated way. There are moments when I feel like I was meant to be exactly where I am right now—running along Lake Union with the running club I found or exploring the city on my own or having adventures with Minh and my other friends. Building a space that's mine, rather than fitting myself into the pockets where people have room for me. I can feel myself stretching, a necessary, beautiful pain.

And in those times, at my happiest, is when I miss Eli the most. There were times in another new city where I was happy, too.

I never wanted to think about the hard times with Eli in New York, but I stuffed the good moments even further down, because they hurt more. Now those memories come to me in pieces until they're a wave.

I think about those first few weeks before we started our jobs and the couple months after, when we carved out ways to make the city more ours. I think about our meandering walks in Riverside Park. The cheap drinks we'd grab at our neighborhood bar, inexplicably named Jake's Dilemma. The puzzle-movie hybrid nights. The early-morning bagels and coffee Eli would pick up on the weekend. He'd crawl into bed, kiss up my neck, along my cheeks until it roused me enough to roll out of bed.

I think of the way he'd pull me into his arms when our neighbor would play the guitar; the music would waft from his living room window to ours, mingling with the sound of traffic four floors below us. It was the perfect soundtrack to dance to, to be in love to.

I remember the everyday things we did together—Eli teasing me about how bad my chopping skills were while we made dinner, watching reality dating shows and arguing over which contestants were the most unhinged. Figuring out the little, beautiful annoyances of merging our habits. Even folding laundry together is a memory that warms me, maybe because it was often interrupted by Eli throwing me on the bed and stripping me out of my clothes.

"Bad news, these need to be washed right away," he'd say, his eyes lit with humor and heat.

"Wow, you're so diligent about laundry," I'd reply, feigning solemnity.

"Could not be more serious about it."

"Better get busy, then," I'd say, nodding to the pile on the floor.

I'd get a wide, wicked grin for that. "I'm planning on it."

"With *laundry*. Since it's so serious."

"Sorry, Peach," he'd whisper, crawling over me. "There's one thing I'm even more serious about."

"What's that?" I'd ask, already knowing the answer. He'd shown me.

But he'd say it still, his smile brushing my mouth. "You."

It's a slow realization that comes to me as I'm sending Eli pictures of Pike Place Market, the view of the city from Kerry Park, of my day on Bainbridge Island. I'm texting, Look at this, but what I'm really saying is, Remember this? And he always responds with his own version of Yes. I remember. Those words used to hurt, and they still do, but it's the pain of having had something special.

The day before my birthday, while I'm at Washington Park Arboretum, it clicks: I love exploring Seattle because it's going to be mine and I want to dig my roots deep. But I also love exploring because it's tethered to my happiness before and I crave that connection to Eli. Those older memories twine with these newer ones, making it all feel connected through time. One never-ending circle.

Maybe that's why I end up with the Converse box in front of me on the living room floor that night. I'm turning the paper ring that Eli left on the cottage nightstand around my finger, thinking about circles and time. Forever-shaped things. Thinking about our week together at Blue Yonder as my eyes catch the flashes of neon nestled in the box. Thinking about the five years before that and how there's nothing tangible to touch here from that time because we pushed ourselves so far away from each other. Thinking about New York and all the years—and rings—Eli gave me before that. The older ones look fragile, but they're still there. Imperfectly shaped, some of them fraying at the seams, but solid under my fingertips.

I'm thinking about the past seven weeks and how much I want to actually see him. Touch him, remember how he feels, wallow in the sandpaper texture of his voice against my skin. Listen to him tell me he loves me.

I look at my phone. The screen is dark, and has been since Eli texted two days ago, asking what my plans were for my birthday.

Dinner with friends, but nothing too fancy since it's on a Monday, I wrote back.

No cupcake with a dollar-store candle
in it?

I stared at his message, my heart heavy and pounding in my chest. It was an overt push into a major milestone in our history, and in my mind I heard his first *I love you*. I wanted to hear it again. I was so hungry for it. I can still feel the growl of it in my stomach now as I take a sip of wine.

It took me at least five minutes to write back with something that acknowledged what he said without tipping us into some dangerous space. He didn't try to fill the silence; he just waited, letting that memory hang between us.

Finally, I wrote, Pretty sure that's trademarked. No one else would dare.

You're right, I'd sue, came his message seconds later.

I wanted to tell him I missed him, no *as a friend* at the end of it. Just that. I missed him, because I do. *Still*. I hear that word in his voice and mine, another intertwining.

Instead I wrote, Wouldn't mind one, though.

His response was immediate, like he'd been waiting for me. Is that your birthday wish?

Yes. My thumbs skimmed over the letters, not quite touching.

Can't be a wish until the candle's in my face, Mora, I finally replied.

Noted, is all he wrote back, and my heart hasn't settled since.

I've come so far in so many ways. I can *feel* it. And yet I'm still scared of these feelings I have for Eli. My life here is good, my happiness more touchable than it's been in a long time. But the way I'm missing Eli is becoming bigger alongside it. Our last night at Blue Yonder, I told him I didn't want to miss him the way I have for the last five years. I thought this friendship would prevent me from feeling it so intensely, because at least I'd have him in some way. And I do.

But somehow, it's still not enough. It's a messy emotion I actually let myself feel. I just wish I knew what to *do* with it.

With a frustrated groan, I set my wineglass down and slip off the paper ring, placing it carefully on the floor. Then I pick up my phone, navigating to my text thread with Eli so I can read his last message.

> The next couple days are slammed, but I'll definitely talk to you on your birthday, okay?

I knew better than to ask whether it was job related, so all I wrote back was, Of course, good luck!

But in the message bubble is an *I miss you* I never sent.

"I miss you," I say to my phone, tilting it so the speaker is at my mouth. Louder, I add, "I miss you and I'm in love with you and I hate being friends with you, if we're being honest. It fucking blows."

It stays dark and silent and I toss it aside with a sigh, straightening my legs.

But I guess the universe decided it's been a while since I've had a disaster on my hands, so in the process I kick the stem of my wineglass.

"Dammit," I gasp, lunging for it. I catch it before it shatters everywhere, but a tsunami wave of wine sloshes over the lip—and splashes right onto the paper ring. "Oh shit, shit, *shit*."

The top layer starts to turn transparent and I reach for my decorative Target throw to sop up the mess, stupidly near tears. It's just a paper ring, but it's the last one Eli gave me, and now I've probably ruined it—

A slash of black against the bright pink stops my thought in its tracks. It's handwriting. Eli's to be specific. The number 211 is written there, followed by a period. After that is what looks like half a word, though I can't make it out.

It takes my sluggish brain a second, but then it hits me hard and fast.

Eli's written something inside the paper ring he gave to me our last morning at Blue Yonder.

Chapter Thirty-Four

I start peeling the paper apart gracelessly in a blur of shaking fingers. I'd feel bad about wrecking something Eli put together with so much diligence if I weren't desperate to see what he wrote.

My urgency is rewarded; seconds later I open it, and my heart stops. It's a list, written in meticulously small block handwriting, scrunched onto the two Post-it notes that made the intricate ring.

207. Because you panic under pressure, but you're magic so you make magic happen anyway.

208. Because you let me in this week when you didn't have to.

209. Relatedly, because you're brave through your fear and you don't even realize it.

210. Because of the bachelor party and your 57 streamers. Also, that red bathing suit, holy shit.

211. Because you don't want me to say goodbye this morning. You don't know yet that with us it's never goodbye. But you will, I promise.

The words blur as I reread them, my brain scrambling to figure out what the hell this is. A list, yes, but of what? And where's the rest of it?

My eyes dart to the Converse box. The other paper rings.

For a long second, I stare at it, unable to breathe. But then I throw open the hinged lid, snatching the first substantial ring I can find. The straw wrappers would've given him away years ago, so I unfurl a worn gum wrapper ring instead.

Sure enough, there's writing inside:

22. Because I'm the first person you look at when you think something's funny.

23. Because you meet me and my sisters at the park when we need to get out of the house, and you scream every time that shitty plastic slide shocks your ass to make them laugh.

24. Because the coffee I make sucks, but you love it anyway. I think your taste buds are defective.

I press the back of my wrist to my mouth with a strangled laugh, throwing the wrappers aside and grabbing for another ring.

76. Because you were so excited to see me when I got to BY yesterday that you ran too fast down the driveway and ate shit.

77. Because you let me carry you inside. Gonna think about your breath on my neck all summer.

78. Because the cartoon Band-Aids Julia brought made you laugh, then you laughed harder when I wiped the dirt off

your teeth. Even like that you're so beautiful. Especially like that.

79. Again, because you were so excited to see me. Fuck, I am so in love with you.

And another one.

184. Because I came to bed at 3 last night and you were asleep, but you turned toward me and let me hold you. Feels like it's been weeks since we've hugged.

185. Because you have an unhealthy obsession with Everything but the Bagel seasoning. On cottage cheese?! Seriously?

186. Because my coffee still sucks but when I made you a cup this morning, your face lit up.

187. Because you smiled at me. You looked happy for a second. I can't dig myself out of this anxiety, Peach. The only thing that makes it go away is work. But it's the thing that makes it worse, too. Why can't I tell you that?

I pull more apart, reading each one as the purpose of the list becomes clear. There are three silent words before each item: *I love you.*

146. Because we share an address now.

1. Because you let me call you Peach when no one else is allowed to.

54. Because trying to parallel park makes you so mad, and then you get even madder when I take over and do it fast.

32. Because you buy me a puzzle every time you see one at a store. I don't have the heart to tell you I'm good on them for five lifetimes.

123. Because you pretend like you don't believe in airport snacks, but you were so into it when I bought you that 7 a.m. Peppermint Pattie. Stop lying to yourself, Peach.

47. Because you were smug as hell when I told you Heather Russo has a crush on me. I love your petty little heart. You know I belong to you, but you don't know how.

89. Because you looked so fucking happy when I told you I was coming to Cal Poly.

151. Because the corner bodega guy knows your name and birthday already and exclusively calls me "Georgia's boyfriend." You find family anywhere.

111. Because you told me you love me.

164. Because you lean on me whenever we're on the subway instead of holding on to the rail. You never lean on me otherwise. You wonder why I don't mind long subway rides—it's that.

The language switches on some of them, and I recognize that they're during our hardest times.

182. Even though you didn't invite me to dinner with Rory. I know you thought I'd be working, but you didn't even ask. I love you for bringing me takeout when you realized I was home.

191. Even though you say "it's fine" when it's not. Even though I can see you pushing me away, and I don't know how to get to you. Or if I even deserve to.

198. Even though it hurts to love you sometimes.

199. Even though I can't make you happy.

Tears fall freely as I read each unraveled ring and unravel along with them. The floor is littered with paper. It's a mess, and I make it even bigger. I spread them out, then line them up in order, taking in the passage of time in the sharp creases and soft wrinkles, in the fresh and smudged ink. I see the ebb and flow of emotion in Eli's handwriting—sometimes it's so careful. Sometimes it's dashed off, each line curving unsteadily.

There's thirteen years' worth of love here. I can see it even in the five years of absence.

I imagine the number doesn't end at 211—no, 212, I realize, remembering the numbered card attached to the anthurium Eli sent. *You're going to do amazing*, he said. *You already are.* I heard his "I love you" there, even if I didn't want to admit it, and I hear it now. Two hundred twelve times on paper, hundreds more out loud. Some that were never said.

Sitting back on my heels, I look down at the winding path the list makes. I'm a list girl, so I recognize the purposeful organization of thoughts. But I've never seen one like this before—it's not meant to keep thoughts or emotions compartmentalized. It's meant to set them free.

My eyes find the most recent unfolded ring.

208. Because you let me in this week when you didn't have to.

209. Relatedly, because you're brave through your fear and you don't even realize it.

Something inside me cracks down the middle. Maybe I've been brave elsewhere in my life, but not with Eli. I've kept myself safe because that's what I thought it took to keep him. But this list shows the best and worst of us, through so much change and turmoil and separate growth. The one thing that hasn't changed at all is him loving me.

And me loving him. It's our tether, the thing that's never let us drift too far.

I recognize, too, that plenty of the things he loves about me aren't easy or pretty, and it makes me think of what I love best about Eli. It's not the perfect things, it's the *real* things. The messy stuff, the way he let me see all of him during our week at Blue Yonder, the way he's let me see him over the past thirteen years. Imperfect, yes, but real. I can't dash off a list this comprehensive, but the one he made for me is an Eli Mora capsule in itself, a way for me to lay out all the reasons I've loved him through time.

I love him because he finds beautiful moments even in the hardest of times. Because of his determination and dedication to the things and people he loves. Because he really is an annoyingly talented parallel parker. Because he's pushing through his anxiety with the same commitment he gives everything. Because of his terrible coffee and his quiet mouth and that crease he gets between his brows when something annoys or perplexes him. Because of his unshakable belief in airport snacks and his sweet little puzzle addiction. Because he assigns nicknames to the people he wants to keep. Because he's bossy when it counts the most.

Because when he's messiest, that's when I see myself reflected in him.

It's a privilege to have someone trust you enough to show you those pieces of themselves, the most vulnerable and tender, the least polished. It's a show of trust to let you see them first thing in the morning, in the middle of a panic attack, right after they've cried. To give you a shaky smile after a messy fight. To come back to you again and again with their heart in their hands.

Eli spent the entire week at Blue Yonder telling and showing me that he wants real and honest and messy. This list is telling me the same thing: he wants to love me in totality. I have to let him. Isn't that the way I deserve to be loved—completely, messily, imperfectly? Isn't that the way I deserve to love myself?

And isn't it what Eli deserves, too?

We can be all those things—good, bad, easy and needy, okay or not on an endless cycle—and trust that the other will stay. Our circumstances are messy, but so is life. It doesn't mean that we can't love each other through it. We already are.

Suddenly I understand what Eli must've been feeling the morning of Adam and Grace's wedding when he said he was done not saying the things he'd held back. I have so much to tell him. I want to say everything. The first thing will be *I love you.* The last thing, too.

"Phone," I breathe out, a blizzard of papers swirling around my swiping hands as I search for it.

My ringtone blares behind me and I whirl, crawling to my

phone where it skidded halfway under the couch sometime during all of this. God, I hope it's Eli.

I deflate when I see Adam's name, but swipe to answer anyway. "Oh, hey."

"Wow," he says, "I've never gotten a more underwhelming greeting, thanks."

"Sorry, I'm—" I look around, overwhelmed. "I wouldn't even know where to begin explaining, actually."

"Do you . . . want to?"

"Maybe after." God, I'm making zero sense, but I need to talk to Eli. "Listen—"

"Are you at home?"

I frown at the out-of-the-blue question and his tone. I think he's aiming for breezy, but Adam couldn't blow the fuzz off a dandelion. "Yes, I'm home, but—"

"More importantly, are you okay?" he interrupts, his voice shifting into what I've come to label as Dadly Concern. He's been experimenting with all of us before the baby arrives in April. "You sound—"

Now it's my turn to interrupt. "I swear to god if you say *feral*, Adam—"

"Would you rather I say *unhinged*? Because it's going to be one of the two." I groan, resting my forehead on the couch. "Are you okay, seriously?"

I look around my decimated living room, my eyes landing on all the words Eli wrote for me, the tiny little declarations transcribed over time. So much quiet devotion.

"Adam," I whisper.

"Georgia," he replies warily.

"I'm in love with Eli."

There's a long pause. And then he says calmly, "Yes, I know."

"You know," I echo.

"I know."

"Like you *know*."

"Oh, I know," he says smugly.

I groan. "Please use more and different words, and also tell me why you sound so chill about it."

"Because I *am* chill about it," he says. "Listen, I know I was all hyped up before the wedding, but that's mainly because you two seemed so off at Nick and Miriam's wedding and I didn't want to put you in a weird position. And fine, also because I was obsessed with the curse thing."

"Minor detail."

He ignores that. "But then you two volunteered to go up to Blue Yonder to help out and honestly . . ." He trails off. "I don't know, you told me things were fine—better than ever, I think were your exact words—"

"That was more a premonition than the truth," I admit.

"Right," he says with a laugh before his voice turns thoughtful. "I didn't *know* know that you and Eli weren't okay, because neither of you stubborn dicks would ever admit it, but I couldn't shake the feeling. And I didn't know if letting you go up together would be a mistake or the best thing that ever happened to you two, but I trusted you'd figure it out."

My throat tightens at how sincere he sounds. How calm and assured.

"I never told you this, but Grace can back me up because I talked to her about it over the years," Adam continues.

"Frequently," Grace calls in the background.

"I always had this feeling you were going to find your way back to each other. Sometimes I just wanted to, like, push and meddle to speed things up, but Grace reminded me—"

"Frequently," she repeats.

"—that if you were ever going to get to this point, it had to be because *you* wanted it, not because I was getting in the middle. She was, as she always is, brilliant and right." Adam's voice gentles. "And you did want to find your way back to one another, George, so in that way I was right, too."

I choke out a shocked laugh.

"I saw it happening when you were vibing on our FaceTime calls, and then when we got there it was really obvious—the bachelor party, the way you leaned on each other through the clusterfuck of wedding disasters, how you both disappeared during the afterparty and no one saw you again for the rest of the night."

He says the last part slyly, but I'm barely paying attention. I'm playing back how unsurprised he was when he found Eli in my hotel room, when he walked into the bathroom in the middle of my breakdown and saw me in Eli's arms. When Eli and I danced together at the reception and I caught his eye over Eli's shoulder. I thought he was in his own world, too blissful to put it all together, but he saw everything.

It wouldn't stop me if he was concerned about this development, but I can't deny it soothes me to hear his steadiness now— and his hope.

"Wow, okay, so you really do know."

"I do," he replies. "And I want you to know that I'm rooting so fucking hard for you two. I always have. One of the things that stuck with me most during your speech was when you talked about me and Grace taking on the highs and lows and loving each other through it. I think you and Eli have done that without even realizing it, but now you get to do it together."

"Oh, god*damn* you," I say, my voice breaking.

"Payback, baby," he crows.

I wipe my face with the sleeve of my sweatshirt. "Ugh. I'm a mess."

As soon as I say it, I think, *I wish Eli could see it.*

On the other end of the line, there's a ding, like a text message coming through. Adam laughs quietly. "Hey, George."

"Hmm?"

"I know it's late," he says, "but I think you're about to have a visitor."

I frown at the clock on my kitchen wall. It's nearly ten. "What are you—"

There's a knock. It's soft and patient. My body recognizes it before my brain catches up, and suddenly I'm standing, staring at my front door. My heart is in my throat. At my feet. On its way to the person it belongs to.

"Adam," I whisper, a hot tear streaking down my cheek.

"Love you, dude," he says, his voice just a little thick. "Tell him I say hi, okay?"

I think I say "okay" and maybe I say "goodbye" but then I'm at the door, unlocking it. Throwing it open.

Eli's standing there with a suitcase at his feet and a bakery box in his hands. He's so beautiful, his expression a heady mix of nervous and sure, that I can't say a word.

But Eli's got me. He steps closer, and I feel the latch of our gazes right in my chest when he says, "Hey, Peach. Happy birthday."

Chapter Thirty-Five

I'm in Eli's arms before I'm aware that I've wildly launched myself at him. He accepts it with a sway and a laughing, "Oof."

"What are you doing here?" I ask into his neck.

His arms come around me, one around my waist, one high across my back. Our hearts pound against one another.

"I came to give you the trademarked cupcake-with-a-dollar-store-candle combo," he says, "since no one else can deliver the experience."

I pull back, drinking him in. Holy hell, I love this man. "It's not my birthday yet."

Eli smiles, his eyes moving over whatever parts of me aren't smashed up against him. "It is in one hour and fifty-seven minutes, give or take a few. I didn't want to risk not being the first person to wish it to you."

"Is that the only reason?"

"Yeah." He curves a hand against my jaw, his thumb playing over the high plane of my cheek. "I'm actually gonna go now, good luck with everything."

I laugh, still stunned that he's here. "*Eli.*"

"Georgia, come on." His voice turns quiet, his eyes warm and happy. "The cupcake is a front. I'm here because I love you."

The past thirty minutes have been so surreal, but it's this moment—Eli standing in front of me, teasing me and loving me when I wished for him to see me exactly like this—that makes it all solidify.

I burst into tears.

Eli's face falls and he sets me down, herding me into the foyer before setting the cupcake box on top of his bag. The door shuts behind him.

"Georgia," he murmurs, and he says my name with so much care that it makes me cry harder. He tries again, a quiet "Peach." He says it the way anyone else would say *love* or *home*. "What's wrong?"

"I'm in love with you," I choke out.

His eyes turn into a starburst of the warmest colors—rich brown, honey, gold. "Is that a bad thing?"

I take a deep shuddering breath, pacing away from him. "No, but I spent all day—the past seven weeks, actually—wishing you were here and thinking about how much I hate being your friend, and then Adam called me to tell me someone was at the door—" I turn back to Eli. He's in my space. He's wearing jeans, a gray sweater with his necklace tucked lovingly under the collar, his old Converse. His hair is mussed, still too long, his stubble grown back. He's here in my *home*. He looks so good in it. "And it was you. It's not bad, it's amazing. It just makes me feel like my heart is going to explode, and that's very unsettling."

He blinks. "You hate being my friend?"

"*Yes.*" Oh god, that sounded violently emphatic. "I mean, no, I love being your friend, but it's not all I want with you."

He takes a step, eyes locked with mine. I can see his hope there, right on the surface. "What do you want?"

"Everything," I choke out. "All the good stuff and the messy stuff and even the bad stuff. I want all of it."

I recognize the look in his eyes—the need to bookmark the moment so he can come back to it as a memory.

Releasing a breath, he reaches out, so I do, too, and our fingers twine. He pulls gently, towing me until I'm pressed against him again.

"I want all of it, too," he says, his voice low.

"Is *that* why you're here?"

One corner of his mouth lifts. "I told you it was the cupcake."

"You're putting a lot of pressure on the cupcake."

He laughs, but it fades quickly, replaced by something far more resolute. "I have things to tell you."

The disaster I made in my living room calls to me. "Me, too."

He nods, as if he knows, but he can't. Not all of it. Not until I say it out loud.

"What if I kissed you first?" he murmurs, his gaze bouncing between my eyes and my mouth.

I let out a shaky breath. "I wouldn't hate it."

He smiles; it's such a tender shape, such a tender feeling when his mouth grazes mine. It's soft, but so quickly it's not. He sighs, parting his lips against mine, and my throat tightens viciously as I open for him. He kisses me, slow and deep, his thumb sightlessly moving up to brush a tear from the corner of my eye. It's a kiss that's so hungry, that's fully satiated, a kiss that ends when he moves his mouth to my cheek, but will never be over.

"I love you," he breathes against my skin, and the feel of it is so familiar that it takes me back to Blue Yonder, to those nights when he'd whisper things I couldn't catch. It comes to me now that he was saying it then. He's been saying it for so long, even in moments I couldn't hear it or didn't want to.

"I love you, Georgia," he says again. He pulls back, his eyes finding mine, holding me in place. "That comes first before anything else we say."

I nod, a tear dripping off my chin. "I love you, too."

His smile is beautiful and quiet. So sure, that I know whatever we say tonight will only make us better. "Okay, then. Let's do the rest."

Eli's crouched on my living room floor, still and silent except for when he lays an unraveled paper ring down carefully and picks up another one. In between reading, I tell him how I discovered his hidden messages. His mouth tips up when I include the part about my shouted declaration to him via phone, his gaze following the path of years' worth of his own.

Finally, he puts down the last piece of paper, rubbing his eyes. He stands and rounds the coffee table to sit next to me on the couch. Running his hand along my thigh, he lets out a breath.

"I wrote all of these, so I *know*. But seeing them like this . . ." He trails off, shaking his head. "I really have loved you for a long time."

My throat crowds with emotion as I nod.

"I saw you sneaking the rings I made when we were at Blue Yonder, so I knew you had some of them," he says, biting back a smile at my shocked squeak, but then his expression turns infinitely tender. "You kept them all, though."

"I did."

His eyes search mine. "Why?"

"Because I've loved you for a long time, too."

His lashes swoop down, pressing hard against his skin. When

he opens his eyes again, they're shining, pinned to me. He seems lost for words.

"Do you want to go first or do you want me to?" I tease, needing to ease his tension and mine.

He blows out a breath. "Maybe we should've written out an agenda."

"If I'd had *notice*—" I stop, triumphant, when he grins.

"Yeah, well, I'm going to live off the look on your face when you opened the door for the next fifty years or so," he says, wiping at his eyes. "I don't mind the agenda being collateral damage."

"I have a late add if you're amenable."

He quirks an eyebrow. "I am."

"Will you tell me why you did this?" I ask, pointing to the rings. "And why you didn't tell me about them?"

"I was going to tell you tonight, just so you know for unofficial agenda record-keeping purposes. I wasn't just here for the cupcake."

"I *knew* it."

He laughs softly, then looks at the rings, sighing. "I don't know, when I first started writing in them, it was to get my feelings out somewhere without it blowing anything up. You and Adam were the only real stability I had in my life at that point, and I didn't want to risk telling you and have it get awkward."

"I don't know how I would've handled it anyway," I admit. I kept him so firmly in the best-friend bracket back then; I needed him too much that way.

"Jesus, you would've crushed my fifteen-year-old heart," he groans. "Good choice there. And when we got together, it felt like something I was building for you, you know? I always felt like saying 'I love you' never really touched how much I was feeling. If I gave you a list that showed all of the times I loved you, cumulatively, maybe you'd see, since that's your language. I had . . ." He huffs out a breath, rubbing a hand along his jaw. His stubble purrs against his skin, a sound I feel everywhere. "Plans like this for it, I guess, but *me* showing you, not a glass of wine doing the grand reveal."

"So inconsiderate of it," I say.

"Thunder stealer," he agrees.

"I'll let you throw it out the window if you want."

His grin is small. "Nah, that's what I get for waiting. I should've known better." His voice quiets as he grows serious. "I *do* know better. When things went bad between us, I used the rings as a way to say things I couldn't say out loud because you were already so far away and I didn't want to push you further. But not saying it did that, too. I think our problem was that we hid the pieces we didn't trust about ourselves from one another."

I nod. "Because if you didn't trust it, or I didn't, why would the other person?"

"Exactly," he says. "I hated the way my anxiety made me feel and act, hated that working harder was the one thing that made it better while making it worse, hated feeling like if I released my foot from the pedal, I'd crash and everything I was working toward would go away. I was ashamed, so I didn't give you access to it. But it was my whole life, Georgia. I woke up and fell asleep feeling that way. Of course you were going to feel shut out."

"I shut you out, too," I say, pressing my knees against his. "I was ashamed of how much I needed you. I was only happy those first couple months, and it felt like so much pressure to rely on you like that, to not be able to find happiness on my own once you really fell into your job. The further away you were, the bigger that feeling got and the more it scared me. I hid how much I needed you when we were together *and* after we broke up, even that week we were at Blue Yonder. I had these Eli Mora lists—"

His eyebrow arches up. "Wait, I had my own Georgia Woodward–made lists? Plural?"

"Don't be flattered," I warn, seeing the spark in his eyes. "They weren't beautiful physical manifestations of the reasons I love you. They were a way to keep my messy emotions in check."

If anything, that spark grows. "Your messy emotions are on my list of reasons I love you, so I'm going to be flattered anyway."

My throat goes tight hearing that. I finally trust it's true. "That's very weird of you."

"Is that on your list of reasons you love *me*?" he asks, one corner of his mouth pulling up. I nod with a helpless laugh and he hums happily.

"Anyway, it didn't work. I still needed you, I just put it in a box. But underneath all my rules, I was still doing all the things I told myself I couldn't—I was still in love with you. I still missed you."

Eli takes my hand, lacing his fingers with mine.

"It clicked for me looking at the rings," I say. "You wrote the things you loved about me in good times and bad, when we were at our highest and lowest. I was wrong when I said before that we're only good at loving each other when it's easy. I think we're good at loving each other out loud when it is, but we've silently loved each other through all of the hard stuff."

"We have," he says quietly. "God, it's so good to hear you say it, though. I wasn't sure."

"I'm trying to be better about saying hard things. It's scary, though."

"But you're doing it," he says, looking proud and windblown.

I nod, then take a deep breath. I'm about to do it again. "That night we argued—"

"I wouldn't call it arguing."

"That night we vehemently disagreed," I amend, raising a questioning eyebrow. When Eli nods his approval, I continue, "You said that doing something means more when you're scared, because you know the risk but trusting yourself ranks above that. Saying I wanted us to be friends was letting my fear drive. In reality, the only honest option is having *everything* with you, even when it's not perfect. Especially then. I love you, and I know that our current logistics are complicated, but I don't care. I can be here and you can be in LA and we can figure—"

"I'm not going to be in LA." He says it so calmly, so matter-of-factly, that it takes me five full business seconds to understand it.

"What?"

"That's my other agenda item," he says. "If you're done with yours."

"I— yes," I manage.

Eli scoots closer, curling a hand around my thigh. "I told you that Adam's bachelor party was the catalyst for my decision to quit my job, but it was also you, Georgia."

"Me?" The improbability that I played into his decision to quit his job five years after we broke up is laced through my voice.

Something flashes in his eyes—an old pain, maybe, seeing my confusion. "Yes, you. A few weeks after Adam's bachelor party, Luce promoted me to VP." His mouth tips up at my gasp, but he continues, "He congratulated me for working my ass off, said I was on the fast track to director as long as I worked even harder to prove I deserved it."

"Oh, *fuck* that guy."

"Right?" Eli says with a short laugh. "I just stared at him while all this shit flew through my head—that I was on my way to being him, someone who had nothing but his work, who went home to an empty house, who would die with a shit ton of money in the bank but no one there to hold his hand."

I take his, just so he remembers that's not his path.

Eli's been looking out the window, back in that moment, but now he looks over at me. "I thought about Adam telling me it was okay that I missed his bachelor party, and you not responding to the text I sent you from the airport when I told you I couldn't make it. I thought about the night you told me you were done, what a turning point it was for you when it could've been a turning point for me, too. You pulled yourself out of our misery even though it fucking hurt. If I took that promotion, I knew I would only be extending my misery. And for *what*? For some stability that was meaningless if I was alone?" His eyes are full of so much emotion, matching the feeling in my heart. "I swear, Georgia, your voice was in my head when I told him I was quitting instead."

Old wounds are meant to stay stitched up, but something inside me breaks open instead with his confession. It feels like relief, like real healing, not just for myself, but for Eli, too.

"I'm so proud of you," I whisper, my voice cracking. "God, you really have been doing work with Amari."

"He's relentless," he laughs, reaching over to brush his thumb over my cheek. It comes back wet. "I'm not saying I wasn't scared after I did it, or that I'm not still. But I know that fear is my anxiety talking and, let's be honest, a heavy fucking dose of being a cog in a capitalistic roller coaster you feel like you can never get off of."

"I know it's an inappropriate time to mention this," I breathe out, "but that's the hottest thing you've ever said."

He throws me the tiniest wink, then leans forward, hooking a hand around the back of my calf, squeezing gently. "The reality is, I *do* have to be a cog and that may feed some of my anxiety. But I want a life that makes me happy. I want something that's going to feel right, not just give me financial stability. I went on interviews in LA and San Francisco. I got two job offers, including the first place I interviewed with and a strategy role at a telecom company in San Francisco."

"Eli," I breathe out. "I— congrat—"

"I didn't accept either of those jobs," he interrupts gently. "You told me you wanted me to choose something for myself, and now I need you to trust that I am. I'm choosing neither of those jobs because it doesn't feel right. I'm choosing you and me because it *does*."

I don't even realize I'm crying until his arms are around me and I'm tucked into the home-shaped place of his arms.

"I can be anywhere, Georgia," he murmurs, running a hand up and down my back. "I'd like to be with you. Here, if you'll have me."

"I just spent a whole huge agenda item telling you I would," I sob.

He laughs, then pulls back to frame my face, taking me in. The look in his eyes is hard to describe, but I know I have time to find the words for it. For now, all I can think is *home*, and it's what I hear when he says, "I love you."

"I love you," I say, and then, because I've promised both Eli and myself we'd say the messy stuff out loud, because it's such a relief to do it, I admit, "I'm still scared."

"Me, too." I thought his paper-ring smile was his happiest, but the one he gives me now replaces it. "Let's do it together."

I nod, crying, smiling ridiculously, and he kisses me just like that—through my tears and my joy. Because of it. He pulls me onto his lap, his mouth turning quickly from grateful to hungry. The talking portion of the agenda is officially over.

I sink fully into my need for him, let it feed the way he needs me. In return, he gives me everything: soft, wrecked groans, his fingers between my legs and then his mouth, his whispered, *it's so good, Peach, it'll always be so good.* A quiet, *I'm so in love with you.* All of it plays on a loop that feels timeless.

Somehow I know this is the end of missing him the way I did before. It dissolves in my blood, an effervescence that follows the path of his fingers as he frames my hips, pulling me down onto him so he can finally slip inside.

Later, when I'm sprawled on the couch, wearing the Denver Nuggets T-shirt Eli packed for me, he turns off the lights as he walks out of the kitchen. He's shirtless and flushed, holding my cupcake. His hand is curved around the candle, protecting the flame.

I think about my birthday years ago with Eli when I wished for him. I trace the fine lines creasing the corners of his eyes as he sits next to me and sings "Happy Birthday." Those lines remind me that eight years have stretched from that moment to this one, that we've circled back to it. That we love each other. Not again, but still.

Time is a miracle. It shows you what you had, and sometimes it brings it back to you. Different. Better.

Eli's done singing. Our eyes catch over the candle and I see the flame in his. It won't extinguish. It never did.

"Make a wish," he says quietly.

So I do.

Epilogue

Eight months later

It's the perfect day for a wedding.

Or evening now, I guess, since the actual marrying portion of the day is done and things have transitioned into a party. It's raucous for being so last-minute and for being such a small group of people, but I shouldn't have expected anything less. Sometimes happiness is loud and messy.

I stand at the edge of the commotion after being in the middle of it all day. I want to memorize exactly how this looks and feels—the sweet breeze that winds over my bare shoulders; the deck filled with friends and family, laughter and clinking wineglasses and music cutting through the summer warmth of the night; the vineyard beyond that, stretching toward the tree-cloaked jut of the mountains; the reaching branches of Big Daddy, the oak tree that's watched so many of my memories at Blue Yonder. The one that provided sun-dappled shade earlier when Eli and I stood underneath it and slipped rings onto each other's fingers.

And the sky. It chased dusk off an hour ago, and now it's a wide blue that's deepening by the minute, so endless it almost doesn't look real.

But it is. All of this is.

I run my thumb over my new wedding band, thinking about

the Post-it and receipt and gum-wrapper rings in my Converse box, still tucked on the bookshelf that's now crammed with my trinkets and Eli's puzzle boxes. The paper ring he handed over three weeks ago during an otherwise typical Saturday at Kerry Park, telling me thickly he'd been thinking about this moment from the first one he gave me. And once I'd read the proposal inside it, the diamond he held up as he kneeled at my feet.

I think about the ring he gave me today, his eyes luminous as he said his vows. I trace the unending circle of it, knowing that every ring Eli's ever given me has meant the same thing: forever.

A pair of arms slide around my waist and I close my eyes, my body melting under the heat of the most devoted touch.

"There she is," Eli murmurs against my skin. "And by *she*, I mean my wife."

"You've called me that approximately four thousand times since we got married."

"And I'm going to say it four million more over the next hundred years," he says stubbornly.

I laugh. "Oh buddy, I have some bad news about that estimate."

"Fine, fifty or sixty," he says. I can feel the smile curling over his mouth when he murmurs into my ear, "All of them, regardless."

"That sounds pretty ideal," I reply, my chest aching at the fact that we'll get it.

Eli tightens his hold on me, resting his chin on the crown of my head. I trace my finger over the arch of his wedding band as we go quiet, soaking it all in together. Grace and Adam are spinning each other tipsily to the music, safe in the knowledge they can party the night away now that Laurie's shuttled three-month-old Penny off to sleep. Jamie and Blake are seated in chairs pulled into a makeshift circle with Eli's sisters, a wine bottle on the ground between them, and my and Eli's dads are chatting easily, arms crossed over their suit-clad chests. Cole, who served as our last-minute officiant, is swirling the wine in his glass and then holding it out for Eli's mom and her fiancé to smell. I can track his ester-volatizing spiel from a mile away.

It really is the perfect day, and it's ours.

As if he's thinking the same thing, Eli turns me until we're facing, wrapping his arms around my waist. I get caught in the hypnotic lock of his eyes, as I always do and ever did—caramel and gold and deep, deep brown, bordered by lashes that are still spiked from his tears during the ceremony.

"I love you so much," he says quietly, grazing his mouth over mine.

"I love you," I whisper back.

"Thank you for marrying me." His hand comes up to cup my face, his thumb moving over the curve of my cheek.

I lean into his touch, lifting a shoulder. "I mean, I had nothing else going on."

He grins, brushing another almost-kiss along my lips. "And thank you for agreeing to do it with such little notice."

"That was a no-brainer. We have a proven track record for planning weddings in a week," I say, and he's still smiling when he kisses me for real.

Originally, we'd planned to come down to the Bay Area for the weekend to celebrate Penny's one-hundred-day birthday, a Korean tradition. After we got engaged, though, Eli requested we extend the trip to the whole week even though we'd just been down in March when Grace had Penny.

Even eight months into living with Eli and six months into his strategy director job at a telecom company (which comes with, among other perks, unlimited PTO), sometimes I have to calibrate my brain to an Eli who suggests time off with such little anxiety. Whose late worknights are few and far between, whose weekends are saved for me and the friends we've made together and separately in Seattle, whose panic and stress continues to unwind itself with time and patience and therapy.

It was an easy yes. I love being in Seattle with Eli, the space it gives us to build a life together, but I miss this other home we have, too. Maybe someday we'll come back. For now, I love where we are, and every trip we make down here feels like a bonus. For a girl who struggled so mightily to know the shape and feeling of home, it's a revelation to have so many places—and people—to call it.

I didn't think anything of Eli's request until we were on our flight down and I looked over to find him staring down at my ring, his expression soft and hungry.

"Pretty, hmm?" I asked, holding it up like we hadn't been gazing at it starry-eyed for the past two weeks. It winked under the reading light.

Eli hummed, then looked up. His eyes locked with mine and I reveled in that clicking feeling in my chest, the way it vibrated through me when he murmured, "Hey, Peach."

"Hey, Eli," I murmured back.

A tiny grin tipped his mouth up, but there was a nervous shake to it. "Do you want to get married this week?"

My laugh was short and clueless, fading when I realized he was serious. "Wait. Are you re-proposing while we're flying over Redding, California?"

"I looked it up," he said. "There's no waiting period to get a marriage license in California, so we could go in and get it, then get married up at Blue Yonder."

My throat went instantly thick. "You want to marry me?"

"I mean." His amused gaze flickered down to the ring. "Yeah."

I shook my head, flustered. "Right now, I mean. This week. There."

"I can't think of any other place I'd want to marry you more." His voice was quiet, his expression warm and hopeful. "This is probably a good time to tell you that marrying you at Blue Yonder was always on my list."

"It was on mine, too," I said, my eyes stinging. We hadn't started wedding planning at all, but suddenly I was desperate to marry him in the place where those first roots of love dug in between us. And I didn't want to wait.

"Okay," I whispered, and for the second time in two weeks I told him yes.

It came together quickly after we celebrated Penny's day. Adam got Blue Yonder squared away for us—"The most equal payback of all time *and* it means you two are getting married? Hell fucking yes," he exclaimed when we asked him to help. "But whose best man am I going to be?" And I learned that Eli had already asked his family to fly out, anticipating that I'd agree to his plan. Jamie, Grace, Blake, and I went shopping and I found an off-the-rack dress like it was fated for me, a strapless number with a sweetheart neckline that made Eli so speechless he stumbled over his vows. We put Adam in charge of music, asked Jamie and Blake to pick up a Costco sheet cake, and had Aunt Julia buy every flower at Trader Joe's for the decorations.

And now we're married.

Eli's mouth softens against mine, pulls back until it's just a graze. It's a tease of things to come. His fingers flex into my waist and he breathes against my lips, "How do we get rid of ev—"

"The Moras are *making out!*" comes a howl from the other side of the deck. *"Let's goooooooo!"*

I look over to see Adam with his hands cupped around his mouth, as if he needs help projecting his voice. Everyone else is gathered around him—Cole wolf-whistling, Jamie yelling "ow-*owwww*"—and it's a cacophony of applause and glass-clinking and joy, until it bleeds into a chant that surely echoes for miles: *kiss, kiss, kiss*.

"Oh my god," I say over the noise, turning back to Eli. "This is ridiculous."

"Absurd," he agrees, but his happiness curves around the word and so it sounds like *perfect* instead.

"They're not going to stop until we give them what they want." I'm practically yelling now; it's a mutiny.

Eli gazes down at me, so much love in his eyes that it almost shocks me, even though I see it all the time. I don't know if I'll ever get used to seeing how obviously he belongs to me. How eager he is to show it to me every day.

"Well, then," he says, and when he dips me, I swear my ears pop thanks to the jubilant, roaring cheer from the people who love us most. Who wanted this day as much as we did, and did everything to make it happen.

I'm still laughing when Eli says against my mouth, "We'd better give them what they want. I have plans for you."

Much, much later, when pictures have been taken and dinner is done, when our euphoric dance party has broken up and everyone has gone home, Eli and I take a familiar path. The sky above us looks infinite, pitch black and sprinkled with stars. We wander past the cottage we'll be sleeping in tonight—*our* cottage—and I kick my heels off, leaving them on the grass as we make our way to the edge of the pool. It shimmers under the moonlight, holds all of the memories we've had and the ones yet to come.

I only intend to dip my feet in for a quick cooldown, but when I look over at Eli, he's grinning, that sharklike one.

"What do you think?" he asks, nodding his chin toward the water. "Wanna jump in?"

"What, like this?" I reply, sweeping my hand over my dress, hemmed in vineyard dirt, and his dove-gray dress pants and white dress shirt, tie and jacket long forgotten.

"Naked works, too," he says silkily. "I'm going to get you there regardless."

I hear the challenge in his voice and straighten, raising an eyebrow. "Are you asking me to *rumble*, Eli Mora?"

"Maybe I am, Georgia Mora."

"Oh my god," I laugh. "My name rhymes. I didn't even think about that."

"I like it," he says, towing me into the circle of his arms. Now his smile is brilliant, the happiest I've ever seen it.

"Me, too," I murmur, eyes stinging.

He brushes his lips against mine, a gentle touch that becomes something needier, and I exhale to slow down the moment. It's a dream. Something real. A memory, but not yet. Something we'll look back on in fifty years, or a hundred if Eli gets his way.

Finally, he pulls away, his gaze tracing over my face. His smile fades, but the happiness is still there. He feels this memory we're inside of, just like I do. "What do you say? A rumble for old times' sake?"

I grin. It's old *and* new, a pattern we'll repeat. "Let's do it."

And then, hands clasped, we jump in.

Acknowledgments

I've always loved reading acknowledgments. It feels like an author's way of cracking the door open, not just to say who got them through the book's creation, but to lay out little nuggets of information about how *they* create. My writer brain loves to know the intimate engineering of every book I read.

So I think if *I*, as a writer, love reading acknowledgments, then other writers probably do, too. If that's you, perfect, I'm so glad you're here, because I'd like to tell you something about this book: it wasn't my first time writing it. I wrote a very different version a few years ago and it died in the querying trenches. It sat on a shelf and waited patiently while I cried over it, while I thought about quitting, while I moved on to something else (very casually, a book called *You, with a View*). It waited until I had the ability to write the story it was actually meant to be.

If you're a writer, you probably know the pain of shelving a project, but I hope this book can serve as proof that your first chance isn't always your last one. Often it isn't (just ask Georgia and Eli). If you're a writer reading this right now and you're stuck in the mud of it all, if you're in the trenches, in the middle of shelving a book, writing your next one in tears, wondering if it's worth it, I can tell you unequivocally that it is. Take a break or a breath or both, and then keep going.

On to my very important thank-yous! First, to my incredible agent, Samantha Fabien. Your belief in me makes me believe in myself, and I'm so grateful for your guidance, your expertise, your excitement. To the rest of the Root Literary family, you are all absolute icons. To Heather Baror, thank you for all the work you've done to get my books into countries I manifest visiting.

Thank you to Kerry Donovan, my amazing editor. Working with you is a dream—not only are we always on the same page, we're consistently reading the same word on that page. You just *get* my writing and then you make it even better. So much gratitude goes Berkley and PRH at large, and specifically the team I'm lucky enough to work with: Mary Baker, Genni Eccles, Anika Bates, Dache' Rogers, Yazmine Hassan, Megan Elmore, and the Berkley social media team for creating the most iconic Theo Spencer thirst trap posts, among other things. Thank you to Emily Osborne and Anna Kuptsova for once again creating a cover that is a literal work of art. Thank you also to my amazing UK team at Transworld: Alice Rodgers, Lara Stevenson, Emma Fairey, and Rosie Ainsworth!

To Lavanya and Kate, the platonic loves of my life: all the New York references are for you, because that city is ours, from Jake's Dilemma to Anya's apartment (thanks for letting me fictionally borrow it for Geli) to John Stephens to MoMA, which we almost got kicked out of.

Massive gratitude to my uber-talented CPs, Livy Hart, Laya Brusi, and Sarah T. Dubb. Thank you for telling me I could write this book when I was sure I couldn't. To Alicia Thompson, my favorite Pisces (and one of my favorite people, period), you keep me sane, and when I can't be sane, you keep me company. To Erin Connor, my book 2 warrior, WE DID IT, BABY. To Lindsay Grossman, who reminded me constantly that I *was* going to finish this book, turns out you were right and I was dramatic, hehe. So much love to the Berkletes and everyone on #TeamSamantha. And to all the incredible authors that I talk to regularly but fear naming in case I miss someone: thank you for always making me feel at home and for writing some of my favorite books.

Thank you to my early readers: Alicia, B.K. Borison (my Celine Dion sister, the iconic creator of my favorite series), Mazey Eddings (I love how we yell at each other about how much we love the other's writing), Tarah DeWitt (what if I live inside the beautiful worlds you create? What then?), Lana Ferguson (you are amazing, DON'T argue with me), Laura Marie Meyers (my soul sister for real), Maggie North (kind heart, terrifying talent), Nicole Poulsen (my true blue from the beginning), Esther (one of my first booksta cheerleaders), Shaina (my OG reader, I love you), and Sofia (your opinion = everything).

Thank you also to the amazing authors who took the time to blurb *You, with a View*: Ali Hazelwood, Alicia Thompson, Rachel Lynn Solomon, Anita Kelly, Mazey Eddings, Denise Williams, Amy Lea, Jen Devon, Chloe Liese, and Ava Wilder!

Thank you to Books Inc., my local indie bookstore, particularly the team at Chestnut Street! I can't thank you enough for your continued support. Other amazing indie bookstores I want to thank: Capital Books; A Seat at the Table, especially Faith Emmert; Rachel Johnson at Content Bookstore (I LOVE YOU); The Novel Neighbor; The Ripped Bodice; Meet Cute Bookshop; East City Bookshop (Destinee!!); and Tombolo Books. To Bree, who hand-sells *You, with a View* like they're lined in gold, and to every bookseller who's read my book, recommended it, written one of those bucket-list little quote cards for it—I owe you so much.

To the readers and bookstagrammers: god, I love you. You showed up for me from the very start. You've shouted about *You, with a View* on Instagram, on TikTok. You've reviewed on retailer sites and Goodreads (I don't step foot near it, but like . . . spiritually I know you're doing it and it means so much). You've written me the most touching messages, have confided in me, have shown me your grief. You've shared pictures of your grandparents and let me know them, too. You've taken photos of *You, with a View* in Zion, Yosemite, in countries all around the world. You made my dreams come true × thousands. Thank you from every corner of my heart.

To the winery experts who helped me get the vibes right, and who opened their doors when I needed to do "research" up in Rutherford, thank you! Anything I got wrong is my own fault (aka don't look too deeply into whether you can actually have multiple cottages on winery property in Napa County, because you can't) (but that's fiction, baby!). To Marjan, who gave me SO much expert advice on investment banking, thank you for making sure Eli's job didn't sound like "idk, he just does money stuff." And thank you to Renske for the intro!

Thank you to all my friends (I can't name you all, but you know who you are) who've known me in other phases in my life and have come on this journey with me so enthusiastically. You really took the initial surprise of me saying "uh, I wrote a book and it's going to be published" in stride.

Thank you specifically to "Maroon," "Labyrinth," "This Love," "Paper Rings," and "You're Losing Me" by Taylor Swift; "Your

Needs, My Needs" by Noah Kahan; "Work Song" by Hozier; and Georgia Parker's cover of Taylor Swift's "Karma."

To my mama, who thinks I'm the greatest—I got it from you. Thank you for making sure your local B&N put me on a display table. To my dad for keeping a dresser drawer full of my school projects because you were so proud of them, and for reading my book even though I told you not to. And to my incredible family at whole, thank for your support and for buying my book (even though I told you not to!!!!).

Gram, you are everywhere. You're reading over my shoulder, in every car with a Utah license plate, up in the sky on the most beautiful days. Thank you for being such a rascal that even death can't stop you from showing me you're with me.

And finally, to my little crew—you are so invested in this journey of mine, and I'm so grateful when you tell your pickleball friends to buy my book (Steve) or when you mention proudly that your mom is an author (Noah). Our house is full of laughter that always morphs into painful hiccups for me, but I wouldn't trade it for anything. I love you to infinity.

Continue reading for a preview of
Jessica Joyce's next book

THE SOULMATE CHARADE

Where the Stars Meet the Sea

By: Helena Wright for *Wander*

My mom once told me that there are more stars in the sky than there are particles of sand on Earth.

I was nine years old and it was the second day of our two-week summer vacation. The second day I knew Stella Point, a city in Northern California nestled between Big Sur and Carmel-by-the-Sea, existed at all.

My family and I had spent the morning exploring downtown, a place that looked like it had sprung straight from a movie set. I'd listened, enraptured, while the owner of The Next Page Bookshop told me the stack of secondhand books I'd set alongside my older sister's brand-new copy of *Anne of Green Gables* were meant for me, before winking at Lauren's sigh, her twelve-year-old skepticism clear. I'd gotten a coin pulled out from behind my ear at Stellar Toys & Novelties, laughing when the mustached employee gasped "Magic" in wink-nudged wonder. I'd stared, mesmerized, at the sandwich board outside a shop that read PSYCHIC READINGS: DISCOVER WHAT THE UNIVERSE HAS IN STORE until my mom hustled us into the arcade next door. Once there, I'd announced I was going to play pinball, then snuck off to feed quarters into a rickety fortune teller machine instead.

Follow the magic, the neon pink paper that spit out of the machine read. *That's where you'll meet fate.*

I slipped it into the back pocket of my jean shorts alongside one of my trusty paper fortune tellers. It felt exactly right, and already true—magic had followed *me* all over Stella Point.

And later, at Luna Beach, it found me again when my mom crouched down next to me at the shoreline with a handful of sand. I'd spent most of the afternoon listening to seagulls cry overhead while I leapt through the crashing waves, pretending to be a mermaid to entice the real ones out from the depths of the ocean. Now, mid-build on a sandcastle, I was crusted with the same sand my mom was holding.

"See all this?" she asked, running a finger across her palm, right over the heart line, spreading the sand so thin that I could see every individual speck of it.

I nodded, picking up a few grains with a fingertip.

"Now imagine a number in the multiple quintillion hundred quadrillions."

My jaw dropped. "Those are real numbers?"

"Very real, and that's approximately how many grains of sand are on Earth. But"—she held up a sand-caked finger at my whispered *whoa*, her patented astrophysics-professor tone telling me this was a lesson—"it's estimated that there are two hundred billion trillion stars in the universe. So when you pick up a handful of sand and see all those little particles, think about how amazing it is that there are an unfathomably higher number of stars above us."

After my mom returned to our family's blanket, I got busy digging in the sand. I imagined each speck equaled however many millions or billions of stars. I thought about that psychic's sign and pictured what an unending universe littered with so many stars to wish on might have in store for me. It shaped itself into a path, lit up with star matter, pointing me exactly where I was supposed to go.

On my tenth or twenty-seventh handful of sand, my fingers hit metal. I pulled a locket with a long silver chain from its nest of infinitely numbered sand particles and star specks. It had stars of its own etched onto one side, what looked like half an H etched onto the other. H, for Helena. For *me*.

For nearly an hour, I walked up and down the beach to make sure it didn't belong to anyone else. When I'd confirmed it, I looped the chain around my neck, repeating the bookstore owner's words: *meant for me*. It was the first of many things that the universe would reveal as mine, still tucked somewhere in the stars.

Nearly twenty years later another reveal would happen overlooking that same spot. Not a necklace, but a ring, this time given to me. It was magic, held so lovingly in the sandy palms of Stella Point's hands. Slid onto the fourth finger of my left hand.

I still think about that fortune all the time. I keep it in my nightstand drawer and pull it out regularly. It's creased with time and wear and hope, the neon pink faded into something soft and beautiful, but the words are as crisp as they ever were, and just as true.

I've found magic in so many moments in Stella Point. I've met fate because of it, again and again and again. And if you stand in one particular spot on Luna Beach, let your feet dig into the nearly unfathomable grains of sand below you and stare up at the equally unfathomable stars in the sky, you might hear the waves whisper this:

You're exactly where you're meant to be.

Chapter One

I am so incredibly lost.

I raise my sunglasses and squint at the two-lane road Google Maps lured me onto as I approach yet another hairpin turn. The yellow line separating my car from certain and unaffordable damage should anyone make a wrong move is chipped to the point of uselessness.

"No, this is great," I say to the pine-thick air wafting in through my open window. It curls around the crumpled Taco Bell bag on the passenger seat, creating a mingling scent that would turn my stomach if it weren't already upside down. "This is really, truly wonderf—"

The trill of my phone interrupts that lie, along with the two hundredth consecutive replay of "If It Makes You Happy" in the last seven hours, nearly sending me off the road. Probably right off a cliff, knowing my current luck.

Okay, that's not true. The thick foliage on either side of this mystery road I followed off Highway 1 would catch my rickety-ass car before it had a chance to get anywhere near the Pacific Ocean again, but I've earned the right to be dramatic.

With my gaze trained ahead of me, I press a finger against my mounted phone's screen with a repeated "Hello?" until Colette's

"Hi!" confirms I've succeeded in connecting to the call without dying.

"Oh, hi, is this my boss calling?"

I smile at her groan, the first time my mouth has seen anything like it since I left San Diego this morning.

"Please don't turn this into a bit," she says. "I can't handle you calling me your boss, given our history."

"But I *love* a good bit, Col."

"You once personally witnessed me throwing up in a trash can at work. I have zero authority over you."

A Porsche zips past me on the other side of the road, shaking my old Dodge Neon.

"In your defense," I say, gripping the peeling steering wheel until my knuckles blanch, "we were twenty-four and had been drinking all day because we'd just found out we were all losing our jobs."

"That's what we got for working at an astrology start-up," Colette says with the nostalgic sigh of someone at least three tax brackets above me.

"Sure was." That dream job died a swift death. "Also, you *will* be my boss as long as I nail this project."

"Are you kidding? There's no doubt in my mind. That's why I called you," she says. "There's quite literally no one more perfect for this job."

My stomach twists. If she only knew.

A month ago, minutes before Colette called with the offer, I was starfished on my sister's guest room floor, staring at the email I'd drafted accepting the office manager position I'd just been offered, my finger hovering over the SEND button. I told myself I was only hesitating because the pay was kind of shitty and the law office gave crypt keeper vibes. In reality, I just didn't trust myself to make the decision. The possibility of going down the wrong path again was terrifying. The last one I'd followed had decimated me.

For so long I'd had an unshakeable certainty that I was on the right path, guided by the loving hands of fate. I knew my purpose, because it was known *for* me. I knew at seventeen that I wanted a career in writing, thanks to the AP Lit teacher who told me I was meant for it. I knew, when I crashed into a guy as I strode out of a ratty bar on my twenty-second birthday and he told me his name, that he was forever. I knew at twenty-four when I was laid off from StarSite that the universe would push me toward an even better job, and a week later it did—a dream role at a dating app touting a fate-fueled algorithm. I knew at twenty-seven, when Wes proposed, exactly what the rest of my life was going to look like.

I knew, I knew, I *knew*, and I followed that magic loyally.

Right off a cliff.

Minutes before Colette called, I was thinking about what my life had looked like since that cliff moment: the death of my relationship and then my dream job, because they wouldn't allow me to work remotely from San Diego and I couldn't afford San Francisco on a single income. Moving in with my sister, because I couldn't afford anything in San Diego, either. Trying to get a full-time writing job and failing over and over again. Feeling like I'd been stuck at the same miserable, gray crossroads for a year with no end in sight.

I used to dream all the time, but it didn't feel safe to dream anymore. Life had turned into a series of choices I hoped wouldn't fuck me up further.

My finger was millimeters from the SEND button when Colette's name flashed on the screen. It had been several years since we'd chatted, but the former CEO of StarSite had just been arrested for embezzlement, so I assumed she wanted to indulge in a joint It's What He Deserves party. The thought of focusing on someone who was having a worse time than me, particularly an incompetent dick who deserved it, sounded like a five-star mental vacation.

Instead, she said, "I need a copywriter for a four-week contract and it has to be you."

That alone wouldn't have moved me. My career had fizzled into patched-together freelance gigs, and a four-week contract would barely fan its dying embers. I needed something permanent, especially because my sister was weeks away from relocating across the country to Charleston for work, and I'd need a regular paycheck in order to pay rent for a tiny room in some stranger's house.

It was like Colette had heard me, or had felt the quiver of my finger over that SEND button like some butterfly-effect earthquake, because she rushed on to say that as long as I nailed the contract, she'd be able to bring me on permanently at the PR firm she worked for.

"And there's no way you won't nail it," she said, but my heart had already taken off. *Permanently* was a lifeline to stay connected to a career I still loved, and the pay was significantly better than the office manager position. It was studio-apartment money. "As soon as I tell you what it's for, you're going to scream."

And I did. Internally, at least, not because of what it was for, but because of *where* it was for: Stella Point, California, the place where I learned what magic felt like, that all I had to do was chase it to know what was meant for me. Where that surety grew to astronomical proportions when Wes proposed there almost two years ago. Where it died when he told me he couldn't marry me three months later, perched on the bed in our romantic little B&B overlooking Luna Beach.

The place where I'm currently headed.

My stomach dips along with the road as it curls to the left.

"Oh!" Colette says. "I was calling for two reasons. Firstly because I want to remind you I have my best friend's wedding this weekend, so I'll be out of pocket."

"I will do my level best not to need you," I promise.

"I mean, you *can* need me—"

Another turn, and this time it's my heart that dips. God, where *am* I? "In the most emotionally healthy sense I will, but in the literal sense, you won't hear from me."

"If you need me in the literal sense, text me. It's just that the wedding is a high-pressure situation because of my best friend's future in-laws, so I'm sure I'll be preventing emotional breakdowns until rings are on fingers."

"I'm predicting a completely uneventful weekend." In other words, I'll be Netflix and chilling with myself.

"Not too uneventful," she replies. I can picture her looking at me from beneath her perfectly plucked blonde brows with the cajoling look we used to give each other. The one that always turned *It's just happy hour, we'll be home by seven!* into *Holy shit, how did we end up on top of a bar at 2 a.m. on a Wednesday?* "Stella Point has a shocking amount of young people these days. Actually, I just read about a new bar that opened up there recently that's fate-themed. I think it's called—"

Her voice cuts out before I get the name, but it doesn't matter. I'd rather jam splinters into my eyelids than endure one minute in a place like that. I try to stay away from bars entirely these days; I spent enough time visiting them when Wes managed one.

" . . . fun Saturday night," she's saying.

"I'll check it out." *At never o'clock.*

"Secondly, and probably more importantly, I sent you an email in preparation for getting started on Monday. It has some of our deliverable dates and an official list of the landmarks you're going to visit while you're there. You don't have to look at it closely until next week, but I wanted to flag it because you have that event at the bookstore Monday night."

"The Next Page, yep. I already put it in my calendar."

Saying the name out loud immediately puts it in my mind: glossy walnut bookshelves built into the wall, stuffed with new and secondhand books. Skylights that suffuse the space with warm golden light when it's sunny, and turn it a quiet, soft gray when the marine layer creeps in. The friendly, recently retired owner who watched me race around her store nearly every day during a two-week stretch with a smile on her face.

I hope it looks completely different now. It'll make what I'm there to do so much easier.

Colette sighs happily. "I'm so excited to work on this with you, Helena. This is exactly what I manifested for this project, and now look at us."

"Look at us," I echo, peering out the window. It's definitely less dark, which means I may be getting out of the (literal) woods, but that could be wishful thinking.

"In fact," she continues, oblivious to my turmoil, "I was just rereading your *Wander* article, thinking about the masterpiece you'll turn this guide into. It's going to be magic."

"Yeah, well," I say, hoping she can't hear the discomfort in my laugh. "That's why you hired me. For the magic."

Stella Point has always believed its own story, the same one it told me and will tell anyone who'll listen: that the magic of destiny lives in the air there. That the stars are a little closer to it than they are anywhere else. Nearly touchable.

And now that story is finding a much bigger audience.

Last year, the film adaptation of a wildly popular romance book about a fateful love story was filmed in the city and its surrounding areas. *Only With You* comes with an intensely loyal fan base, and city officials are banking on those fans making pilgrimages to Stella Point once the movie comes out on Labor Day weekend in two months. It's why they hired Colette's PR firm—they want to capitalize on the convergence of their reputation and fans' feral love of the magic woven into *Only With You*'s plot.

And *that* is why Colette called me. Because I wrote a love letter to Stella Point in that *Wander* article. Because she read it and showed it to her boss when they got the project, and Rayan told her to hire me, saying that as long as I did a good job, Colette could bring me on permanently as the headcount she'd been begging for.

And because now, I'm going to somehow replicate all those magical words I wrote nearly two years ago when I still believed in the kind of luck that existed in Stella Point *and* my life. I'm going to infuse it into an interactive guide describing all the city's landmarks featured in the movie so it can launch alongside the film and I can get this permanent job back in San Diego.

It's a path lit with arrows, one I'd be stupid not to follow, and I can't deny that it makes me feel better that I was basically forcibly shoved down it. There was no SEND button I had to push. It was Colette calling me with the job offer. Lauren saying later that night that the sale of her condo had officially closed and we both needed to be out by the middle of June—right when the contract started. Her eyes narrowing when my voice cracked on "Stella Point" as I told her about the job, and her replying, "It's the perfect opportunity for you to stop rotting, Len. Don't give that place more power than it deserves while you're up there. Seriously. It's *just* a place." My friend Neve telling me the next day, while I was fretting about my imminent houselessness because Colette's firm was only willing to pay for a three-day stay in Stella Point, that I could stay at her parents' rental there until they put it on the market in July, as long as I didn't mind a little residual remodeling dust.

In the end, the only decision I had to make was getting in the car and allowing Google Maps to take me on this side quest. A decision I am, of course, now regretting. But it can only go up from here, right?

"Okay, I'm going to let you go, but I lied—I have three reasons for calling," Colette says. "I wanted to make sure you got there okay. Are you all settled?"

The intricate ceiling of branches is finally starting to thin out, letting in more meaningful slices of late-afternoon sun. Enough that I need my sunglasses again.

I let out a breath, running a finger along my necklace chain in a long-ingrained soothing gesture. "I'm going to be totally honest. I took a wrong turn off the freeway, so I've been lost this entire phone call, but I'm fairly certain I'm almost there."

Colette lets out a happy squeak. "*Ah*, I legitimately have chills."

I reach a three-way intersection and hook a left at Google Maps's insistence, then a hard right. Almost immediately the air thickens with salt, pushing back the crisp scent of pine as I'm spit out onto a familiar road. One I traveled twenty years ago. One I traveled for the last time more than a year ago, with Wes and then without him.

And yep, I have chills, too. But probably not Colette's kind.

"Hold on," she gasps. "I just had a feeling."

My heart sinks. "Like a *feeling* feeling?"

"Very much a *feeling* feeling."

She used to get them constantly when we worked at StarSite.

Our desks were practically on top of one another in our concrete slab of an office. She'd announce it while I was in the middle of writing Taurus moon's write-up, right in my ear, knowing I'd turn in my seat with an exhilarated "Tell me, tell me, tell me." Twenty-four-year-old Helena lived for signs and feelings, those sister emotions to fate and *meant to be*.

Now I want to beg Colette to keep it to herself.

And I would, respectfully, if a familiar sign didn't come into view at that moment. It's shaped like a cresting wave, dotted with hand-painted stars and swooping letters. The sun slices through trees overhead, creating a lattice pattern of light along the wood.

WELCOME TO STELLA POINT, it announces. Somewhere stuffed in the back of some drawer next to that old fortune I got when I was nine is a picture I begged Lauren to take: me standing in front of it, knobby-kneed and toothy-smiled, dressed in a cymbal crash of colors and patterns. That little girl who gave her heart to everything and everyone she thought was meant for her is preserved forever on faded photo paper.

It's just a place, Lauren's voice echoes, but I can't quite look away.

"I have the strongest feeling," Colette says, and those words sound so deeply ominous that I wince, "that you're about to get a sign that the next four weeks are going to be smooth sailing."

I'm so busy staring at the literal sign that I don't notice the light ahead turning yellow, or the car ahead of me braking abruptly for it instead of blowing through it like any self-respecting Californian.

And then it's too late.

My skills are rusty after so much disuse, but I have to assume that as far as signs go, getting into a car accident two minutes after arriving in Stella Point is a bad one.

JESSICA JOYCE grew up a voracious reader who quickly learned how to walk and read simultaneously to maximize her reading time. Thanks to a family full of romance-novel-adoring women, she discovered love stories and never looked back. When she's not writing, you can find her listening to one of her chaotically curated playlists, crying over TikToks, eating her way through the Bay Area with her husband and son, or watching the 2005 version of *Pride & Prejudice.*